Distant Cousin
REGENERATION

A Novel

Al Past

Distant Cousin: Regeneration

Copyright © 2009 by Al Past

All rights reserved. No part of this book may be reproduced or transmitted in any form or by any means without written permission of the author.

Cover 'author' photo by permission of juliesjungle.com

Also by Al Past

from iUniverse:

    Distant Cousin

    Distant Cousin: Repatriation

    Distant Cousin: Reincarnation

from Charles Colin Music Publications:

    Baroque Duets from
    Themes of Famous Composers

Distant Cousin:
REGENERATION

Chapter 1

No matter how bad the day had been—or how good, for that matter—deciding to have someone killed never failed to brighten his mood. At the moment he felt better than he had in months. Compressing his thin lips in satisfaction he swiveled his chair to face the bulletproof plate glass window behind his desk and stared absently at the bleak day outside.

The street lights had come on even though it was the middle of the afternoon. A mixture of snow and sleet slanted down through the murk, graying the lanes cleared by the snowplows only hours earlier. The boulevard below had four lanes in each direction yet the sparse traffic stayed to the outside, keeping one lane each way relatively clear. The temperature would probably be -20º C. by the time he left the building, but that was not a problem. He would never be exposed to it. He had people to do that for him.

He was content. Well…relatively content. His right elbow hurt like the devil, as it usually did when the barometer dropped. The best rheumatologists in the world said there was no cure, nor for his aching wrists and right shoulder. Yet the physical pain didn't bother him as it usually did. All was well. He was in control.

Shortening his focus to the window rather than the freezing city beyond, the reflection of a pair of crossed dueling sabers and trophies arranged on the wall behind him became clear, glowing quietly under recessed spotlights. They were proof that he wasn't merely one of the richest men in the country, not just the son of the richest and most powerful man in the country, nor only a supremely successful businessman. Not at all: he was more, much more! He was a Cossack! A warrior and a sportsman! And not just any warrior or sportsman, but the best swordsman in all of Russia!

Or he had been. Of all the thousands of matches in his life he'd lost only two, when he was still a boy. The two who defeated him he had later humiliated time and time again, to his vast satisfaction. But that was a long time ago and those opponents were ancient history now. More recently he had lost a fraction of his speed and flexibility, and that had been enough to dethrone him and leave him looking back to better times.

The excuse he confided to intimates was arthritis due to aging, but he kept the real reason a secret from everyone: he had not lost a match at all, but a true sword fight, and not to a satisfyingly valiant opponent but to a mere girl. His jaws clenched at the memory: a damnable slip of a girl in a strange uniform had broken into his father's house in the middle of the night accompanied by a male thug in black. His father had shot the thug, but that girl—that girl from hell! She was no expert with the saber, but he could never get the advantage over her. Her style was idiosyncratic but unbeatable, and against all odds she had somehow managed to severely injure him—she could easily have killed him had she been less merciless. His eyes narrowed to slits. It was her mistake that she was not, by God! Now that his investigator had discovered who she was, it would be his turn! He would arrange her death, very slowly and very painfully, no matter the cost, however long it might take. He smiled at his reflection. That investigator would make it happen. It would be wonderful.

The lunch period at Juarez Academy in Las Cruces, New Mexico, was almost over. It was a small school, and accommodated the entire student body in its cafetorium, the elementary students at one end and high school and middle school students in the other. They had mostly finished eating and were laughing and talking amid the clatter of dishes, utensils, and trays. One ninth grader, however, had quietly slipped out onto the gallery facing the playground, despite the chilly wind which gusted out of the northwest. He was huddled on a bench, bent over a book in his lap, holding down several sheets of paper which he studied closely.

His classmates knew him as Harry Saenz, but his real name was Heriberto. His family liked old-fashioned names. Some were handed down from ancestors but others might have come from the Bible—he had no idea. Although he was one of the many scholarship students at Juarez Academy and had been given a

90% tuition grant, his mother still had to pay the other ten per cent. It was difficult for her, and he was trying his best to fulfill his side of the bargain. Calling attention to his weird name would have been embarrassing.

At some point he realized someone was standing close. He looked up in surprise. It was one of the elementary girls, a fifth grader. She was just standing there, looking at him. He stared back for two beats.

"Hi," she said.

"Uh, hi."

"I'm Clio Méndez."

"Yeah, I know. I know your brother. Julio, right?"

"Uh huh."

"We, uh, we helped each other with projects last week."

"Cool."

Everyone in the school knew Clio Mèndez. She was a funny-looking little runt, small, skinny, Spanish-speaking but with chestnut hair too light to be pure Hispanic, kind of a pointy face, and nearly invisible eyebrows over keen pale hazel eyes that seemed to see straight into things. The wind was whipping her hair behind her. The word was she was one of the smartest kids in the whole school, next to her twin brother. She was making him nervous. Why was she standing there? What did she want? What should he say?

"I'm Harry."

She spoke again.

"You come to school with two dogs every morning, right? Are those your dogs?"

"Huh? Yeah."

"Where do they go while you're in school?"

"Home."

"By themselves?"

"Yeah."

"Is it far?"

"About a mile, I guess."

What was that to her?

"And they don't have trouble with traffic or other people?"

"No."

"And they come back in the afternoon to walk home with you?"

"Yeah."

"How do they know what time it is?"
"I don't know. They just know."
"How did they learn to do that?"
"I taught them."
"Awesome. Have you taught them other things too?"
"Yeah. I guess."
"Can you do that with other dogs?"
"Probably."
"Do you like animals?"
"I do."
"That's so cool. Can I meet them sometime?"
"The dogs? Uh, sure...."

The bell five feet over his head clanged loudly. He jumped and the wind instantly ripped the notes from under his hands. At practically the same moment, the girl snatched both out of the air, one in each hand. Her body hadn't moved but suddenly her arms were in front of her holding the flapping sheets by the corners. She put them together and handed them to him with a smile. He took them and looked at her. Had she really done that? Finally the clamor of kids and dozens of chairs scraping the floor leaking through the window behind him called him back to his senses.

"Thanks. Got a math test next period. Better go."
"Me too. I'll see you later...about those dogs? OK?"
"Sure."
"Good luck on your test."

"J-Man!"

Julio Méndez, wearing only a pair of shorts, was standing at a table in his room with his back to the door. His shirt and Nikes and socks were in a jumble on the floor. He was looking down at an open book, sliding a pair of parallel dividers across some kind of map, pencil ready in his other hand. He didn't look up even when Clio dropped her gym bag, making a pronounced 'plunk.'

"Hey, J-Man! Whatcha doing?"
"Huh?"

She repeated the question in Spanish.

"¿Qué haces?"
"Oh. Nothing. This book just came in. I'm looking at it."

"You been bicycling?"

"Uh-huh. What about you? Swimming?"

Clio was wearing a silver leotard.

"No. Gymnastics. I did a double flip today! Coach couldn't believe it!"

"You look like a fish."

"You gonna clean up?"

"Yeah."

"Well, get moving. I'm next."

"That's OK. You can go first." He turned back to the table. Still leaning against his door jamb she watched him a minute. Foosh, one of the family cats, ambled down the hall, delicately sniffed the gym bag, and began winding around Clio's ankles.

"Hey, you know a kid at school named Harry?"

"Huh? Harry Saenz? Yeah. What about him?"

"He said he knew you."

"Yeah. He's taking algebra II. He was having problems solving rational equations. He caught on pretty quick when I showed him how they were just like fractions."

"He said you'd helped each other on projects."

"Right. I was doing that folklore report for Mrs. Bianchi. He told me a bunch of stories his grandmother had told him."

"His grandmother? What kind of stories?"

"Oh, you know, like about 'la llorona,' the ghost of a mother who drowned her children, and 'la lechuza,' the owl with the face of a woman. Stuff like that. He said she was a curandera."

"No kidding! She's a faith healer?"

"Yeah. Reminded me of you, with all your herbs and junk."

"Is she still alive?"

"I think so."

"Cool!"

"Why did you ask if I knew Harry?"

"You've seen the dogs that come to school with him every morning, right?"

"Uh-huh."

"He trained them. They go home and then they come back when school is over. I wanna see what else he's taught them and how he does it."

"You would." He glanced at the alarm clock next to his bed. "Uh-oh. Dinner's in ten minutes. I better go clean up."

"¡Muévate! I get half of that!"

"You hope...fish-face."

It would have been a warm summer afternoon in Miami, except it was really late winter, as Michelle Stratemeyer strode into the cool lobby of her building, nudging the strap of her shoulder bag further up her shoulder. She took advantage of the one minute ride to the twelfth floor to hastily blot her face and run a brush through her hair.

"You have people waiting for you," the receptionist whispered as she approached.

"I know. I'm headed there now."

The receptionist made eyes at Michelle.

"Two men! One's a hunk!"

Michelle smiled slyly. Linda hadn't worked there long enough to meet all the big wigs who came by infrequently. She decided to tease her a bit.

"I know. One is a big-time journalist and the other is a former Seal."

"A Seal? Seriously? Which one? Is he married?"

"The journalist is the tall one. He's Ana Darcy's brother-in-law. The Seal is single."

Linda's eyes gleamed. "Purrrfect!"

"Down, girl. His little black book is probably legal size."

"I don't care! Introduce me when you're done and your next lunch is on me."

"That's the best offer I've had all day. I'll do it."

She winked and headed down the hall to the main conference room. The two men waiting inside had pulled chairs to face the bay while they chatted. They turned when they heard her enter.

"Hi, Scott, Rob. Sorry I'm a little late."

They stood. Scott Zimmer was closest and hugged her quickly.

"Great to see you again, Michelle. You look lovely."

"Thanks. I don't feel lovely. Kinda hot today. Hello, Rob."

Coombs, the former Seal, hugged her fractionally longer and closer than Zimmer had. Zimmer wore a brown blazer, khaki slacks and a gold tie over a white shirt. Coombs, several inches shorter than Zimmer's six feet, sported a crisp, pale blue dress shirt, maroon tie, and gray slacks. A navy blazer was draped over a nearby chair. Zimmer was semi-trim but Coombs was square-shouldered and compact and gave the impression of perfectly controlled strength. Irrationally, Michelle loved the dimple in his chin.

"Long time, Michelle. I've missed you!"

"Oh, Rob. Between keeping New York City safe and juggling girl friends you couldn't possibly have thought about me."

"I promise you," he said, looking into her eyes, "I have."

"Well...."

"And speaking of keeping things safe," he continued after a pause, "what's this all about? Is Ana Darcy going to need the services of World Security again soon?"

"Uh, well, maybe, but that's not what this is about. Yes, there's been some talk of a trip, but that's top secret for now, OK?"

She glanced at Zimmer.

"Hey!" he protested, "if I outed Ana Darcy, her sister would tear my face off! Don't worry about me!"

"I'm not worried. Well, I always worry about her, a little. But that's still to be decided. For now, the truth is I'm not sure what this is about."

"So, Scott and I dropped everything and came down here together and you don't know why?"

"Strange but true. The three of us have a meeting with someone very important we all know, but none of us have ever met in person. Or even seen a picture of...."

That stopped them.

"In fact," she added, "a picture would be impossible."

Finally Coombs spoke quietly.

"You couldn't possibly mean...Counselor Hleo?"

"You got it. He's been arranging this for a month, having me check your schedules for a time when you both were relatively free. That's why now."

"Counselor Hleo?" said Zimmer.

"Right. What do you know about him?"

"He's the Thoman who came here with Ana, isn't he?"

"He is. Let's sit down and I'll tell you about him. Do you all need anything to drink?"

Zimmer glanced at Coombs, who shook his head.

"Maybe later."

Michelle pulled a chair towards the window and sat with the others.

"I probably know him better than anyone except Ana. I lived with him!"

Coombs looked skeptical.

"When the people of Thomo sent Ana to locate the signals they'd been receiving from Earth, Hleo came with her. He had been a senior adviser and long-time retainer of her family. The way I understand it, he was quite elderly at the time the expedition was ready to take off, and he allowed his brain to be copied into a computer so he could accompany her. He managed their little station on the moon. He still does, I guess, It's weird. He's real, but he exists only in electronic form. I know he follows events on Earth, using the internet and other electronic media, and he helps Ana with things when she needs. He has more brain, or memory, or data banks than twenty of us. There's no telling how much information he has stashed away."

"We're meeting with him?" Zimmer marveled.

"He usually uses email, but he has a voice too. He had us hook up speakers for this afternoon."

"So we're going to meet with a dead person from a planet twenty five light years away who's living on the moon?"

"Well, basically, yes. But he's plenty alert! You'll see."

"I've dealt with him," Coombs said, glancing at Zimmer. "Ana and I went to Eastern Europe to untangle that mess her brother in law, uh, excuse me, Scott, her first brother in law, that other Thoman, that Harrison guy, had got messed up in. Hleo helped us with navigation, target location, and strategic planning. He was invaluable. He's a crusty cuss, but he's for real."

Zimmer nodded slowly. "I heard about that during the get-together we had, what, four years ago? It had to do with some kind of godawful weapon Russian fatcats were using to suppress some peasants somewhere, right?"

"That's right. Sedlakia. Ana and I went over there and destroyed them."

"Right," said Zimmer. He thought a second. He looked at Michelle. "You lived with him?"

"Yes. You were with her when she was kidnapped, ten years ago. I bet you remember that."

"Like it was yesterday."

"She promised that Mafia fellow that she would disappear, so he set her free. Everyone watched her fly back to the moon on television, right?"

"Right. His name was Cellini, Antonio Cellini."

"Yeah, but the person you saw leaving on the Thoman shuttle wasn't her."

Light dawned in the two men's faces. Coombs spoke first.

"Don't tell me! It was you?"

"Uh-huh. She fixed me up with a disguise and I took her place. I stayed in her station on the moon for three months, until the Thoman shuttle went back on a regular run. I sneaked back with it. While I was there, Hleo taught me to speak the language and all sorts of things about their history and culture. We became good friends. He calls me *prodcera*, 'goddaughter' in Luvit."

Coombs sat back in his chair.

"I'll be damned. I never knew that! I had no idea where Ana Darcy was during that time."

"My mother knows, you two know, and Ana's husband Matt knows. That's all. I'd like to keep it that way."

"Is that cool!" exclaimed Coombs. "You lived on the moon with an electronic alien from another planet...and became friends with him! What a yarn!"

"So, Rob, does that put me back on your list of girl friends?"

He smiled. "You were never off it, girl friend. And it isn't as long a list as you think."

He winked at Zimmer.

"This is the only woman who ever pinned me in a wrestling match. How could I not love her?"

"He let me, Scott."

"I did not! OK, I was weakened by a couple of beers. But I'll give you a rematch any time you want!"

"You're on, Rob. But not here in the office. Besides, I think Linda, the receptionist out front, has dibs on your next match. It's almost 2:30. Let's dial up Hleo and see what he has in mind for us."

The three keys to success: connections, money, and secrets! Viktor Reznik was certain of that. He'd studied successful people for years, to learn how they'd achieved their status. He had worked to acquire all three and now it was all coming together. He was headed for much greater things. He knew it.

He had excellent connections: he'd gone to school most of his life with Oleg Serbanov. Being in Oleg's good graces was the best possible connection. And now he worked for him!

He had money. Actually, his father had money, not nearly as much as Oleg's father, but adequate for a luxurious life, including a dacha, even if it wasn't quite up to the Serbanovs' palace. Enough of his father's money trickled down to him for a nest egg with which to make much, much more in the future.

And he had secrets, valuable secrets. His good friend Oleg had hired him to manage the security branch of his father's energy conglomerate, replacing an elderly Communist Party apparatchik who was well past his prime, living off his reputation and no longer firing on all cylinders. Viktor made a good impression early on by identifying the troublemakers who had thwarted the Serbanovs' plan to take over the energy reserves of tiny Sedlakia. It hadn't been difficult. All he had had to do was find and interview the sergeant who had been in charge of security at the Serbanov dacha where the troublemakers had appeared.

The sergeant, Dmitri Bondaruk, had told him two people, a man and a small woman, had been caught rifling the desk in Serbanov's office. He had marched them before the great man himself, who ordered him to call out the rest of the household guard, leaving two men to guard them. When he returned with a squad of men the two were in the process of escaping. Most lamentably, a hail of gunfire hadn't been enough to stop them. Vasily Serbanov, the old man, was in bad shape with a bullet in his chest, while Oleg was in perhaps worse shape, with at least thirty saber wounds in his body. None were fatal but he'd lost a lot of blood and most of the joints in his arms and shoulders had been punctured, some more than once.

Sergeant Bondaruk described both intruders in some detail, which was fortunate, because later, when Viktor went to Sedlakia to investigate the destruction of the weapon, he had found the entire country buzzing about the reappearance of some ancient Sedlakian warrior queen who had promised thousands of years ago to return to defend her people in time of need. A Russian living in Sedlakia told him there was a picture of this queen on a Sedlakian patriots' website. Back in Moscow, Bondaruk identified the person in the picture as the same woman who had taken a sword to the son of his employer. Her hair looked different but he was almost sure it was her.

Viktor made some cautious inquiries with the picture and determined that it apparently was a photo of Ana Darcy, the woman supposedly from the planet Thomo, the one who'd saved the planet from meteoroids after winning a half dozen medals in the Olympic Games. She was a worldwide celebrity. Even the kulaks knew who she was.

The story seemed too incredible to Viktor. First, what were the odds Ana Darcy, well-known as a publicity-shy and peaceful woman, would interpose herself into two countries and lay waste to private property, laboratories, and buildings? Why would she attack and nearly kill two corporate magnates? What were the odds she could prevail with the saber over the world's best swordsman, at least in his age category? It seemed as likely to him that the person in question really was the former queen of her people—certainly they believed it, anyway.

But Oleg wouldn't hear of it. He was certain his attacker had been Ana Darcy. He declined to explain to an underling like Viktor why he thought so but he ordered him to do whatever it took and spend however much it cost to get to her. Viktor smiled to himself. The stupendous sum he'd be paid if she were killed would be doubled if she were captured and turned over to Oleg alive. For that kind of money Viktor didn't care if she were Mother Teresa. Her days were numbered.

Such lovely secrets! He had another one, an even better secret. Vasily Serbanov, the old man, had taken him aside one day when Oleg was flying his MIG to offer him money under the table to report back to him on his son. The reason he gave was that he was concerned Oleg was wasting millions on fruitless weapons development, but Viktor learned the real reason from Olga, the old man's administrative assistant, during a drunken evening last New Year's Eve. Vasily was worried Oleg was preparing to push his father aside and take the whole company over for himself.

Secrets! Connections! Played skillfully they could lead to more money than his father had ever dreamed of! Yes, luck was a factor too, but whichever way this went, he would either please the old man with his loyal service or please his current employer with the body of some unfortunate small woman. Alive or dead, it didn't matter. He couldn't lose.

Chapter 2

The Rio Grande wears many personalities in its 2000 mile passage from its source high in the mountains of Colorado to its mouth among the salty sand bars of the Gulf of Mexico. It can be majestic, wild, happy, romantic, dangerous, even pitiful, but nowhere is it more sweetly domestic than in its passage through the Mesilla Valley of southern New Mexico, roughly 100 miles of fertile, elaborately irrigated land squeezed between the stark Rocky Mountains on the east and the blinding, empty Chihuahuan Desert to the west.

Francisco Coronado, in 1540, and Juan de Oñate in 1596, were the first Europeans to explore the area, but serious farming didn't begin until the early 1800s. Today the valley is a progression of stately commercial pecan groves, dairies, and fields of chilies, onions, and other produce. Historic Highway 28 meanders through all, following the river most of the 50 miles from Las Cruces to El Paso. Cool, shady, pecan groves alternate with tiny historic villages, some thriving, some not, irrigation canals, and a scattered assortment of small businesses and homes, a few new, most old, and some very old.

One of the older homes, occupying three acres fronting on Highway 28, belongs to Reyes Méndez, an 89 year old widow and materfamilias of the 120 year old Méndez estate. On the other side of the highway one of her fields extends to the river on the west. The main house lies comfortably in the center of the property. Behind it to one side is the home of the estate's last foreman and his family, now long gone, and on the other side is a barn, no longer used for purposes of agriculture. An adobe wall surrounds all, including eleven large cottonwood trees,

On this Saturday morning the only sign of life in the whole compound was a pair of quivering golden Rhodesian ridgeback dogs, eagerly working their way through bowls of food at the back of the foreman's home, renovated and occupied by Sra. Méndez' grandson Matt and his wife and two children.

The gate to the patio of the house opened and a young girl emerged. She closed the gate, brushed the crumbs of dog chow off her hands, patted the dogs, and strode to the back door of the big house with a quick, light step.

Sra. Méndez' hearing wasn't what it had been. She avoided wearing her hearing aids unless she had company because she couldn't stand their squealing as she adjusted them, so she wasn't aware she had a visitor until she heard the screen door off the kitchen slam. It was her great granddaughter, Clio, who already knew to speak louder to her great grandmother.

"¡Hola, Abuelita!"

"¡Buenos dias, mija!" replied the old lady. "¿Cómo amaneciste?"

"Muy bien, gracias," replied the girl, delivering a polite kiss to her cheek. "¿Y usted?"

Her great grandchildren's splendid manners often reminded the elderly lady of the social graces of her own, long-past youth. The twins learned them from their mother, she was sure.

"Muy bien, gracias a Diós."

"What are you doing, Abuelita?"

"I'm pitting cherries. These are early cherries, still tart, but they'll make wonderful pies. I'm going to take some when I visit my sister next week and I'll freeze the rest. You still like cherry juice, don't you?"

"Yes, ma'am! So does Julio!"

"Tell me, mija. What brings you over here on this bright, chilly morning?"

"I...I was wondering, Abuelita. Do you know a lady named Dolores Saenz?"

"Hmm. Dolores Saenz, you say? Sí, I think I know of such a person—not well, but I know someone by that name. Why do you ask?"

"Well, I heard she might be a curandera."

"Ahh." She wiped her fingers on a wet cloth and sat back and looked at Clio. "You miss Tia Fani, don't you?"

Clio's eyes began to glisten.

"Of course you do. She was a good friend to you. She taught you a lot, didn't she? But she was old, child, even older than I am. She's been with God for, how long, two years now? I told you I knew Epifania Guajardo when I was a little girl and she seemed old to me then. It was a blessing you got to know her and learn from her. ¿Y ahora qué? Have you found another hierbera to study with?"

"Maybe. A student at school told me his grandmother was a curandera. He asked her and she said she'd like to meet me. Dad's going to take me this morning."

"I see. What's her grandson's name?"

"Harry. Harry Saenz."

"Where does his grandmother live?"

"He said near La Union."

"Ahh. That's not far from here. Dolores Saenz. Sí, I remember her now. Her husband was a famous wrangler along the river. Do you know what a wrangler is?"

"Yes, ma'am. A wrangler works with horses."

"That's right. Don Emilio could do anything with horses. He was the best trainer of race horses in the valley. He worked right up to the day he died, God rest his soul. I'm afraid I don't remember his son, Harry's father."

"No, ma'am. Harry just lives with his mother."

"Well, something must have happened to him. Several of my friends have gone to see Doña Dolores with problems. They say she's very good. But she's just a young thing, thirty years younger than I am!"

She chuckled at her own joke as the polite toot of a car horn sounded outside.

"Oh! Dad's here! I've got to go. Bye, Abuelita! Thanks!"

A quick hug and she was out the door. Her grandson really should have come inside to say hello before hurrying off, but ni modo. Even if the children had better manners than their father he was still a good man, and a good grandson también. She took a sip of tea and turned back to her cherries.

Harry Saenz cursed his bad timing. He'd arrived a few minutes early in front of the tendajo where he worked from time to time so that Mr. Méndez wouldn't have to wait for him, and who should be coming down the sidewalk but a swaggering group of Tirilongos, boys from the neighborhood gang. Harry had grown up with most of them. They were the reason he was so glad to be going to Juarez Academy. They saw him before he could duck inside.

"¡Ese! ¡Carnal! ¿Qui hubo, Galgo?"

They prided themselves on their street slang. He did a handshake routine with them but not their gang sign. He wasn't in their gang, though they wanted him to be. Lito, the vato calote (the big guy), tilted his head back, narrowed his eyes, and invited him to come to their headquarters and drink a few birrias. Harry begged off, saying he had to work. Cande, who would have been a ninth grader like Harry if he had stayed in school, suggested that while he worked he could steal them a couple cartons of cigarettes. All Harry could think of to say was "Not today."

They loved nicknames. Their name for Harry was "Galgo," literally greyhound, but on the street it meant thin, puny-looking. The vatos locos (cool dudes) watched him pull open the door of the store. Lito made a pistol with his fingers and pulled the "trigger."

"We want you, man. You need to be with us. Orale, we're your family, 'mano. Sooner or later you gonna join us." He winked. "Ahí te guacho, cucaracho" (See you later, alligator).

He made a subtle gesture with his tattooed forearm and the rest of the kids sauntered after him. Harry stepped inside the store. Nicho (short for Dionisio) Silvas was watching from behind the cash register. Evidently he'd been sticking prices on canned tomatoes. Bar code technology had yet to reach most neighborhood tendajos.

"Buenas, Harry. Those kids bugging you again?"

"Yeah. They don't need me. I don't know why they think they do."

"They give you any trouble, you let me know. I'll call the cops on 'em."

"That's ok. But thanks."

"You grocery shopping, or you come in for work? You not supposed to be working today."

"No, I'm waiting for someone. I just ducked in here to get away from those guys. There's my ride. Thanks, Mr. G. I'll see you next week."

A white king cab pickup had pulled up out front. Clio's head was visible through the passenger side window. It wasn't a new truck by any means. He had wondered what kind of vehicles the Méndez family might drive. They were prominent people around the school, but it looked like Clio's dad drove an ordinary pickup. Clio pushed open the door.

"Hi, Harry! Let's go! I'll sit in the middle."

As he climbed in, Clio added, "This is my father Matt Méndez. Dad, this is Harry Saenz."

Matt reached across Clio and they shook hands lightly and exchanged greetings. Just as they pulled away, a tricked-out metallic black Escalade with dark windows and custom chrome rims glided past and turned the corner right in front of them. Mr. Méndez braked and shook his head but said nothing. Harry had seen the vehicle before, usually with several Tirilongos standing near, but he too said nothing.

Once under way, Clio and Harry chatted and Mr. Méndez asked about his grandmother's family. Her father seemed friendly enough, not that different from the typical male customer in the grocery store. He was wearing pressed jeans, a western shirt, and nice-looking but well broken-in boots, perfectly respectable for meeting his grandmother. Harry was relieved to find he didn't feel quite as awkward as he had feared he would.

Was it something about curanderas? Matt wondered. He'd never forget the day he'd walked Clio a mile down the acequia behind their house to meet Tia Fani. She must have seen something in Clio immediately. Whatever, they bonded right away and went inside and left him standing there. Pretty much the same thing had just happened with Sra. Saenz. The four of them had greeted each other normally enough, but when the herb lady shook Clio's hand she paused, squatted down and looked closely into her face, and immediately invited her into her house with the briefest apology to the two men. He and Harry had little choice but to wander around outside and chat.

It was an interesting house, at least: old adobe but in good repair, with a crowded garden out front full of ornamental plants in colorful pots, benches, and religious statuary. The front wall of the house had a lovely Virgen de Guadalupe on painted ceramic tiles set into it. Below was a fountain, some ofrendas and flowers arranged on the ground underneath. Behind the house there looked to be a chicken coop, a vegetable garden (were those herbs?), a wind chime, a wind sock, and more statuary.

He thought Clio's visit might conclude when two women pulled up out front in a dusty old Taurus with a large black exhaust smudge on the back bumper. The younger, perhaps 60, helped the other, much older, white-haired and using a cane, up the walk and into the house, but nothing came of it. Clio stayed inside.

The two of them ended up leaning against a corral several houses away, idly watching the horses within. After some initial reticence, Harry began to open up and actually talk to him.

"It's tough working while you're in high school," Matt was saying. "If your mother has a good job being a secretary at the county health office, do you really have to?"

"Well...yeah. She told me I could go to Juarez Academy if I wanted, but I'd have to help pay for it."

"Hmm." Matt knew Harry was one of many students who got 90% tuition grants. The thinking was that having to pay something themselves would help them feel fully enrolled and invest them in their own enterprise. Harry and his mother were struggling but they'd done it for three years successfully and he seemed determined to continue. That was good—not easy, but good. "What are your plans for the future?"

"I don't know. I'd like to do something with animals."

"Oh, yeah—Clio was impressed with your dogs and what you'd taught them. So you're good with animals?"

"I guess. Horses, mainly. I like horses. We don't have any, but I like them."

They watched a colt capering about inside the corral.

"What can you tell about these horses?"

"Huh? Well, the mare and the stallion over there are dam and sire. The other stallion is jealous. He'd like to challenge the other one. See how nervous he is?"

"You can tell that? I can see he's more active but I couldn't have told you why. How can you tell?"

"I don't know. I just can. He shouldn't be in there. He might hurt one of them. Maybe I can calm him down."

He began making a clucking sound with his tongue. All four horses looked at him. Finally the unrelated stallion began nodding his head up and down. He snorted twice, dragged a front hoof through the dirt, and took a couple steps toward the humans. Harry changed to kissing noises and extended his hand over the top board. Cautiously, the horse approached, eyes wide. Harry kept making an odd assortment of sounds, more softly as the animal neared.

Matt, fascinated, didn't move a muscle. When the horse got within six feet he extended his head and sniffed loudly several times. Another step...another...he shook his head, sending his mane flying. Finally his nose actually touched Harry's hand. He drew back, snorted, and took another step.

"It's ok," the boy said quietly. "It's ok." The skin on the animal's back quivered. He took another step, still sniffing. Finally Harry was able to rub his hand along the horse's jaw. The eyes were no longer wide. Harry patted him and began stroking his neck.

A sudden shrill peep caused the horse to start. Damn! His cell phone!

"Excuse me," Matt said, stepping away from the corral and fishing the squealing gizmo out of his jean pocket. Harry coaxed the horse back into range while Matt listened. "OK, mija. We'll be right there. Bye." To the boy he said, "She's done. Vámonos." Harry was still rubbing that horse. It was the damndest thing he'd seen in a good while.

"Did you like Sra. Saenz?" Matt asked as he slowed to ease past a line of vehicles, including a stake truck, a tractor attached to a tank of diesel fuel, and several pickups parked just off the shoulder of Highway 28. There was activity out in the field—planting something, from the look of it.

"Uh-huh," answered Clio, watching a tractor pulling an implement slowly along with a file of men and women following with bags over their shoulders.

"I guess what I really mean is do you want to see her again, is there something you can learn from her?"

"Oh! Yes," she said, paying better attention. "She doesn't know as much about animals as Tia Fani did, but she really knows about plants. She studied with a curandero in Mexico a long time ago. She said he was an Indian, a Chiricuahua, really old, and knew everything about thousands of plants. She's going to help me with mushrooms."

"Mushrooms?"

"Uh-huh."

Matt decided not to pursue the topic of mushrooms.

"What happened when those two women came in?"

"Doña Dolores treated one of them. I was going to leave but she asked me to stay. It was interesting."

"Yeah? How so?"

"It was funny. She told the lady what her problems were before the lady could tell her. I don't know how she knew but the lady said she was right. Then they prayed, and Doña Dolores brought out some ointments and dried stuff for teas. She told the lady that I was her assistant. She asked me which ones would be best for her. I wasn't sure but she wanted me to say, so I smelled and tasted them and told her which seemed good. She acted surprised, but she gave them to the second lady and told her how to use them."

"Hmm," said Matt, nonplussed. He was having visions of FDA inspectors knocking on his door inquiring about his twelve year old daughter practicing medicine and asking to see her license. But what did he know? Curanderismo was a centuries-old practice and he'd never heard of a suit resulting from it. He decided to knock on wood as soon as he could and hope his daughter had more in mind for herself than just being a herb woman. He wanted to know something else anyway.

"Why do you think Harry wanted us to let him off at that grocery store again? His house couldn't be that far away. I'd have taken him all the way home."

"Well, I don't know, Dad. He's really shy. I think he's embarrassed."

"Embarrassed by what?"

"Oh, maybe about his house, or his neighborhood. They're pretty poor."

"Ahh. Could be."

He should have thought of that. As far as he knew all societies were stratified socioeconomically and the one they lived in was very finely stratified indeed. In truth, there were great differences from bottom to top. Those near the bottom would think the Mendez family was near the top, which they might really be though they lived quite modestly. Yes, they were heirs to an old, prominent family, and yes they lived on a lot of land in comfortable buildings, but except for that they lived simply and mixed freely with all their neighbors. If those neighbors had any inkling of how well off they really were there'd be lots of consequences.

Matt had no idea how much money his wife had stashed away, millions, probably. And if they knew that Matt's wife was actually the first human to come to earth from another planet, there'd be even more consequences, most of them awkward. Anneyn Darshiell, more commonly known as Ana Darcy, was a name familiar to probably 98% of the people in the country if not the world. Under her married name, Ana Méndez was a local wife and mother. Despite keeping the lowest of profiles she pulled a lot of strings, like at the school their children attended, and helping direct the foundation that funded the mobile migrant education trailers that followed migrant workers' children through six states. His wife was probably the one responsible for Harry's 90% tuition scholarship at Juarez Academy. OK, then: credit Harry with good instincts.

"Well, no big deal. He seems like a nice kid. What kind of student is he?"

"He's always studying. He had some trouble with algebra II but Julio helped him. He does OK, I guess."

"That's good. He told me he wants to work with animals. Y'know, the more he studies the more possibilities he'll have. He seems to realize that, fortunately. You like animals too. If you want to invite him over some time that might encourage him. That is, if you can stand him."

He took his eyes off the road long enough to glance sideways at his daughter. She was soberly examining a Styrofoam cup of cuttings Sra. Saenz had given her.

"OK, Dad." A beat passed. "I can stand him."

"All right. If I can make this thing work we can start." Michelle consulted a sheet of paper and punched some keys on the computer before them. "Hleo is using some voice encryption thing and I have to enter a code…let's see…what day is this?" She mumbled to herself and punched a few more keys, checking the paper again. "Now, let's see. Counselor Hleo, are you there, sir?"

Muffled static came from the speakers. Zimmer frowned. Coombs leaned in his direction and whispered, "He's on the moon. There's a five second delay for a signal to reach the moon, and five to get back. You'll get used to it."

"I am here, my lady. I hope I see you well this day, *prôdcera* dear."

She replied with a liquid string of Luvit, evidently a standard greeting, and then switched back to English. "We are all three here, sir. We are at your command."

"Excellent! My warmest welcome and best wishes to the estimable Mssrs. Zimmer and Coombs. I am so appreciative of your goodwill and cooperation, gentlemen and lady. You do the people of Thomo great honor. I will endeavor not to impose too greatly upon you, but your help will be of the greatest value to the amicable unity of our two peoples."

Coombs rolled his eyes at Zimmer. He had some idea of how elaborate Thoman etiquette could be. Zimmer shrugged back at him. He was married to a Thoman and he knew it better than Coombs. In fact, there was much to be said for it. It did actually make interpersonal relations smoother, even as it made determining one's true feelings difficult. He had several Japanese friends with whom he'd felt the same uncertainty. He got along splendidly with them, but whether that was merely polite behavior or genuine friendship was sometimes hard to tell. He'd learned not to worry too much about it. That seemed to be the point.

"If I may, I would like to begin by explaining the task before me and how you may help it be accomplished, if you would be so kind. My apologies if any of what I shall say is already known to you.

"I am certain that you are aware Thoman culture deeply values tradition. Ever since those far distant days of our translation to Thomo our people have been aware of our uniqueness as a separate entity with connections, dim but very strong, to Earth, our original home. In the age before we learned to preserve the tales of our history permanently, in writing, we did so orally, taking great pains to preserve our narratives and honoring those among us who did so. Similar practices are not unknown on Earth, from the time of Homer among the ancient Greeks to the griots of Africa today.

"Our epic tales are recited on ceremonial occasions, festival days, and for entertainment and the education of the young. They define our very identity; they recount our challenges and our responses to them; they are standards for us to emulate. No one can call himself Thoman who does not know and cherish them. They are more than mere history: they are culture, they are literature, and they are art. I am proud to say that my honored goddaughter, the esteemed Ms. Stratemeyer, has read several of the most famous ones. Is that not so, my dear?"

"It is, sir, thanks to your kind guidance. I continue to explore them to this day, with the help of the Thoman website maintained by his excellency Ambassador Darshiell."

"You honor us, my dear. And soon, with the blessing, there shall be a new epic, a crowning epic, to add to those of yore! It is time to compose the story of the Honorable First Daughter of Clans, Anneyn Darshiell, daughter of The Honorable Leader of Clans, Heoren Darshiell, who fulfilled our people's goal for the ages: to reconnect us to our original home and bring the entire history of our people full circle. As you know, she did this on her own initiative and in the face of the most extraordinary difficulties. It is a thrilling tale, and a monument to humanity.

"I have seen to it that the basic facts of her efforts, and those of our tiny Thoman delegation, have been transmitted to Thomo. I began this thirteen years ago, which means that the first news will be arriving at Thomo in another twelve years. I now judge it the proper time to sum up what has occurred to date, to express it in the finest epic verse of which I am capable, and present that to the people of Thomo. It will be the culmination of the story of our people for the last three thousand years."

Coombs raised his eyebrows at Zimmer, who silently puffed out his cheeks. Hleo continued.

"You three have been more deeply involved with First Daughter Darshiell than anyone else except her husband, whom I will contact separately. I know the broad outlines of your experiences together, but I must beg you to allow me to ask you to supply some of the details which I do not yet know. Such details are as crucial to a history as they are to a work of art. I have asked Ms. Stratemeyer to make available separate communication channels for each of you. It will be possible for us to communicate simultaneously yet separately, and in so doing I would estimate the total time required would be one day only, tomorrow, if you will. This afternoon perhaps we may lay out the substance of what is to be covered tomorrow. I pray that will be agreeable to you."

Michelle glanced at her companions.

"It will, sir. We will be honored, of course."

"Uh, Counselor," Coombs leaned toward the microphone, "Excuse me. Ana Darcy and I only worked together about a week, and you were in communication with us for nearly all of that time. Just what can I tell you that you do not already know, sir?"

"You are correct Master Chief Coombs."

Hleo had somehow learned his rate in the Navy four years ago. Using it now seemed excessively honorary—no one had ever called him "Master Chief Coombs" anyway. "Chief Coombs" was the accepted form. Maybe it was a Thoman thing.

Hleo continued. "I must emphasize that a Thoman epic is not merely a history. Character is paramount. For example, First Daughter Darshiell twice went among Sedlakian guerillas and convinced them to aid her. When you two were captured, she fought three soldiers and enabled your escape. I was not present at those times. You were. Those are the events for which I would like a more personal description."

"Now I understand, Counselor. I wish you could have seen her use a sword. I would never have dreamed it possible! It was...."

"Exactly, Chief Coombs. And as for Mr. Zimmer: you, sir, were present when she was kidnapped, as well as when she was attacked by a martial arts master. I know the basic facts, but I shall be most grateful to have your first-hand narrative. And my esteemed goddaughter likewise was present during a foiled assassination attempt. Beyond that, my dear, since you have been with her in many social settings, perhaps you would allow me to ask about more quotidian matters."

"Quotidian?"

"Yes, that is, the way she has integrated herself, adapted, as it were, to a quiet life as a wife and mother, while still retaining the ability to act on a more formal, public scale as a Thoman representative, when the occasion presents."

"I see, sir. We all do." She paused a moment. "We look forward to tomorrow, then."

"Excellent, Honored Goddaughter. You do us great honor. I shall weave your collective memories into the crowning epic of the Thoman people—and you, my dear, shall be the first to read it!"

After a few more formalities, Michelle shut the computer off. Zimmer drained the last of his coffee and Coombs pushed his chair back from the table.

"Man," he said. "Just thinking about that sword fight has got me going again. I've seen my share of combat, but never anything like that. She's a small woman and she went up against a tall, expert fencing champion and she totally whipped his ass. It was beautiful!"

Zimmer set the empty mug down. "I could say the same thing about that Russian giant. At the time I was terrified for her but looking back on it, it's as if the fellow never had a chance. By the time he actually touched her, he was already done for."

Michelle smiled. "I guess I have a similar tale for Hleo, but right now I'm remembering her with her children, up in the mountains on the Williams' ranch. So gentle, and such sweet kids—just like their mother, really. You'd never imagine...."

"No, you wouldn't," said Coombs.

Chapter 3

Viktor Reznik mopped his face for the third time and tossed the towel into his locker as his boss emerged from the shower. Oleg was in excellent shape for his age, lean and hard. He was smiling, and Viktor knew why.

"Good match, Mischka! One day I think you will beat me!"

"I pray it be soon," he replied. "If it happens I will demand a certificate. No one would believe it otherwise."

It never hurt to suck up to the big man. Viktor thought he could have actually beaten him today at squash, but even if he could have he wouldn't have dared. He wasn't stupid. He didn't mind "losing" to the man who paid his salary. What he did mind was being called by the diminutive form, Mischka, of his middle name, Mikhail. It was a subtle or not-so-subtle indication of the difference in status between him and his old schoolmate. In school Oleg had had a nickname like everyone else, but now that he was so powerful he assigned others nicknames. No one else ever risked being that familiar with him, at least not in his presence.

Oleg chuckled and began toweling himself off. Viktor noted the scars on Oleg's chest and ribs, and, when he turned to his locker, the ones on his upper back. There must be more than two dozen. Thanks to his interview with Sergeant Bondaruk he knew those scars came from the fencing match Oleg had lost, with that girl. He had never told Oleg that he had talked to Bondaruk or that he knew about the match. He wasn't stupid.

"So," said Oleg, removing his pants from a hangar, "how are things in Security, eh? All smooth?"

"Yes, very smooth indeed. In fact, there are developments you will be interested to hear about."

"Ah? Having to do with that unrest in Tajikistan, perhaps? Have you smashed that?"

"No. Having to do with that, uh, with that person you asked me to locate."

He looked around automatically. They were alone. Oleg, buttoning his shirt, froze. He spoke quietly.

"You mean...*her*?"

"Yes."

Oleg looked around too.

"Excellent. I'll be in my office. One hour."

Exactly one hour later, Viktor found Oleg looking crisp and taut, with a Dior tie that would have cost the weekly wages of the common citizen snugged up under his collar. Oleg was not the sort to work with a loosened tie. With his black hair freshly slicked down his face looked harsher than ever, like a hungry wolf.

"Ah, Mischka. Come in. Sit down. Coffee? Vodka?"

"Neither, thank you. Sadly, it is too late for one and too early for the other."

"As you wish. You have news of *her* already?"

"It would be safest to say 'possible news.' It comes from our man Genady at the United Nations, who heard it from Ambassador Levitov himself. It was in connection with that G8 Summit Conference taking place next month in Milan."

He paused. It was so gratifying when he knew the questions Oleg would ask—and the answers to them. He could have said it all in one sentence but it was much more satisfying to drag it out a bit at a time, dramatically.

"What about it?"

"One of the themes of this conference is to be philanthropy."

"So?"

"And one of the special invited guests is to be Ambassador Darshiell, of the planet Thomo."

"Ahh...."

"Yes. And as you know, the person most directly responsible for the philanthropy of the people of Thomo is the woman, Ana Darcy."

A steely glint came to Oleg's eyes.

"I must stress that we only know that Ambassador Darshiell has been invited to address the conference. But it is also worth assuming that his niece will accompany him, whether or not she speaks. It would be a considerable publicity coup for them."

"In Milan, you say...."

"Yes, in Milan. I have taken the liberty of alerting our best intervention team. They began training for all possible eventualities three days ago. In addition, I have sent a team of agents to Milan to scout out the venues the conference will use, and to study the hotels and likely travel routes between them. If and when circumstances come together properly, we shall be ready."

His boss stared at him as if he were considering killing and eating him for his next meal.

"Excellent. Well done. Remember, alive if possible. But if not...."

"I remember."

"Keep me advised."

Oleg stared out his window for ten minutes after Reznik departed. Today the only snow remaining was in small patches in shady places. Traffic was flowing freely on the boulevard below. Tiny green spears were emerging from the bulbs in the planter outside the window. He noticed none of it. He swiveled to his desk and picked up the phone.

"Get me Petrov."

While he waited he focused absently on the sabers in the case on the wall.

"Piotr? Yes, very well, thank you. Tell me, Piotr, how soon can the yacht be ready for sea?"

"Two weeks? Good. I feel like doing a little archeology. I want you to sail in two weeks to Corsica. Find a harbor with first class accommodations and make the arrangements. Check the moorage carefully. The Galaxie is too big to fit in some harbors. Let me know once you have done so. Do you understand? Very well, then. Goodbye."

He swiveled back to the window and resumed staring at nothing in particular, thumbs tapping against the arms of his chair.

Harry Saenz massaged his aching bicep and stared out the dusty bus window as the scenery rolled past. Stupid Tirilongos, anyway. He'd spent a couple hours this Saturday morning at Mr. Silvas' tendajo restocking shelves. It was a small store and the job was easy, but when he was about to leave Mr. Silvas asked him to drop off a half gallon of milk and a bag of sugar at Sra. Lerma's house, and that's when it happened. The poor old lady was too sick to walk to the store and she had no family, so he couldn't say no. The problem was her house was next door to the old body shop where the Tirilongos hung out. That Escalade was parked on the far side and he could see people standing around inside the building. They seemed to be giving each other stuff but the bright sun made it hard to see people in the shade.

He'd dropped off the groceries and headed back to the through street when several Tirilongos confronted him. They were insulted that he didn't want to join their gang, and things got a little rough for a minute. He was no fighter and he didn't think fighting would help even if he was. He managed to get away just as the bus pulled up. Forty-five minutes after transferring to the third bus his arm still hurt where Moco had punched him.

He saw the long adobe wall he was looking for over the bus driver's shoulder. He pulled the cord and the bus groaned to a stop and let him off. As it roared away in a cloud of diesel exhaust he crossed the road and headed through the open gate. Two large dogs within raced toward him barking loudly but he quickly convinced them he was friendly and soon they were competing with each other to be patted.

At the sound of a shrill whistle the dogs whirled and streaked around the left side of the big old house in front of him. Clio appeared from behind it. She shouted "Hey, Harry!" and beckoned. He waved and started walking.

So this was the Méndez place. It was nice: spacious and shady under the cottonwoods, soft grass everywhere except for a garden against the left wall. He wouldn't have been surprised to find a swimming pool and a Suburban or Lexus but he saw nothing flashy at all. The only vehicle he noted was the back end of Mr. Méndez' old white pickup visible on the far side of a smaller house to his right. An assortment of wrought iron patio furniture was scattered around a concrete slab behind the main house. Clio was waiting for him next to an old barn, rubbing the dogs.

"Hey, Harry, you made it!"

"Yeah. No problem. How you doin'?"

"Good. Ooh, what happened to you?"

"Huh? What do you mean?"

"You've got a cut on your forehead. It's bleeding!"

"Huh?" He reached up and touched it. Damn! She was right! "Oh. It's just a bump."

"I can fix that. C'mon in here."

She led him through the open door behind her into what had probably been a feed room when there were livestock about, but it seemed to have been renovated for...for...well, he had no idea. There were shelves on both walls, good lighting overhead, a counter with a number of electric appliances lined up, and...was that a microwave oven? And under the counter a little refrigerator? On the shelves were rows and rows of jars and boxes. The jars all bore labels and seemed to contain a variety of dried leaves, flakes, and powders. On the far wall, bunches of shriveled plants hung from hooks. Clio was looking in the refrigerator.

"Here we go," she said, producing a shallow glass dish. Removing the lid, she wiped up a small blob of whatever was in it on her middle finger. Turning to him she said, "Now, hold still."

He flinched.

"What's that?"

"It's an antiseptic, silly. Plus there's an astringent to stop the bleeding and some aloe to help it heal. Be still."

Pursing her lips, she dabbed the goo on his cut. It stung a little but it also felt cool.

"There. How's that feel?"

"Um...it feels good. Where'd you get it?"

"I made it."

"You made it?" He felt stupid asking but he really wanted to know.

"Yeah. I didn't invent it. It's a folk remedy, actually three, but I combined them. Curanderas know about all of them. I found you can mix them and store them a long time if you keep them cool, that's all."

"Huh. Thanks." He looked around. "So what is this room, anyway?"

"It's just my shop. Mom and Dad gave us this room at the back of the barn. Mine takes up half and Julio's takes up half. His is through there."

"Neat! So, what do you do in here?"

"Whatever I want. I've been collecting the herbs and plants that I've learned about and experimenting with them. You wouldn't believe all the stuff they're good for. Mostly, I use them on dogs and cats and other animals. You'll be my human experiment for this stuff."

She set the dish back in the refrigerator and closed the door.

"OK. What's all that?" He pointed to a retort, Bunsen burner, coiled copper tubing, and other vessels clustered next to the sink.,

"That's a still."

"A what?"

"A still. It's used to distill essences, like for perfume and medicine." She grabbed a small bottle from the counter and pulled the stopper. "This morning I distilled a bunch of petals from some of Mom's roses. Here, smell this."

A strong, flowery, rose-like scent hovered around the top of the vial. It was overpowering.

"Sweet! What are you gonna do with this?"

"I guess I could make perfume, or lotion, or put it in soap. It might have medicinal properties; I don't know. I'll keep it until I think of something."

"Way cool!"

"You want to see the rest of this place?"

"Yeah. Sure!"

He lost track of time as she began showing him around her "shop." Normally he would have been embarrassed by his ignorance, but she was so open and happy to talk that he forgot to feel awkward. It was fascinating. She must have collected hundreds of herbs and plants, some of which she said she had ordered over the internet from other countries. He knew about curanderas but he'd never once considered that what they did out of tradition might be something worth studying. Clio was actually doing it. He was impressed.

She let him peek into Julio's shop too, a totally different place, full of electronic equipment, junk, spools of wire, a dirty computer, and machines and tools of all kinds, some obviously purchased and some cobbled together seemingly haphazardly. Sheets of paper with graphs and columns of figures littered the counters and the floor was crunchy with bits of wire and, he guessed, blobs of solder.

"What is all this?"

"I have no idea. You'll have to ask Julio. He's in the house, working on some correspondence course he's taking. Maybe we'll see him later."

His questions prompted descriptions of how she macerated some plants, infused others, and ground still others into a powder, using the traditional molcahete and mano, and a mortar and pestle. She was demonstrating reducing a thimbleful of chili pequin seeds to a highly potent powder when there was a soft knock at the door. It was Mr. Méndez.

"Hi, guys," he said. "You all having fun?"

"Yessir," he replied, shaking hands quickly, his shyness suddenly returning. Mr. Méndez glanced at his forehead but thankfully said nothing.

"Good deal. Sorry to interrupt. Hey, Harry, I remembered our talk last Saturday, when you said you wanted to work with animals. I called a fellow I know, Hank Stallman. Ever heard of him?"

He shook his head.

"He runs a stable down towards Anapra, near the race track. He trains race horses and quarter horses. He told me his track supervisor could use a part-time assistant, and he was willing to have you meet him. You got anything you need to do this afternoon?"

Harry shook his head again.

"Well, would you be interested? If he hires you, you could get there on the same bus you took to come here."

"Yes, sir!"

"All right! Clio, why don't you finish up out here and you two come inside for lunch? Afterward, I'll run Harry out to Stallman's place and we'll see how it goes, OK?"

As Matt headed back to the house, Harry turned to Clio, thunderstruck at his good fortune. She was dumping the chili pequin powder onto a sheet of paper. She rolled the paper into a cone and tapped it gently so it slid into a tiny jar. Her father's stunning offer didn't seem to surprise her at all.

"Dad's cooking today. Mom's off watching some sporting event. But it'll be all right. He's not too bad a cook."

Matt and Hank Stallman watched the track supervisor, a small sunburned man named Tony, walk off down a long row of stalls with Harry. Clio tagged along with them. Stallman, tall and ruddy-faced, with sandy hair turning to white, said, "They might be a while. Got time for a beer, Matt?"

"You bet."

The little field office was tucked among a half dozen other metal buildings including an equipment shed, a feed room, and a couple other structures Matt could only guess at. The air inside was cool and moist, a pleasant contrast to the dry heat outside. An evaporative air conditioner hummed in a window. In a corner a muted television was showing a baseball game. Stallman pushed a couple of chairs to face the window and pulled two dripping bottles of Negra Modelo out of a cooler next to his desk.

"This stuff all right?" He wiped the water off one with his hand and passed it to Matt.

"Yeah, love it! Thanks," Matt said, raising his bottle in Stallman's direction. He took a modest sip.

"There's a lot of activity going on here. You working up to some horse races maybe?"

Stallman took a pull on his own bottle and swallowed slowly.

"Nawww, the racing season is really pretty quiet now. Most of that action is movie people, believe it or not. They're filming a western, mostly in their studios in California, but they needed some scenes in New Mexico and they wanted a place where they could keep animals, so I was willing to help out. You wouldn't believe how they spend money."

"Well, I guess that's all right with you, huh?"

"Damn straight. Until racing season gets going, there's not a lot of money coming in at all. This year'll be different, thanks to Hollywood."

They paused to watch a horse gallop around the track beyond the window. The jockey was up off the saddle, moving fluidly with the horse. The hoofbeats barely sounded over the hum of the air conditioner. Mount Cristo Rey, in the distance, looked like cutout sheet metal against the sky, bluer than the gray of the more distant mountains on the horizon.

"Your daughter's a cute little thing. She doesn't favor you much, does she?"

"Lucky for her. People say she looks like her mother. My son is the one who looks like me, poor guy."

"Now, that other kid, Harry Saenz. Tell me about him."

"He goes to school with Clio. She's in the fifth grade. He's a ninth grader, good student, from a poor family. They struck up sort of a friendship because they both love animals. I got to watch Harry operate around horses last week. I was impressed—he seems to be on their wavelength somehow. He told me he'd love to work with horses, so I thought of you."

"It's that name, Saenz, that's got me wondering. Do you know anything about his people?"

"Not much. He lives with his mother. I've not met her. His grandmother lives near La Union. Her name is Dolores."

"Dolores Saenz? No kidding? Does she have a husband?"

"She's a widow. I think her husband died some time ago."

"Well I'll be damned."

"What?"

"When I was a kid my dad had a trainer named Emilio Saenz. That man was an ace, the best trainer in the valley. His horses made so much money for my father he was able to buy this place. Don Emilio! I remember him—a wiry old fellow, very gentle and quiet, but he could talk to horses in their language. I don't know what he died of but it was sudden and too early. His son worked here a while but he wasn't worth much. And so this is his grandson?"

"I guess."

"I'll flat be damned. Maybe the gift skipped a generation. I'm gonna be real interested in what Tony has to say about young Harry Saenz."

They chatted companionably another twenty minutes until Stallman was about to offer Matt another beer when Tony returned with Harry and Clio. Stallman opened the door and ushered them in. He pointed to the cooler.

"You kids like some sodas? Help yourselves. No beer, now—not with your dad watching!" He turned to Tony. "So, how'd it go?"

"I think we might have us an assistant trainer," he replied, "as much time as he can give us."

"Good deal!" said Stallman. "How about it, Harry? You want to work for us?"

"I...yes, sir, I do!"

"Consider yourself employed, then. You and Tony work out a schedule and I'll tell our business manager to draw up a contract for you. Glad to have you with us, Harry."

They shook hands. Tony cleared his throat diplomatically.

"Uh, there's something else, Mr. Hank."

"Yeah? What?"

"The movie people...."

"What about them?"

"They want to hire Mr. Méndez' daughter." He turned to Matt. "I told them they'd have to talk to you about that. I'll show you where to find them."

Matt stared at Tony. Then he looked at Clio. She was smiling like a cat—a cat with canary feathers stuck to its snoot.

As soon as Matt cut the engine Clio hopped out to run tell Julio about her new job. Ana still wasn't home. The tournament must be running long. His wife dearly loved the martial arts. She wasn't competing, fortunately—it was apparently more a demonstration tourney this time. He stepped into the house for a restroom break and to check supplies in the kitchen and then headed out the front door to see what Abuelita wanted to do about supper, but mainly to tell her about her great granddaughter's first paying job.

She was on the phone, but that was good because it meant she had at least one hearing aid in place. She waved at him and ended her conversation after only five minutes more, hanging up but not slowing her flow of speech.

"Buenas tardes, Matt. You won't believe the visitor I had while you were out! You met Dolores Saenz last week, didn't you? Well, she just stopped by. Such a lovely person. She'd been visiting in Las Cruces, and she just had to tell me about meeting Clio. She says she's a born healer. She's never seen anyone who was so gifted at diagnosing and treating people's problems. She said two ladies stopped by last week when you were there. Did you see them?" Matt nodded but Abuelita barely paused. "Clio knew just how to treat Mrs. Estrada, she even had ideas that Sra. Saenz hadn't thought of. She spoke to the ladies so quietly and sweetly that they thought they were hearing the voice of an angel! An angel, Matt! But that's not all! She also recognized a problem her daughter, Sra. Campos, had, that she hadn't even known about herself, and Clio told her to see a doctor, and three days later she did, and the doctor said she came in just in time. Matt, it's like a miracle! ¡Dios mío!" She crossed herself. "Can you believe that, grandson? ¡Un milagro!"

Abuelita paused to take a breath. Matt shook his head.

"That is unbelievable, Buela, de veras. It's funny, too, because I have more news about Clio. You won't believe this either."

Those were the magic words. He had her attention.

"I just took Clio and her friend Harry out to Stallman's stables to see about getting Harry a job training horses. They liked him. They hired him—but get this, Abuelita. There was a big crew of people from Hollywood there, making a movie. There's a scene in the movie where a mountain lion jumps on the back of the hero. They had three mountain lions with them. The cat trainer was shocked when Clio walked up to their cages and all three came to greet her. They started purring, and she reached through and petted them! The trainer nearly died. She told me mountain lions are dangerous and difficult to work with, but they calmed down when Clio was around. She begged me to bring her back, to work some more with them. She said she'll not let her in the cages, but anything that makes the animals more manageable will be save a lot of expensive time for the director. She'll pay her! What do you think about that?"

Abuelita sighed audibly, clasping her hands to her breast.

"Ay, ¡qué niña! Matt! ¡Qué santa niña, bendecida de Diós! ¡Ay, pero que cosa, Matt!"

She crossed herself again, kissed her fingers, and pressed them to the magnetic Virgen de Guadalupe on her refrigerator. Matt forgot about planning supper. He was making a mental note to ask Clio about diagnosing a genuine medical condition. God was one thing, but Caesar and Caesar's laws better not be ignored either.

"Hey, Mom, you wanted to see me?"

"Hi, Michelle. Yes. Come in please, and shut the door."

That was a little unusual. Michelle usually saw her mother several times a day in the Second Planet Foundation offices, but a private conference was rare. They were not unknown, though, and Michelle had an idea what the topic would be.

"I've been talking with Rothan Darshiell."

Rothan Darshiell was the senior of the three Thomans who joined his niece Ana Darcy several years after her own arrival on Earth. The matter of seniority among the rank-conscious Thomans was a bit confused: Ana, being the eldest daughter of the head of clans of Thomo, should have been senior, but her marriage to Matt Méndez removed her from the Thoman clan hierarchy, leaving Rothan in charge. Since then, however, Rothan had married his niece and Matt a second time, under Thoman law, thus uniting his "clan" and hers and ostensibly restoring her position. But it was muddled since the Méndez clan had no ranking on Thomo, she was separated from the Thoman clan structure by twenty five light years, and cared nothing for rank anyway. She preferred to live privately as much as possible. The result was that Rothan remained senior in practice, consulting her as required. He was a jolly, gentle man with a keen mind and he loved being Ambassador to the United Nations.

The other two Thomans were not factors: Ana's next-oldest sister Ianthe had originally been married to the fourth Thoman on Earth, Herecyn Cymred, but when he violated Thoman law, disgracing the Thoman people in the process, Rothan granted Ianthe a divorce. She remarried American journalist Scott Zimmer. Herecyn had since roamed the margins of society on his own.

Michelle took a seat as her mother continued.

"Rothan is going to attend the G8 Conference in three weeks. The leaders of those eight countries represent 65% of the world's economy, and they're having a special summit session on philanthropy."

Michelle could see it coming. The Thoman U.N. delegation would provide Ana's security. Her mother continued: "He's going to invite Ana to attend with him. It makes sense, really. She'll accept, won't she?"

Michelle was practically a scholar of Thoman culture, and she knew Ana as well as anyone except her husband. She nodded.

"Yes. No doubt about it. She'll feel obligated."

"Right. So we'll need to provide security."

"Sounds like a job for World Security Services."

"I agree. They're good and we've used them before. Ana likes them. How about I call Darlene Pizzoli and see if she can set it up? Maybe she can get Rob Coombs to be in charge."

"Exactly what I was thinking. Where's the conference going to be?"

"Milan."

"Milan? Wow, I may have to go along to help! I'd love to visit Milan!"

"I suspect it'll be a nightmare. Milan is a big, industrial city. Previous G8 conferences have always attracted protesters. There've been riots and mass arrests, complete with bombs and tear gas. I think you'd better visit Milan another time."

"Maybe you're right. Too bad. Well, I hope three weeks is enough time to set things up properly."

"I do too. I'll call Darlene right away."

"Does Ana know about this?"

"No. Not yet. I'll let you contact her. Just let me know what she says before we go home. We can't afford to waste a minute."

Chapter 4

Matt loved doing man things with his son. He enjoyed doing things with his daughter too but there was just something special about two guys, father and son, working together on a project. When Julio was younger Matt had generally been in charge, but nowadays a few of their joint projects were so technical that Julio was sometimes the more knowledgeable one. That was OK with him, and probably good for Julio too. Other times, like now, they were nearly partners in full. Matt would remember these moments for a long time. He hoped Julio would too.

This evening they were going to work on repainting the pod, the escape vehicle Ana had used to come to Earth from the moon thirteen years ago. It was roughly the size of a minivan, but originally only had two seats. Matt had added two more seats behind the two in front to accommodate the whole Méndez family.

Julio loved the pod. It was the only thing in the family (not counting his mother) that had come from Thomo, 25 light years away. Its propulsion system endlessly fascinated him, though Matt warned Julio not to mess with it. The vehicle remained, after all, Thoman property, and Ana had estimated it had cost a billion dollars to create, more or less. Like the two larger Thoman vehicles, one on its way back to Thomo with a load of trade goods and scientific and cultural material, and the other now parked on the moon, plus the bus-sized shuttle that traveled back and forth to Earth, they all somehow used gravity for propulsion. It could hover and it could fly faster than sound, yet its engines made almost no noise. It did not, however, have the thrust necessary to leave

Earth orbit. Ana had employed it on several important missions, but since its existence was secret it had to be used with extreme discretion.

The "paint" they were to reapply was crucial. Formulated by Hleo, it contained metallic compounds that, when connected to a box of electronic components he had also designed, caused the pod to absorb electromagnetic radiation rather than reflect it—especially in the high frequencies used by radars. As long as it worked, the pod was invisible to radar. The paint wore off in flight, however, and had to be reapplied every couple of years.

Julio liked visiting the "secret hangar," partly because it was secret and partly because it contained the pod and a number of large power tools: an air compressor, a drill press, an arc welder, and more. Clio wasn't interested in working on the pod and had stayed home. She valued it as a means of transport but didn't share Julio's regard for it as a gadget, and she thought of the hangar merely as a garage which formerly had been something else, a place for processing and warehousing pecans. The owners of the orchard had built a larger facility closer to El Paso, so Matt was able to lease the building as a family "machine shop." It actually wasn't a secret building, but access to it was controlled because pecans were a valuable crop and the orchard owners employed fences, gates with keypads, and regular security patrols to keep people out.

Julio was eager to begin.

"Hey, Dad, what pressure do you want the compressor set to?"

"Ninety p.s.i., son, please."

"OK, Dad."

Further conversation had to wait while the powerful electric motor chugged into action. When it quit, with a tired-sounding wheeze, Matt found Julio at his elbow.

"Need help with that, Dad?"

"Yeah, sure. See how I'm doing this?"

"Uh-huh."

He had been carefully pressing masking tape around the edges of the windshield and then taping sheets of newspaper onto those strips of tape. Julio started on the other side and they worked toward the middle together. In fifteen minutes they were taping the last sheets of newspaper in the center.

"So you're not gonna paint the windshield?"

"No! It'd be hard to see out if I did."

"Well, if the paint absorbs radar, then won't the windshield reflect radar? Won't the pod be visible?"

"Oh. Well, I guess it would. Hleo's instructions were not to paint it, though."

Julio looked thoughtful. He and Hleo were old friends, by email, at least. He had great respect for "Uncle" Hleo.

"But you're going to paint all the rest of it, right?"

"Right."

"Well, Hleo must've figured that the windshield would have a tiny radar signature anyway, and only from a radar in front and above. Since most radars would be on the ground I don't guess that would matter."

"Hmm...probably not." Matt had never thought about that. "OK, that's done. Now we need to mix the paint. You can help with that."

"OK, Dad. But don't you need to jack up the pod so you can paint the bottom?"

"Nope. We'll paint it in two stages, top first. Then I'll use the pod's remote to raise it up six or seven feet and we'll just let it hover there while we paint the underside. How about that?"

"Cool!"

Matt knocked on the side.

"Good ole pod. It feels tough."

"It is," Julio replied.

"Yeah? What's it made of, I wonder?"

"Glass."

"Glass? You're kidding!"

"No. I asked Hleo."

"Glass breaks!"

"It's not regular glass. The molecules in regular glass are random. These are lined up, or something like that. Hleo didn't explain it completely but he said it's way stronger than steel."

"Wow. Good ole pod! I'll set out the cans of ingredients. Why don't you get the electric drill and chuck the paint stirrer? You can also bring the spray gun off that shelf over there."

"Right. Hey, Dad, aren't we doing this early? You said at Christmas we'd paint it over the Easter break."

"Yeah, I did. But that was before I found out Abuelita was going to visit her sister for a week. I'll take her up there and stay a day or so. And then the family is planning a reunion over the spring holiday, because it's close to Buela's ninetieth birthday and they want to celebrate that. It'll be at our place and we'll have folks everywhere. There'll be no time then to sneak off and paint the pod. What's the matter?"

Julio was looking stricken.

"How many people?"

Matt measured out a quantity of pale gray fluid and poured it into a large can.

"I don't know. Maybe as many as twenty. So what?"

"Will there be kids, little kids?"

"Probably. Why?"

"They'll get into my lab and mess it up. They'll wreck my room."

He consulted a sheet of paper, selected another small can, and began prying the lid open.

"Well, let's lock up your lab. We better lock Clio's shop, too. We don't want any guests getting electrocuted or zonked on Clio's herbs. You'll just have to put the goodies that are in your room in the lab for a few days, that's all."

A strong smell of solvent filled the air. He poured an amount from the small can into a measuring cup and dumped it in the large can too.

"It should be all right. Besides, you'll meet relatives you've never seen before. You might even like some of them. Stranger things have happened. Hand me that drill, please, mijo. And let's put those breathing masks on. It's going to get thick in here for a while."

It was twilight when Matt and Julio returned home. Matt headed for the laundry room to scrub the paint stains off his fingers. When he finished, Julio was standing by the door.

"Dad...."

"Yes?"

"Clio isn't feeling good."

"Yeah? What's the matter with her?"

"I dunno. I think you better go see."

He sounded worried.

"OK, sure."

He headed across the patio to Clio's room.

"Dad?"

"Yeah?"

"She's in her shop, Dad."

He found her leaning back in a chair, her arms crossed over her middle, a worried expression on her face.

"Mija?"

"I don't feel good, Dad. I'm sick. I think."

He knelt at her side and studied her closely. He felt her forehead. It was cool.

"What's wrong? *How* do you feel bad?"

"I...I don't know. Dizzy."

"How long have you felt like that?"

"Umm...not too long."

"What have you been doing in here?"

"I was making something...over there."

He looked in the direction she nodded. Several jars and bottles sat on the counter, some containing liquids, a funnel, wet filter paper, spoons, and...was that a bottle of *vodka*? He rose and looked closer.

"Vodka? Where did you get this?"

"From Abuelita's pantry."

"Mija, what the blazes did you want with a bottle of vodka?"

"After lunch Abuelita gave me a tiny sip of her blackberry brandy. She said it made her feel better sometimes. It was good! So I looked on the internet and found a recipe. I wanted to make her a liqueur out of cherries, that's all."

She hugged herself while he put two and two together.

"I see. And you tasted it, right?"

"Uh-huh. I had to balance the sugar. It was hard to get just right, not too harsh and not too sweet."

"So you tasted it several times?"

"Uh-huh."

"Mija, do you know what vodka is?"

"It's a kind of wine, isn't it?"

"No, girl. It's nearly pure alcohol. It's four or five times stronger than wine. Exactly how much did you have, do you think?"

"Uh, four, no five, tablespoons, I think."

"That's all? You're sure?"

"Uh-huh. Dad, am I going to have to go to the hospital?"

"I doubt it, sugar. I think you've just learned what it feels like to be half drunk. Let's see you stand up."

He lifted her to her feet. She could stand, but she didn't look happy.

"OK, you can sit down. I think you just got a buzz on. You should feel better in an hour or so. We'll go eat something and that'll help."

"Don't tell Mom, Dad!"

This had good possibilities for a funny story, but maybe not. Ana had a lively sense of humor but he was pretty sure she would not extend it to her half-blasted daughter.

"Well, OK, I won't. If she asks why you're moping around, just tell her you're tired. Don't let her smell your breath, either. Maybe that'll get you through to bedtime safely. I hope you'll remember what you learned about the power of alcohol."

One of the jars on the counter was half-filled with a dark red liquid. He poured a little into a glass and took a sip. It was delicious, full-bodied and tasting of fresh cherries. He tipped the rest into his mouth and savored it: nice! Very nice! Sweet, fruity, with a smooth, potent finish. Excellent!

"This is very good, Clio! Sweetheart, if you try this again, come get me to do the tasting for you, OK? Don't worry—I'll wait for the right time and give this to Abuelita privately. I'll tell her it's from you but it's a secret. We don't want Mom to know her daughter experiments with vodka. I'll clean up these things and walk you back to your room."

Julio was watching somberly by the door.

Without changing his expression he said, "Doofus."

The first few times Harry and Clio were chauffeured back and forth between their homes and Stallman Stables they felt like movie stars. After a number of such trips, though, the novelty had worn off. Besides, the "limousine" was just a rented Mazda and the driver was a local woman between jobs and just happy for the work, no matter how dull. She was pleasant enough but seldom said much. That was all right—the two youngsters never ran out of things to talk about. The car was comfortable, gliding smoothly down Old 28 under the canopy of pecan branches, norteño music playing softly on the radio.

"No joking. I'm serious. How did you learn about all those plants?" Harry asked.

"From a curandera several years ago, and from a biologist, and a chemist. Also a nutritionist, and now your grandmother. Plus I've done some reading."

"Really? Where did you find all those people?"

"I don't know. My mom and dad found them."

"Found them?" He was feeling stupid again.

"Located. They located some of them. Then later I asked them to find some others, like the chemist. Now they're looking for a mycologist, someone who knows about mushrooms. I want to study mushrooms for a while."

"So...you study with them?"

"I guess. I call them tutors."

"Does Julio study with you?"

"He has his own tutors now, mostly. When we were little we worked together with the same people, a music teacher, an artist, like that. Now there's a physicist who helps him. And an engineer, I think. I'm not sure what kind."

"Is that how you learned all those languages?"

"We learned those when we were little. We had babysitters who spoke different languages with us. I remember a couple of their languages, but I've forgotten some too."

"You mean, your parents hired these people?"

"Uh-huh."

Not for the first time Clio suddenly felt the great divide between her upbringing and Harry's. He was feeling embarrassed, and so was she. She changed the subject.

"How about you? How did you learn to train dogs and horses and stuff? Did someone teach you?"

"No, I just like animals. They like me. Dogs are better friends than most people. So are horses." In a lower voice he added, "I don't mean you."

"My abuelita said your grandfather was the best horse trainer in the valley."

"Yeah, that's what Mr. Stallman said too. I never met him."

"The trainer said you already broke two horses."

"I didn't 'break' them. I just calmed them down and showed them that they didn't have to be afraid of a bridle and a saddle. I taught them to trust me. I started with a hackamore."

"That's so cool."

"I still don't know how to train them to race. I don't know a lot of things."

"I couldn't do that. I like cats. Horses are so big. They scare me."

"Oh, no! Horses are smart! They're really friendly, once you understand them."

His exposition of the equine personality and the strategies for working with it could have continued all the way to Albuquerque, but it had to end at the entrance to the Méndez compound, where they stopped and Clio hopped out. With the car back up to speed and headed to his neighborhood, he reflected that Clio had every reason to be a *ricacha* (a rich bitch), but she didn't act like one at all. She was the friendliest, most interesting human he knew.

The driver let him off in the tiny parking lot in front of Silvas' tendajo, now closed up tight and looking lonely under the pale white security light. It was full twilight as he trudged to the corner and headed toward his house three blocks away, thinking of the homework waiting for him.

It was the dinner hour. Not a soul was in sight, nor any vehicle moving. A dog barked in the distance. As he passed a vacant lot in the second block, a metallic creaking from a junked car startled him.

"Galgo!" a voice called. "¡Hola, 'mano!"

He peered into the dimness. Was that Mando?

"Mando?"

A shadow emerged from the weeds, steadying itself against the rusty car door. A second person was behind him: Mando and J. D., two of the lesser Tirilongos, probably high on something.

"Hey there, 'mano, whatcha doing?"

"Going home."

"Orale, hombre. What's you hurry? You want some stuff? Good stuff, 'n' we got plenty, man."

Mando was squinting as if the fading light hurt his eyes. J. D. rubbed his wrist on his nose.

"Uh, not tonight. I gotta get home. Check you later."

"Hey, man, you always sayin' 'not now,' 'maybe later.' How 'bout now, 'mano? Now's a good time."

"Better not. Mamá will call the police if I'm not home for supper."

"We'll go with you a ways, man. C'mon, J.D.."

It was awkward. Harry didn't feel he could walk off and leave them but they shuffled along at half the speed of his normal walk. Mando wanted to talk.

"We need you, man." Mando's voice was hoarse. "Lito says you good with numbers. We gonna have a lot of numbers soon, Galgo. We need someone to add 'em all up, keep everything good. You gotta join us, 'mano. Hey, we all hermanos! ¡Somos hermanos del barrio!"

Harry said nothing to that.

"You walk everywhere, man. You need a car. You need a car bad. We all gonna have cars soon, bro. Lito's gonna fix us up."

"Yeah?"

"Yeah. He's already started. He got him a Mustang! He's talking with Duque, man! You know who's Duque? Duque, he drives that big Cadilaque. You've seen it, I know you've seen it. Duque's tight with the Zetas, man! Yeah, really! 'N' the Zetas, tu sabes, they're Mexicanos, man, they're the real deal, they're with the Colombianos, man! That's big time, hombre! Duque, he's gonna be their agent, you dig? 'N' us Tirilongos, we're gonna be their dis...we're gonna dis...dista...d...."

"Distribute?"

"Yeah, distribbit, we gonna distribbit for them. We all gonna get rich, bro! You'll see! You gotta join us! No other choice, hombre."

Harry stopped and turned to them. Mando halted, wobbling in place. J.D., five feet behind, was sniffling.

"Listen, guys. You had enough for today. You're tired. Go home. Get some sleep, OK? Get some sleep."

He held out a fist. Mando, sighting on it carefully, extended his arm slowly and knocked knuckles.

"You'll feel better tomorrow. Hasta mañana, primos."

He turned and headed for home.

Matt set his iced tea on the little wrought iron table, swallowed, and crossed one leg over the other. With the foot on the concrete he pushed himself gently back and forth on the glider and contemplated his wife, gardening happily sixty feet away. She was wearing a green sleeveless shirt, tail out, over khaki shorts. Her chestnut hair, dyed to match her daughter's, was gathered into a pony tail which swung this way and that as she moved. She pulled up a carrot, inspected it, dropped it into a basket, and moved down the row, looking at each plant closely. No wonder their fresh vegetables were so good—each one was personally inspected by the gardener.

It was a spectacular spring day, unmarred by the too-frequent dust storms that made spring the area's least pleasant season. Most places, spring was the best season, but it was the opposite here on many days. The temperature in the dappled shade of the cottonwoods was nearly perfect. Ana reached the end of the row and moved to the next, facing him this time. She looked up, saw him watching, smiled, and resumed her scrutiny of the plants.

He smiled back, thinking of the waiter who carded her a month ago to make sure she was old enough to have a glass of wine. A stranger who looked closely at her in good light might have guessed she was somewhere in her thirties, but that stranger would never have believed the truth, that she'd been born something like a hundred years ago. She'd spent twenty five of those years traveling at nearly the speed of light, living proof of Einstein's claim that time slowed down as speed increased. That twenty five years probably only added one year to her biological age. Then she'd spent another fifty years in some kind of suspended animation on the moon, only being awakened every five years or so to check on what her station manager, Hleo, had been observing on Earth. Even Ana couldn't say exactly how old she was. All the same, if he'd been a bartender he'd have checked her ID too.

Rajah and Rani, their two Rhodesian ridgebacks, dozed in the shade of a cottonwood tree by the wall, close to Ana. Rani was on her back, feet in the air, seemingly dead to the world. He took another sip of tea. Ana raised one leg behind her and brushed something off her ankle. She did her gardening barefoot. She had told him years ago that it was a custom on her planet to be in intimate contact with their "mother" whenever possible. Matt had had a little difficulty understanding it at first. Thomans weren't animists and didn't worship Thomo as a god or anything, but they did feel physically connected to their world and going barefoot at certain times, as when gardening, "grounded" them, apparently. He finally came to realize it wasn't a bad concept. A little more concern for the poor, abused Earth on the part of its human passengers wouldn't be a bad thing at all.

Ana reached the end of the last row. She picked up the hose, sprayed off her legs, retrieved her basket, and came to join him.

"Is that tea? Can I have a sip?"

"Sure. Help yourself."

"Mmm! Delicious! You bought some Mexican limes, didn't you?"

"Yup."

She put the basket of vegetables down and moved a cushion from the back of the glider to the arm rest. Sitting next to him she lay back on the cushion and lifted her legs onto his lap. It would have been an ideal time to tickle her feet but he had learned early in their relationship that that was a very bad idea. She couldn't stand being tickled, and until he learned better he inevitably ended up in some bizarre hand lock begging for mercy. She could move much faster than he could react. Even when he knew it was coming he couldn't prevent it. Years ago he had tried the "this little piggy went to market" routine with her toes, and in less than three seconds she had almost broken four of his fingers, dislocated his shoulder, and given him the goosing of his life. So, they reached an accommodation: he wouldn't tickle her and she wouldn't inflict excruciating pain on him. It was a good compromise.

He affectionately wiped the remaining water droplets off her calves, tracing the tiny scar on her left knee, the result of a childhood accident, she'd told him. She wiggled her off-limits toes in pleasure.

"How you feeling, babe?"

"Great!"

"Not tired?"

"Of course not."

"You ready to tell the twins yet?"

"Not yet. It's only been nine weeks."

"So, when?"

"The doctor said we can't be sure until maybe 15 weeks. Then we can announce it."

"Abuelita will go crazy."

"It'll be good for her. She'll love it."

"Can you handle the family reunion, week after next?"

"Sure."

He rubbed her shins.

"You say 'sure,' but you haven't met a lot of them. Don't be too certain about that. What about the two days I'm taking Buela to Las Vegas? Will you be OK then?"

"Of course."

"And then, let's see, that summit conference you're going to afterward. That won't be a problem, will it?"

"I don't think so. It's not the best time but it should be all right. Uncle Rothan is so looking forward to it. It'll be a great opportunity to spread the word about our philanthropic initiatives. More foundations may decide to join with us."

"That cell phone thing is amazing. Who'd have thought selling cell phones to poor people would be so successful?"

"Charlene Stratemeyer was embarrassed by all the money it was making. She used it to buy more phones for the program. Hey! Down, girl! Stop that!"

Rani had waked up and joined them. She was pushing her big black nose into Ana's side, dangerously close to a tickle. Apparently realizing she was on thin ice, the dog sat back on her haunches and whined pleadingly.

"Silly girl! I'm not going to play with you now!"

She pulled herself erect and began rubbing the dog with a foot.

"Another sip, please?"

He passed her the glass.

"Fresh tea! Mmmm."

"Did Clio tell you about her most recent lion taming?"

"She did."

"Whaddya think?"

"Most kinds of cats are pretty much alike. Clio and I understand cats."

"Another of life's little mysteries."

"How so?"

"You and cats. Clio and cats. Never mind. It's a mystery."

She stood up and looked into her basket.

"How about some new potatoes and a fresh salad tonight?"

"I'll make the salad," he said, "and open a bottle of that new chardonnay. But not for the kids!"

"Of course not," she said, picking up her basket. "None for me either. Children and alcohol don't mix."

"Tell me about it," Matt said.

Chapter 5

Matt's great aunt Lourdes was so happy to see her sister Reyes—Abuelita—that they barely stopped talking when Matt ducked out to head to Albuquerque the next day for a quick meeting at the Mobile Migrant Education office. After the meeting, he returned to Las Vegas (New Mexico) to visit a little more with his aunt, heading home early the next morning. Tia Lourdes was ten years younger than Abuelita but not quite as spry. She carried a cane when she went out and Matt overheard her recite a litany of all the prescription medicines she was taking to Abuelita. Frailty notwithstanding, she was looking forward to the upcoming family reunion.

It would have been faster to have headed home on Interstate 25, but he preferred New Mexico Highway 54, some 60-70 miles east, less crowded and ever so much more scenic. The road wound through a picturesque sampling of the Rocky Mountains, gentle valleys, scrubby piñon forests, ranches, stretches of desert, always something to delight the eye. His old truck hummed along smoothly, which was a slight surprise. It shouldn't be humming at all, but it was, literally. He'd varied his speed, rolled down windows on both sides, and checked the gauges. As best he could tell the humming was coming from under the truck. It didn't affect the handling so he decided to stick to his schedule and make a beeline for home.

One of the trendier executives at yesterday's meeting had taught him a term he could use on his return trip: "bio-break." He'd stopped in Tularosa for just such a bio-break and a bottle of tomato juice and now he was a little over an hour from home and approaching his favorite stretch of highway, where the road passes through New Mexico's ski areas and drops from Cloudcroft down a spectacular, steep, six-mile decline to Alamogordo and the desert floor below. White Sands National Monument, a dramatic, blinding expanse of pure white sand (actually gypsum), awaits at the bottom. Signs warning about using low gear and others directing runaway trucks to emergency pulloffs add a note of drama. At some point during the descent his ears always popped, which was why he almost missed his cell phone beeping. It was his wife.

"Matt? Are you on schedule?"

"Pretty much. I'm leaving Cloudcroft. I should be home in a little over an hour."

"Could you do me a favor, Matt? I got a little carried away cooking supper and I can't really leave the house right now. Would you be able to pick up Julio at 4:30?"

He checked his watch: 3:15.

"Yeah, sure. No problem. If I'm late for any reason I'll call but I should make it about right."

"Gracias, marido. I promise, supper will be worth it."

"You got it, love. I'm looking forward to it. I'm hungry! See you soon!"

He parked in front of the Tipton Air Charter office at 4:35 feeling pleased at his timing. Once inside, he knew to step around the short counter cluttered with aeronautical piffle—a cylinder head, a broken holdback fitting from a carrier-launched plane, an ancient leather flight helmet with isenglass lenses—to the desk behind, where Debbie Lama Tipton could usually be found. Distantly related to the Tony Lama bootmaking family of El Paso, her love of flying led her to marry a former Air Force pilot. Now they were spending their golden years running a small charter service. Her desk was stacked with manuals, paperwork, and radio equipment. Martha Stewart was icing cookies on a small television off to one side.

"Hi, Debbie! How's it going this afternoon?"

"Hey there, Matt! Going fine, thanks. About to close up, soon as Sleepy gets back."

"Is my son with him?"

"He is. They're a few minutes late. If you look to the right you might see them landing."

"I see a single engine plane lining up way out there. That must be them."

"Yup. I bet your son is going to land it. I hope he does, anyway."

"I hope so too. I still can't get used to the idea of him flying a plane."

"Sleepy said he's a natural—plenty smart, cool-headed, careful."

"That's Julio. How'd he do on that written test?"

"He aced it. You'd be surprised how many people flunk it the first couple times. Julio must've done his homework."

"Yeah, he was all over that correspondence course. He loves stuff like that. Hey, if you'll excuse me I'll step outside and watch them land."

"Sure, go ahead. I'll be shutting things down in here."

Matt stepped out on the apron and shielded his eyes. A small, single-engine, wing-over-fuselage plane was just about to touch down. The wings dipped gently left and right and then leveled off. Perhaps thirty feet over the runway the nose came up slightly and he heard the throttle cut back. The plane settled gently to the tarmac, the three wheels touching at almost the same time. The engine throttled back still more as the plane rolled towards him. He could make out Sleepy Tipton behind the windscreen pointing; Julio, evidently still in control but barely visible, taxied up to the office and killed the engine. The two of them sat inside finishing the lesson, perhaps, or maybe filling out Julio's log book. Finally the doors swung open and they climbed out.

"Hiya, Matt!" Sleepy called, shaking his hand. "Lemme secure this thing while we talk. It might get windy out here. Julio, run that log book inside and get my wife to stamp it for you."

"You don't look as stressed as I would be, Sleepy. Smooth flight?"

Sleepy, who looked anything but, pushed the plane a few feet and began tying it to the cloverleafs sunken in the tarmac.

"Oh, yeah. Very smooth. Your boy's practically a born pilot. He remembers everything I tell him and he's a bear for flying by the book. Good eyesight and spatial sense too. He'll be ready to solo in no time—it's a shame he has to wait until he's sixteen."

"Easy for you to say, but I'm his dad. I shudder to think of him driving a car at sixteen."

"Well, if he drives like he flies I think he'll be all right. Good kid, Matt."

"Yeah, thanks. And thanks for teaching him. We'll be back next week, OK?"

"See you then, unless the sand is blowing."

On the ride home Julio surprised him by asking after Tia Lourdes, who he'd only met twice. Matt wondered if he was genuinely interested or if some of his wife's Thoman manners had taken, but he didn't ask. He was curious about Julio's flying lesson.

"So, did Mr. Tipton have you land the plane?"

"Uh-huh. That was my fourth landing today."

"Looks like you got the hang of it."

"It's not hard. It'd be different at night, though."

"I bet it would. Is it fun to fly around up there?"

"Uh-huh. It was bumpy. It'd be a lot more fun in the pod."

"No doubt. That's kinda why you're taking these lessons. Are you learning some stuff that'll help you fly the pod?"

"Sort of. The pod flies a lot better, easier, than an airplane. But I'm learning about flight patterns and corridors and beacons and frequencies and stuff. Those are important."

"Excellent. You can be Mom's copilot, or she can be your copilot!"

Julio smiled as if he hadn't thought of that.

"Hey, Dad, what's that sound?"

"Huh? Oh, you mean that hum? I don't know. It's coming from under the truck. It started on the way home this morning. You're welcome to try to locate it when we get home. Maybe you can fix it."

"OK, Dad, sure."

Even though he had been gone only two and a half days, it was a good feeling to reach the final stretch of Old 29 and turn into the old family compound. The early evening sun rendered the adobe wall around it a buttery caramel, while the grounds were entirely in deep shade. The place looked quiet…no, hold on: Rani was busy in the back corner, prancing and dancing around something in the grass. Playing with Rajah? No, Rajah wasn't in sight. He wasn't that playful anyway, to Rani's frequent disappointment. But she was having a wonderful time with something.

He drove around Abuelita's house and pulled in beside Casa Méndez, next to Ana's Corolla. Julio grabbed his log book, hopped out, and headed for the patio gate.

"Thanks, Dad."

"Sure, mijo."

He didn't immediately follow. Instead he stood at the corner and watched Rani. She was barking and yipping, dashing forward and backward and feinting from side to side, ears flying and tail wagging. What had her so excited? She was facing away from him, but he saw nothing. Quietly, he walked closer. He got within twenty feet when out of nowhere a cat rose up out of the grass and hissed loudly at him—but it wasn't just any cat, not even close!

"Holy shit!" he said. Rani jumped aside at the sound of his voice.

It was an enormous cat...a goddam *mountain lion*? Surely not, ¡por dios! It wasn't that big, though it was nearly as big as Rani. A juvenile mountain lion? Wait! The ears—what the hell was the deal with its ears? The animal had the lean, muscular configuration and sandy coloration of a mountain lion except for the ears, which were black and large, more than doubling the height of its head, with long tufts of black hair rising from them making them look even taller. The cat hissed again, showing fangs an inch long. It had eyes like lasers. It was easily the fiercest thing he'd ever seen up close that wasn't in a cage. The tufts of ear hair wavered in the breeze.

"Sweet Jesus!" he whispered, backing away slowly, very slowly, desperately reviewing his options. With one hand behind him he finally touched the house and eased sideways toward the patio gate. The cat crouched back down, disappearing into the grass. He felt the latch, opened the gate, and slipped inside the patio in a flash. ¡Madre de dios! His family! Were they safe? He called to Julio and Clio. No answer. Clio? Could Clio have something to do with this? *Clio?* Dammit, if that kid....

Heart pounding, he strode through the patio to the house's original back porch and let himself in to the living room. Ana was cooking away in the kitchen. Julio was seated at the dining table near her, his log book in his lap. She saw him and smiled radiantly.

"Matt! Welcome home!" Her hair hung down her back in a loose braid. She gave him a warm hug and kiss. Then she sensed his agitation.

"What, Matt?"

"I...there's...what...."

"Matt? Are you all right?"

"You...," he swallowed, "Did...."

"Oh, Mom," said Julio, "Dad probably saw Clio's new cat. It's OK, Dad."

"Is that it? Did you meet Raisin? Isn't she sweet?"

"*Raisin*?" None of this was making any sense. "Clio's new cat? That thing is Clio's?"

"You know how sad she's been since Mork died. Mork was her special cat since she was a baby. She's missed him terribly. But now she has a new cat!"

"That...the...what kind of cat is that?"

"It's a caracal."

"A what?"

"A caracal. They're natives of Africa, but they're domesticated there and in India. Some people train them for hunting. They get along quite well with people. Isn't she beautiful? She's so sweet!"

"Domesticated? It was about to eat Rani! I thought it was going to eat me!"

"No she wasn't, Matt. She and Rani were only playing. Rani loves her too. You just need to be introduced. Clio's out there somewhere, probably in her shop. Julio, please ask your sister to bring Raisin in to meet Dad."

"OK, Mom," said Julio resignedly. Leaving his log book on the table he headed out the front door.

Matt's heart had finally slowed to a trot.

"Where the hell did she find that thing?"

"The animal trainer with the movie crew gave it to her. She's moving to Australia and had to leave her behind. When she saw how well they got along with each other, she offered to give her to Clio. She brought her the afternoon you left."

Matt collapsed in Julio's chair. He shook his head slowly.

"Oh, me. Ay de mí. Que familia."

His nose reminded him he was starving.

"What smells so good?"

"I got a little too busy in the kitchen. I'm sorry you had to get Julio. Things just got out of hand."

"No problem. I was coming by the airfield anyway. What's cooking?"

"A special meal for your homecoming! I was thinking about coconut shrimp, but with a Thai variation. I had to run to town to get some green curry paste to mix with coconut milk and whole leaves of fresh basil, like the Thais use. It's so marvelous, but it's really hot, so I knew Julio wouldn't eat it. For him I decided to use some of the shrimp in a more Mexican way, with lime, cilantro, and a mango salsa. That's what I'm making right now. You probably smell the shrimp and lime, and maybe the potstickers I made earlier. Oh, I better check them!"

She lifted the lid off a simmering skillet and poked something with a fork. Matt scanned the dishes and bowls and utensils on the counter, the blender, the food processor. When Ana got herself in high gear things happened fast. At least the food would be so good he'd be happy to clean up the mess.

"Oh, well, they're supposed to stick," she mumbled. "That's probably why they call them that."

She poured in a little water and replaced the lid.

The front door opened and Julio entered followed by Clio. A few seconds later the head of her new cat appeared. It—she—checked the occupants inside keenly. When she saw Matt she hissed again.

"Oh, Raisin! Don't be silly," Clio said. "That's my dad!"

She leaned into her father, rubbed one of his hands between hers, returned to the cat, and held her hand out to be sniffed. Raisin did so, delicately, with her mouth slightly open. Matt noted the cat's head was bigger than a softball, not counting those awesome ears. Clio rubbed its throat and shoulder blades and shut the door. Ana turned off a burner.

"Dinner in ten minutes, familia. Wash up and set the table, please."

Matt didn't budge.

"Um, if I get up, will she rip me to shreds?"

Julio, the scientist, said, "Probably not. Try it and see."

"Just ignore her, Dad," Clio advised. "Let her get comfortable with you. It won't take long."

Fortunately, Raisin attacked no one. Except for being a little watchful toward her surroundings she acted pretty much like an ordinary house cat. Thanks to his wife Matt had lived around regular cats for years and knew their conservative nature. Once they were comfortable in a place, knew all the nooks and crannies, they were fine. This extra-large tawny version seemed little different. She was spectacularly beautiful—long and lean and taller behind than in front. He couldn't get over those elegant black ears that tapered into long tufts, and the pale blue eyes. With more leisure to observe he noted the powerful haunches, and the subtle white lines around the eyes, cheeks, and tip of the muzzle. She would look fierce even asleep, he figured. Eventually she spread out on the floor between Ana and Clio. Ana's aged cat, the devoted Eleanor, ignored everyone and snoozed on the front window sill.

Matt's stomach convinced him to table the feline issue in favor of eating. Five minutes later, he exclaimed over the Thai shrimp, "This is fantastic, babe, y muy picante, como diciste."

He could feel sweat popping out on his forehead.

"I know. I like it that way. Is it ok, mija?"

"Yes, ma'am. But Dad's right. It's really hot."

"How's your lime and cilantro shrimp, mijo?"

Julio avoided spicy food and was less than enthusiastic about seafood.

"It's good. My favorite is the potstickers."

Matt was finally feeling much better.

"Pass the Mexican shrimp, please, son. I want to try that too. Everything is delicious. Magnificent, esposible! Thanks!"

"It was my pleasure," she said. "Would you pass the rice, please, daughter?"

"Sure, Mom."

Matt dribbled some peanut sauce onto his plate and looked at Clio.

"Well, mija, your new cat doesn't appear to be too ferocious, at least not at the moment. But we could still have problems."

"No, Dad!"

"For one thing, she's too big to stay in the house all the time like Eleanor and Foosh. She needs a place outside."

"We can make her a place in the barn."

"Yes, we can. We can build a pen in one corner of the barn with a door to the yard. But she's a big cat. She'll need exercise and she'll have to spend some time outside. That's when there could be trouble. Cats like to explore. What if she runs off? What if she goes to visit the neighbors? One of them might shoot her."

"She won't run off, Dad! She's very territorial! As long as she's fed well she won't go wandering! Anway, she'll be with me!"

"Well, that's fine, but we can't be sure. You weren't with her when I came home. I know, you were in your shop, but if you get distracted by something and she gets out, we'd have to find her fast. She needs a collar, for sure—probably a tracking collar."

"No, Dad! They're ugly!"

She had stopped eating. She looked down at her plate.

Julio spoke up.

"They're clunky and expensive, and the batteries wear out. Why not use a gravity tag?"

"A what?" Matt asked.

"A gravity tag!" Ana said. "That's a good idea, son. How did you know about gravity tags?"

"I found some in the pod. I asked Uncle Hleo what they were."

She looked at Matt.

"The pod carries a number of gravity tags. I'd forgotten about them—I never used any. The designers tried to think of all the tasks the pod might be needed for. One use was working with things in space, outside the mother ship. If there's a tool or an item floating loose, it's easy to lose. You can't tell how close it is and you can't see it very far away. The gravity tags are to help you locate things."

"They have stick-on pads," Julio added, "but the actual tags look like thin wires. A short piece of one could be inserted beneath the skin and never be noticed."

Matt glanced at Raisin, peacefully reposed in a C shape by Clio's chair, eyes half shut, her side rising and falling evenly. He didn't want to be the one to insert it.

"That's a good idea, son," said his mother. "Why don't you ask Hleo if a short piece would work?"

"And if it's safe for cats!" added Clio.

"That might be a good idea," Matt admitted. "How far can you detect detect them, anyway?"

"Um, I think I remember the distance given in the manual was, uh, let me convert the units...hmm, maybe a hundred miles. If the wire were shorter it might be less. See what Hleo says about the length too, will you please, mijo?"

"Sure, Mom."

The driver who met Viktor Reznik at Milan Malpensa Airport was a small, swarthy, stubble-cheeked man of unidentifiable ethnicity. With a fierce, hooked nose, unruly black hair, and a missing fingertip on the scarred hand that gripped the steering wheel he would have made a fearsome pirate in an earlier age. He smoked the whole hour and a half he drove and said not a word. The first ten minutes Viktor was rather afraid of him. He liked to see a person's eyes but the man wore wraparound sunglasses. Finally he realized that this ruffian, one of the company's most elite soldiers, might simply be wary of driving the world-wide head of the company's security division, the boss of his boss's boss.

Yes, surely that was it. Viktor relaxed slightly.

He'd never been to Milan before, but on this trip tourism was out of the question. The day was overcast and showery anyway, and traffic was heavy. In his two years with the company he had directed several violent episodes, but always from a distance. Usually, bribes and political machinations were the order of the day. This was the first time he'd ever stepped into a "situation" personally, and he felt a little anxious. Despite two years in the army, no one would say he had a military bearing. Instead, he'd try to achieve a "businesslike" bearing.

The driver seemed to be taking one of the loops around the city center, which was unfortunate. The one thing he really wanted see was the famous duomo, the 600+ year old cathedral in the old section. But there was no time for that—maybe on the way back to the airport.

They had reached an industrial section: warehouses, low office buildings, security gates, parking areas with rows of trucks, containers, and cranes. The pirate drove carefully, evidently heeding the company policy of keeping the lowest possible profile. They turned onto a wide arterial road, then onto another, and finally onto a two-lane street with high walls on both sides. He slowed and turned in at a gate, spoke into a microphone, the gate opened, and they pulled into a parking area before a low, modern metal building. Viktor knew no Italian but the sign over the entrance seemed to boil down to "Energy Gaznik Field Office." It was one of the company's subsidiaries.

The manager, Salvo Monterossi, was gratifyingly deferential toward the VIP. Viktor's businesslike demeanor worked perfectly as friendly condescension. Monterossi ushered him to a private room for his "important meeting." Monterossi would never know how important.

Kirill Lebedev was waiting for him. He rose and they shook hands in a businesslike fashion. Lebedev was a truly scary man. Despite his Russian name he had a distinctly German appearance: solid as a tree, with a square, ruddy, hard face topped by a sandy crewcut. He wore civilian clothes styled like the uniforms he had worn most of his life. Viktor knew him to be a scholar of the lethal arts, and utterly without mercy.

"Smooth trip?" asked Lebedev briefly, in a small concession to sociability.

"Yes, quite. Tell me, who was the driver?"

"The driver? Ah. That was Afrim, Afrim the Albanian."

"I had not met him before. What is his position on the team?"

"Sniper. The senior of four. Fifty caliber rifle. Deadly at two kilometers."

"Very good. So, show me your plans."

Lebedev locked the door and unrolled a map across the desk, weighting it down with an automatic pistol and three clips, and began explaining. He started with what was known: where the main summit venues would be, where press conferences would be conducted, speeches made, and banquets held. Next he covered the inferred points: where the heads of state would be staying, what their most likely travel routes would be, and possible lines of fire for snipers, including along the probable routes to the airport. After fifteen minutes he tossed down his pencil and made a sour face.

"There are problems," he said, and began ticking them off.

"One: we only assume our target—the woman—will attend. Her uncle will be present but we do not know when or how he will arrive or where he will stay or if the woman will be with him.

"Two: the security services of eight nations, including our own, have the public appearances of all the important people covered as tightly as a saddle on a pig. We cannot get close to her at those times.

"Therefore, three: the highest priority, capturing the woman alive, is extremely unlikely, unless we can enlist the cooperation of our own nation's security forces to help us gain access to her. I recommend we do so."

Viktor interrupted.

"No, that is out of the question. My instructions were clear: this is a company operation only, strictly an internal matter. No one but our team and Director Serbanov are to know of it. If word of this gets outside the company we have failed. And we must not fail."

Lebedev sat back in his chair. His face was emotionless.

"Very well, then. Since that is so, we must abandon our first priority, abduction, in favor of the second: the woman must be killed. That means it will have to be done outdoors, when she is in transit or getting into or out of whatever conveyance she uses. And since we are unable to pinpoint her precise location at any time, it will have to be an operation for snipers. They can more easily adjust for variables."

Viktor thought about that. Lebedev was right, but regrettably so. True, a basic assassination would be simpler and more certain than an abduction, but it would also mean a smaller bonus for him. Well, it was still a nice sum. And for however little it mattered, it would be easier on the unfortunate girl.

In his most businesslike voice, he said, "Good. Make it so."

Chapter 6

Matt tossed his empty carton of orange juice into the trash barrel, slid his lunch tray to the perspiring woman in the kitchen with a "Gracias, Sonia," and headed down the hall to room 112B, the meeting room next to the principal's office. Kids and teachers were heading off in all directions, but Clio and Julio were nowhere to be seen. He waved at one of the math teachers, noting the dust storm whipping the trees through the windows outside. With a little luck, the damn thing would blow itself out overnight.

He introduced himself to the disconcertingly young man in 112B, a reporter from *Newsweek*, whom he'd seen talking to the principal at lunch.

"Thank you for agreeing to meet with me, Mr. Méndez. I appreciate it very much."

"You're welcome, Mr. Mathiesson. I'm not sure what I can tell you, though."

"Well, as I said at the luncheon meeting, *Newsweek* is doing a piece on the new trend in smaller schools, many of which are excellent. Juarez Academy figures to be in our top 100, and perhaps the top 10, nationally. The principal told me your children were among the best in the school right now, so I wondered what you might have to say about the curriculum. I know you and your wife are on the board."

"Yes, that's right. I'd love to say we played a big role in making this school what it is, but the truth is we mostly just attend the meetings, and advise along with the rest of the board."

"So, how do you explain your children's remarkable records?"

"Actually, our twins were mostly home-schooled. They only attend here a half day, because we felt they needed the company of peers to develop socially. My wife and I are big believers in early education. Our children read early, were exposed to mathematics and languages early, and encouraged to follow their curiosity. That's not to shortchange the role of the school, though. The main advantage of Juarez Academy is that no class has more than 15 students. That's expensive, of course, but try that ratio in any public school and you'd increase its effectiveness exponentially. The public isn't willing to pay for it, and we get what we pay for. Juarez Academy also has a highly flexible curriculum that allows the students to study all kinds of subject areas well above their grade level, and the faculty is exceptionally well qualified. It's just that our kids may not be the best example of what you're after.

"If you want to see what this school does best you should talk to some of the scholarship students. Most of them could never have hoped to find such a stimulating environment, and many are excelling in unexpected ways. Look up a young man named Harry Saenz, for example."

"Harry Saenz," Matthiesson said, jotting down a note. "I'll do that. Thanks. Tell me, then, aside from home-schooling your children, would you say Juarez Academy has been good for your twins?"

"You bet! They've made friends across the full spectrum of local society and have been exposed to more people and ideas than would ever have been possible at home. Harry Saenz was one, for example."

Whew, Matt thought a half hour later, easing his truck out of the school's parking lot, one more potential crisis averted! All he needed was an inquisitive reporter poking into his family. It was not hard to conjure up a nightmare: your children speak Thoman, Mr. Méndez? Come to think of it, your wife looks a little like that woman who came from Thomo...hey! Could she actually be....?

Brrr! He put that out of his mind. He switched on the headlights to make himself more visible through the murk. Damn dust storm, anyway. He made a distinction between dust storms and sand storms, and this was a dust storm. It turned the day a dirty gray rather than brown and you couldn't feel the grit on your face, in your eyes, and in your mouth, or hear it hissing against glass or metal like you could with blowing sand. The wind had been gusting out of the west since lunch at the school. Occasionally these went on for days, but perhaps this one would blow itself out by nightfall and be clear tomorrow. He hoped so, for everyone's sake.

It was a relief to get home and inside where the air was cool and clean. Most everyone in the area used swamp coolers, though he hated that name. The nearest swamp had to be 800 miles away. He preferred the term "evaporative air conditioner," since the units were simply big fans that pulled damp air into the house through soaking-wet filters: simple, cheap, and effective in a dry climate. He had to hose the grit out of the filters every month during the spring, but that was easily done.

Clio's room was at the end of the hall.

"Here's something for you, sugar," he said, setting a fat envelope down on her dresser and sorting through the rest of the mail. "It's from Northern Biologics."

"Thanks. That should be my *flammulina*."

"Your what?"

"Mushrooms. Enokitake. They're edible."

"Oh. Goody."

She was propped up on her bed, reading. Raisin was draped over her shins, regarding him with slitted eyes. Front paws to tail, she stretched all the way across the single bed. Fortunately, she had finally accepted him. Ana was right: she really was a sweet cat.

"No lion-taming today, huh?"

"Nope. Too dusty."

"Hey, daughter, I've been meaning to ask you about your diagnosis of that woman at Sra. Saenz's last week. What did you tell her?"

"Huh? Oh. Well, I could see she was worrying about something. I gave her some teas and things to help her relax."

"Didn't you tell her to see a doctor?"

"Yes, because her eyes were yellow. I mean the white part, pale yellow. That could be a sign of a thyroid or liver problem, lots of things, really."

"So you didn't give her anything for that?"

"No, dad! I couldn't tell what was wrong, just that she needed to check it out."

"Ah. I see. Well, that was good, then. Sra. Saenz told Abuelita that the lady's doctor said she'd come just in time."

"That's great. I'll ask Doña Dolores. Can you take me next week?"

He knelt down and began scratching Raisin's jaw. She raised her head to allow him better access, purring like an idling diesel pickup.

"Maybe. We'll see. Let's wait until we recover from the reunion."

"Oh, yeah. How many people will be there?"

"At the big party in town, maybe 200. But don't worry. That's just Saturday. I think maybe twelve or fifteen will stay at Abuelita's overnight and Sunday."

Raisin slowly stretched out and grabbed his forearm, pulling it to her.

"Ow! Dang, cat, easy there!" He dislodged her claws. "What's the deal with this cat, anyway?"

"What do you mean, Dad?"

"I mean, where does she think she fits in? You know, in our family."

"I think she sort of feels Mom is her mother. Julio and I are her, uh, litter mates, I guess. That's how she acts, most of the time."

Clio pulled one foot from under the cat and then the other. She got up.

"Where are you going?"

"I told Mom I'd join her for exercise." She tugged on some tennies. "I forgot. I better get moving."

"OK, sugar. I'll look in on you all in a bit."

He scratched the top of Raisin's head, pulling her black ears affectionately. Counting the tufts they must be five inches high. Her fur wasn't silky like their house cats, but it still felt sleek, almost like horse hair. She stretched and yawned, pink tongue curled between gleaming fangs, eased to her feet and glided noiselessly to the floor to pad after Clio, her tail swaying gracefully this way and that.

Litter mates? So what does that make me? he wondered.

Rather than cross the patio through the dusty air he followed Raisin down the hall to the old part of the house. Setting the mail on a table he continued around the other side back to Julio's room.

"Hey, son."

Julio was peering at his monitor, probably working on a project or a game. The only internet-connected computer was in the living room: Dad's rules.

"Hi, Dad."

"I noticed the truck isn't humming any more. Did you look at it?"

"Yessir."

"What was it?"

"A loose heat shield over the catalytic converter."

"Aha. How'd you fix it?"

"I fastened it with some of your stainless steel wire."

"Good. That oughta hold it."

"Will you teach me how to weld, Dad?"

"Sure. I'll show you what I know, but that's just the basics. Our arc welder wouldn't weld thin metal like a heat shield or an exhaust pipe anyway. It'd burn through. If I'd been smart enough to find the problem I'd probably have used stainless steel wire too. Thanks, son."

"Sure, Dad."

"Have you asked Hleo about that gravity tag thing?"

"Uh-huh. He thinks it would work. The metal is inert and he thinks the detection range would be proportional to the length of the wire, maybe 20 miles for a piece 5 mm. long."

"Did he have any ideas for how to insert it?"

"I'm working on that. I made a little gun from an empty ball point pen refill. A spring-loaded plunger pushes it out. I tried it with a little piece of stainless wire on an apple and an orange and it worked. Hleo thought that would be OK."

"Good deal. Some brave soul can install it on Raisin. You reckon Clio's the one least likely to be mauled by her own cat?"

"Maybe."

A staccato whappity-whappity-whappity sound floated into the room from the hall. Julio pushed back from his desk, almost tipping his chair over.

"The speed bag! Mom's going crazy! I gotta see this! C'mon, Dad!"

Raisin was already there, crouched low in the doorway, eyes wide. Ana, in shorts and t-shirt and fingerless gloves was practically playing a tune on the bag. She was using her knuckles and the sides of her hands to make the light-weight bag rocket back and forth too fast to be seen. The rhythm was pronounced, in three/four time. All that was missing was the melody and harmony.

Matt knew she was speedy but it was seldom in evidence like this. Julio said it: she was working out seriously. The beat changed to two/four; the speed increased. Her hands were moving in quick little circles in front of her chest, elbows out from her body, eyes unfocused, as if she were daydreaming. Kids, husband, and cat watched in fascination for several minutes until she began using her forearms, producing a thumping bass note. Julio and Clio began applauding.

"Way to go Mom!" shouted Julio.

She slowed the pace until she clasped the bag between her hands, smiling sheepishly.

"That's so fun," she said, puffing. "I can barely make the body bag move, but I love this little one. Thanks for getting it, Matt."

"You're an ace, Mom!"

"Coach Washington showed me how to use it. It's great exercise," she replied, pulling off the gloves.

"Did you have anything like that on Thomo?" Matt asked.

"No, never. But we should have!"

Clio spoke up from her stool in the corner.

"You think we could learn to do that?"

"Sure! Any time you want!"

Matt imagined watching Clio on the speed bag some day. As far as he could tell she seemed to have inherited her mother's speedy genes. There was no telling what tune she might play. She swiveled to face him.

"Oh! Hey, Dad?"

"Yes, mija?"

"I want to show Mom some new moves I learned at judo. Would you be the bad guy?"

"The 'bad guy?'"

"Yeah, you know—try to grab me and stuff."

"What? So you can throw me around and beat me up?"

"No, Dad. Slow motion! I just wanna show Mom a couple things. Please?"

"Well, OK, mija, but don't hurt me. Please don't hurt me."

The next evening Clio was dialing home on her cell phone while thinking about what had happened during her judo demonstration the previous afternoon. Fortunately, her mother answered and not her father.

"Mom? Is it OK if I have supper with Harry and his mother tonight? He has a math final tomorrow and we want to practice graphing quadratic functions.... No, ma'am, I won't be late. I'll call when I'm ready to come home.... OK, I will. Thanks, Mom. Bye."

She slid the phone into a pocket and turned to Harry.

"It's OK. We're good." To the driver she said, "I'll get off with Harry, Mrs. Del Bosque."

Harry seemed relieved.

"I sure appreciate your doing this."

"That's OK. You know how to do those graphs, but it never hurts to review."

"So you're gonna miss the last school day?"

"'Fraid so. Dad says people will be coming early to the family reunion. I'm supposed to help set things up."

"What about your job?"

"They might've finished shooting today. They're gonna check the rushes tonight to be sure."

"The what?"

"That's movie stuff. I've learned a lot about making movies. Rushes are the raw footage they take during the day, before they edit them into the movie. They think they got the lion attack just right but they want to be sure."

"I don't see how they get those cats to do that. The trainer said you were better at it than she was."

"No way. But I probably know the three cats better. Today I could tell that the males, Corbett and Darby, were not in the mood, but the female, Sterry, was. I helped set her up so she'd jump from that tree."

"That just seems impossible."

"Not really. Cats love to perform. Seriously. You just have to show them what you want so they'll understand, that's all. Have you seen circus cats perform?"

"On TV, that's all."

Darn. He'd never been to a circus. She changed the subject.

"What about horses? Do they enjoy performing?"

"Some do. The ones I work with love to run. They actually like to compete with other horses. Today, for instance...."

The driver let them out by Silvas' Market. The sun was low in the sky, not yet an orange ball but perhaps a half hour from it. The air was crystal-clear, yesterday's dust storm a bad dream. Clio got out first. When he emerged from the car she was looking at something down the block. The sun was in her face, her hair a luminous, shimmering gold, her eyes glowing hazel. She almost had freckles. It hit him like a hammer: he used to think she was funny looking, but she wasn't, not at all. She was beautiful. How had he not seen that? Suddenly he felt clumsy.

She smiled.

"Ready? Let's go."

They were chatting their way down the second of the three blocks, Harry doing his best to forget the lump in his throat and keep his mind on what he was saying, when he abruptly ceased his narrative.

"What?" Clio asked.

"Over there. Bad news, probably."

He was looking into the weeds next to a tumbledown house. The doors of a junked car swung open and two boys got out.

"Do you know them?"

"I wish I didn't."

"¡Ese! ¡Galgo!"

"They call you 'Galgo?'" She giggled.

It was Mando and J.D. again. They didn't seem totally wasted. Maybe it was too early.

"Hey, ¿cómo 'stás, 'mano?"

Harry tried to walk on, holding out an arm to herd Clio along.

"Wait up, bro! I got news, important news!"

Harry stopped reluctantly, turning toward them.

"Yeah? What? Be quick. I'm late."

"I bet you late! You late gettin' tu ruca a tu crib, ¿que sí? Una minina para un galgo, ¿verdad?" ("A kitten for the greyhound, right?")

"Never mind that. What news?"

Mando came closer, his expression serious. He lowered his voice.

"Listen, man. I'm in trouble. You got me in big trouble, 'mano. Lito says I shouldna said nothin' to you 'bout Duque, see? Unless you a Tirilongo, unless you one of us, you ain't 'sposed to know that, you dig? Lito said you gotta join us, bro. If you don't, my ass is grass, man. ¡Me van a chingar!"

"I didn't get you in trouble. You did that by yourself. That's your problem, primo."

"¡N'ombre! La culpa es tuya! You gotta come over, man!"

"Olvídalo, Mando. Eso no va a pasar." ("Forget it, Mando. That's not going to happen.")

"¡Que sí, y prontito! ¡Te digo!" ("Yes it is, and soon! I'm telling you!")

He gave Harry a sharp push.

"Don't you touch him!" Clio said sharply.

"¿Cómo que?" ("What's this?") Mando looked askance at Harry. "Díle a tu ruca que se calle el hocico" ("Tell your broad to shut her snout").

J. D. had sidled even with Harry, facing Clio. Harry never took his eyes off Mando.

"Leave her out of it. Your business is with me."

"Sí es. De veras." ("Yes, for sure.")

He pushed Harry again to emphasize his point.

"¡No lo hagas, tu!" said Clio. ("Don't do that, you!")

"¡Cállate, niña!" said J.D. ("Shut up, kid"), stepping toward Clio and raising an arm to give her a shove.

That was a mistake. Clio repeated the move she had used on her dad the day before, grabbing his arm and pulling him toward her while falling backward. J.D., already moving in her direction, would have fallen on top of her except she placed both feet in his midsection and shoved him all the way over her. He flew through the air and slammed hard onto the sidewalk.

She sprang to her feet and moved toward Mando. Mando had produced a switchblade, waving it at both of them. Clio raised a threatening hand, Mando followed it with his eyes, and she kicked him in the crotch.

"C'mon, Harry. Let's go," she said, tossing his knife into the weeds.

He took in the spectacle of his two acquaintances groveling in pain on the sidewalk. She had put them both down in ten seconds. He looked at her, his mouth open. She was beckoning him to get moving.

He got moving.

The Saenz home was small but respectable, one of many like it in the neighborhood. It needed new paint but so did many others. The yard was fenced and neat, as if the owner valued clear lines of demarcation. Inside there was rather too much furniture, Clio thought, but it was all clean and orderly.

"Mamá will be home in an hour or so. I'm supposed to fix supper. Let's see what we have."

A few minutes of searching produced some side dishes—tortillas, frijoles, cheese—but no entrées. Clio finally made a suggestion.

"There's enough stuff here to make tortilla soup. How about that?"

"Tortilla soup? You know how?"

"Sure! It's easy! Why don't you dice that tomato while I sauté some rice and garlic. Let's add that avocado too. It'll be yummy!"

They began working side by side. Harry couldn't get out of his mind the picture of his small friend taking down two punks in seconds, and the way her eyes burned holes in Mando. Clio must have been thinking similar thoughts.

"I hope I didn't make more trouble for you with those two."

"Probably not. They're just dopers. Don't worry about it. Where'd you learn to do that, anyway?"

"Oh, my mom has always liked martial arts. I've worked with her trainers and she's taught me some stuff too."

"Your mom?"

She'd always struck him as a gentle, friendly woman, not the ninja type at all.

"Yeah, and my dad too. He's big on...."

She paused. Harry noticed the same noise.

"That's Mamá. She comes in the back door."

When she appeared, he introduced Elida Saenz, a small woman, no taller than Clio's mother if not quite as trim. She was professionally dressed and made up—permed hair, nails, the works. Clio remembered her dad had said she worked in a county office somewhere. Unlike Ana Méndez she wore perfume and only rarely modified her habitually serious expression to smile. She welcomed Clio warmly, however, excusing herself to go change her heels for flats. Harry set the table while Clio served the soup.

The meal proceeded companionably. There were compliments to Clio on her dish, though she herself thought the Saenz's overcooked salsa detracted from it somewhat. To her embarrassment, Mrs. Saenz thanked her several times for "all she had done" for Harry. She tried to turn the thanks aside but felt herself blush, and when she saw Harry noticing she blushed even more.

Mrs. Saenz insisted on carrying off the dishes by herself so Harry could arrange the dining table for his studies. He and Clio were soon absorbed in mathematics, barely looking up when Mrs. Saenz told them she was going to bathe and watch TV in her bedroom.

Harry was enjoying the graphing. Either he remembered more than he expected or Clio gave him the confidence to plunge ahead. She mostly watched, offering comments only rarely or kidding around, something her brother had never done. She even came up with an easy memory aid he never would have thought of. He was feeling a lot better about his exam tomorrow.

"What's that?" Clio said out of the blue.

"Huh? Sounds like a Coke commercial."

"No, out front. Listen."

It was a car engine being revved up. In the blink of an eye four things happened: there was a loud pop out front, the sound of breaking glass in front of them, the curtain over the living room window twitched, and something thwacked into the wall behind. In a heartbeat Harry dived at Clio and they both crashed to the floor. He lost count of the gunshots—there must have been four or five.

Out front, an engine roared, tires squealed, and a car (or truck—who knew?) sped away. From the back of the house his mother was shrieking.

"Harry! Clio! Are you all right?"

He rolled off Clio and sat up. She hadn't cried out or struggled once.

"Yeah, Mom. We're OK. Are you OK?"

"¡Ai, Harry! ¡Ai, mija!" A quick glance convinced her they were indeed uninjured. She had a cordless phone in her hand. Shakily, she dialed 9-1-1.

What the hell? Two police cars, light bars flashing, were parked in front of the Saenz house. A small group of neighbors stood around on the sidewalk. Clio had mentioned no emergency on the phone. The whole way over he had been a little put out with her, still feeling the sore shoulder he had acquired when she had thrown him yesterday. He outweighed her by over a hundred pounds, but the force of gravity had trumped "slow motion combat" and now he was paying the price. He forgot all about that as he stepped through the rubberneckers and hurried through the gate to the door. There were three spidery bullet holes in the front window.

Inside, Clio ran to hug him.

"Are you OK, sugar?"

"Yes, Dad."

"What happened?"

"A drive-by shooting."

"Jesus! Anyone hurt?"

"N...no."

"Sir? Are you this girl's father?"

"I am, yes."

"May I see some identification, please, sir?"

"Sure."

He pulled his drivers license out of his wallet and handed it over. The officer jotted a note and passed it back.

"Thank you, Mr. Méndez."

"What happened here, officer?"

"Your daughter and this young man," he nodded at Harry, talking with his mother to another officer, "were doing homework," he nodded at the book and note paper and pencils on the table, "when a party or parties unknown fired six bullets at this house."

Matt looked around the room. A third officer was digging a slug out of the wall with a pen knife.

"Any idea why?"

"Young Mr. Saenz says the local gang has been after him to join them. Most likely they were making a point. But it doesn't have to be the local gang and it doesn't have to be for any reason in particular. It could have been anyone."

"So, what are you going to do?"

"We'll canvass the neighbors, see if anyone can ID the vehicle or the shooter. We know the local gangbangers, most of 'em. We'll roust them and maybe get a lead. But probably not. We'll do frequent patrols through the neighborhood. We'll type the bullets and check 'em against any guns we may confiscate. We'll keep after 'em. A Neighborhood Watch program wouldn't be a bad idea. In the meantime, it's a good thing Mrs. Saenz keeps the drapes closed. Here's my card, in case you want to check back later for any reason."

"Thanks, officer. Are we done here?"

"Yes sir, you can go."

"Good." To Clio he added, "Let me have a word with Harry's mother, mija."

While he tried to comfort Mrs. Saenz, Clio took in the scene. The living room was a mess—furniture pushed around, two chairs turned over, three policemen busy doing police things, her dad talking to the jittery Mrs. Saenz while clasping her hands in his, and Harry, standing by himself and looking shipwrecked. She walked over to him.

"I can't believe how brave you were," she said.

"Me? I didn't do anything."

"You protected me! You could have been killed!"

"No, I...I didn't even know what I was doing."

"Well, I knew."

Her father was saying, "Remember, if there's anything we can do, please call us. You have our number."

He turned to his daughter.

"You ready, sugar?"

Impulsively, she hugged Harry.

"Thanks, Harry. I'm glad everyone's all right. I'll see you after the reunion."

"Take care, son," Matt said, patting him on the back. "Next week, OK?"

Harry watched them depart, stepping carefully around an officer taking pictures of the living room window.

She had hugged him! His mother hugged him sometimes. Not often, though. His whole body was tingling. This wasn't the same thing at all.

On the way out of the neighborhood a TV truck from a local station sped past them. Clio barely noticed. She was thinking about Mrs. Saenz, and about Harry, and remembering the odd sensation of feeling him on top of her, holding her down tightly and flinching every time the gun fired.

"Sugar?"

Her dad had been saying something.

"Uh-huh?"

"I was saying we're going to have to tell Mom about this."

"Oh."

"I suggest you let me do it. I'll explain what happened but I'll try not to alarm her more than I have to, OK?"

"Sure, Dad."

It went a little better than he expected, partly because Clio didn't seem visibly upset, which was helpful. Ana didn't like guns, but that part couldn't be avoided. She was not happy, very not happy, that kids from some gang had fired a gun on a peaceful street, and that several of the bullets had hit the Saenz house. But she didn't panic. She embraced Clio, said she was happy no one was hurt, and sent her off to feed her cats. Then she turned to Matt.

"That's terrible, Matt!"

"It sure is."

"Is that really what happened?"

"That's basically what the police told me. We've heard about drive-by shootings for years. Clio and the Saenz family happened to be in the wrong place this time."

She sighed and shook her head.

"Why do things like this happen? What can we do about it?"

"It's the old story: educational and economic problems, family problems. We're already doing more than most private citizens, way more."

"I wish there were something else."

"I can think of one thing. Tomorrow morning I'm going to town to see if the Knights of Columbus Hall is set up for the reunion like we asked. On the way back I'll stop in at the Doña Ana County Sheriff's Office and find out more about this kind of thing. Maybe they'll suggest something."

The visit to the hall took longer than he had estimated, so it wasn't until 11:30 that he reached the Sheriff's office. He was directed to Deputy Braga, a husky young man in uniform—including shorts—who said he was headed to lunch and invited Matt to go with him. After a quick call home so Ana wouldn't wait for him, he followed, joining the deputy at an unpromising looking restaurant tucked into an old strip mall.

"I thought you said the place was 'Tornillo's,' Matt said.

"Oh, right. Sorry. As you can see, it's really 'Treviño's.' We call it 'Tornillo's' 'cause so many cops eat here."

Matt chuckled at the bilingual joke. "Tornillo" meant "screw."

"The food's better than average, and it's cheap," he added.

"What's good, Deputy?" Matt asked, scanning the menu.

"Call me Sonny. I like the carne adobada. The chile caribe marinade they use is outstanding."

"Say no more. I'll have that too."

Matt loved carne adobada but they didn't fix it often at home because the marinade was fairly elaborate, and the meat had to marinate overnight. If the restaurant used good red chiles, it would be a treat, something to bring his family to try some day.

The waiter departed with their orders as Braga stirred sugar into his iced tea. Matt dipped a tostada chip into a shallow bowl of salsa.

"So," Matt began, "You're in the Community Policing Division. What is that?"

"It's sort of like a partnership with the communities we serve, kind of a problem-solving task force. We try to reduce or deter crime. It's hard to say how many crimes have *not* been committed because of us, but I think we're pretty good at it. There are twenty-eight of us in the division. We even use bicycles and four-wheelers some of the time. That's why I'm in shorts today—bike patrol this morning and maybe another this afternoon, unless the sand starts blowing."

"That's a good idea," Matt said.

"We probably need to publicize it more. I thought you might be a journalist, but the desk sergeant said you'd been the victim of a drive-by."

"Not me; my daughter was. We live on Highway 28. She was visiting a schoolmate on Belva Way. That's where it happened. No one was hurt, but my wife and I do take an interest in the community. We work with the Mobile Migrant Education Program and also with Juarez Academy. I guess I'm looking for background, mostly, in case there's some way we could help."

The deputy squeezed some lemon into his tea. Matt noted he shielded it with his off hand to prevent errant sprays of lemon juice. Good manners for a community cop, he thought.

Braga stirred in the lemon juice, nodding.

"I get it. Well, I gotta tell you, that's one of our most intractable problems."

"Drive-byes?"

"Gangs. There've been gangs around here since before I was born, but lately they're starting to get out of hand. It's one of our biggest law enforcement problems."

"Why lately?"

"Drugs. There've been drugs in this area since forever too, of course, but now the problem is worse than ever. I guess you're aware of what a mess things are downriver. From El Paso and Ciudad Juarez on into the interior of Mexico it's like a war, with cops and politicians being assassinated, squads of goons shooting up towns. Hell, west of here, across from Columbus in Las Palomas, they can't hardly keep any police. The parents are afraid to let their kids go to school."

"I've read about that," admitted Matt, "but why here? Why now?"

"I'm no expert, but I'd say it's because the Coast Guard has been so successful at pinching off drug smuggling over the water from Colombia. The drug lords there have spread inland to Mexico. Our long, empty border is a paradise for smugglers, and the Mexican druggies are nearly as ruthless and clever as the Colombians. As to why here, it seems that as resourceful businessmen they're trying to expand their market. Do you know what 'cheese' is?"

"Unless you mean an ingredient for enchiladas, I guess I don't."

"It's a new recreational drug. By that I mean a 'starter drug,' like for hooking junior high kids. It's a blend of a tiny bit of heroin, about a tenth as much as a full dose, and Tylenol or similar drug. It gives a quick, short high, and it's cheap, like a dollar or two. They even give it away. It's all over the place."

"Jesus! I had no idea!"

"Yeah, see: that's one way to gain customers. It's happening, right here. Even worse, the Mexican dealers are linking up with area gangs, to act as distributors. Not only do the gangs know the territory, they're eager to make the money. It's a godawful problem."

Braga looked past Matt's shoulder.

"Ah! Here comes our order. Nothing like a morning's bicycling to give me an appetite!"

"I bet," agreed Matt. "Let's come back to this topic later. It's too depressing over good food."

"Sure. I wanna ask you about Juarez Academy. My wife and I would love for our daughter to go there but it's way out of our price range for a private school."

The waiter set down two plates loaded with colorful food, the pork buried under a luscious bright red sauce. The smell was heavenly.

"Yes, it is expensive, but maybe you didn't know that three-quarters of the kids there are on graduated scholarships of one sort or another. You should talk to their admissions person, Dr. Saldivar. I'll give you her number after lunch. Wow, this adobada is delicious."

It was a quarter to two by the time he got back home. The afternoon was breezy, with high bands of thin clouds speeding over the Organ Mountains. There was no sign of blowing sand. Perhaps Officer Braga would get in his afternoon patrol.

Ana was sitting on the glider behind Abuelita's house, watching Julio and Clio fooling around at the back of the compound. It looked like they were doing something with Raisin.

"Hey, babe. Sorry I had to miss lunch."

"That's OK. Did they give you any ideas for things we might be able to help with?"

"Uh, not really. I had lunch with a deputy who works in community relations. He gave me some background on the gang problem, mainly."

"Is Harry in a gang?"

"No, nothing like that. But there's a gang in his neighborhood and they want him to join. He refused and that may have been the cause of the ruckus yesterday."

He congratulated himself for avoiding saying that Harry's house had been the gang's target. He changed the subject completely.

"So how you feeling? You up to the reunion tomorrow and Sunday?"

"Yes, of course. I'm glad you insisted on a caterer for tomorrow, though. Now I don't have to worry about a thing."

"And your trip, uh, out of town, on Wednesday?"

"I'm ready for that too."

"Will it be safe, you think?"

"I hope so. Uncle Rothan has arranged security for the Thoman delegation. World Security will handle my personal travel. I think they'll assign Rob Coombs."

"The Seal? Excellent. I liked that guy. He seems cool and competent."

" He ought to be cool. He used to, how do you say, unfuse bombs?"

"Defuse. He may need to be. Those G-8 conferences get pretty wild, I seem to remember."

"We'll be careful. You shouldn't worry about me."

"You know what I always say, babe: that's my job!"

The twins joined them.

"Hey, Dad, we just shot Raisin with the gravity tag. She didn't even mind!"

Matt spotted the cat at the back of the property, crouched down and twitching her tail. It looked as if she might be having second thoughts.

"Nobody got clawed? Great! Now we need to test it to make sure it works, right? We need the pod to do that, only we can't risk getting it out until the reunion is over. Let's do it next week."

"Can I fly it?" asked Julio.

"Sure. We can take Mom and your sister too. All we need is Raisin to be here in the barn, right?"

"Oh! Hey, Dad," Clio blurted, looking to the back fence. She made a pssst pssst sound and Raisin rose up from her crouch, those formidable ears swiveled toward them. Clio repeated the sound and the cat ambled in their direction.

"Watch what she can do, Dad! Julio helped set this up."

Matt looked around.

"Where are the dogs?"

"I put them in the barn. They get in the way when we're training. Watch this."

She knelt by the cat and draped an arm over her, holding her in place lightly. Julio had retreated to the cottonwood tree, where he fished something out of an ice chest and fastened it to a cord which looped high into the tree.

"Those are chicken pieces," Clio explained.

Raisin seemed to know what was coming. She had begun quivering with excitement. Julio pulled on the loop and the chunk of meat rose into the air. Matt now saw a second cord fastened perhaps 15 feet up in the tree, extending to another tree at the back of the compound, the catenary drooping lower at the midpoint. The ascending scrap of meat rose to some kind of wire trolley with wiry spider legs dangling beneath it. They captured and held the piece of chicken.

"Ready?" Julio asked.

"Uh-huh," Clio replied.

Julio jerked the cord, and the trolley, with the chicken piece dangling underneath, began rolling toward the other tree. Clio held the cat a few seconds and then released her, saying "Dhava!"

Raisin darted a couple yards and froze, lowering her body almost to the ground, still quivering, eyes on the prey moving high in the trees. Staying low, she scooted a few more feet, focusing intently upward. Suddenly she accelerated in a blinding burst of speed and, just as the trolley reached its lowest point, leaped impossibly high into the air, grabbed the chicken piece with her paws as her front end switched places with her rear end, and plopped to the ground. Crouching low, she checked to see where the humans were and then began consuming her catch, her ears turned outward.

"Great God almighty!" said Matt. "I don't believe that! ¡Híjole! How high was that, son?"

"About eight feet."

"Holy moly!"

"She can jump five times her own height, Dad."

Matt was thunderstruck. He shook his head.

"Awesome! Truly awesome! What did you say to her, sugar?"

"I told her to attack, in Hindi. That way English won't confuse her."

"¡Diós mio! She even obeys—she stays, she sits."

"I told you, Dad," said Clio, "caracals can be trained for hunting. They'll even attack larger animals, like antelope. You just have to know how to understand them and talk to them. You've heard her hiss, right? She has different hisses for different things."

"I've noticed that. She has a funny chirping sound too, doesn't she?"

"Uh-huh. I bet she can catch that woodpecker that pecks Mom's tomatoes."

"No, mija," Ana said. "That's a pretty bird, just trying to live. I'll protect my tomatoes with cages."

A screen door slammed behind them.

"Uh-oh," Matt whispered. "Here comes Abuelita. She likes Raisin but you better not show her what a spectacular predator your kitty is. Might give her nightmares! ¡Buenas tardes, 'Buela!"

"Good afternoon, grandson, granddaughter, nietos! You're playing with your cat, I see."

"Yes, ma'am," Clio said tentatively.

"I was watching from the house. She's quite the jumper! I'd love to see her do that up close but it has to be now, if you can, please. Tia Lourdes will be here for supper and if she sees that cat leap like that she'll faint dead away. I bet Raisin can take care of that woodpecker for you, Ana!"

Chapter 7

The younger members of the Méndez family seldom took naps, though the senior member, Abuelita, rarely missed her daily siesta. On this Saturday afternoon, however, Ana, Julio, and Clio were all sneaking a half hour to recharge after a hectic morning. Visiting had proven considerably more taxing than they had anticipated. Even Julio, normally the most reserved Méndez, had had so much fun that his nerves needed quiet time to reset.

The day had begun with a major thrill: an early morning hot air balloon ride, a surprise birthday present to Abuelita but also an exciting novelty for the twins and seven lucky relatives who won the drawing to ascend with her. Festivities continued afterward, culminating in a massive catered luncheon at the Knights of Columbus Hall, taking several hours to wind down afterward as the more distant relatives made their farewells. Afterward the Méndez family and nine close relatives returned to the home compound to rest and get ready for the evening meal. In the Méndez house, only the cats, Eleanor and Foosh, were awake.

Reluctantly, Clio awoke to Foosh's insistent claws kneading her tummy. Feeling for her flip-flops, she slid off her bed to dish out the afternoon cat food. Rattling the kibbles to attract Eleanor, the other house cat, she measured out two rations into bowls and stepped across the patio to look in on Julio.

"¡'Ito!" she whispered, leaning on his door jamb.

"¡Ese!" she said, a little louder.

No response.

"Ding Dong, wake up!"

"Mmmm, make me, Tister," he grumbled, blinking in her direction.
"Up with you! Sleepy-head! Every time you nap you wake up cranky."
"So what?" he retorted, proving her point.
"One hour till we eat at Abuelita's. Unless you plan on sleeping through it."
"Let's skip it. Maybe we can hide in the barn."
"Abuelita said to come over an hour before dinner."
"The relatives I liked all left. Everyone staying at Abuelita's is dorky."
"False! Aunt Lourdes isn't dorky."
"Right; I forgot about her. Everyone else is, though."
"Well, Abuelita, and Grandpa Bert and Grandma Julia?"
"Except for them. Like Aunt Bess, and Marky."
"Lovely Aunt Bess. You might be right about her. C'mon, let's go."
"You go ahead. I'll come in a minute."
"Don't you dare forget."
"I won't."

He stretched slowly and turned his back to the wall. Shaking her head in frustration Clio headed out the back gate.

"How those coals looking?"
"Just right, Dad."
"Good. Don't want 'em too hot. That smells wonderful."

Matt painted a little barbecue sauce on the chickens, poked the brisket with a fork, flipped over the sausage rings, and shut the lid on the smoker. Rajah and Rani, spread out on the grass, watched Matt closely as he returned to the chair next to his father. Their long noses swiveled in tandem like a gun turret, making sure he didn't have any food in his hands. The two men reposed in companionable silence a minute, contemplating the back half of the Méndez compound. The slopes of the Organ Mountains, visible over the back wall and under the canopy of cottonwood trees, loomed rocky and golden in the distance as the afternoon sun threw the canyons into sharp relief.

"This place is sure looking good, son. You all have done a wonderful job on it."
"Yeah, it's very comfortable. Very homey."
"I remember how it was at Abue's seventy-fifth birthday party, before you came back. There was mostly bare dirt back here, trees struggling, no garden. The barn was falling down and the wall was in bad shape. It was sad. Now it

looks better than I can remember." He took a sip from his beer bottle. "Whatcha doing with the renovated barn, anyway?"

"The main part is a shop, more or less. The feed and tack rooms at this end are workrooms for the kids."

"Abue' told me Clio has a new super-cat. You keep it in there too?"

"Yeah, there's a pen at this end of the main room. See that little door? That's it. She can also climb up in the loft and look out the vents up there. She might be watching us right now."

"Hmm…can't tell. Too many shadows. Abue' says it's quite a cat."

"It is. Might be the most beautiful animal I've ever seen. I can't get over how she's just like a regular house cat, only bigger and smarter. She and Clio have bonded. I swear, it's almost like they're sisters."

"You gonna give me a look at her?"

"You bet. Let's wait until our guests depart in the morning. She's leery of crowds, like most cats."

"OK. Good."

Matt's father's 65 years had left him a bit round-shouldered and with a noticeable paunch but his hair was still thick and black. He looked like what he was, a man who had worked hard all his life and was now enjoying living at a slower pace. Matt admired the way his father observed much but said little. That had rubbed off on him a bit, he thought. His dad tipped back his beer bottle at a steeper angle this time.

"You ready for another beer?"

"No hurry. Finish yours first."

A gate latch clicked to their right. Clio appeared, headed for Abuelita's house. Her path took her within twenty feet of the two men.

"Hi, Dad. Hi, Mr. Méndez," she said in passing.

Both men waved. Matt's father chuckled.

"Such old-fashioned manners. That's Ana's doing, I guess. Must've learned them in Argentina. Your kids just won't call me Bert, or even Grandpa."

"They do, actually, but not when you're around. Not sure why."

Matt leaned to his left and flipped open the cooler between them.

"How 'bout that beer?"

The back of Abuelita's house, built long before air conditioning, had a screened porch off the kitchen for protection from mosquitoes, always a problem along the river. A girl was seated inside, her back to the door. So as not to startle her Clio didn't let the door bang shut as she usually did. It was Sara, the 16 year old granddaughter of Abuelita's sister Lourdes. She was bent over, working on something, her face hidden by shiny black hair in a chin-length bob.

"Hi, Sara."

"Oh. Hi, Clio."

"Whatcha doing?"

"Peeling potatoes."

"Need any help?"

"No, thanks, that's all right."

"Where are John and Vanessa?"

"Uncle John took them on a walk down by the river."

"Are the others still sleeping?"

"I dunno. I hear a few voices now and then."

"What are the potatoes for?"

"Mashed potatoes."

"Sara?" a shrill voice boomed out of the kitchen.

"Yes, mom."

"Are you working?"

"Yes, mom."

"Don't eat all the potatoes! Leave a few for us!"

A high-pitched cackle followed.

"Yes, mom."

Sara looked sheepishly at Clio, who was clearly nonplussed.

"Mom says I'm fat. She's sending me to a fat camp this summer."

"To a *what*?"

"Well, that's not what they call it. They call it a nutrition and exercise camp. But it's for fat kids."

"You're not fat!"

"Thanks, but Mom says I am. I'm a little heavy, I know."

"No, you're not! You're fine!"

"How do you stay so slender?"

"Me? I don't know, really. I never thought about it."

Sara sighed and carved off another sliver of potato skin.

"Abuelita says you're practically a curandera."

"Well, not really. I study with one. I'm learning."

"I wish you had something that would make me thinner."

"Gosh. I don't know of anything like that." She thought a second and added, "But...."

Sara paused, peeler in midair.

"But what?"

"There might be something else...."

"Like what?"

"Do you drink tea?"

"Uh-huh. With no sugar..." she lowered her voice, "...if Mom is looking."

"Well, I know a herb that will make you less hungry. I have some. I could mix it with regular tea and you can drink a cup before a meal. It should take the edge off your appetite. You might eat less."

"Really? Oh, that would be soo cool!"

"The thing is, it won't do it by itself. You have to work with it—you gotta remember you're not as hungry. It'll help you eat less but still feel satisfied."

"I can do that!"

"OK. I'll mix some up tonight. I'll put it in a regular tea tin. I have some empty ones in my shop. You can tell your Mom that I gave you some tea as a gift and maybe she won't drink it."

"I hope not. She needs a barrel of it herself."

Sara had peeled all of half a potato while they had talked. Clio had another thought.

"Hey, don't you go to that fancy high school in Las Vegas?"

"United World College. The high school part of it. Yeah, why?"

"I heard someone say that you're good in math."

"Uh-huh. And physics, too."

"Did you know Julio loves math and physics?"

"No. For real?"

"Oh, yeah. He knows stuff I can't even begin to understand. He has a shop where he makes things. You'd love it. Why don't you get him to show it to you? I'll finish those potatoes for you."

"Gee!" She looked down at her potato. "I better not. Mom told me to do this."

"Oh, phooey. Let me do it. If she says anything I'll make up a story. It'll be fine. You see the side of our house, the windows down the back? Julio's is the second from the end. Go knock on it and tell him, tell him, oh, tell him I said to show you his star charts. That'll get him started. Gimme the peeler and you get going."

There were only a dozen or so large potatoes and she was sure she could peel them four times faster than Sara. The peels began flying as she smiled to herself. She would present Sara with a tin of her mother's store-bought tea (after she broke the seal on the can and stirred up the contents), but she was confident that Sara would indeed not feel as hungry as she might have without that placebo. At the same time, she'd also figured out a sneaky way to get Julio out of his room and interested in their guests, or at least one of the guests.

She had three potatoes to go when she heard a new voice in the kitchen. There was a pantry on either side of the door from the porch to the kitchen, and the short hallway they formed seemed to be acting like a funnel, sending kitchen sounds straight to the porch. The voice of Sara's mother Marky was high and sharp. The new voice was smoother and lower, Aunt Bess, it sounded like. The smooth voice was speaking.

"Did you get a nap?"

"Oh, not really, but I rested."

"So did I. It's peaceful here, isn't it?"

"More like dull."

"It's so much quieter than Vegas—our Vegas, not your New Mexico one. It's beautiful. I wonder how they do it."

"Pass me the sugar there, Bess. Thanks. How they do what?"

"Pay for all this."

"Well, it's family land."

"Yes, but I mean all the improvements. They're nice but you'd expect more. There's no pool, no paved drive, they drive old cars. I bet they're barely making it."

"I never thought about that!" she said with another cackle.

"I mean, Ana doesn't work. Matt seems to work only part time. How do they keep this place up so well? I bet Mrs. Méndez senior is helping them."

There was the sound of a spoon stirring something in a bowl.

"On Social Security? That couldn't help much."

"Not Social Security. John told me this family used to be well off. She must have certificates of deposit salted away somewhere. I hope she doesn't spend them all just to make the place look nice for her grandson. They send their kids to an expensive private school. She probably helps with that too."

Rattling pans and the oven door being pulled open drowned out Marky's response. The low voice continued.

"Ana doesn't have a college degree. I wouldn't swear she even has a high school diploma. And Matt only has a master's in English, for heaven's sake. Where's the money in that?"

"I couldn't say, Bess. Hey, do you see the cinnamon in that rack?"

Clio heard small jars rattling against each other at the same time she noticed movement out in the yard. Julio was walking to the barn with Sara, a head taller, alongside. Her mother was talking with Matt and his father. She patted Matt's shoulder and headed towards Abuelita's back door. It slammed behind her. Within seconds a shrill voice from the kitchen rang out.

"Sara! You better not be running off!"

Ana smiled at her daughter and passed into the kitchen.

"It's just me," she said. "How are you all this evening?"

The smooth voice answered.

"Oh, hi, Ana! We're fine, thanks. We were just talking about what a wonderful reunion this has been. You and Matt did such a tremendous job arranging everything!"

"It's been fun. Abuelita has certainly had a lovely birthday."

The high voice, surely Marky's, responded.

"She sure did. I can't believe she actually went up in that balloon. I'd have been scared silly. I heard she was complaining that it didn't go far enough or fast enough. I'll wait for the pictures, myself. There." The oven door slammed again. "That's done. I'll set the timer for 40 minutes. I'm going to go change clothes. I'm all sweaty! Y'all excuse me please. I'll be back."

The smooth voice resumed.

"The food at lunch was delicious. The caterer outdid himself."

Ana agreed.

"Yes, he did. White Stripe Catering is supposed to be the best in this area."

"I'm sure it was expensive."

"I don't know, but everyone contributed. I imagine it was covered."

"I hope so. If it wasn't, please let us know. John will be happy to kick in the rest."

"That's very kind, but please don't worry about it. Hmm. You're near the spices. Do you see the chili powder? I'm going to make a quick salad."

"Here it is. How's Abuelita's health these days, anyway?"

"Her health? Just fine! She's slowed down a bit over the time I've been here, and she does love an afternoon nap, but she has no major problems. Excuse me. I need to get the cucumbers out of the refrigerator."

Clio, still listening on the porch, realized that gave her an opening. She picked up the pan of peeled tomatoes and went into the kitchen.

"Here are the potatoes, Mom. Can I peel the cucumbers too?"

"Yes, you can! Thank you, mija!" As Clio headed back to the porch her mother went on. "I see there's a pot of water simmering on the stove. Bess, could you put these potatoes in to boil?"

"I'll be glad to."

Back on the porch Clio heard a series of moist splashes as Aunt Bess resumed talking, but in a lower voice that was harder to hear, at least on the porch. She must have moved to a different part of the kitchen. There were gaps.

"My mother wasn't as fortunate as Abuelita. She had several strokes...her seventies. She...and the...found a nursing service that was terribly expensive! ...outrageous...so instead I...wetback...for less than minimum wage. I insisted she live in and...by the week. It saved ever so much money....might remember that if ever Abuelita...."

"We'd never do that," Ana replied. "If Abuelita needs nursing care that's just what she'll get, no matter what it costs."

"You say that now, but...can change...me ask you something...move these potatoes to a larger burner."

Clio heard footsteps and several more clunks and scrapes. Bess continued, her voice a little clearer. She must have moved closer to the pantry.

"You know, you and Matt are sure to inherit this land, and probably Abuelita's entire estate too."

"Goodness! I have no idea!"

"Well, you have to think it'll happen that way. Who else would it be? Have you given any thought to what you'll do then?"

"No. What do you mean?"

"It'll probably be a lot. You'll have money to do all sorts of things you can't do now, I mean, like travel, for instance. Have you ever gone on a cruise?"

Clio stopped peeling. What was she talking about?

"A cruise?"

"Sure, like take a cruise of the Mediterranean. Wouldn't you love to do that some day? I would. We could go together!"

"I don't...."

More footsteps. Marky's voice boomed out loud and high.

"Mmm! Something smells good! I wonder if that's a pie!" she whooped. "I'm getting hungry again! Gosh, I feel better now. I was so hot in those long sleeves!"

A high-pitched chuckle. Aunt Bess spoke.

"It *is* warm in here. I think I'll go freshen up too if y'all will excuse me. Please call me when it's time to eat!"

Clio realized that gave her another opening. She grabbed the pan of cucumbers, waited for Aunt Bess's departing footsteps, and headed into the kitchen.

"Here they are, Mom."

"Thank you, mija."

"I'll take the peels out to the compost pile."

"Good. Ask Dad how the meat is coming, please."

"Sure, Mom."

Once those tasks were done she ducked into her own family's house to emerge a minute later and head for the barn with a small bundle under her arm. She put a cup of water in the microwave and set it for two minutes. When it dinged, she knocked on the door separating her shop from Julio's and opened it. Julio and Sara were standing by Julio's telescope. He was apparently demonstrating how the celestial tracking mechanism kept it focused on a star while compensating for the Earth's rotation.

"Hey," she said.

"Hi!" answered Sara. She looked like a different person, cheerier and more animated, eyes bright.

"I made you a cup of tea," Clio said, setting a mug down on Julio's counter. "You can try it before supper. Here's the rest," she added, handing the tin to Sara.

"Oh, wow!"

"Careful! It's hot! Remember, you have to work with it."

"Oh, I will. I really will. Thanks!"

She picked up the mug and blew a puff of air across the top. Clio glanced at Julio. Neither twin needed to say a word. Julio knew something was up but his face registered nothing. Clio spoke again.

"Dinner's in twenty minutes. Don't miss it!"

"We won't," Julio answered.

"I gotta get back to the kitchen," Clio said. "Julio can give you a look at my shop if you want."

"This is so fun!" Sara exclaimed. "Thanks so much for the 'tea!'"

"It was my pleasure," Clio replied, realizing she'd just spoken a phrase her mother used. "Good luck!"

Outside, she saw Grandpa Bert going in the back door carrying a big platter of meat. Her dad, surrounded by swirls of smoke, was loading a second platter at the grill. She ran to hold the door for him.

In the thirty minutes she'd been gone Abuelita's kitchen had become a hive of activity. Grandpa Bert and her dad were standing to one side balancing giant trays of beef and sausage and chicken while her mother, Abuelita, and Grandma Julia were getting other dishes ready. Marky bustled by carrying two pies to the dining room.

The men were in jeans and flashy guayaberas. Abuelita and Grandma Julia wore long dresses covered with bright Mexican embroidery, while Marky had on a muu-muu a size or two smaller than it ideally should have been, but mercifully muted in color. Her mother wore her favorite little brown leather flats with the leather bows, round-toed and scuffed (which fit Clio as well). With her jeans and white cotton shirt with the tail out, she looked more like one of the kids than the adults. Clio suspected she had chosen something with sleeves because she was embarrassed for her lean, muscular arms to be noticed.

Grandma Julia, a cheerful, active woman who taught high school Spanish in Albuquerque, seemed to be the one coordinating everything.

"Bert, could you take the meat out to the sideboard in the dining room and carve it up, please? Matt, that big pot of beans needs to go out there too. Marky, if you could find the salad dressing and barbecue sauce in the refrigerator, that could go to the table. Ana, the salads need to go into the pretty bowls and be taken out too. I'll get the ice out and put the limeade and the tea on the sideboard. Abuelita, would you and Clio like to set the table?"

No one bumped into anyone else, at least not too violently, no dishes were spilled or broken, and in a matter of minutes things began coming into order. Clio and Abuelita had almost finished setting the table ("Let's use the good china," Abuelita told her.) when Grandma Julia called Clio aside.

"Clio, honey, would you go tell Aunt Bess that we're ready, please? She's probably in the blue bedroom."

"Yes, ma'am," Clio replied with a sinking heart.

Upstairs, she found Aunt Bess seated at a table before a mirror, doing something to her eyes.

"Excuse me, Aunt Bess. Supper's ready."

Aunt Bess was clearly not in a hurry.

"Why, hello, Clio. Come in, young lady. We haven't really talked all day. You've gotten so big and pretty since I saw you last! You're just darling! How are you?"

Clio cautiously advanced into the room a few feet.

"Fine. What are you doing, Aunt Bess?"

"Oh, just touching up my makeup."

She seemed to be performing delicate surgery on her eyelids.

"Does it hurt?"

"Not much. A little pain is the price of beauty, you know." She set down a tiny tool and picked up another. "Clio, sugar, are the boys after you yet?"

"Ma'am?"

"Do you find boys always hanging around you at school? Calling you at home?"

"Uh, no, ma'am."

"Well, it won't be long, I'm sure. You're getting so gorgeous!"

"Thank you," Clio said, very softly, after a short pause.

"Pretty soon, you're going to have your pick of all of them. I know you will."

Clio said nothing to that. Bess continued.

"The more ready you are, the better you'll do, you know."

"Ma'am?"

"Beauty, young lady. We can't just rely on nature. Beauty is a cruel business. If we were going to be here longer I could show you how to maximize what you have. You're so pretty, but there are a few simple tricks—your hair, for example. You have such lovely hair, but it's so fine and straight! It just lies there. You can spruce it up, put a little flip in it, give it some life!" She turned to Clio and laid a finger under her chin. "Your features are delicate and nicely structured—a little highlighting will bring them out wonderfully. Your eyebrows are so fine you can hardly see them. We could bring them out to set off your eyes. You'll knock them dead! But," she turned back to the mirror and selected a third brush, a larger one with softer bristles, "we just don't have time this visit. Your mother could show you. Actually, she could benefit from a few tips herself. She's quite attractive, but she could be twice as attractive with a little effort." She lightly backstroked her cheeks with the brush. "Do you have a boyfriend, Clio?"

"Ma'am? Oh. Well, I have a friend. He's a boy."

"Good for you! And are his parents well off?"

"He's...I...I don't know."

"That's important, Clio. In another year or two when the boys start crowding around, you need to select the best of them. Pick one who can support you in style. I had to learn that the hard way. It took me three husbands to finally get it right. You can do better than I did."

"Uh...."

There were footsteps on the stairs.

"Bess! Clio!" Grandma Julia called. "Come to eat! We're sitting down!"

"We'll be right there," replied Bess. She mashed her lips together and checked her image in the mirror one more time. Pushing back from the table she whispered, "We can continue this later. You'll be such a beautiful young lady! I just can't wait to see you in action!"

Abuelita's dining room came into its own during big parties. The house had been built for a large extended family and was still reminiscent of the hacienda of a prosperous landowner. The interior walls had been originally papered in a loud Victorian pattern, but the paper had been removed and the underlying adobe painted a soft cream. Old paintings hung in ornate frames and two wrought-iron chandeliers supplied adequate light. Someone had lit the candles in the sconces next to the Virgen de Guadalupe at the head of the room, and the candles on the dining table and the sideboard sent out a subtle, festive glow.

With all the leaves installed, the big table easily accommodated fifteen people, seated in approximate order of seniority: Abuelita at the head, her sister Lourdes to her right, and in descending order Julia and Bert Mêndez, Matt's parents; Bess and John Gonzalez, Aunt Lourdes' oldest grandson and wife; Marky and Ricky Gonzales, Aunt Lourdes' youngest grandson and wife; Ana and Matt; Sara, Marky's oldest daughter; Clio and Julio; and, sitting on several volumes of the Encyclopedia Britannica, Vanessa (Ricky and Marky's youngest daughter); and James, John and Bess' six year old. There were so many different dishes, on so many large platters, that the diners were continually getting up to visit the sideboard and have a little more of this or try a little of that. Most of the early conversation concerned the food. John was impressed with the chicken, and said so.

"This chicken is outstanding, Matt, really different! What did you do to it?"

"It's as close as we could get locally to Jamaican jerk chicken. Glad you like it."

"It's hot and sweet and smoky—awesome! What's in the sauce?"

"Ana handled that. You tell him, babe."

"It's a paste of ginger, thyme, scallions, peppers, and allspice. The recipe called for allspice berries, and allspice wood to smoke it, but we had to do without those. Matt used mesquite."

"Man, it's good. Bess said you made the cucumbers too. How?"

"Oh, that was simple. They're just soaked with lime juice and then sprinkled with a little chili powder."

"I'm gonna tell Salvatore about that chicken. He's one of the chefs at the new Royale Milano."

"That's a new hotel going up in Las Vegas. John's got the contract for the drapes," Bess inserted.

"Yup. They're going first class. Drapes a thousand dollars per room times a thousand rooms—quite a tab. I know most of the staff by now."

"Wow," said Ricky, Marky's husband.

"Are these Papá's frijoles?" asked Tia Lourdes.

"Sí," Matt replied.

"I knew it. You remember that story about him getting the recipe from Charlie Goodnight's chuck wagon cook, don't you?"

"I do. The man was born around 1850, right?"

"It was 1848, as father told it. Those frijoles got his vaqueros all the way to Kansas."

Abuelita nodded. "That's right. The cows they sold got our brothers through college. We owe a lot to those vaqueros, and to those frijoles."

"It's a good thing we don't have to rely on cows to get our kids through college today," Bess said. "Drapes are going to get our kids through."

Marky cut her eyes to Ricky. "Natural gas is going to get our kids through. We hope."

"What's going to do it for your kids, Matt?" Bess asked.

"Well, uh..."

"Are you planning that far ahead?" she asked sweetly.

"Well...yes, I guess we are. Actually, I think Julio has it covered, for him and Clio too. Right, son?"

Julio looked up from his sausage.

"Yessir."

There was complete silence at the table except for young James, crunching a carrot stick with his mouth open.

"Julio?" Beth asked.

"Uh, yeah. With royalties from his invention."

"His invention?" Beth was beginning to sound like a straight man. "What invention?"

"When he was back in the first grade, he built a robot car. He showed it to a physics professor at the university, who realized that the power control circuit he invented could be used in automobiles. So he patented it for Julio and sold it to Toyota and Honda. He and Julio are partners. Those circuits are in most Toyotas and Hondas sold now."

"Oh," said Bess, "how nice!"

"Excellent!" exclaimed Sara. "You gotta tell me about that after supper, Julio!"

"OK," he said, reaching for a tortilla.

"Don't think Clio won't contribute her part," Abuelita added. "You're going to save what you made last month, aren't you, mija?"

"Yes'm," Clio murmured, looking down at her plate.

Abuelita went on, oblivious to Clio's discomfort.

"Clio made $9000 last month in an after-school job."

"Good grief!" exclaimed Marky. "How?"

"She handled the mountain lions for that company that made a movie here," Abuelita replied primly.

"She did not!" Marky blurted. Then she noticed Clio, her head still lowered to her plate, looking at her over her eyebrows. She actually looked a little like a mountain lion. Marky giggled. "How wonderful!"

It seemed a good time to change the subject. Bess spoke up.

"Ana, does your Corolla have your son's circuit in it?"

"I think it does."

"I was going to mention to you that John's getting me a new Jaguar this fall. He buys me one every two or three years. I always choose the same color so our neighbors won't know. I'd be happy to sell you this one if you like. It'd be a great deal, and it's so comfortable, so smooth. I'm sure you'd love it."

"That's very kind of you. I appreciate your thoughtfulness, but I could never sell my Corolla. It's the perfect car for me, and besides, I have a...an emotional attachment to it."

"Because of Julio's circuit?"

"Oh, no. I wouldn't know one circuit from another. It's because he bought it for me."

"Oh," said Bess, realizing it was the second time she'd said that. "Well, it was just a thought. If anyone else would like a fine, gently used luxury car, just let me know."

"Right now," broke in Bert, "I would like another glass of wine. Anyone else?"

John, Ricky, and Matt pushed their glasses forward simultaneously. Bert poured. Abuelita looked round the table.

"If anyone would like a twenty-five year old Grand Marquis, just let me know. It was only driven by a little old lady."

"Not likely, Abuelita," chuckled Bess. "The next owner of that car will probably live in a trailer."

"We live in a trailer," Marky said quietly to a quiet table, adding sub voce to her husband, "but at least we don't work for the Mafia."

"Well!" Julia inserted brightly, "I think it's time for the birthday cake! Bert, do you have a match?"

Everybody had to sing and Abuelita blew out the candles. Fortunately there were just two: one candle on the "9" and another on the "0." The cake was soon reduced to crumbs.

"What a wonderful cake!" exclaimed Marky. "Who made it?"

"Julia did," said Abuelita. "The icing was heavenly. What was in it, Julia?"

"Mostly cream cheese."

Marky giggled again.

"But it's still nutritional," Julia added. "It's a zucchini cake."

Marky let out a whoop of delight. Julia smiled.

"Bert always hated zucchini. I started making it just to prove him wrong."

"Well," Bert rumbled, pushing his chair back from the table, "maybe I was wrong about zucchini. I'd eat cat food if you'd put enough cream cheese on it. This whole meal was delicious. Thanks, everyone. Happy birthday, mamacita!"

The adults began getting up and clearing the table. Marky, balancing a stack of dessert plates, looked at her teenage daughter.

"Are you feeling all right, Sara? You hardly ate anything!"

"I'm fine, mama. I ate all I could hold."

As her mother headed for the kitchen Sara glanced at Clio. Clio smiled a tiny smile back.

Four hours later the only windows showing lights were in Matt and Ana's house. Matt was putting the serving bowls on a high shelf when Ana padded in in her terrycloth bathrobe and flipflops, settling on the couch where she could see her husband. Matt hung up a dish towel, opened the refrigerator, and poured two small glasses of grape juice. He handed one to Ana as he eased down next to her. They sipped.

"Well, we did it," he said. "Long day, but we survived."

"It was fun," Ana said, setting her glass on the coffee table. Matt set his down next to hers and laid an arm over her shoulders, pulling her to him. Her damp hair was cool on his cheek. It smelled of honeysuckle.

"We'll see them off in the morning and then we're done. I hope none of it bothered you."

"Bothered me? Certainly not. What do you mean?"

"Oh, the undercurrents, the little jabs and cutting remarks and stuff."

"Of course not. I understand those."

"Yeah? Like how?"

"Well, Ricky is Marky's second husband. Sara is the daughter of her first husband, who teaches biology at a community college somewhere and Marky isn't sure she should have divorced him because she was better off than she is now. Bess used to be a fashion model, but got too old so now she sells clothes at a department store. She has children by each of her three husbands. Each husband was wealthier than the last. Her oldest child is a college student, majoring in English, which upsets her. James is her only son by Juan. She told him to change his name to John. They have homes in Hawaii and Acapulco. So it makes sense there should be some jealousy between her and Marky."

"Good grief! You know more about my family than I do! How did you learn all that?"

"I asked Abuelita, days ago. Families are important to Thomans. Politics is unavoidable, especially family politics."

"Did you have reunions on Thomo?"

"Of course. You wouldn't believe ours. Yours was tiny by comparison."

"Yeah? I guess that makes sense, with your clans and all."

"The last one I attended, the year I left, there were 600 people. That was a small one."

"Sheesh!"

"They're usually very structured, with officers and a program and entertainment. There are contests and arguments and even fights, sometimes."

"Wonderful! Then our little reunion must have seemed tame to you." He picked up his glass and sipped. "So, you didn't get too tired?"

"I'm tired...normal tired...normally tired? Is that right?"

"I guess. You know, you could have announced we're expecting. It would have made a sensation."

"It's still not 15 weeks yet. I didn't want to attract attention. That's why I wore a shirt with the tail out."

"Ah. How about your trip, day after next? How you feeling about that? Everything arranged?"

"Yes, mostly. I need to make a final check with Hleo and Rob Coombs, but I think it'll go well enough. I should be gone four days."

Matt kissed her damp ear.

"I'm gonna worry about you. I'm your husband. That's my job."

"This trip could be very helpful. Some of the larger philanthropic institutions are beginning to coordinate their activities, so instead of a medical program, or economic, or agricultural, or educational, several large-scale combined programs are being tried. Then they follow up, to be sure the progress isn't lost. If I can get even more to participate, it could make a difference, a permanent difference. You shouldn't worry about me."

"If you say so. Let's call it a day, shall we?"

Giving her shoulder a little squeeze, he leaned forward and picked up the two glasses with one hand. They drained them. He was thinking of her phrase 'you shouldn't worry.' She'd said that on other occasions. He planned to worry anyway.

The after-breakfast farewells the next morning went smoothly enough, delayed only by the curious custom of one man on one side of a car talking to the driver and a woman on the other side talking to his passenger, with neither pair wanting to stop since the other was still talking. But somehow it ended, and John turned the key to start his wife's Jaguar.

There followed a prolonged cranking sound, several startling backfires, and the knocking of a badly-timed engine struggling to start. Two nasty black clouds billowed out the sporty dual chrome exhausts as the engine shook the whole vehicle before settling into something resembling the purr of a luxury car. Clio, on one side of the car, cut her eyes to her brother, on the other. He was already looking at her, his face determinedly rigid. In a fraction of a second, whole paragraphs of twin metacommunication were exchanged.

The departure of the John (formerly Juan) Méndez family was soon followed by that of Ricky, Marky, Vanessa, and Tia Lourdes, after which Clio introduced Grandpa Bert to Raisin, released from captivity to sample the new scents in her domain. Bert, duly impressed by his granddaughter's majestic and coolly reserved super-cat, collected his wife from Abuelita's kitchen to depart. With that done, the five resident Méndez family members returned to the kitchen to recall the highlights of the past three days, and Abuelita's family reunion was over.

Chapter 8

Afrim the Assassin carefully stretched an arm forward to make sure the legs of the bipod supporting the muzzle of the sniper rifle were fully spread and solidly planted. They were. He eased back and began setting the windage and elevation knobs on the sighting mechanism to the values he had calculated: total range 1.63 kilometers, wind to be determined. It would be a long shot, but an eminently makable one. He was confident he could place a bullet within a three inch circle at that range, even if the target were walking. Two years ago he'd completed a contract on a Tajik cabinet minister who'd been riding horseback two kilometers away. This would be easy compared to that.

It was a pleasure to work for Kirill Lebedev, a consummate professional with an apparently limitless budget. Afrim considered himself a complete professional as well, one who took pride in his craft. He'd done some sloppy work in his desperate early days as a beginner, but he'd survived with a little luck and now he was at the pinnacle of his trade. This shot would be perfect. He had located the best possible vantage point and Lebedev had quickly secured it for his use: a corner hotel room on the tenth floor of a building facing away from the convention center. From the edge of its tiny balcony there was a clear, narrow path through three long blocks of other buildings to the main entrance to the center. Flight time for the bullet would be 2.97 seconds and the sound of the muzzle blast, such as it was, would be so dissipated by nearby buildings that those at the other end would not likely hear it at all. Best of all, there were flags at the point where the limousines would let off their passengers, allowing him a final adjustment for windage.

He was sprawled on the narrow balcony, out of sight of police helicopters by virtue of having stretched the cheap green carpet that covered it some twelve inches off the cement. From the air the balcony would look like any of the other hundreds of balconies on that side of the hotel. The muzzle of his rifle was completely out of sight from above and below. It was hot under there, but the discomfort was trivial next to some of the places he had been.

He squinted through the scope. The plaza of the convention center came into sharp focus. Police and other security people were everywhere. The flags indicated a breeze of perhaps eight miles an hour. If he had known any of the people down there he could have recognized them through the scope. This would be his first contract on a woman, but that didn't bother him. Whether she stopped for photographers or simply strode into the building, she would never know what hit her.

The escape plan Lebedev provided was a good one. In the hotel room behind him were a large but lightweight video camera and two cases of accessories big enough to hold his disassembled rifle. When he left, he would look like a television reporter rushing to a story. Lebedev had even cobbled together a press pass for him to hang around his neck. The man overlooked nothing. It was a privilege to work for someone with such concern for others.

He wiped the sweat from his eyebrows and took another look through the scope. He opened and closed the bolt on his rifle. The freshly-oiled action was smooth as silk. Everything was in place. In less than twenty-four hours it would all be over.

The seat back in front of her moved several inches closer as its occupant adjusted it to a more comfortable angle. This second and final leg of her flight, from Dallas/Fort Worth to New York City, would be nearly four hours. She reclined her own seat a bit, not glancing at the people on either side. The type of person she was disguised to be would not have been too friendly. The first leg, from El Paso, had been bumpy, thanks to a dust storm blowing through west Texas. She still felt queasy, but the little air nozzle overhead was blowing directly on her and the coolness helped.

Her disguise was working nicely so far, as long as she didn't get sick. The last time she was pregnant she had had to fly the pod, but unlike now, there had been no one to care when she had started retching. If the flight attendants would just hurry and bring some ginger ale she'd feel a lot better. So far, no one had paid her any attention at all, at least not until a teenage boy with unruly hair, ragged jeans, and t-shirt sporting a grimacing green monster over the crimson words "Have a Nice Day, Asshole," claimed the aisle seat. After he had squirmed himself into position he had leaned over and asked her, "Whatcha listenin' to?" Thinking quickly, she pulled out the (silent) ear bud from her right ear and said in a chilly, low voice, "Bach." After that he left her alone. Whenever she traveled alone she could take on ten or more "looks" without requiring much in the way of extra clothing, but this particular disguise was a first for her.

Ah! Two flight attendants rolled a drink cart up the aisle, headed for the front of the plane. Hurry back, please!

She turned a page of the book in her lap but she was absorbed in her own thoughts instead of reading. It was curious—she lived a peaceful, rural life with enough time to herself, so why did she generally do her most reflective thinking on airplanes? It must be because she was separated from her family. She'd been gone all of three hours and already missed them. But she had to make this trip. It would be all show and ceremony, heads of state and cabinet ministers, banquets and bowing, but that never bothered her. She had grown up in that kind of atmosphere, and Thoman culture was quite ceremonial anyway. In spite of the elaborate formalities, this trip would matter. After years of planning, several of the world's biggest philanthropic organizations were finally beginning to work together, pooling their efforts in public health and education. The combined effect would be multiplied, and with a sound follow-up program the gains would not be lost. Millions of lives would be improved. If she could help in any way, even if only as a glitzy celebrity, she would do so. She owed it to both of her planets.

The plane dropped drunkenly. She forced herself to ignore her nausea and think ahead to meeting Rob Coombs at the airport. She liked Coombs. They had worked well together on a dangerous mission four years ago. There was an expression in Luvit which described him that was similar to a phrase she had read in English: roughly, "happy warrior," but the Luvit phrase added the connotation of "pleasant companion," which fit him perfectly. They would fly to Italy together where she would discard her disguise and join the luminaries at the G-8 conference. At the moment she was totally anonymous, but by this time tomorrow she would be anything but.

She glanced forward, through the narrow gap between two seats. The drink cart was two rows away! Ginger ale! She would make it! She thought again. *We will make it!*

Rob Coombs hated airports. They were enormous, crowded, chaotic despite their all-encompassing organization, and, given his current occupation, dangerous. His Seal training had had nothing to do with this kind of environment, being more wartime and technical, but his more recent career with World Security Services frequently involved work in crowds of people. He had learned to continually employ unobtrusive surveillance techniques, making himself exceptionally aware of his surroundings, but he still didn't like it.

The one thing that made this assignment welcome was that he would once again be working with Ana Darcy, his only friend from outside the solar system. Their week-long evolution together, four years ago, remained the highlight of his career to date, even when he took into consideration the fact that he had been shot. Ana had turned out to be a petite, attractive young woman, composed, compassionate, with a firm sense of honor, and utterly unflappable. She even had a subtle sense of humor. He had known she was an incredible athlete—the whole world knew that—but he'd been totally blown away to see her in combat. Seals, who knew they were the best fighters in the world, were far too lofty to gasp in admiration at the martial skills of a civilian, but he had at Ana's. All the same, he prayed those skills would be irrelevant on this trip.

The last bit of coffee in his cardboard cup was cold. He checked his watch: forty minutes to the flight. He tossed the cup and stepped out of Starbucks to regain his bearings. Gate 72 was at least a quarter mile to his left. He headed that way.

The concourse was crowded with the predictable sorts of travelers, the majority seemingly summer vacationers. Casually, he doubled back once, and ducked into a mall store another time to check if anyone was following—apparently not—while his mind rambled on. Four years ago he'd been disappointed to learn Ana Darcy was married. Later he had met her husband and twin children and changed his mind. He liked Matt, and their two kids were smart and lively. He had decided he was happy for her. What were the odds, to travel twenty-five light years and find true love? He lived in New York City and hadn't been able to do that.

He was almost at gate 72. This was an international flight, and the crowd waiting for it included fewer people in shorts and flipflops, except for one boisterous group of college students chattering animatedly near the check-in counter. One of them approached him hesitantly, a young man with a wispy goatee, gray windbreaker, and Russian worker's cap, backpack over his shoulder.

"Hey, man," he said, "can you change a twenty?"

"No," he said automatically.

"C'mon. You sure?"

"I'm sure." He scanned the crowd.

"You lookin' for somebody?"

Coombs looked more closely at the speaker. He was short. He had high cheekbones, narrow chin, and deepset eyes. He looked Slavic, like a Russian student radical on holiday. His voice was reedy…oh, hell! It was Ana Darcy, with a twinkle in her eyes! Dammit! Gotcha!

It was all Coombs could do not to laugh. Instead, he said, "Maybe I do have change," and reached for his wallet. They exchanged bills and struck up a phony conversation. Ana passed him a book, he looked at several pages, and they faked talking about it as they looked for two vacant seats where they could sit together. Coombs pointed to a pair at the end of a row by the windows. Ana took the end seat and he sat next to her with an unhappy six year old on his other side. The child's mother, patting a squalling baby, sat on the other side of the kid. He doubted they'd be interested in what he and Ana might say to each other. Through the large windows the ground crew was bustling around their plane. It was now fully dark but the plane was lit up from one end to the other.

Handing the book back, he spoke in a low voice.

"Man, you really faked me out, shipmate. Lookin' good! How are you doing?"

She riffled through a few pages and handed the book back to him.

"Thanks! I'm fine. How are you?"

He looked down at the book.

"Much better, now that we've met up successfully. Are you sure this is the way you want to travel?"

"Yes. My uncle is already there. He said the American President invited me to fly over with him, but I was afraid that might…might…what's the word?"

"Co-opt?"

"Well, politicize my appearance. I'd rather not be seen as taking sides. I'd prefer to avoid as much, uh, excitement? as I can."

"Hullaballoo?"

"What?"

"Hullaballoo, uproar."

"What a funny word! Do you have a pen?"

"Yeah."

"Write that word in the back. I want to remember it."

He did so, passing the book back to her. She looked at it, shaking her head.

"So many words. I'll never learn them all."

His reply was cut short by the announcement that their flight was boarding. People began standing and collecting their belongings. She slid the book into her backpack. Coombs looked at his boarding pass.

"We have assigned seats, so we'll be apart during the flight. But if anyone tries to speak Russian to you, I can help translate. I've been working on my Russian."

They stood. She stuck some ear buds into her ears. The wires disappeared into a pocket.

"It's not likely. With these in, no one bothers me at all."

"So much the better. Let's try to get as much sleep as we can during the flight. We're going to have a hell of a long day tomorrow."

"Grandson, pass the chicken, please."

"Yes, ma'am. Here you go."

"It's just wonderful. You did such a good job with it."

"Well, thanks, but the credit goes to Ana. She found the recipe and she made the sauce."

The Méndez family, minus Ana, was digging into the leftovers from the reunion dinner. Raisin was stretched out full length along the top of the couch behind Clio's chair, reposing in dignity, head erect and turned toward the dining table, eyes shut. The light through the windows was a weird purplish gray, the residue of dusk seen through a dying dust storm.

"Julio, won't you try some?" Abuelita asked.

"I already did. Thanks."

"Too spicy, isn't it? Well, that's all right. I'll be happy to finish it."

"Dad, where's Mom right now?" Clio asked.

Matt glanced at the kitchen clock.

"Well, let's see, if she's on schedule she should be over the Atlantic, headed to Italy."

"Why's she going? I forget."

"She's going to the G-8 Conference, which is mainly for the leaders of the big, industrialized countries. There are nine countries represented—they really should call it the G-9, I guess. One of the main topics this time is philanthropy. Mom's going to try to get all the big organizations to work together."

Abuelita shook her head.

"¡Ay! To think, three days ago she was cooking for my birthday dinner, and now she's talking to kings and presidents! ¡Que cosa, grandson!"

"Not that many kings," Matt said.

"If our family only knew, they would go crazy!"

"We don't want them crazier than they already are. Let's not tell them."

"And her from so far away! Here with us one day, and the next with leaders of the world! ¡Que milagro!"

"Un milagro de veras."

"Dad?"

Matt tore a tortilla in half, putting one piece on his plate and the other back on the stack.

"Yes, mija?"

"Harry says he'll teach me to ride a horse. Can you take me tomorrow?"

"I think so. In the afternoon? For a couple hours?"

"Uh-huh. After lunch."

"I thought you were scared of horses," Julio remarked.

"I am. I was. Harry says I shouldn't be. He's going to teach me."

"Good idea, actually," said Matt. "Maybe he can teach you too, Julio."

"I'll wait to see what happens to Clio," Julio replied.

"Since we'll be close, I might go over to Sunland Park Mall, check out the sporting goods and stuff. Would you and Abuelita like to go along?"

"I'm still tired from the reunion, grandson. I think I'll take a nap tomorrow afternoon."

"Son?"

"I have a project to work on."

"OK, then. You and me, Clio." He mopped up the last bit of barbecue sauce with his tortilla and popped it in his mouth. "I'll clean this stuff up if you two want to run along."

"I'll call Harry," Clio said, pushing her chair back. Both youngsters gave Abuelita a quick hug and headed toward their rooms. Matt stood to gather the dishes. Abuelita watched Raisin stretch and hop soundlessly to the floor to follow Clio. She set down her tea cup gently.

"I think your daughter is sweet on that young man, Matt."

"You do? I don't know. They're friends, as far as I can tell."

"Perhaps you should be looking into his family."

"Oh, surely not. It's way early for that kind of thing."

"Oh, no, Matt. Children have always matured too early—I should know—but now it's earlier than ever. Clio is smart as a whip, pero eso no vale ni un pepino ("but that's not worth a cucumber") when the heart is involved."

"Well, I take your point, but so far I think it's mostly animals that connect them."

"Exactly. That's what you should be worrying about."

Coombs grabbed his duffel bag out of the overhead compartment and followed Ana out of the plane and up the jetway at a discrete distance. She flowed with the throng of passengers to the right, toward the baggage area. The concourse was crowded with people coming and going, including an impressive assortment of security personnel and police, but no one paid her any attention that he could see. After all, who would recognize Joseph Stalin's great-grandnephew?

She stepped onto a moving sidewalk. He did the same. As they silently flowed down the concourse, inside a weird translucent blue tube, he eased up to three feet behind her and spoke in a low voice.

"Got any luggage?"

She shook her head imperceptibly.

"OK. Good. I don't either. Head straight to the street and we'll get us a taxi."

The front of the airport looked much like any other: crowded sidewalk, clogged traffic lanes, people everywhere. The pavement was wet. There were puddles at the curb. To the far left three limousines were parked, with police and photographers standing around—transportation for G-8 VIPs, Coombs figured. Buses and taxis were to the right.

Their driver turned out to be an ancient man with a thin, spiky crewcut, week-old beard stubble, and gnarled hands. From the back seat, Coombs ventured a "bon giorno" in a speaking voice, but there was no response. He tried a little louder. The man looked over his shoulder and said "Eh?"

Coombs tried again, much louder: "BON GIORNO!"

"Ah, si! Bon giorno!" the driver replied, adding another couple phrases he understood not a word of. Ana leaned forward and handed the man a slip of paper, adding, "Prego. Grazie."

The man read it, nodded, and began easing the car through the traffic. In a few minutes they were on a four-lane highway headed to downtown Milan. The wind and engine noise were considerable. Coombs winked at Ana.

"I think we can talk. Did you get any sleep?"

"A little, yes. Did you?"

"Some. I'll be fine. You can't possibly get by with just the contents of that backpack, can you?"

"No. Uncle Ro...uh, my uncle brought what I'll need."

"Good. We're actually a little early. We could sightsee a little, but it's not a good day for it." He peered through the window on his right. The air was hazy with the mist flung into the air from other traffic on the wet highway. Dark clouds hung low and solid over the countryside. "Too bad. I bet it's beautiful country."

"It is, or at least the parts I've seen are. Our family was here two years ago. We visited Rome and Florence."

"No kidding? How'd that go?"

"Fine. We were just another family of tourists. We could only see a fraction of what we wanted, with so little time and two active ten year olds along, but the experience was good for them. I enjoyed it too. Everything old was new to me!"

"I bet it was. Did you go anywhere else?"

"Oh, yes! We spent three weeks visiting lots of beautiful places. Some day I'll tell you about it. You've probably been to all of them."

Coombs grabbed for the armrest as the driver swerved suddenly into the left lane and accelerated past a line of trucks. The windshield wipers seemed to be losing ground to the dirt and mist. Coombs prayed silently for the both of them.

"I doubt it. The places I've been aren't very popular with tourists."

The ride took over an hour. Somehow, despite speeding through several hard showers, they survived. It seemed a miracle that the only accident they saw was in the lanes going the other way.

The driver delivered them to a majestic older hotel surrounded by iron railings and with a canopy, fortunately, out to the street. At the entrance they had to pass through a station not unlike airport security, and once inside, hand over their passports and state their destination. Coombs noticed Ana's passport was for "Dusan Janacek," complete with "his" picture. Only after a clerk had made a phone call and confirmed they were expected were they allowed into the elevator.

The door to Ambassador Darshiell's room was opened by a young man who embraced Ana warmly, laughing at her disguise. She introduced him to Coombs (Pavel Sugarek, the Ambassador's secretary) only seconds before the Ambassador himself bustled in.

Coombs had met him twice at functions in New York City but he didn't figure to be remembered. Before he or Ana could say anything, the Ambassador held out his hand and said, "Chief Coombs! So delighted to see you again, sir! I pray your trip was smooth?"

Still the "Chief" business, Coombs thought. These Thomans are certainly on the cutting edge of etiquette. How did he know? Could the Ambassador have been talking to Hleo? He did his best to respond in kind.

"The pleasure is mine, Mr. Ambassador. Yes, sir, the trip was good. I hope you and your delegation are well."

"We are splendid, sir, all the more so now that you and our honored niece are among us. Please, come in and be comfortable. Pavel, some refreshments for our guests, if you please." He turned to Ana and indicated a nearby doorway. "Dear niece, you may wish to first alter your appearance, might you not?"

"Indeed I do, Honored Uncle, and thank you."

While Ana changed, Coombs chatted with the Ambassador and his secretary. Their choice of topics was Ana's disguise: how she had learned to be so proficient at the process, what her recent appearance was intended to suggest, and so on. He was only able to tell them what Ana had told him, that she had learned from a drama student specializing in theater makeup, many years ago.

What Coombs wanted to talk about was security. It didn't take him long to learn that security was everywhere, that the convention center was only a kilometer away, and that they would travel to it in an unarmored limousine. He wasn't entirely happy with that, but then he never was. If security wasn't tight with nine world leaders on site, it never would be.

Ana emerged, looking relaxed and like her old self in her familiar black tailored slacks and deep blue silk blouse. Coombs was no fashion expert but he thought the blouse was a little more frilly than the shirts he'd seen her in before—could it be French? Or maybe Italian? The Ambassador asked her how it felt to walk around in disguise. Coombs, used to examining people minutely, asked if she'd changed her ears, which made secretary Sugarek snort, but her reply made him smile in wonder.

"Oh, yes. I had some plastic ears made. Men typically have bigger ears than women and mine are small anyway. So I slip on the larger ones and stick them down with a little latex paste. You'd be surprised how much that changes my appearance by itself."

Coombs also thought she had modified her nose, cheeks, and eyebrows as well, but he didn't comment on that. She was very skillful, however she did it.

Finally, the Ambassador shifted to a more timely topic.

"Allow me to caution you to restrain yourselves over Pavel's delicacies. There is a luncheon at the conference shortly, and it's certain to be lavish."

"What is the schedule in general, Mr. Ambassador?" Coombs asked.

"The luncheon opens the day. I expect many ministers to attend, but it will be minimally ceremonial. There will be sessions and meetings all afternoon, a pause in the early evening, and then the formal banquet, followed by a party which will doubtless extend into the morning.

"The Thoman delegation will depart before it concludes, without returning here. I therefore suggest that you take your belongings with you when we leave," he checked his watch, "in two hours, if you please."

The Ambassador noted Coombs' surprise.

"It is for our safety. We are sharing the security forces of nine nations while we are here, but the arrangements for our departure are left to us alone. You will see how that is handled. I believe you will approve."

Coombs nodded. He was Ana Darcy's personal security force and nothing more, with neither responsibility for, nor command over, anything else. He hoped the Ambassador was right. It would have to do.

The cell phone in his shirt pocket vibrated against his chest. Afrim the Assassin pulled it out and pressed it to his ear.

"Ja," he said.

"Subject's here," a voice whispered. "Just left the hotel. Black limousine, no flags. Five minutes."

"Ja," he replied, and replaced the cell phone.

Most unfortunate: it was raining, raining hard. He wormed under the narrow space beneath the stretched green carpet and peered through his scope. He could barely see the next block, much less to the conference center. Nevertheless, he'd wait it out. It might let up in time. If not, he would stay close until she left. The entrance to the convention center was nicely illuminated and he had two spotters watching the entrance from a building across the street. Sooner or later, she had to leave.

When he was in his professional mode, Coombs' mind was immune to boredom. It was part of the job. The difference this time was that he had no duties to concentrate on. Security within the conference center, and no doubt outside it as well, was already tight as a drum. Those personnel not actually on duty somewhere were stationed in suites of rooms along both sides of the main hall. Fortunately, some of the rooms had windows through which he could see what was happening on the floor, if not in the meeting rooms.

It was amusing to see the stir Ana's entrance caused among the several hundred present for the luncheon. From his high vantage point he could watch the awareness spread: shoulders were tapped, elbows poked, heads tilted, necks twisted, and people aligned themselves so as to be able to actually see the reclusive woman from the planet Thomo in person. No one seemed much interested in the man at her side, though both were dressed similarly. She had added a black blazer over the blue blouse. Her uncle wore a gray suit with a blue shirt the same shade, but her honey-colored hair made her more easily identifiable from his window one floor above.

It took a while for her to be shown to her seat. She and her uncle must have shaken sixty hands each. The Ambassador probably bowed twenty times. Ana employed a graceful little curtsy instead, and her hand was kissed often. Her smile lit up the vicinity like a flash grenade. She was really working the crowd.

The round tables seated eight, and she had to shake hands with, or curtsy to, everyone at hers before they would sit down. Once they had, heads at neighboring tables continued to turn in her direction. Coombs chuckled: there were three prime ministers down there that he recognized. They seemed as star-struck as everyone else.

When the diners began chatting over their meal he lost interest. He wouldn't mind something to eat himself. He sauntered over to the buffet table at the other end of the room and spent five minutes assembling a meal: prosciutto and cantaloupe, two slices of oddly appealing potato pizza, several tempting biscotti, and a bottle of something called Aranciata Rossa, whose label seemed to promise orange juice. Hand it to the Italians: they knew how to set a table. A little wine would have been a nice touch, but tipsy security people would doubtless be frowned upon.

On his way to a table he spotted someone he knew.

"Hey, Bunny!" he exclaimed.

"Robboman!" came the reply. That had been one of Coombs' Seal nicknames, pronounced "Robb-o'man," alluding to his name, Rob, and also to his robot-like steadiness when dealing with high explosives.

Bunny Duggan and Coombs had shared several duty assignments in the Middle East and Caucasus years earlier. Duggan was a Seal poster child, except for his face. He was a tall, robust man with endless endurance, but his nickname came from his unfortunate dentition and big ears, giving him something of a rodent-like appearance. That was misleading, however. On the job, he was more like a bulldog. Coombs took a seat next to him.

"How did you sneak in here, man?" Coombs asked.

"Presidential detail. You knew I was Secret Service now, didn't you?"

"No! No kidding? So you're still one of the elite few, huh?"

"I guess. Damn bureaucracy's all through the Service too, though. Semper fubar—the old story. Can't get away from it, can you?"

"Oh, I don't know. I don't have much any more."

"Yeah?"

Coombs took a bite of the pizza. It was wonderful. Potato pizza! Who knew? The rosemary set it off just right. Savoring his food, he shook his head at Bunny to indicate "no." Bunny continued his interrogation.

"Well, you're obviously not part of the American delegation. What's your assignment?"

Coombs swallowed and took a pull on the bottle of orange juice.

"I'm guarding Ana Darcy."

Duggan's face went slack.

"No way."

"Hey, Seals don't lie and I ain't joking, man."

"You son of a bitch."

"She's a sweetheart, man."

"You dirty bastard!" Bunny leaned forward. "You really know how to hurt a guy! What's she like?"

"I just told you: a sweetheart. Seriously, she's great fun."

"God damn it! And I get stuck with the freakin' President! So, she's cool?"

"Wicked cool. I wish you could see her in action."

"In action? Like what? Sports?"

Coombs leaned toward Bunny and lowered his voice.

"Just between us, OK? I saw her fight once, for real—life and death."

"Yeah?"

"Yeah. I can't tell you what we were doing, but I swear, she dropped two armed guards in three seconds, disarmed a third, and fought a fourth with a sword—I'm not kidding, a sword. He was an ace swordsman, but she beat him like a drum."

"Damn! A sword fight? For real? You saw that? What the hell were *you* doing?"

"The third man winged me twice. I was out of it. She saved my ass."

"Oh, God! Please, promise me you're not just pulling my chain."

"Bunny, I'm serious as a heart attack. I made her an honorary Seal because of that fight. Now, that's top secret, ok?"

Duggan sat back, lost in thought. He looked wistfully at Coombs.

"You gotta help me, Robboman. Seals stick together, right?"

"Always. Whatcha need?"

"Do you think you could get me her autograph? Please?"

Duggan went on duty shortly after lunch, leaving Coombs no one to talk to. The luncheon conferees had gone off to their meetings and sessions. Idly, he watched several squads of maintenance people swarming around the convention floor. The tablecloths were changed and more tables brought in and set. Curtain walls were opened at the far end of the room and a dais brought out, a speaker's stand set up, and plants, columns, and other adornments arranged behind it. In the opposite back corners, several backdrops appeared, lights were rigged, and tripods and flash umbrellas set up. Coombs had the thought that Ana Darcy would probably get sunburned if she let everyone who wanted to take pictures of her. On the far side of the room, what appeared to be a band stand was taking shape.

Other crews ran wires, set up microphones and television cameras, while still others checked lights and sound. It looked chaotic, but in about two hours all was shipshape—very efficient.

At 7:30 waiters loaded down tables along the far side with snacks, bottles, and glasses, evidently an aperitivo. More and more delegates wandered in to munch and drink and talk. He couldn't identify the food from his vantage point, but two bartenders were pouring lots of sparkling wine from bottles that looked like Prosecco and another was decanting mostly from bottles of a red liquid, probably Campari. He hated that stuff—too bitter. Let them have it. A bustle behind him diverted his attention: the hotel staff, with more food. This time he'd go for the pasta. There were several types he'd never seen, each with different sauce and garnishes. He could take his time and savor the novelty.

By 8:30 most of the seats down on the floor were filled and a small chamber orchestra was playing something classical—he had no idea what. The lights had been dimmed and a small army of waiters was scurrying about serving the formal banquet. The attendees had changed into tuxedos and an assortment of splashy party gowns and dresses. Ana Darcy and her Uncle Rothan were seated at a table near the dais on the far side. As best he could tell in the low light, Rothan seemed to be wearing something similar to a tuxedo, but with a blue sash across the chest and several medals over the left breast. Ana's back was to him. She was wearing a high-waisted gown of a color he decided should be called "Thoman blue." It had long sleeves but left her shoulder blades bare. Would she be wearing heels? He guessed she would be.

It took two hours for them to reach the coffee, tea, and dessert stage. People appeared at the lectern and the evening program began: a welcome, introduction of luminaries, and speeches, the first five of which yielded polite applause. Speaking were three leaders of G-8 countries and two Very Important People: an ex-American President deeply involved in global philanthropy, and a billionaire industrialist who had donated most of his fortune to world betterment. Coombs was surprised when Rothan Darshiell was invited up to the podium to be the sixth to address the audience. He moved nearer the speaker that provided the audio feed from the floor. Whatever would he say?

He made a speech that left the whole hall buzzing. He began pleasantly enough, thanking the hosts for their hospitality and the conference for inviting his delegation, making the point that on behalf of the entire planet of Thomo, he was delighted his people were finally reunited with those from whom all Thomans sprang. There was applause to that. He went on to stress how much Thomans would benefit from the richness of Earth's cultures, and in return, how eager his people were to contribute to the welfare of their home planet. Philanthropy was one way. Another, he added, was to employ Thomans' legendary negotiating skills in mediating conflicts on Earth, something he had already begun doing. Finally, he ran through a brief list of Thomans' scientific and technical contributions, and concluded with a proposal that made Coombs sit up straight: the Ambassador offered the people of Earth the use of the Thoman shuttle to undertake a voyage of exploration to Mars. This was greeted with great applause, drawing the audience to its feet. When the clamor died down, he made a final announcement: thanks to the gracious cooperation of the Italian government, the G-8 Board of Directors, and Milan air control, the Thoman shuttle would be landing on top of this very building precisely at 2:00 am. Any and all conferees were invited to take a look at it. He concluded with more polite remarks about everyone's hospitality, and left the podium to resume his seat.

The audience was on its feet once again. Rothan smiled and bowed at his place, invited Ana to stand, and they both bowed.

Coombs shook his head: that was cool, very cool, of the Ambassador. From a political and philanthropic standpoint, the conference was evidently a success for the Thoman delegation. For his part, from a security standpoint, it had also been a success: nothing bad had happened. At least, not yet.

Who was she posing with? Ana tried her best to remember: several diplomats, but from where? She was so light-headed she was barely able to calculate that she'd been 36 hours with very little sleep. If she could endure one more hour, it would all be over. The umbrellas flashed for the hundredth time, she shook hands with the diplomats, and stepped away from the backdrop. Her smile felt funny. Did it look funny as well? Her mouth was dry. People were crowded around the photographers but she saw no waiters with trays of drinks that weren't champagne.

Uncle Rothan, chatting with a group of people, beckoned her to him and put his arm lightly around her shoulders. She smiled again, trying to make her eyes work. Who were these people, and what were they saying?

Beyond Rothan, pairs of people were swirling to a waltz, which didn't help her swimming vision. Twenty feet away, someone in another group was looking fixedly at her. She tried again to focus. He was a tall, gaunt man who resembled that American President...Abraham Lincoln? Was she hallucinating? He approached.

"Excuse me, Mr. Ambassador. A word with your niece, if you please?"

Rothan nodded. The man drew her aside.

"So pleased to finally meet you, Ms. Darcy. You don't know me, but I know you. You autographed my harpsichord!"

The strangeness of the man and his comment jogged her mind back to her.

"Oh! Was...was that at the home of Dr. Charles Hodge?"

"It was!" he said, "You remember!"

"Yes. As I recall, Dr. Hodge said you were doing surgery, in Africa. Is that it?"

"I was! Extraordinary!"

"I felt bad signing my name on your beautiful French harpsichord without asking your permission. I hope you didn't mind."

"Good heavens, no! I show it to everyone who enters the house! And now, after all these years, I can thank you in person!"

It dawned on her that it truly was odd to meet this man at this place.

"It was my pleasure, sir. And so here we are...."

"Oh, excuse me! I should have introduced myself. I am Dr. David Schwartz. For the last three years I have been the director of Surgeons to the World, the organization I was volunteering with when you visited Charles in Durham. Our group has joined forces with four other medical and health-related organizations to improve our efficiency and increase our coverage in the third world. Thanks to your efforts, we are soon to be eight groups!"

"That's wonderful, Dr. Schwartz!"

"It is, truly. In fact, Ms. Darcy, the first of next month I will be part of a combined medical team tending to the people of the midlands and highlands of Peru. Other agencies have been there for some time, working in educational and economic areas. The idea, you see, is to employ a comprehensive and long-lasting program that will continue to improve the lives of the residents after the teams have left. It is just the sort of effort you encourage."

"It is, indeed. I shall look forward to hearing how well it succeeds."

Schwartz smiled.

"I believe it will succeed nicely, if not perfectly. It is a pilot program, after all. Perhaps the greatest drawback is that the world community is barely aware of it. You could be an immense help with that, Ms. Darcy, if you were to visit with my team."

"Oh, my. I haven't made a site visit in over a year. The first of next month? That's quite soon. I don't know, Dr. Schwartz. I'd love to, but I'm almost exhausted from this trip. As much as I regret it, a visit is probably impossible. I will consider the matter. May I contact you through Surgeons to the World?"

"You may, absolutely. It would be such an honor to serve with you, mademoiselle."

They shook hands again as Uncle Rothan appeared before her. Fortunately, she didn't have to focus to recognize him. His sash gave him away.

"It's getting late, Honored Niece. Would you like to dance one dance before we leave?"

"I hope you are joking, sir. I'm not sure I can walk safely, much less dance."

"Yes, a jest, a poor jest of course. Let us work our way to the exit and then make our escape, shall we?"

"Give me your arm, Dear Uncle. Lead the way, sir."

Coombs' cell phone was vibrating against his thigh. He fished it out of his pocket.

"Yes?"

"Mr. Coombs, it's Pavel Sugarek. They are leaving, sir."

"Copy. I mean, got it. I'll meet you."

The plan was to meet in the Thomans' room on the twentieth floor. It was the plainest of rooms, but only their luggage was in it. They would collect it and depart. He looked at his watch: 1:17 pm. Time to get moving.

"Ja?"

"Subject has left the floor. Should be exiting soon."

"Ja."

He hung up. The skies had cleared. He worked his way under the carpet and sighted through his scope. The mercury vapor lights around the front of the conference center were adequate. People were crowded around the entrance, groups breaking off as their limousines pulled up to the curb. He counted the time it took a given person to cover the carpeted distance to the car: eleven seconds. Plenty of time. Even if photographers were lined up on both sides, his elevated, head-on vantage point gave him the perfect line of fire.

Coombs checked his watch and knocked on the door: 1:26 pm. He was wondering if the ambassador had turned into a pumpkin at midnight when Secretary Sugarek opened the door and let him in.

The room was moderately upscale. It could have been a hotel room in any hotel anywhere in the world, except perhaps for the six small framed pictures of fantastically sleek and colorful women's high-heeled shoes on one wall. Italian, he assumed, probably Milanese. The drapes were drawn. A luggage cart with three suitcases on it rested by the door. Ana's gray nylon backpack and a fourth suitcase were open on the far bed. The Ambassador was speaking Luvit into a cell phone at a little round table in the far corner.

The Secretary opened a small refrigerator.

"Would you have some refreshment, Mr. Coombs?"

"Uh, no, thank you very much. I'm...."

The door to the bath area opened and Ana Darcy came out in slacks and blue shirt, barefoot. She was carrying a pair of shoes and her blue gown over her arm.

"I hope it's years before I have to wear these again. Hi, Rob. Why are you smiling?"

"Hey there, shipmate. Oh, I made a bet with myself that you would wear high heels. Now I don't know whether I won or lost."

The heels were not quite two inches high. She tucked them in the suitcase, folded the gown and laid it on top, and sat on the bed. She began massaging her feet.

"We both lost. I dare you to stand for three hours in shoes like that."

Coombs smiled again.

"For enough money and no one to see me, I'd take that dare."

She unzipped something inside the backpack, pulled a cloth bag of bulky objects from it, and set it on the bed. Then she began wrestling with the backpack.

"What are you doing?"

"Watch."

She was turning the backpack inside out. She slid the cloth bag back inside and zipped it into place. As she pulled the thing into shape, Coombs realized it was now a classy leather businesswoman's shoulder bag.

"Well, I'll be! Is that slick! You have your disguise stuff in that bag, don't you?"

She extracted a pair of lace-up black flats from the suitcase and slipped them on.

"Oooh. These feel so much better! Yes. I can look like a dozen different people with what's in this. I can live from this bag for a week."

"Where did you get that?"

"I had it made, in New York City. It was expensive."

"I bet it was. I'd like to know...."

He paused as the Ambassador snapped his phone shut and stood.

"We're on schedule," he announced. "Chief Coombs, do you require anything from your suitcase before it is removed?"

"No, sir."

"Pavel, if you would do us the honors with the luggage."

"Yes, sir," he replied.

Ana zipped her big suitcase closed and the secretary added it to the stack on the cart, opening the door and wheeling it out. The Ambassador checked his watch.

"We'll follow in five minutes," he said, closing the door gently.

Coombs thought he knew what would happen when the three of them finally stepped into the elevator, so he wasn't surprised to see the Ambassador press the button for the roof. There must have been two hundred people waiting there, behind a row of security people guarding a cleared area. Automatically, he looked the crowd over quickly and carefully. Most were peering into the night sky, but he didn't bother. He'd flown thousands of miles in Ana's smaller escape pod and knew he would feel the shuttle before he saw it.

At 1:59 he sensed a low frequency vibration in the air. The bottom of the shuttle was emerging from the darkness, perhaps 200 feet overhead, slowly sinking toward the lighted area, amid a throbbing hum and flashes from cameras. Coombs remembered how stunned he had been the first time he had seen Ana's pod land next to him. This night, he watched a vessel as big as a boxcar float down like a balloon slightly low on helium, to a gentle landing fifty feet away—very impressive. The guests began applauding.

An hour later they were finally in the air headed for home. All two hundred visitors had been toured through the vessel, from the cockpit to the living and dining areas, the galley and head, the sleeping quarters, and the surprisingly capacious cargo areas. The propulsion room, aft, was visible only through a window in the hatch leading to it. Coombs hadn't seen anything through it that looked like any propulsion system he was familiar with.

Once in flight, it was completely quiet inside. He could feel only the slightest vibration when he pressed his hand against a bulkhead. From the living area he could see the Ambassador standing at the hatch to the cockpit, behind their two guests, sitting in the pilot's and copilot's chairs. Both were astronauts, one from NASA and the other from the European Space Agency. They were absorbed in conversation and looking at the control panel. Pavel and Ana, again minus her shoes, were crashed on a sofa, water bottles in hand. He joined them.

"Tired, shipmate?"

"I can barely stay awake."

"Mr. Secretary? Are you tired too?"

"Pavel, please. I'm just a language major from CUNY, originally from San Diego. My dad is an electrician and my mother is a photographer, and here I am, flying in a machine made on another planet! I should be tired, but I'm so excited that I don't feel it at all. This is so cool! Isn't it unbelievable?"

"It really is. Funny to think of it going to Mars, huh?"

"Maybe they'll need a translator," Pavel said.

"How long till we're back in New York?"

"Eight hours," Ana replied. "We're keeping it subsonic—more time for the trainees to get oriented, and more time for us to sleep."

"Good deal. Show me which bunk is mine and I'll start on my part."

Ana eased to her feet.

"Take any one on the right. What's the Navy word for that?"

"Port! That is, the left side, looking forward."

"Yours too, Pavel. Mine is on the other side...?"

"Starboard."

"That's it. I'll remember now. Thanks for everything, Rob." She hugged him quickly. "See you in New York!"

Chapter 9

Viktor was reasonably hopeful Oleg was not going to have him killed. Surely he wasn't that angry. Would he invite someone to his yacht only to tie a heavy weight to him and throw him overboard? Probably not. Still, that was just the kind of gesture Oleg was known for.

Oleg couldn't possibly blame him for the failure. He knew what a long shot, literally, the mission had been. Who could have predicted the Thoman shuttle would carry the woman away from the hotel's roof? The smart thing, the courageous thing, for him to do was assume Oleg realized that, and play straight with him.

Even so, it had been a terrible shock to find a stranger at his hotel door saying "The boss wants to see you." He wasn't much relieved to find himself delivered to a private airport where he was ushered into a tiny blue helicopter with a pair of dueling sabers painted on the side. The cabin was the size of one of those horrible little Smart Cars, and once in the air it was noisier than a chain saw and hotter than hell's kitchen.

After an uncomfortable hour, he woke from his musings when the helicopter tilted sideways into a sweeping circle. Below was a port city of some kind. He could see vehicles on the streets. They were almost low enough to see individual people.

"Where is this?" he shouted at the pilot.

"Genoa," the man shouted over his shoulder.

They clattered through the turn, fishing boats and small freighters appearing below in the shallows. In the near distance, two larger merchant vessels were leaving wakes behind them. As they passed over a breakwater dividing the deep blue of the Mediterranean from the lighter blue of the harbor, a line of moored yachts, all shiny as new cars, came into view. Two of the three smaller ones had fishing rods mounted from their sterns, like giant whiskers. Oleg's yacht was obvious: four times as big as any of the others, streamlined as a bullet, and a dark, metallic blue like the helicopter. The pilot was flying towards a platform mounted a deck above, and a bit forward of, the fantail.

He was met by a bearded man in an unfamiliar uniform sporting gold-striped shoulder boards, who said merely, "Mr. Reznik? This way, sir."

"This way" turned out to be down a steep stairway (Viktor's naval friends called them "ladders"), along a passageway, up two more stairways, and then forward until the passageway opened onto a broad, ultra-luxurious lounge with curved windows the width of the ship. The view was spectacular. Oleg was seated in a leather chair fit for a king, with a glass at his hand.

"Viktor. Welcome aboard the Galaxie. Take a seat. Something to drink, perhaps?"

Oleg's voice was warm enough, but he did not rise and did not smile. His smiles usually portended bad news for someone, so maybe that was for the best.

"Thank you. Yes, I think a little vodka if you please."

Oleg nodded at the man who had led him forward. Viktor sat down. The man left.

"Pleasant flight?"

"Very. Scenic! Lovely helicopter. It stays with the ship?"

"Of course. You entered the ship through its hangar. It is small, I am sorry to say, and its air conditioner needs work. It will be fixed, but I am in no hurry. I am negotiating the construction of a new ship."

"Indeed?"

"The Galaxie has given good service, but it is rapidly becoming outdated, I'm afraid. There have been so many yachts built in recent years. These are good times for buyers, and for builders. The new vessel will be state of the art, and the biggest afloat, at least for a while. And it will be built in a Russian shipyard, and designed by Russian designers! Though I admit, the Italians are hard to beat for style."

"Excellent!"

A waiter in a white jacket appeared carrying a gold tray. He set a small decanter and glass next to Viktor, poured the small glass full, and retreated.

"Yes, it will be a ship worthy of Mother Russia. In addition to a larger helicopter and several speedboats, it will carry a submarine!"

"Incredible!"

"One of my areas of interest is archeology, marine archeology. With a submarine I shall be able to explore practically all of the coastal Mediterranean, much more thoroughly than with scuba equipment only."

"I wouldn't have thought it possible."

"Yes. Well, it will take several years. For now...."

He raised his glass. Viktor raised his and they both drank off their vodka. Oleg regarded his empty glass and set it down gently.

"Now, as to the attempt in Milan. I am disappointed, of course, though I am pleased with the performance of our squad. Where are they now?"

"All have been retracted, or nearly all. Two remain to clear out all traces. That should be complete tomorrow."

"Very well." He sighed. "I must tell you, Mishka..."

Viktor's esophagus shrank around his vodka. Here it comes.

"...that to be completely honest, I am just as pleased the woman survived."

Viktor couldn't keep the surprise from his eyes.

"Yes, that's true. I prefer her alive. I would like to meet her in person. I would like to 'reason' with her, you see." He poured another shot from his decanter into his glass. "We will try again, and if we fail, we shall try yet again. It is not unlike the case with my new yacht. Patience is required to achieve the objective, patience and continued effort. Cost is no object. Are you up to that, Mishka?" His brows rose fractionally over his hooded eyes.

"Certainly. Of course."

"Good. I expected no less."

Viktor poured his own shot. He tried to keep his hand steady. They tossed down the liquid. Oleg continued.

"The conference the woman attended had to do with philanthropy. Philanthropy is a noble pursuit. Even I endorse it. Helping the less fortunate eventually helps us as well, does it not? Among the attendees were a number of our countrymen, friends from the embassy, and friends of our friends. Tomorrow night there will be a grand ball at the Hotel De L'Empereur in Monaco. I have reason to know that many who have attended your conference will be there."

He poured himself another shot and nodded at Viktor. Viktor copied. How could he not?

"Tonight we will sail to Monaco. It is not far to the west. You and I shall have a grand evening at the ball. We shall keep our heads about us, and we shall see what we can learn about the woman who flew off in the shuttle that is going to Mars. Won't we?"

He looked coolly at Reznik. Together, they tossed off their vodka.

"*Animopsis Californica*. Reduced to a poltice, good for burns and sores," the printout said. It was annoying to have to look stuff up on the internet in the living room, print it, and then go back to her workshop. If Dad would only let them install a wireless system, she wouldn't have to. "Coarsely ground," it said.

Hierba mansa (*Animopsis*) had been difficult to obtain, but Doña Dolores had come through. She pulled the leaves off the stems and piled them in the molcahete, adding the dried fragments that had fallen to the paper underneath. Picking up the mano, she began gently pulverizing the dried leaves. One benefit of printing everything out was that she could put the page in her notebook for future reference. What was that cool word for that? "Pharmacopoeia." She had learned that from the internet too.

"Yo, Coo-Coo," said a voice from the door. It was one of her brother's nicknames for her, along with "Tister," both from their baby days. In return, she called him "Buster," "J-Man," or worse, depending on how bothersome he was at the moment. Julio had no outside door to his shop, which was closest to the north wall around their compound. He accessed his room through Clio's.

"J-Man," she replied, concentrating on her grinding. "What's up?"

"Not much. Gonna work on my vehicle. I'm close to getting the power I need from the battery."

"Is Mom still asleep?" she asked.

"I think so."

"How come she's sleeping so much? She's been home two days."

"I dunno. Jet lag?"

"Is jet lag that bad?"

"I guess. Don't you remember when we got home from our trip two years ago?"

"Not really."

He passed behind her and opened the door to his shop. He leaned against the jamb.

"You don't? You were grouchy for a week."

"I was not!"

"Even Mom got tired of it. You don't remember?"

"No." She paused her grinding. "Hey, J-Man. Has Mom seemed different to you since she got back?"

"Different? Not really. I dunno. Different how?"

"I mean, besides sleepy. She hasn't been exercising as much. She put those chocolates Dad gave her in the freezer. She looks different, too."

"I haven't noticed. But *you're* different. I noticed that."

"C'mon, I'm serious."

"I'm serious, too. Ever since you started riding horses."

"Well, I found out I like horses."

"You used to hate horses."

"I thought they were big and stupid and dangerous, but they're not. They're smart, once you understand them."

"Harry showed you that?"

"Yeah. What of it?"

"So, you like Harry?"

"Yes. I do. So what?"

"Just be careful, that's all."

"What do you mean?"

"I mean, like, don't let his friends take any more shots at you."

"That was just an accident!"

"You hope, Tister. You hope."

Byron Thormodsgaard, the best dentist in Iowa Falls (the only dentist in Iowa Falls), reflexively clenched and unclenched the $2000 wad of receipts in his pocket as he stared up the avenue hoping to see their returning tour bus. He was totally at the end of his patience for touring, and so was his family. His wife was sitting limply on a divider under the shelter of the magnificent porte cochere of yet another magnificent hotel, clutching a pitiful bag of overpriced souvenir piffle. Their daughter Julie, whom he was on the point of donating to the next rabble of gypsies to skulk past, slumped next to her mother, huffing in boredom after an endless day of looking at things, grumbling bitterly about not even having seen a movie star. Byron Junior was scanning the harbor with his father's fine Nikon mini-binoculars. He would probably drop and break them any minute. Whose idea was it to visit Monaco, anyway? Europe was expensive, but Monaco was the last damn straw! A miserable lunch for four at something resembling a second-rate MacDonald's had cost him over $300!

"Ooooh, wow!" breathed Byron Jr., the binoculars to his face. No one bothered to ask him to elaborate. After a few seconds he continued.

"Sports car! Red! Sexy! Rolling out of that gi-normous yacht! Far out!"

Terrific. Another kajillionaire flaunting his inconceivable wealth. Byron Sr., DDS, had had a bellyful of those types today. He checked the avenue in the other direction. It was getting dark. No tour bus. Dammit! He had a headache, his feet hurt, his back hurt, and worst of all, his wallet hurt.

"It's coming toward us!" exclaimed Junior.

Byron Sr. turned to look. An outrageously sleek, flashy, red sports car was indeed headed their way. As he watched, it turned in to the hotel drive. What kind of megabucks jackass would drive eight blocks to a hotel?

"Hot damn! It's coming here!"

"Junior! Watch your mouth!" his mother snapped.

It pulled to a stop not ten feet away, the engine dropping from a throaty purr to a husky rumbling that vibrated the whole porte cochere. The overwhelming splendor of the close-up vehicle softened Byron Sr.'s disgust.

"See the little horse on the front?" Senior whispered to Junior. "That's a Ferrari. Probably cost a quarter million dollars."

White-coated attendants opened the doors and two men wearing elegant tuxedos emerged. The driver was tall and slim, with slick black hair and shoes polished to a mirror shine like his car. He would have been handsome except for his harsh, hatchet face pitted with imperfections like people used to have from smallpox. He looked around casually, said something inaudible to the attendant, and pressed some bills into his hand. The Thormodsgaard family and several of their fellow tourists stood frozen in place. Had he smiled everyone might have relaxed, but his face was cold and fierce, utterly without emotion. His glance hadn't even registered the human beings standing there, but instead looked through them—they might as well have been peeling paint. The coldness of the man's casual insult right to their faces left the small group of tired tourists stunned.

The man walked around the front of the car and he and his companion headed into the hotel. The attendant got in, put it in gear, and rumbled carefully off to the parking area.

"Whoa! Jeez! That sure wasn't a movie star!" said Julie. "Who was that?"

"Some rich jerk," said her father. He didn't know and he didn't want to know. He wanted that goddam bus to come, and come this very minute.

Oleg and Viktor strode past the doormen holding the doors.

"We have a suite. Get the key," Oleg muttered to Viktor.

The suite was sumptuous. By some miracle, Oleg already had clothes hanging in the closet neatly above a couple suitcases on the floor. Viktor had only his tuxedo, and he wouldn't have had that if Oleg hadn't had a tailor aboard.

Oleg made a number of phone calls, both had a shot of vodka, and they headed to the ballroom. At the entrance, the maitre d' gushed that he had reserved a prime table for his two eminent guests, and Oleg sent him off to claim it, saying he'd be along in a minute. Viktor paused just inside, long enough to observe Oleg, reflected in a mirrored column, with his hand on a waiter's shoulder, sliding something into the pocket of his white jacket. Thanks to a hunch yesterday, he now could guess what Oleg was doing. Oleg had been called to the bridge to take a call from the port captain. Viktor, summoning his courage, arose quickly and poured a small amount from Oleg's decanter into his own glass and tasted it: water. No wonder Oleg was famous for keeping his wits about him. Viktor decided to spend the evening drinking mixed drinks, not vodka, and not too many of those.

He took in the surroundings from his table. Clearly, this was not Moscow, with its ultra-modern, high-tech, deafeningly loud clubs, exclusive as those were. This was an Old World place, elegant, comfortable and confident, seemingly hundreds of years old. The lighting was low and on each table, but enough to have recognized people halfway across the room had he known any of them. At the far end, a band was playing tunes from the 1940s and 1950s, but the sound was not overpowering. A few couples danced.

A waiter approached, eyebrows raised. The words "A highball" sent him off quickly. English seemed to be the language here, though he also heard French. His own French was functional, but barely. Halfway around the room Oleg's lean and hungry silhouette was visible, chatting with people at this table and that, seemingly the picture of bonhomie. It was hard to imagine Oleg in a genuinely jolly frame of mind.

The waiter brought his drink. He sipped slowly, for form's sake. He didn't know anyone in the room, and he needed a strategy. He thought through several as he continued to sip.

As soon as Oleg joined him at the table, a waiter appeared as if drawn by his personal magnetism. Oleg ordered vodka.

"There are at least five people here already who attended the conference," he said in a low voice. "They are at the tables in front of that blue brocade." His eyes continued to scan the room. "Unfortunately, I may not be able to interrogate any of them too closely," he continued. "You shall have to do the biggest part, dear Mishka."

It was not his place to ask his boss the reason. He took another tack.

"Perhaps it would help if I were to be a philanthropist myself, one who regrettably missed the conference but who nonetheless would like to know about it. I could use my own name, and claim to be an executive of one of our subsidiaries."

"Excellent," Oleg replied, his face angled to an approaching female form, a smile beginning to take over his face. He rose.

"Tanie, my dear!"

"Oleg, darling! How lovely that you are here!"

Viktor stood as well, while Oleg and "Tanie" exchanged air kisses, hugs, and a hand kiss. At first he thought the woman a fashionable ingénue, but closer inspection revealed her to be far from young, painfully thin, heavily made up, and wearing a smashing peach gown that had to be some couturier's pride and joy.

"You are more radiant than ever, Tanie, my love."

"And you are as big a liar as ever, my noble Cossack."

"Au contraire! Cossacks always tell the truth, my sweet. It is a matter of honor! Tanie, may I introduce my good friend Viktor Reznik, president of Gaznya, the largest supplier of oilfield technology in eleven time zones. Viktor, it is my privilege to introduce to you her excellency Tainaya Brinkoeter-Ledesért, Marquess of Northern Saxony."

"Marquess, I am honored," Viktor improvised, daring to kiss the proffered hand.

"What a charming man you are, Viktor," the marquess purred. "And so handsome! We absolutely must become acquainted."

Oleg held her chair while she sat, and the two men seated themselves. A waiter appeared. The marquess ordered a single malt scotch.

"Eleven time zones! *Ma fois!*" she exclaimed. "You must travel continually."

"I do," Viktor said. "It was my great good fortune that my first day of leisure in months brings me to you, madame."

"You are *cattivo*, dear Viktor. May I call you Viktor? I already like you. You are a friend of my good friend Oleg so how should I not? Where are you from, sir?"

"Oh, a tiny village of no consequence near Minsk, madame. Yet you! I have not had the good fortune to meet anyone from Saxony before. How very exciting!"

"Bah! Saxony is a relic of history, Viktor. Only my title survives. In that I am more fortunate than your regal friend here, whose title has been lost; yet nonetheless I envy him greatly. His title remains manifest in his youthful bearing! I ask you, have you ever seen a more princely man? Of course you have not. Is leisure your sole purpose this evening, Viktor?"

"Your intuition is most keen, madame. I confess it is not. My company is very profitable, so much so that I believe it the appropriate time to become involved in more humane endeavors. Unfortunately, I could not attend the recent conference in Milan, especially the associated sessions on philanthropy. If there are those here who did attend, I would be eager to establish contacts that might assist me in furthering that goal."

"Splendid, Viktor! How compassion becomes you, does it not, dear Oleg? A toast to you, my saintly man!"

Viktor sipped his highball, Oleg his water (probably), and the marquess drained her scotch, leaving a smear of lipstick on the glass. Oleg traced a circle in the air with a finger at the nearest waiter, who bowed and disappeared. The marquess swallowed and resumed her verbal momentum.

"And to think, I am privileged to start you on your humanitarian quest! So thrilling! I would tell my grandchildren, if I had any. Do you see the man over there?" She twisted her head and waved a skinny finger tipped by a long, peach-painted nail, in the general direction of the blue brocade Oleg had mentioned. "...the distinguished-looking man with the silver hair? Do you see him, Viktor?

That is a most unusual man, sir. He comes from nowhere you have ever been, nor anywhere you could ever go. What do I mean, pray tell?"

"Madame, now it is you who are being *cattiva*."

She guffawed a rusty shriek.

"A hit! A palpable hit, sir! How entertaining you are! But I say no more than the truth. That man was born not on Earth but on another planet! Do you follow? That is the extremely honorable Herecyn Cymred, one of those Thomans who came to Earth some years ago. He is the former brother in law of Ana Darcy, who created a sensation at the very conference you mentioned. He is certain to be a devoted philanthropist himself. I have no doubt of it."

The waiter returned and set new drinks in place. The marquess seized hers immediately and raised it to Viktor.

"You have only to ask him, my dear. Sir! To your success!"

Viktor endured fifteen more minutes of jousting before excusing himself to search out the philanthropists present. He minded his steps, not certain whether his fuzzy-headedness was a result of two and a half highballs or the marquess's cleverly disjointed but probing dialog. Both, perhaps. He was able to realize, however, that Oleg could not help because he had a history with Herecyn Cymred. Cymred had sold him some sort of Thoman technology which Oleg had turned into a highly effective weapon, only to have both models destroyed, apparently by Ana Darcy, Cymred's former sister in law, or at least so Oleg believed. That aside, Viktor was content to do the investigating without his boss along.

From his chair, Oleg observed the marquess watch Viktor move away, her lips pursed and a gleam in her eye. Viktor was a useful subordinate. If he was not up to the games of the aristocracy that was unimportant. There was no need to waste time making fun of him, which is what he expected this withered old she-wolf was about to do. He would change the subject first.

"So, Tanie, love, do you know Mr. Cymred well?"

"Only socially, dear Oleg. That is enough to know one need not know him better."

She extracted a cigarette from a gold case. As Oleg retrieved his lighter, a passing waiter did the deed. She inhaled deeply.

"What sort of fellow is he, if I may ask?"

"Of course you may ask. I am delighted you have asked. I specialize in answering such questions." She paused and blew a plume of smoke to one side.

"Mr. Cymred is a marvelously courtly, highly agreeable, and delightful fraud, I must say." She took a sip of scotch and another drag on the cigarette. "When I say fraud, I do not mean that he is not who he says he is. I suppose he is from that planet; who am I to say he is not? He is a fraud in the sense that he does not belong among us here, on our level, as it were. We have money, but we do not think about it, we do not burden ourselves with it. It is simply there, a precondition, as it were. For him, while he does have some amount of money, it is not enough. He has no stately yacht, like *some* of the more adventurous among us, my dear." She patted Oleg's hand. "He has no assortment of mansions or castles scattered about the civilized world. His purpose here seems to be to search out a suitably wealthy wife, you see, using his unique status as a lure. Thus, he is a mercenary, a grasping mercenary and poseur, and no patina of exquisite manners will suffice to conceal that fact. It is so…tacky—is that the word the Americans use?—in poor taste. Do I explain myself, heart of hearts?"

"Eloquently, *comme d'habitude*, my sweet." He twiddled his lighter between his fingers. "What about his compatriot, Ana Darcy? What do you know of her?"

"It pains me deeply to admit I know next to nothing, little more than anyone else knows. She's a reclusive former athlete, apparently a simple soul, though not without courage. She must have money, though it would seem she gives most of it away, poor fool. It's scarcely to her credit that men seem to like her. Women too, even though her fashion sense is dreadful. Did you see a picture of her in that gown at the conference? An empire waist? Please, dear prince! So eighteenth century! One suspects she acquired it at a consignment store! But I'm sure she's harmless. Why do you ask, old friend?"

Oleg almost slammed the table. She was *not* harmless! Her ability to inflict harm had been on his mind every day for years. That "harmless" woman had destroyed his two proton weapons and the technical data to build more. She was the reason his left elbow and right shoulder were killing him this very moment! Swallowing his anger, he responded with an icy smile.

"I should think Mr. Cymred would have an opinion, would he not?"

"Ha!" she chuckled. "Most insightful of you, sir! Why, only last week, I was having afternoon tea with the Duchess of Middle Batavia at her chalet near Berne. She said Mr. Cymred had been seeing her daughter Eloise. Eloise was flattered by his attentions at first but ultimately found him entirely too self-absorbed. He has little sense of humor, though in social settings he does try to be entertaining. Occasionally he succeeds. The only time Eloise saw him lose his composure was when she asked him about Ms. Darcy. He became quite indignant, claiming that far too much was made of her, that she was an ungenerous, disloyal, ungrateful, spiteful person. He forbade any further mention of her name! Thus, you are quite correct, my perceptive Oleg. He does have an opinion!"

Before he could reply, another elderly couple wandered by their table in search of diversion, two more irrelevant aristocrats of no conceivable use. Oleg's thoughts wandered darkly.

At the other end of the room, the band, assisted by a stout, middle-aged singer, began playing "Stormy Weather."

"You want a taquito with a scrambled egg, son? With a little sausage in it?"

"Sure, Dad. Thanks," Julio replied, over a spoonful of cereal with a strawberry slice balanced on it.

"Clio?"

"That's OK, Dad. I'm good."

"Coming right up, son."

Matt didn't remember his own eating habits when he was Julio's age, but growing boys were famous for eating everything in sight. Maybe Julio was starting a growth spurt. He cracked another egg into the bowl and whipped them into a froth. The sausage chunks in the pan were about ready. The aroma was mouth-watering. Through the window over the sink the tops of the trees toward the river were turning golden in the new morning's sunlight. The egg slurry sizzled as he poured it over the sausage.

"You want salsa with that, mijo?"

"If it's mild."

"Got some."

He fished the jar of Julio-strength salsa out of the refrigerator while the eggs fried.

"You gotta be there at 9:30, right?" he said, checking the kitchen clock as he set the jar on the table.

"Yessir."

"To see Dr....Dr. Chatterjay, or something like that?"

"Chatterjee."

"Right. About batteries?"

"Uh-huh."

"So, what's a professor at UT El Paso doing with batteries?"

He flipped over the mess of eggs and sausage.

"Dr. Jameson said what I was doing with super ion discharge batteries was similar to what Dr. Chatterjee was doing in his lab. He thought we might like to share ideas."

"Ah; good deal. Here you go."

He laid tortillas on two plates, divided the scrambled eggs between them, and set the plates on the table.

"Yum. Thanks, Dad," said Julio, reaching for the salsa.

"Dad?"

"Yes, mija."

"What time are you coming back?"

"By noon, sugar."

"Well, then, could...."

"Buenos días, familia," said their mother, padding from the bedroom in robe and flipflops.

The three at the table responded with a chorus of greetings, Matt adding, "¿Amanaciste bien?" ("How are you this morning?")

"Bastante bien, gracias," she replied. ("Fairly well, thanks.")

She had washed her face and brushed her hair, but signs of recent awakening were visible in her face.

"What can I get you, love?"

She took a seat and reached for the orange juice.

"Oh, I don't know." She looked over the cereal boxes, fruit, taquitos, and salsa. "Maybe some of those refritos from yesterday...no...oh, let me think about it a minute."

"Uh, Dad?"

"Yes, Clio. You were saying?"

"Could you drop me off at Stallman's and pick me up on the way back, please?"

"Are you going to see Harry?" asked her mother.

"He'll be there. Yes, I'll see him. But...."

"You're spending a lot of time with him lately, aren't you?"

"Mom!"

"Well, it just seems like every chance you get...."

"Mom! I'm taking some horse medicine to Mr. Stallman!"

"Dad could drop that off for you."

"I need to explain how to use it!"

"Well, fine. There'll be no one at home all morning. Except me."

"*Mom!*" Clio shouted, "That's it! I know what it is! You're pregnant! Aren't you!"

There was complete silence at the table. Ana began stammering.

"I...uh...we...." She looked at Matt and sighed. "Uh...yes. Yes."

"Oh, wow!" Clio hopped out of her chair and ran to embrace her mother. Julio looked at his father, nonplussed. Matt winked at Clio.

"Very good, daughter. How could you tell?"

"I don't know. It just hit me all of a sudden."

Ana was hugging her daughter tightly, her eyes misty.

"Eres muy lista, mija." Matt said. "Hey, I have an idea. Why don't we all go for a drive and do our errands? We can talk while we roll."

They had such a good time in the car, his mother sitting close to his dad with her head on his shoulder and hugging his arm, that Julio was surprised to realize that his dad must have meant for the trip to be like this. Julio was adept at science and technology, but the idea that people could be managed as well as numbers and materials had never occurred to him—and his father seemed to know how to do it. Interesting! Maybe he should pay more attention to his dad.

Viktor found Oleg having an open-air breakfast on the hotel's fourth floor balcony, with the harbor spread below in the morning sunlight. The sea was light blue and the sky clear. There was no trace of the showers of yesterday. The Galaxie was not quite the biggest of the eight or ten largest yachts moored at the T-heads, but it was easily the most noticeable, with its streamlined shape and deep blue color.

"Mishka! Join me," he said, almost companionably.

He was the picture of sophisticated ease, a trim vest over a pale gray shirt and maroon silk rep tie, a bottle of champagne in a sweating silver bucket with arm's reach. Of necessity, Victor was wearing his white formal shirt from the previous evening, and the same pants and suspenders. He hoped those who noticed him would think he was ending an all-night bout of revelry with a quiet morning meal.

"Thank you," he said, taking a seat.

"Breakfast?" Oleg waved at the baskets of pastries and fruits on the table. "...or would you rather order?"

"This will be fine, thanks. I'm late. I apologize. I was running down some details."

"Ah. And what did you learn last night?"

Viktor speared some fruit onto a plate and pulled it in front of him.

"I think we have two leads, perhaps. Sparing you the details, while at the conference, the woman was overheard being asked to attend two events. One is the next annual conference on Thoman civilization, at the City University of New York. That's in October. The other was to take part in a visit to a combined philanthropic program in Peru, on behalf of Surgeons of the World, a little over a week from now. She declined both offers, my sources say."

"Is that so?" he said, buttering a roll. "And what do you make of that?"

"I checked this morning. This is the seventh such Thoman conference. She and her uncle attended the first. Her uncle has been present for three others, the last two years ago. The woman has not been back since the first." He reached for a croissant, paused, and added that and a brioche to his plate. "In recent years, she has visited several sites at which her foundation has been a participant, though none in South America. This event is a demonstration project that was discussed a great deal at the Milan conference. Her foundation is once again involved."

"She turned down both, eh? What are your conclusions?"

"It is possible she declined for form's sake, because she was in public. Both would be high visibility appearances, but I think we should not assume her refusals were sincere. It will be easy to put an agent in position to watch the preparations for the Thoman conference. I believe, however, that her philanthropic endeavors are closer to her heart. I would consider it a better chance that she will take part in the Peruvian tour. In view of the nearness of the date, I would recommend that we begin immediately acquiring more details about this tour and planning our own possible 'visit.' Our team is still assembled and their training level is high."

Oleg sipped from his champagne flute, set it down gently, and looked at Viktor.

"Excellent. My thoughts exactly. The company has exploration crews in Peru at this moment, under our chief of development, Kornei Vukovsky. He knows the territory and he has transportation. I will tell him to give you full cooperation. Begin as soon as possible."

Viktor wrapped the brioche and croissant in a napkin.

"I shall start now," he said, rising from his chair.

"And Viktor," Oleg added, "remember, I prefer her alive."

"I remember," he replied.

The prey was close. Focusing intently, she crouched low and froze. Lift one paw, move it forward slowly. Set it down quietly. Creep forward, precisely balanced. Quiver. Move the other paw forward. Slink forward again. The prey turned away! Now! Attack! She leaped!

"Raisin! You're mashing the mint! Come here, you bad cat!"

Clio rubbed the cat's shoulder and continued harvesting her epizote leaves, stacking them carefully in the basket next to the aloe she'd already gathered. Two more bunches were enough. She stood up and stepped out of the chicken wire enclosure along the north wall. She made a tsk tsk sound with her tongue and the cat hopped over two rows of herbs and joined her. She fastened the gate.

"Silly kitty! The catnip won't be ready for weeks! I promise I'll give you some, but we need most of it to keep off the mosquitoes. C'mon, now."

She headed back to the barn. The cat sat in place a moment, the tufts on her ears bending gently in the wind, and then ambled after Clio, checking the surrounding territory as she did so.

The sound of a hammer clanking against metal attracted Clio to the barn's main room. Julio was chipping slag from a weld under the eyes of his father.

"OK, that's good. Now clamp it to the first piece and tack them together."

While Julio fished around for a C-clamp and fiddled with the vise, Clio sat on a stool to watch.

"Whatcha making, J-Man?" she asked.

"An axle bracket, maybe," he replied.

"He can run a nice bead, now," Matt said. "I think that bracket will work. Make another just like it and your driving wheels will support some real torque. Whatcha got there, mija?"

"Oh, just some herbs from the garden."

"Gonna make some more horse medicine?"

"Uh-huh, and some mosquito repellent."

"Good deal!"

"Dad?"

"Yes, sugar?"

"Why can't we get a wireless router, so I can get the internet in my shop?"

"I thought about that, mija. It would be really convenient. But Uncle Hleo says it would be a bad idea."

"Why?"

"Because it works by broadcasting a signal into the air. It doesn't travel very far, but Hleo said it would be fairly easy for someone outside the wall or in a car on the highway to pick it up and eavesdrop on us. I know we're careful about what we say online, but you can never tell what someone might figure out. There are things that we don't want people to know about us, right?"

"Well, yes."

"I'm sorry, sugar. I know it's inconvenient, but it works pretty well like it is right now. We'll just have to make the best of it."

"Dad?"

"Yes, son?"

"I'm ready."

"Can I watch?" asked Clio.

"Uh, sure. Grab that helmet over there and watch through the lens. Don't wanna burn your eyes."

There were two blinding flashes of brilliant white light, and then Julio started hammering the slag off his welds as a fan dispersed the smoke.

"Looks good, son. Nice tacks."

"Matt?"

Ana was at the door of the barn.

"Hey, wife!"

"Why did Raisin run out of the barn just now?"

"Oh!" exclaimed Clio. "I forgot about getting her away from the welder!"

She picked up her basket and rushed out the door.

"Do you two need a drink?"

"I could use some tea. What about you, son?"

"No, thanks. Can I finish this?"

"Sure. You see where to run the beads now, right over the tacks? You'll do fine. Let's go, babe."

Five minutes later they were sipping tea on the cement slab under the cottonwoods. The tips of Ana's hair tumbled in the breeze. The door to Clio's workshop was open. Raisin looked out, sauntered over, chirped softly, and hopped up next to Ana. Matt had finally gotten used to the big cat's vocabulary. This trilled sound was friendly.

"That cat sure loves you."

"She's so sweet and smart," Ana replied, gently scratching the feline's chin and throat. Raisin purred like a Lexus. Matt rocked the glider gently. More hammering clanged from the barn.

"Our son is a better welder than I am."

"He really enjoys creating things."

"He does. So does Clio, in her way. I mean, she's good at folk medicine."

"How did she know I was expecting? Did you tell her?"

"No. But you know how sensitive she is to medical stuff. There's an old saying that pregnant women have a special glow about them. I bet she noticed a lot of subliminal things and put them together. Remember how she detected that problem with the woman seeing Dolores Saenz? And somehow she knew that Abuelita's blood pressure had gone up—the doctor increased the dosage, remember that?"

"I guess so. I wonder how she does that."

"No idea."

Matt moved a lock of her hair behind her ear. Raisin had her chin high in the air, eyes closed, while Ana rubbed her throat.

"So, what have you been up to this morning?"

"Oh, making arrangements with Hleo and World Security for next week."

Matt shook his head.

"You're sure you wanna do this?"

"I'm sure."

"How long will you be gone?"

"Well, a day to travel there, a day there, and a day back, more or less. About four days."

"You gonna be all right?"

"I think so. The morning sickness isn't as bad now. I don't think air travel will bother me this time."

"I know it's for a good cause, but I still don't like it. It seems to me like expectant mothers should stay closer to home."

"Thoman women are tough, Matt."
He traced her elf-like ear with a finger.
"That's what we're counting on, babe."

Chapter 10

"Yes?"

"Your 3:00 o'clock is here—Mr. Coombs."

"Thanks, Linda. Send him down."

Linda's voice dropped to a whisper.

"He's back!"

"Easy, girl friend!"

Michelle stood and slipped off her crocheted vest. The foundation didn't go in for casual Fridays, but her favorite long, slinky, white-with-blue-polka-dots chintz spring dress came dangerously close. The collar and sleeves saved it. If it had had spaghetti straps it would have been too sexy for the legal community. At least a discerning person could tell she was a swimmer, or so she hoped. Tossing the vest behind the door, she walked to meet the sound of footsteps.

"Hi, Rob."

"My favorite lawyer! Hiya, Michelle!"

A quick hug and kiss and then they were seated. He was all business. Why was that dimple in his chin so beguiling?

"So, are you up on this tour?" he asked.

"Not really. It happened too fast. What can you tell me?"

"She gave me the basic skinny by email. I'll know more after I'm down there and check things out. She's going with an outfit called Surgeons To the World, or 'For the World,' I can't remember."

Michelle pulled a tablet over and made a note. Coombs continued.

"They fly down Monday. She knows the fellow in charge, a Dr. Schwartz. His group is working in concert with three or four other entities—an economic development group, a Peace Corps-type bunch of teachers and developers, and an outfit that coordinates local workers in building basic medical clinics. She wants to draw publicity to this shotgun-style assistance program. It's the new thing, apparently.

"Dr. Schwartz is going to visit four villages in six days. She'll only go along on one, probably the first, and then split right away, thankfully. Her presence will be a secret until she actually gets there. The media will be with them, and they'll probably go crazy once she pops up. But she'll be gone before word gets very far.

"I'm going to arrange things so it'll be a clean in-and-out. It's impossible to control all the details in a situation like this, but the element of surprise should work for us."

He sat back and looked at her.

"Whaddya think?"

Michelle looked at her notes.

"I'm not wild about it, but then I never am. The outline sounds good. I'll get the names of the other organizations. More than likely, the Second Planet Foundation is working with several. I'll get one of our media people down there. We'll play it for all it's worth. What can we do to help?"

"I can't think of anything right now. Just stand by; be handy. What else do you need from me?"

"The details, as soon as you get them."

"All right, then!" he said, "End of business meeting."

He loosened his tie and leaned back.

He looked much better with a loosened tie. She set down the pen.

"When are you leaving?"

He looked at his watch.

"Gotta be at the gate in two hours."

"So soon?"

"Yeah, bummer. I wanted to ask you out for a night on the town, but time's awasting."

"Rain check?"

He smiled.

"I have a better idea. You got any plans for next weekend?"

"Huge plans. Gonna clean out my refrigerator."

"Well, if you're willing to delay that and also skip work Friday, why don't we fly to the Bahamas and hang out a few days? It's summer there, too, but no hotter than it is here. How about it? You can call the shots. I'll even promise to be a gentleman, if you really insist."

"I don't know. I need to think about that, Rob. OK, I've thought about it. Let's go."

"Great! And the gentleman part?"

"Let me get back to you on that."

He'd covered a good part of the world in his career, but never South America. After arriving in Lima in the wee hours Coombs crashed at an unexpectedly nice hotel right at the airport, the Hotel Ramada Costa del Sol, awakening to the insistent beeping of the alarm he'd set only six hours earlier. After a decent breakfast he went in search of the air charter service he'd found online days earlier, Aviones del Sol, apparently the only such business at the airport. "Sol" (sun) seemed a staple of Peruvian names. "Sol" was even the name of their currency.

The town where the tour would start had one scheduled commercial flight per day, but only Monday through Friday. The eight hour drive was out of the question.

The charter agent insisted on the full amount up front for an all day charter, checked his passport, passed it back, and pointed him to a Cessna four-seater, wing-over plane that looked to have seen better days. After a scenic hour of bumping through the air over incredible mountains (the "cordillera," according to the pilot) he was on the ground in Huánuco, a fairly large town on the east side of those formidable peaks. The pilot helped him scare up a taxi driver, a compact Quechuan man. Coombs requested a tour in his best elementary Spanish, but the man seemed to prefer his own elementary English, replying, "You bet! Is no problem." Well, fine, then. Maybe their conversation could meet in the middle. The man introduced himself as "Weelie," which Coombs elected to consider a variety of "Willy."

An hour later he had acquired a basic knowledge of Huánuco. It was a surprisingly civilized little town. He'd seen nicely maintained schools, including one for some kind of higher education (a "tecnológico," his guide said), churches, a plaza, many small businesses and several office buildings, including one bearing the mother-and-child logo of one of the organizations Ana Darcy was going to visit, and a plaza where a group of children in Inca costumes were serenading an assortment of citizens. The surrounding countryside was arid, with scrubby trees and smallish clumps of undergrowth. The weather was perfect, cool and dry. A vigorously flowing river divided the town, a tributary of the Amazon, he learned.

Willy told him the jungle was "up in the mountains," and that he would be happy to show him remains of early Inca civilization, the earliest known in the hemisphere. Coombs asked a different question.

"Do you know where Qotosh is?"

"Ah, yes, no es muy far," the driver nodded. "Es where mis grandparents live."

"I'd like to see it. Can you take me there?"

"Ai, sí...pero..." he shook his head, "...will cost you more...."

"No problem. ¡Vamos!"

While the elderly Toyota labored up a winding, one-and-a-half-lane-wide road, Willy continued his running travelogue. The valleys produced coffee, bananas, cacao, and an assortment of other fruits and grains, like quinoa, which Coombs had never heard of. The pueblo of Qotosh, an Inca name, subsisted mainly on cattle, vicuñas, and exotic spices, apparently—the driver didn't know the English names and Coombs didn't know the Spanish.

After thirty minutes, the road became so curvy with switchbacks Willy had to slow down. Finally, he braked to a stop with the jungle looming over the road on both sides.

"Jesus!" said Coombs.

They had halted at the brink of a steep river gorge, the impenetrable vegetation dropping out of sight in front of them and resuming on the other side, perhaps 200 yards away. The driver pointed through the windshield.

"Allà. Qotosh."

An assortment of what looked like stone or mud buildings were scattered over the opposite ridge. Connecting that ridge to the place where they were was, of all things, a rope suspension bridge, "paved" with boards.

"Son of a bitch!" Coombs exclaimed. "You can't drive over that, can you?"

"Sí, you bet," said the driver, releasing the brake and easing forward.

Coombs considered himself a courageous man, but his heart was in his throat as the vehicle bumped slowly over the groaning planks. The bridge didn't appear to be swaying, but he swore he felt it moving back and forth. Christ! Fifty or sixty feet below them was yet another rapidly flowing river, not more than 100 feet wide, but dark and green. The damn bridge creaked! Well, he told himself, others have done this. The driver sees no problem. Steady as she goes.

They made it.

The pueblo of Qotosh looked like a good place for philanthropy. Not more than 200 people seemed to live there, and a fair proportion of those were small, dirty children wearing mismatched layers of ragged garments, staring at the rare vehicle among them.

"Is there a medical clinic here?" he asked.

"Sí."

"Let's take a look."

Willy eased the car up the only street, over the ridge, and turned left, calling out and waving to women carrying pots on their heads, old men seated on steps, and children. Some waved back. He pulled up before one of the larger buildings, a one story house-sized thing with the mother-and-child logo on the front wall.

"I'm going inside," he said, opening the door.

"Bueno," replied Willy. "I go see mi abuelita. You honk the horn when you ready to go."

Coombs got out and approached the building. A woman carrying an infant emerged, saw him, averted her face, and hurried down the hill. Inside was a tiny room with a woman sitting in a chair, a toddler in front of her. The child turned to its mother and buried its head in her dress. The woman looked startled.

"Perdón," said Coombs, backing to the doorway.

He knocked on the frame and called out.

"Hellooo?"

A minute later a young woman wearing a white coat stepped from an inner doorway and studied him briefly. "One minute, please," she said, disappearing back inside.

Coombs waited in front of the building. In a few minutes, an ancient man emerged with a bandage over one eye, carrying a tube of something in a gnarled hand. A few seconds later the young woman appeared.

"Yes?" she said, regarding him warily, moving one of several locks of brown hair away from her face.

He introduced himself and explained he was an advance man for Surgeons of the World, and wanted to inquire if anything was needed for the visitors expected Monday. The woman relaxed slightly and introduced herself as Dr. Sandrine Closset, with Doctors International. She was looking forward to the visit, she said. She was trim and neat, in her thirties, with tiny crow's feet at the corners of her eyes and a contained, businesslike brusqueness about her.

"OK, good," Coombs said. "I'll tell Dr. Schwartz that everything is fine here, then."

Her face softened a bit.

"Doctor Closset, you seemed surprised, a minute ago. Is everything really all right? I'll help if I possibly can."

"No, all eez well." She had a lovely French accent. "It's just that others have visited lately."

"Oh? Who else?"

"Two men were here, uh, jeudi? Thursday. They said they needed medicine for a cut, but I didn't see anyone with a wound."

"What kind of men?"

"Germans, maybe. No...Slavs, probablement. Maybe Poles. They spoke English with an accent, but I do not understand well the English accent."

"I see. Where did they go?"

"They walked on toward Tlingel, to the right from the bridge. Later, I heard a helicopter. It was probably nothing."

"Probably. Well, thank you, doctor. I will see you again on Monday, then. Thank you for your time."

"You are welcome, Mr. Coombs."

"Oh, do you have a phone, Doctor? May I have your number in case the schedule changes?"

She recited a number, he jotted it in a little notebook, and thanked her again.

She retreated inside, waving the waiting woman and child to the back room.

Coombs honked the horn of the Toyota, leaned back against it, and checked out the village. A badly paved road did indeed lead from the bridge around a ridge to the right. On this side, the road the Toyota was parked on played out at the edge of the village, diminishing to a trail that wandered along the steep gorge over the river. A man was driving three odd animals, probably vicuñas, toward the village. He carried a thin stick, but the animals were walking placidly without its encouragement.

Willy appeared and they headed back to Huánuco. Coombs barely noticed the suspension bridge, his thoughts absorbed in pondering Dr. Closset's visitors. Once across the bridge, and having negotiated a rickety bus coming the other way, he asked him about the gringos.

"I not sure," he said. "Two men land un helicóptero at the aeropuerto jueves, digo, Toorsday, and take off again. They head north. I no see them again. Petroleros, I think. You know, the ones who look for petróleo."

"Ah," said Coombs. Land men, most likely, an exploration crew. Still, it was unsettling. That narrow road bothered him most of all. If Ana needed to get out of there fast, it could be a problem. He'd planned to fly her out of Huánuco in an airplane, in his current charter if possible, but if she got stuck in Qotosh there was no way it could reach her. Maybe he could convince her to appear at one of the other places Dr. Schwartz was going to visit. They couldn't all be this isolated. He'd check those out and also inquire as to the charter of a helicopter.

The news was no better in Lima at Aviones del Sol. The agent, who was in the process of closing the office, told him they had three helicopters. All were out on charter—to a Russian oil company. Coombs left a large deposit to secure the services of his Cessna for four more days.

He did what he could on Sunday. Using contact numbers from his boss at World Security, Darlene Pizzoli, he retrieved a diplomatic package from the embassy (a nine millimeter pistol and three clips of ammunition), got a list of Ana's tour sites from the officer in charge of the U. S. Agency for International Development, and contacted the Foreign Commercial Service officer at home. That gentleman told him that indeed, a Russian petroleum company was in country exploring, but in the southern part, the officer thought. When Coombs asked if someone in the Peruvian government might know more, the man told him not to bother. The minister in question was way too buddy-buddy with well-to-do international businessmen, and would never give him a straight answer.

He ended the day by studying a map of Peru. Only the last site on the schedule would be near an airport. It was unlikely Ana would want to sit around for days and wait for that. He wouldn't be happy to have her wait that long himself. Crap. He'd never yet been on an operation where all the details fell neatly into place. All he could do was be loose and alert. The ever-present uncertainty was not his favorite part of the job.

Ana was pleased to find how well she remembered Durham from her one visit twelve years earlier. It was still a bustling, energetic place, but she had learned a lot in the intervening years. Thriving, urban areas were less novel now. She loved the elegant neighborhood the taxi took her to, and she even recalled the percentage Matt had recommended to tip the driver after their long ride. Before, money had been just numbers. Now she knew the total fare could have fed a poor family for a week.

The home of Dr. Charles Hodge was the same stately, two-story brick house of her memory, set comfortably on an extravagantly gardened yard behind a wrought iron fence. Flowers were everywhere in showy profusion. As before, he opened the door just as she closed the gate and headed up the short walk. A tall man with thinning silver hair, he was crisply dressed in a lightweight brown checked blazer, teal shirt and red and blue striped tie. His tassled loafers shone.

"Ms. Darcy!" he said softly, hugging her gently. He smelled terrific. "So delightful to see you again at long last!" He held both her hands and gleamed at her affectionately.

"The honor is mine, sir," she replied. "I will never forget your spontaneous hospitality in my time of need. I was unworthy of it."

"Not in the least, my dear! Those memories have warmed me ever since. I am in your debt for them, I assure you. You are well, I hope?"

"Yes, sir, I am, despite my appearance."

Before he could reply a voice sounded behind him.

"Ms. Darcy?"

"Dr. Schwartz! I pray you are well, sir!"

"I am, I am, thank you, ma'am. What an honor to have the star of the Milan conference in our humble home. You outshone the prime ministers, Ms. Darcy."

"'Ana,' please, sir, and thank you. I would outshine no one today. I was just apologizing to Charles for my appearance."

"No need, Ana, no need. Charles has told me of your clever disguises. Anyone who saw you outside just now would think you were a mere student, come to consult on your thesis, perhaps. Appearance could not be farther from reality! Please! Let me take your bag."

Hodge intercepted the backpack and disappeared with it into the interior of the house, leaving Schwartz to usher her into the living room, still beautifully and sparingly furnished, still dominated by a splendid blue and gold harpsichord in one corner.

"Ah. Josephine!"

"You remember!"

"She's so beautiful!"

"I wonder if I could impose on you, Ana, to sign her one more time, but in our script? None of our friends can read Luvit. Some, I fear, believe the photograph a hoax."

"I'd be happy to, but you must play me something in return!"

"Delighted! After supper, perhaps?"

Hodge appeared at the entryway and offered her tea, which she accepted. Feeling much more confident of her handwriting than she had before, she signed the instrument a second time, next to the first, with the sharpie he provided. Dr. Schwartz waved her to a pristine wing chair.

"Are you ready for tomorrow?" he asked.

"Yes, I think so. As we arranged, I shall travel in disguise, as your assistant, if that suits you."

"Of course. There will be many medical people along. So as not to require you to share their professional chatter, perhaps you should travel as my amanuensis, at least until we arrive on site."

"'A man'...what?"

"Pardon me. A better term would be 'secretary,' that is, one who takes notes and keeps records."

"My goodness! What was that word?"

"A-man-you-in-sis. I beg your pardon, my dear."

"Oh, no. I love learning new words. But there are so very many!"

Hodge entered with tray and teapot and the three passed a pleasant, chatty, musical afternoon and evening. They were the most delightful hosts she had ever met, she thought, preparing for bed that night. She had sent a text message to Matt and the twins and slid into bed, luxuriating once again in the unaccustomed feeling of silk sheets. Would Matt enjoy silk sheets? They were surely expensive, but it might be something to try. Mmm...so nice. And then she was asleep.

"Where's Mom right now, Dad?"
"Umm...in the air somewhere, on her way to South America, I reckon."
"Oh," said Julio, helping himself to a second slice of cherry pie.
They had just completed Sunday dinner with Abuelita, who had headed back to her house for a nap. Matt finished loading the dishwasher.
"You want more pie, mija?"
"No thanks, Dad."
He pressed a sheet of plastic wrap over the pie and set it in the refrigerator.
"I miss Mom," Clio said.
Matt poured a jot of tea over the remaining ice in his glass, set the pitcher in the refrigerator, and eased into his chair at the table.
"I do too, sugar."
"Why'd you let her go, Dad?"
"Huh?"
"Why didn't you tell her to stay here?"
"Well, I'm not her boss. I don't control her. She makes her own decisions."
"But she's pregnant!"
"Yes, but it's early yet. It's the first trimester. Do you know what that is?"
"Uh-huh."
"Airlines generally let pregnant women fly up until the middle of the third trimester."
"Yeah, but...."
She set her elbow on the table and rested her cheek on her fist.
"Would you let me go to South America? By myself?"
"Not this year, no. I don't think so."
Julio spoke up.
"You said you'd think about letting me go to India, for High School University."
"Right. I did. I will check into it."
"I'd be going alone."
"Well, yes and no. The airline will keep an eye on you in the air, and you'll be with a group once you arrive. Someone will be in charge. It's for high school

students, anyway. If you were a high school student, you could probably go on your own."

"That's not fair, Dad," Clio whined.

"It's pretty fair. Guys! We're your parents. We're responsible for you until you're eighteen. Remember James, Uncle John's six year old? Suppose he wanted to eat Vienna sausages and nothing else, just Vienna sausages morning, noon, and night. Should his parents let him do that?"

"Nooo," said Clio, letting her voice drop as if she knew where this was going.

"Of course not. It wouldn't be good for him, and his parents shouldn't let him. That's what they're supposed to do. But when James gets to be, like, eighteen or older, he can eat Vienna sausages until he gets a vitamin deficiency and his teeth fall out."

Clio made a grimace of disgust. Julio stuck a forkful of pie in his mouth.

"Look, you guys already make most of your own decisions. Nearly everything you do is something you decided, and Mom and I help you do it. But you can't drive a car down the highway, and you can't solo in an airplane, son, and you can't get married, because you're still minors. That's the law and we're your guardians and that's just the way it is. You won't be minors much longer. It's not really that bad, is it?"

"Oh, Dad."

A repeated clinking sound came from the kitchen. Raisin was licking a dinner plate which had slid up against a cabinet. Foosh sat off a distance and watched respectfully.

"Son, when you finish that pie, please put your plate and Raisin's plate in the dishwasher, OK?"

"Sure, Dad."

Chapter 11

"Yes, sir. You are...?"

"Gizmo Crowse."

"Uh, hmm...I don't see it here."

"It might be listed as Lawrence Crowse, C-R-O-U-S-E, not K-R-A-U-S."

"Ah, there it is. Good. Welcome, Mr. Crowse. I'm Dr. Schwartz."

"Doc. Glad to see you."

"Who are you with?"

"Miami Media."

"Very good. Let me see...."

Crowse watched the doctor scan the three vans parked off the tarmac. The guy must be six and a half feet tall, he thought. He was wearing khaki pants, a blue button-down shirt, and hiking boots. With that curly black hair and aristocratic schnoz, he might have been a safari guide to the stars. The doc looked from the vehicles to the large duffel bag at Crowse's feet.

"You've got a lot of stuff there."

"Yeah. Hence the name Gizmo. Video gear, mostly."

"OK. Let's put you in the lead van. Back seat, if you don't mind. Your bag can go next to you."

"Sure. Fine. Thanks."

He hoisted the heavy bag and headed for the first van. The second and third vehicles were half full of doctors and nurses, except for one print guy he knew from Atlanta. The back ends of their vans were piled above the windows with boxes and luggage. Three people stood outside the lead vehicle. The one leaning back against the front door had to be the driver—a stocky, dark, round-faced man in a narrow-brimmed straw hat, smoking casually. He nodded at the fellow and continued to the other side. A man and a woman were chatting by the side door.

"Hiya," he said. "Gizmo Crowse, Miami Media."

"Mr. Crowse," responded the man, shaking his hand. "Rob Coombs, security detail."

"How do you do, sir," the woman said. She had a firm handshake. "I'm Anne Davis, Dr. Schwartz' secretary."

"Ma'am," he answered. "Nice to meet ya. The doc assigned me the back seat. I'll stow my gear if you don't mind."

"Have at it," Coombs said. "Looks like we're about ready to go."

The gear bag took up as much room as a person. Crowse considered strapping the seat belt over it but instead leaned it over and wedged it against the far side, leaving the zippers facing him in case he needed his video camera in a hurry. Coombs and Davis took the bucket seats in the middle row. The driver got in, started the engine, and Dr. Schwartz, after a few words with the second driver, got in the front passenger seat, and they were off.

Crowse studied his travel partners from behind. Coombs was an average sized fellow, maybe 40, but in athletic shape, with solid shoulders and narrow hips. He moved efficiently. Crowse liked that. Coombs wore a cargo vest with things in the pockets. He liked that too. A man needed his gadgets. The woman was graceful, wasting no motion swinging over to her bucket seat. She was small, with shoulder-length straight brown hair and slender legs. She seemed small topside too, but the matter wasn't certain. She had on a green windbreaker with a mother and child graphic over the left breast. Couldn't tell about her eyes, either—sunglasses. Hard to determine her age—maybe 30, 35? She was cute, for sure. She and Coombs were consulting over something on a clipboard, probably a schedule. She had nice hands. No wedding ring! If they happened to end the evening in a bar, which he dearly hoped they would, maybe he could get a little liquor in her and become better acquainted. He leaned forward.

"Is that a schedule?"

"Yeah," said Coombs.

"How 'bout some highlights? Help me plan the shoot."

"Sure."

Coombs explained they were headed to a village named Qotosh, memorable mainly for the interesting bridge they'd be seeing soon. The second and third vans would drive on from there to drop the medical people off at the next village down the line, where the docs would set up a surgery for several weeks. Then the two vans would return to Qotosh empty. Dr. Schwartz would remain at the clinic in Qotosh until mid-afternoon, when all the vehicles would return to Huánuco.

"Does that help?" Coombs asked.

"It does. I guess I'll go with the others and cover the surgery setup. I can return to Qotosh and we'll head back, right?"

"Yes, sir," said the Davis woman. "In the next four days, Dr. Schwartz will visit other locations where several foundations are helping with agricultural projects and economic development. There should be some excellent opportunities for you there, too."

"OK. Got it," he said. "Thanks."

Five days with Anne Davis! He still couldn't get a read on her eyes, but her complexion was fine. Lovely smile! "Excellent opportunities," she had said—indeed. Sometimes these overseas assignments had their benefits!

The sound of barking dogs reached Matt through the kitchen window. He put down the newspaper, got up, and peered outside. A bus was accelerating slowly past their gate.

"What is it, Dad?" asked Julio, not taking his eyes off the computer monitor.

"A bus. The dogs don't normally bark at the bus, but it probably stopped for that crew fixing potholes on the highway. I bet they were shouting back and forth and that set them off. I guess we don't have to worry about being attacked by buses or county road men." He went back to his paper.

In her shop in the barn, Clio barely registered the dogs, but a few minutes later when Raisin slunk to the door and hissed a warning, she noticed.

"What is it, girl?"

She peeked out. The cat was staring toward the back of the compound at the double-wide wrought iron gate her dad and Julio had rebuilt, her ears adjusting like fire control antennas. Clio looked more closely. Was that a hand gripping a bar of the pass-through gate? She could make out the hand was connected to an arm...and to a shoulder. The top of a head was resting against the gate. She stepped outside and Raisin hissed again.

Halfway there she could tell it wasn't a man; it was a smaller person. It was...it was Harry!

"Harry! What are you doing here?"

When he looked up she stopped in her tracks. One of his eyes was swollen shut. There was a bruise on his forehead. He held a bloody handkerchief to his mouth.

"Oh, Harry! What happened to you?"

She undid the lock and let him in. He was limping. His jeans were dirty. One knee was torn.

"I need some repairs," he said, shakily.

She supported him by one elbow and guided him into her shop. He collapsed into a chair.

"Oh, me! Harry! You're a mess! Is anything broken? What happened?"

"I don't think so. I was on my way to work, but they caught me before I could get on the bus."

"You mean those guys who wanted you to join their gang?"

"Yeah. Four of them. They worked me over. I thought maybe you could fix me up."

"You need a doctor, Harry!"

"No. No doctor. We can't afford it. And then the cops would come. That would just make it worse. Do you still have that stuff you put on my cut?"

"You need more than that! Oh, poor Harry."

Her nursing experience had been mostly with dogs and cats and the occasional horse, but there was nothing to do but start. She pulled out a box of freshly-laundered cloths she used for processing her herbs and a bottle of hydrogen peroxide and started blotting and wiping his abrasions and applying the antiseptic ointment he had requested. She couldn't do much for his swollen eye or his cut lip. Fortunately, her dad had given her and Julio a first aid kit which included a box of band aids of various sizes. The big square ones were perfect.

"Do you have any puncture wounds, like from a knife?"

"No. They didn't want to kill me. They need me, if you can believe that."

He sighed several times, catching his breath when she touched a tender spot. Finally, he noticed Raisin staring from a counter top.

"¡Hijo! What is *that*?"

"Huh? Oh, that's my cat. Her name is Raisin. Hold still."

"Your cat? That's your *cat*?"

"Well, maybe I'm her human. Yes, she's my cat."

"What kind of cat? She looks dangerous!"

"She's a caracal. No, she isn't dangerous, not as long as you behave yourself. She helped you, you know! She told me you were outside."

She handed him a cup of water and two acetaminophen tablets.

"Take these. I'm going to fix you some tea."

"I don't like tea."

"Ni modo. You'll like this tea. Even if you don't you're gonna drink it."

She put a cup of water in the microwave and punched it on. Taking a second cup over to her herb drawers, she collected bits of yarrow, sage, chamomile, and wormwood. After a bit of searching she added a little winter savory, and for good measure a pinch of catnip.

"What are you doing?"

"Making your tea."

"I thought you bought tea in the store. What is all that stuff?"

"Antiseptics and febrifuges."

"What?"

"They'll help keep your wounds from getting infected and prevent a fever."

The microwave beeped. She extracted the cup of boiling water and poured it over the herbs.

"It needs to steep a couple minutes."

Harry looked dubiously at the swirling mat of sludge floating on the steaming water. She stirred it.

"Don't worry. I'll filter this out. And I'll get a straw so you can drink it."

He seemed skeptical, as best she could tell from his damaged face, but twenty minutes later, he was looking a little better—sitting more erect, and moving gingerly.

"Do you want me to get Dad to take you home?"

"No! I can't let mamá see me like this!"

"She has to, Harry! You'll be weeks getting over this!"

"Ay...." He shook his head, slowly.

"You could tell her, uh, tell her a horse kicked you."

"Yeah! That's good! I fell off a horse!"

"But if you won't let Dad take you home you'll have to go home on the bus. I think you better spend the night here and go tomorrow."

"I don't want your dad to know! You already got shot at because of me. After this, he won't let you have anything to do with me. I'll stay here, but I'll sleep in the barn. Just don't tell him!"

"Well, if you say so, but you still need to call your mother. You can't just disappear overnight."

"Yeah, you're right. Oh, me."

"You could tell her, uh, tell her you had to spend the night with a sick horse. Would that work?"

"Yeah! One of Mr. Stallman's mares is about to foal. I could be staying to watch her!"

"Right. You were dizzy anyway, because of your fall. So you just stayed there, right? Here's my cell phone. Call her right now."

He opened the phone and looked at Clio.

"Me has salvado, hermanita. ("You saved me, little sister.") I'm glad you're my friend."

"I'm glad you're my friend too. Later this evening I'll sneak you something to eat. Now call her."

Damn third-world roads, thought Crowse. Even a modern van with decent suspension would need new shocks after six months of this. Rollins, his acquaintance from the *Journal Constitution*, was jotting notes in the front seat. Fine; go nuts, man, get eye strain. He didn't have to: he was getting time and a half for this gig because he was one of the few TV reporters who could also write. His story was already on tape, chock-full of ailing people, devoted doctors, lots of hope. Not worth a Pulitzer, but not bad.

The van jounced around a curve and there was Qotosh through the windshield, and that damned suspension bridge. Once more unto the breach, dear friends....

The village was even more decorated than it had been earlier this morning. Flags, bright posters, people wearing multiple layers of colorful weavings and decorated hats, were everywhere. As he pulled his gear bag out of the van he could hear a musical ensemble playing enthusiastically in what passed for a plaza. It seemed like an awful lot of festivity just for a tall, skinny doctor in hiking boots.

The driver from this morning was leaning against his own van, munching on something wrapped in a corn shuck. Maybe he spoke English.

"Why is everybody so happy?" he asked the man.

"Eh?" he replied, swallowing.

"Why happy? Happy about doctor?"

"Ah. No. Anadasi!"

"What?"

"Anadasi." He nodded toward the plaza.

Crowse shook his head. The man took a slug from a bottle labeled "Pilsen Callao." What the hell was he saying?

"Sí," he repeated. "Anadasi. You know: woman. Woman from...." and he gestured skyward.

Crowse glanced up into the jungle-covered slopes that surrounded them on all sides. This was making no damn sense at all. He was getting nowhere. He shrugged at the man and headed toward the sound of the music.

A surprisingly large crowd had gathered for such a small village. He was taller than most people there, and once he eased his way through the outliers he could see a trio of men playing panpipes in the middle. OK, good enough. He unzipped a pocket on the bag and pulled out a video camera. People moved aside to let him through. The whole world understood a media guy with a camera.

Folks in the center were clapping and laughing. He pressed "record" and captured the band and the crowd watching a troupe of children dressed like Peruvian dolls dancing in the center. He pulled the shot wider. The kids were mostly facing to one side, and many of the adults were looking that way too. He panned and zoomed to follow, where three adults on a bench were laughing and smiling. The two on either side were looking at the one in the center, with a tiny, dressed-up child in her lap. She was holding its arms, helping it clap in time to the beat. He zoomed in some more.

Huh? It was Anne Davis! No, hold on—she was dressed like Anne Davis, but this woman was blonde. What the hell? He zoomed to her face. Whoa! He knew that face! What the hell? It was Ana Darcy! God damn! The picture jiggled as he started in recognition. Keep it steady, man. Damn! Anne Davis...Ana Darcy. He pulled back to the group on the bench. Now all the hubbub made sense. "Anadasi," for Christ's sake! He'd ridden here in a car with a woman from another planet! God *damn!*

He continued taping, getting the crowd from several sides, the musicians and kids, and most of all, Ana Darcy and the revelers around her. This was a serious scoop, even if it meant he'd not have a bar room tryst this evening, at least not with Ana Darcy.

An hour later he had taped everything of possible interest he could find: the village from a distance, the clinic and patients, a tiny chapel, the suspension bridge and rushing river, a rustic bar, seven inquisitive alpacas in a corral, a battered bus covered with advertisements, a seated woman weaving at a loom tied from her waist to a post, a grizzled harpist plucking merry tunes, a small market area with colorful displays of vegetables and grains, and more. He zipped his camera back in the bag. To one side of the plaza, Coombs seemed to be assembling the caravan. He strolled over.

"We about ready?" he asked.

"I hope," Coombs replied. "Gotta get Ana away from her fans."

Ana was holding another child, chatting with a crowd of women by the bus.

"Man, you guys sure fooled me."

"Don't feel bad. You're not the first."

"She's absolutely the last person I'd expect to run into in this corner of the globe."

"She loves it. Look at her."

They were all laughing about something. Dr. Schwartz and the French doctor joined Ana and the women.

"She must speak Spanish."

"Yeah, she does. Pretty good, far as I can tell."

Schwartz shook hands with the French doc, embraced her quickly, and came over to the van.

"Those women and children are headed to town," he said. "Ana wants to ride with them on the bus. You see any problem with that?"

Coombs frowned. The women were laughing uproariously. Ana had tried on one of their hats.

"I guess not. It's a straight shot, half an hour. Ought to be all right, if we stick together."

Schwartz made a thumbs-up gesture to Ana. She replied with an exuberant "come here" wave to Coombs. Crowse tagged along. Her face was alight with excitement. She hugged the baby and handed it back to its mother.

"Come with us, Rob! You too, Mr. Crowse! It'll be fun!"

"Fun?" Coombs said, looking sidelong at Crowse. "Well, if you say so."

The three of them, with perhaps twenty chattering women, piled on the bus. They ended up sitting in the middle near the side door. Some number of village men, perhaps not looking to travel with noisy women, loaded into the second and third van. Crowse could see Rollins talking to Dr. Schwartz. Both got into the lead van with several other villagers. Way to go, Rollins, interview the doc's ass off, he thought. I've got Ana Darcy!

The bus groaned to life in a cloud of diesel exhaust as the first two vans eased past. The driver pulled out while the last van finished loading. As they turned onto the approach to the suspension bridge, Crowse's throat tightened. The first van was nearly across and the second was right behind. The bus followed. Three vehicles on this damned bridge? Coombs was tense too.

"Is this safe?" Crowse asked.

"I hope so," said Coombs tightly. "I guess we'll find out."

The bus slowed to a stop. Coombs peered ahead. The van in front had stopped too.

"What's the matter?" asked Crowse.

"Not sure," Coombs replied, getting up and squatting slightly in the aisle to see better. "What the hell!"

"What?"

"We're blocked. There's an oncoming vehicle at the end! Dammit! I don't like this."

Coombs stepped to the side door and began trying to force it open. Crowse reflexively grabbed his video camera and started recording. The women in the bus were silent, except for Ana.

"What's the matter?" she asked.

Crowse stuck his video camera out the window and pointed it at the head of the bridge. In the monitor he could see an SUV diagonally across the road at the end. Four men had jumped out of it. He zoomed in. They had guns. They wore stocking masks. They ran to the lead van and yanked the people out and forced them down. He heard gunfire.

"What's happening!" shrieked Ana.

"Don't know. Sit tight," Coombs growled as he forced the doors apart and stepped out.

Crowse pulled the zoom back to normal, acting from instinct, with no thought that he was making a tape that next April would finally win him the Pulitzer Prize.

Coombs knelt on the boards below. Crowse pointed the camera down at him as Coombs produced a pistol from a shoulder holster, actuated the slide, aimed, and fired. Keeping his right arm straight, braced with the left, he squeezed off another shot, and another. The sharp, percussive bark of the pistol cracked against Crowse's ears. Oh, Christ, he thought, turning the camera forward. One of the masked men staggered backwards, lowering a rifle. He fired again, the man fell, and Coombs whirled around, staying low. Crowse followed with the camera. Two men were crouching behind the doors of a vehicle blocking the other end. Coombs fired four quick shots and turned back to the ones in front.

"They want me!" Ana screamed. "They're after me!"

"Stay down!" Crowse shouted, but she was already out the door. More shots came from the men up front. Coombs returned fire. Crowse turned the camera down again, catching Ana saying something to Coombs. Then she leaped up on one of the heavy ropes of the bridge.

"Hey!" she shouted, six feet from his camera. "Hey!" She clapped her hands and waved. "Hey! I'm here! Here I am!"

And then she turned, flexed her knees, and jumped off the bridge. Crowse got it all: her arms widespread in the most graceful swan dive he'd ever seen, down, down, down, blonde hair streaming behind, down, down, rotating to the vertical at the last instant, arms clasped over her chest, ripping into the dark green water feet first. He kept the camera on the bubbles, moving rapidly downstream. Coombs was cussing.

"Shit! Fuck! Shit!"

He charged the men in front, throwing down one clip and jamming in another. One man was dragging his downed comrade towards their vehicle. Another was pulling open the driver's door while the fourth quickly shouldered a rifle and fired. Coombs skidded to a halt and fired three times. The man lurched, dropped the rifle, and staggered to join the others. As he jumped in, the vehicle backed away from the bridge and turned around. Coombs pivoted and began firing at the vehicle behind. Crowse followed with the camera. The windshield shattered as it backed away, roaring up the incline toward the road. He turned the camera back to Coombs, staring downstream.

"Goddammit!" He pounded the ropes in frustration. He pounded them again. "*Goddammit!*"

They looked downriver.

There was no sign of her.

She was gone.

Chapter 12

Nothing was better for a reporter than a disaster. This Ana Darcy business was putting his name before the whole world! After finding a techno-nerd in Huánuco late that night and uploading his videos to the Miami headquarters, it didn't take long for the world to come calling. He'd spent two days in his new friend's house and out on the street, being interviewed by major news organizations. He didn't even mind answering the same questions again and again.

No, no one knew what had happened to Ana Darcy.

Yes, the Peruvian government had sent a helicopter to fly the river for ten kilometers downstream, finding only her green windbreaker, snagged in some undergrowth at the edge of the river, about a kilometer downstream from the bridge.

Yes, people along the banks had been alerted to search for her, but there weren't that many people, or villages, nearby.

Yes, one of those villagers, a fisherman, had found a blonde wig, four kilometers downstream.

No, that didn't mean the woman who had jumped off the bridge was not Ana Darcy. He had been right next to her when she jumped, as his video tape had clearly shown. He had seen her with brown hair earlier in the day, while in disguise. Probably the wig was to cover hair that she normally kept dyed.

No, she had not been wounded. Didn't you see the tape (you idiot)? The best guess was that she jumped in order to save the lives of innocent people, one of whom had in fact been shot (but who was expected to recover). No, he didn't know what she had said to the security man before she jumped. He'd ask him next time he saw him. His name was Bob Coonce, or something like that.

Yes, she was reported to be a strong swimmer, or at least an Olympic gold-medal diver. But the distance to the water was about 60 feet (20 meters for the non-American interviewers), and even a clean entry would have been a terrible shock, capable of knocking her out. Yes, the water was very cold.

No, they had no idea who had attacked the vehicles. The government blamed an offshoot of the Shining Path guerillas, but a spokesman for the Shining Path had denied it. Besides, Ms. Darcy's presence had been a closely guarded secret until that morning. The attack wasn't being ruled out as a random act of terrorism.

No, no trace of the terrorists' vehicles had been found—it was an extremely isolated area.

This is Gizmo Crowse reporting (for the umpteenth time). Back to you at the studio.

He felt bad about Ana Darcy, but there was nothing he could do about her. He'd totally missed one night's sleep with all the interviewing, but on this second night, well, there was a bar down the street, and he bet himself he would not have to pay for a single drink.

Coombs' Seal training had never left him. He didn't brag about it, but he never forgot it. He worked hard to maintain his edge despite the passing years. Seals never despaired. Seals never quit. Seals never cried.

But he was very close. The past two days had been horrible. Probably the world's best beloved celebrity, a sweet young woman he also knew as a wife and mother—he was half in love with her himself—had been his responsibility, and he'd let her down, and possibly watched her die. He was doing everything he could to find her, but the cold truth was he was helpless. That gnawing fear lay in his guts like a stone.

The hardest thing he'd had to do was call Counselor Hleo with the news. The Counselor must be one tough hombre. He'd been clearly upset but not accusatory, nor did he pepper Coombs with useless questions. It was professional to professional, all the way. He said he would get the news to Matt himself, so Coombs could stay on site undistracted. As if that were possible.

There were many things to be done, for sure. One of the first was to ask a visibly upset Dr. Closset, in her clinic at Qotosh, what amount of money would be considered a king's ransom by the local citizens. About $1000, she told him—four years' wages. He asked her to put out the word that that amount would be the reward for any information about Ana Darcy, and that he would also cover the expenses of local fishermen who were willing to take their vessels up and down the banks of the river. She said she would try, though her Quechua, the first language of most locals, was not the best. He left his cell phone number with her.

He searched the area of the ambush before the police arrived from Huánuco. The attackers had left one AK-47 behind. It was in prime condition, he determined: the action was oiled and smooth and the trigger pull had been fine-tuned by someone who knew what he was doing. It didn't look like one of the millions of such knock-about rifles in the hands of third-world ruffians. Nor had the attackers behaved like ruffians. They had been disciplined, with a well coordinated plan. As soon as Ana had jumped from the bridge, they split. There was a long smear of blood where the first man he'd shot had been dragged to their vehicle. It was dark red, suggesting a major wound. He hoped he'd killed the son of a bitch.

He found his pistol clip where it had lodged between two boards. There were five cartridges still in it. That left one full clip, and, once he could transfer those rounds to the second clip, a second nearly full one: 25 rounds total. He couldn't hope to obtain more in Huánuco. These would have to do. He left the AK-47 where it had fallen and put the handkerchief he had handled it with back in a pocket.

The government helicopter that flew the river before nightfall failed to impress him. It made one quick pass each way at perhaps 30 knots. He was amazed they found her windbreaker, but that proved nothing, nor did the wig. Both could have floated to the mouth of the Amazon for all it meant. A policeman told him there were falls five kilometers above Qotosh and ten kilometers below. That meant the government would probably not be able to bring in a boat and would not likely mount a serious river-level search.

Things got even more depressing when he considered the situation from Ana's point of view, if she had survived. Assuming she remained conscious after her dive, and swam with the current around the bend 300 yards downstream to pull herself ashore in the dense undergrowth (not all that easy), she would be scared, in pain, and freezing cold to the point of exhaustion. Since her attackers had come out of nowhere and were evidently well organized and well equipped, she might think a search helicopter was hostile too. She might think the same of slowly moving boats. He'd certainly worry about that if he were in her place. His Seal background had given him the knowledge to survive in such conditions. He'd eaten worms in training and he could do it again if necessary—worms and worse. Could she? Would she know how to work her way back to civilization? Would she even have the strength to do so?

He put out of his mind looking for the bunch who had done this. Sooner or later, he would find them. The result would not be pretty.

In the morning at first light he would hitch a ride on one of the boats and call out to her as it motored up and down the river. If that failed, he would trek up and down both banks, no matter how thick the undergrowth happened to be or how long it might take. If he could find one, he'd take a tracker with him. It was all he could think to do.

Somewhere far away, an insistent beeping was demanding attention.

He looked down. A hand lay on the couch. There was a phone in it. Both looked foreign, as though they belonged to someone else.

Slowly concentrating, he willed the thumb of that hand to move over the "off" button. He stared at it until it pressed down. The beeping stopped.

What had he been thinking about?

There were the knees of his blue jeans. Beyond them, slightly out of focus, was a colorful Mexican rug.

Counselor Hleo. Counselor Hleo had just called him on the telephone. He'd never done that before. But he had had good reason.

On the rug was a low table, and a shiny wood floor on the other side. Raising his head, he regarded the bookshelf against the opposite wall. On the top shelf was a small, framed photograph of two children and a woman standing with three bicycles. Behind them was a narrow irrigation canal, a green field, and in the distance, dun colored mountains. They were smiling.

Those were his children.

That was his wife.

Ana.

What time was it? Nine fifty-five. The twins were in bed, almost certainly asleep. There was nothing to be gained in telling them tonight. Tomorrow. Abuelita too. He took a slow breath, got to his feet, and padded to the double door that opened onto the patio. There were no lights visible in either twin's room. He gently shut the doors and turned on the television, muting the volume.

The screen warmed up to a sleep aid commercial. Then a prescription drug for acid reflux. Another for pickup trucks. Finally, the logo of the evening news broadcast with the coming highlights, cutting to a picture of Olympic Ana in a warmup suit, hung with medals. Another of Ana addressing the United Nations General Assembly, followed by a map of Peru with a red dot somewhere over the midpoint of the country. Then two serious and perfectly coiffed news readers, cutting to shots of a car accident, a house on fire, a weather map, the news logo again, and more commercials.

While they ran he looked around the room. It felt different somehow. Would this be where he and his twins would live, just the three of them, from now on? The house felt empty.

There was Ana on the screen again. He fumbled with the remote, finding the mute button. One of the news readers was speaking.

"...is missing following a terrorist attack in the Amazon jungles of Peru. The whole thing was captured on video by a reporter with the group. It was over in less than a minute."

It was an astonishing sequence: a few seconds of Ana playing happily with costumed children; armed, masked men roughing up people in a van; Coombs (it looked like Coombs) firing at them from right below the camera; Ana standing on a thick rope, calling out, turning, and diving into a river. He watched her fall as the sequence slowed to frame by frame. It was a beautiful dive. His heart froze as she disappeared beneath the dark green water.

The news reader was still speaking: "...Peruvian government has mounted a massive ongoing search effort. Since her Olympic performances, Ms. Darcy has been active in...." He tuned them out. It sounded like an obituary.

The double doors rattled lightly. Through the glass he could see Raisin picking at the jamb with her claws. When he let her in she trotted back to the bedroom. He turned off the TV and sat back down on the couch.

The twins shouldn't see this. He wouldn't tell them it had been taped at all. They might happen to see it eventually, but that would be later. He couldn't control that.

Raisin soundlessly appeared on the rug in front of him. Her ears swiveled outboard, back, then to the front again, the long black hairs waving ever so slightly as she did so. It hit him with a jolt: if Raisin were lost in that jungle, they could find her: the gravity tag. God damn it, why didn't Ana have a gravity tag?

The big cat looked directly at him, eyes wide, making trilling noises deep in her throat.

"You know, don't you?"

The cat looked quickly at the doors over her shoulder, then back at him.

"I don't know, girl. I don't know. It doesn't look good."

The email waiting for Oleg with his morning coffee said only "CNN, world news." That was smart of Viktor—emails were never secure. With the press of a button Oleg slid open the door to the television cabinet, turned it on, and resumed cutting a bite off his pastry. By the time the cabin boy had delivered his eggs Benedict, Ana Darcy's picture flashed on the screen. He turned up the volume and watched the story closely. When the next piece followed, about a typhoon tearing up the Philippines, he turned the set off.

Well. It was interesting to finally see his team in action. They had had a good plan, and they followed it to the letter. One never knows about such things. Who could have foreseen that the security man would have been so quick and fearless—and so accurate? Who could have guessed that the woman would be in the bus rather than the first vehicle? No one could have predicted that she would choose to jump to her death rather than be captured. Admirable, actually. Worthy of a Cossack.

Viktor and his team had earned their bonus, even if the woman had not been captured alive. He'd wait to pay it until the body had been recovered, of course. He patted his lips with the linen napkin and pushed the plate away.

Where were his guests? He wandered out of the captain's stateroom and headed above deck. They were already sunning themselves on the fantail.

"Good morning, my friends. I trust everyone slept well?"

They had. He turned the conversation to a more desired thread.

"Stavros, you mentioned a newly discovered Roman shipwreck last night. Where was that?"

"Off Naxos. In the Cyclades."

"Greece! Excellent! I feel like doing a little archeology. Would you and your friends care to join me?"

They agreed (they had nothing better to do), so he summoned the sailing master to make the arrangements for a night departure. Paros, the island next to Naxos, had a suitable harbor at Naousa. Excusing himself from the sun-bathers, he went below to personally check out his scuba gear, even though his bosun's mate had already done so. One couldn't be too careful. He smiled to himself at the memory of the single good idea he had learned from the American President, Ronald Reagan: "Trust, but verify."

When Harry awoke he not only wasn't sure where he was, he wasn't sure he was alive. He couldn't see and he couldn't move, but for some reason he didn't panic. If he was dead, why panic? Wherever he was, it was completely peaceful. There were no traffic sounds, no beeping medical equipment, nothing. He breathed deliberately for a long time. The air smelled good, like hay. Finally, with effort, he got one eye open. He was in…he was in a barn…oh, yeah, the Méndez's barn. There were faint cracks of sunlight visible between the boards on his right side. Right: he'd made himself a bed here, out of a discarded quilt and some old straw. Why couldn't he move?

He tried a few tentative motions, and that's when the pain started. Now he remembered. He'd had the hell beaten out of him yesterday. Clio Méndez had nursed his wounds and given him shelter. He lay there a little longer, until it occurred to him that what he'd learned to do with race horses might be applicable to him too. He wiggled his toes. They responded. He wiggled his fingers: OK there, too. He lifted both forearms. That hurt, but not too much. He began gingerly massaging his arms and thighs. When those loosened up he raised his knees and worked on his calves. Then he moved to his chest. When working a particular spot caused too much pain he skipped it. Finally he made an effort to sit up.

That hurt, but things looked better sitting up. He swiveled his head, loosening his neck. Was this what it felt like to be old? He cautiously reached behind himself and worked the muscles over his kidneys. He had to pee something fierce. After a little more massaging he slowly got to his feet, hanging on to part of the stall he was in with one hand to fight the dizziness.

When it passed he shook out his legs gently and tried a few steps. It took a while, but he made it to the barn doors at the end, opened one, and peeked out. No problem: they opened to the back of the compound, out of sight of the house. He eased around between the barn and the wall and relieved himself literally and figuratively. The next item was obvious: he was thirsty.

Clio had faucets in her shop. Slowly, using whatever support that offered itself, he shuffled through the door at the back of the barn to the former tack room, now Clio's domain, and drank until he was satisfied. He was finally moving a little better, thankfully. It was no problem deciding what to do next: he sat in her chair, folded his arms, and dozed.

He woke up hungry. He could see nothing to eat except bushels of herbs, hardly promising. He got up carefully and checked her little refrigerator, but there was nothing inside recognizable as food. He sat down again and thought about his problems, which were many. Halfway through the list for the second time there was a fumbling at the latch to the outside door.

It was Clio, with two bananas, three thick slices of dark bread, and a plastic water bottle full of what looked like milk. In the same instant he realized something was very wrong. Her face was red, eyes puffy and moist, and she looked even smaller than usual. She spoke before he could say anything. Her voice was shaky.

"Morning, Harry. I snuck you some breakfast. Sorry it isn't better."

She set the food on the counter, sniffling.

"Ai, Clio! What's wrong, girl? You look terrible!"

She burst into tears and hugged him desperately. It hurt like hell but he hugged her back. She was sobbing so hard he could barely understand her.

"It's Mom. She was traveling, and...she got hurt, hurt bad, maybe...and we don't know...don't know...oh, Harry!"

He held her a long time, until the shaking subsided. She stepped back and wiped her face.

"You don't look so good yourself, Harry."

"Ni modo, Clio. I'll be all right. But what about your mom?"

She collapsed into the chair.

"There's another chair in Julio's shop. Go get it and eat your breakfast, please."

He did so. She kept sniffling and blotting her eyes. The bread was wonderfully restorative.

"So, what about your mom?"

"We don't know anything, Harry. We're just waiting to hear. We might have to leave. Or not. I don't know."

"Ai, poor Clio! Poor family! What can I do?"

"Nothing, Harry. Here. Here's some money for the bus. I have to go back inside now. I don't know what's going to happen. Just get home safely and be careful, please."

Another hug and she was out the door. He thought a minute and then ate the second banana, polishing it off with the last of the milk. Poor Clio! He thought he had problems. But even with all of hers, she had still remembered him.

Chapter 13

Coombs was furious with himself. His alarm had beeped at 4:30 am, but he had stretched and closed his eyes and the next thing he knew it was 6:45 am. He'd planned to be at Qotosh at first light, but now he couldn't count on finding a guide and hitting the river until 8:00 or 8:30. He had been exhausted, but Seals should do better than that.

He called his driver, Diego, and told him to come by at 7:00. He strapped on his shoulder holster and checked and inserted the 9mm pistol. He patted himself down. The Seal combat knife was in place on his ankle. Check the cargo vest: satellite cell phone, GPS unit, hand-cranked battery charger, Swiss Army knife, zoom monocular, two spare pistol clips, first aid mini-pack, LED flashlight, sunglasses. Everything seemed to be there.

His hand was on the doorknob when the cell phone beeped.

"Hello?"

"Mr. Coombs?"

"Yes."

"This is Dr. Closset, Mr. Coombs. I have your friend in my clinic right now."

"You *what*?"

"Yes, that's right. A local herder brought her in about midnight. She needed to sleep very bad...very badly. That's why I waited to call, so I could examine her."

"What's her condition?"

"She could be better, but I think she can travel. I don't want to go into detail on the telephone. Can you come for her soon? I recommend that."

"Yes, ma'am! I'm leaving this minute! I'll be there in forty minutes. Thanks, doc!"

Ana Darcy! Alive! Thank God! A tremendous load lifted from his soul. Diego didn't need to be told to hurry, but Coombs told him anyway. Should he call Hleo? No. Call him on the way back, when he actually had her with him. He'd chartered the Cessna for the week. They could be in Lima by noon. Outstanding! Freaking marvelous!

At the clinic he jumped out of the car before it had fully stopped. Dr. Closset ran to meet him, her expression as alarmed as his was hopeful.

"Doc? Is something wrong?"

"She's gone, Mr. Coombs!"

"Gone? Whaddya mean, gone?"

"She ran away! See that truck?"

Down the slope toward the bridge, a Suburban-like SUV was parked at a haphazard angle 200 yards distant. Coombs recognized it all too well. The windshield had been shot away.

"Five men got out. They came this way. She ran there!"

The doctor pointed to the narrow trail following the river downstream.

"Damn! How long ago?"

"Twenty minutes."

"She ran, and they followed?"

"Oui...sí...yes. Sorry."

"Where does that trail go?"

"To the next village, eighteen kilometers. It is very high over the river, very, uh, thin, very many curves."

"Thanks, doc. Wish me luck."

"Mr. Coombs...."

"Yeah?"

"She is not well. She ran fast from here, but I do not think she can run far."

"I hope you're wrong, doc."

Near the clinic the trail was wide enough for a four-wheeler, but it narrowed as it sloped down toward the river. It got no wider as it rose to the next steep hill and curved around it out of sight. He moved at a quick trot until he reached that curve, probably 150 feet over the river. Staying close to the vegetation he peered around it. The terrain on both sides of the river looked to be a series of narrow, steep outcroppings, like fingers, plunging down to the deep gorge where the river flowed. The trail continued around the next outcropping, going in and curving back out, in a giant U. No one was on it. He ran that section more quickly, until he could see around the second outcropping.

This one stood further out over the river than the first. Looking carefully around it, he could see downstream perhaps a mile. A series of four more steep outcroppings extended to a distant bend in the river, hazy in the early morning mist. No one was on this U-shaped section of the path either. Ana and her pursuers had made good time. He started around it. At the inside of the U, a rickety bridge made of limbs tied together with rope allowed travelers to pass over a rivulet running down the inside.

He crossed the little bridge and trotted on to the third curve. When he peeked around, he saw two men on the trail ahead. They might have been 300 yards from him on a direct line, but perhaps 600 yards by the trail. The doc had said there were five men, so these were probably the laggards. They were trudging rather than running. The one in the rear was twenty or thirty yards behind the man in front. He had some kind of equipment bag on his back, which bulged in several places. His hands were on the shoulder straps. Coombs knelt in the undergrowth and pulled out his monocular. They were wearing the same kind of camouflage pattern he remembered from the Monday attack. The first man was carrying a rifle, from its shape, an AK-47.

He zoomed the monocular. The first man had passed out of sight round the curve. Coombs got ready to run as soon as the man with the bag disappeared after him. He was tensed to sprint when a person darted out of the undergrowth behind the man and pushed him over the cliff into the river. He caught a flash of long, brown hair. Was that Ana? She darted back into the undergrowth. Coombs froze in place. He realized instantly what she was doing. He pulled the monocular out again and focused it.

A minute later, the man who had gone ahead returned. He looked back down the empty path and then stepped to the edge and looked down. Big mistake: Ana darted out again, and that man went to join his associate.

Before she could hide, a third man rounded the curve. Coombs nearly had a heart attack as the man raised his rifle, but Ana was faster. She darted toward him in quick zig-zags. By the time the man fired she was under the muzzle. The rifle flew up in the air, her arms flashed two or three times, and she stepped back. The man stood there like a statue, the rifle swinging from his neck on the sling. Ana stepped closer and pushed him. He fell back, half on the path and half off. Turning on his side, knees drawn up, he put his hands to his throat and slowly rolled over the edge.

Ana was still standing there. Why, dammit? Run, girl!

Even at this distance, Coombs could tell she was unsteady on her feet. He couldn't see her face, but she seemed to be swaying back and forth. Why didn't she dive for cover?

From his angle Coombs could see two more men coming around the curve. These two, one a large man and the other much smaller, were alert, with their assault rifles at the ready, having heard the third man's rifle fire. They were way beyond the range of his pistol. For an instant Coombs considered shouting or firing a couple shots or even running towards her, but it was too late for that. Ana saw the men. The men saw her.

She wobbled even more. As the men raised their weapons she sank to her knees and fell on her side. The men froze in place, both muzzles pointed at her at point blank range. Coombs' heart was in his throat. Ana was on her back, arms outspread, hair over her face, motionless.

The big man lowered his weapon and said something to the other. The smaller man approached Ana carefully, looked her over, and then knelt, removing something from his pocket. He tied her wrists behind her, tied her ankles, and stood up. The big man looked over the edge of the trail to the river and made some comment to the other. Handing his rifle to the smaller man, he bent down and checked Ana's pulse. Apparently satisfied she was alive, he picked her up and slung her over his shoulder like a sack of flour. Holding her in place by her thighs they started down the trail toward Coombs.

Jesus! Coombs looked back down the path he had just covered. Halfway to the little bridge over the waterfall there was a good-sized clump of foliage. Well, if the tactic worked for Ana maybe it would work for him. He pushed his way into the thickest part of it and lay flat several feet off the trail. He slid his pistol out of the holster and worked the slide quietly, checking to make sure it picked up and chambered a cartridge. Sliding the safety off, he stretched his arm in front of him. He pulled a branch with large leaves from a bush and laid it from his head to his arm. He waited.

It was ten minutes before he heard the sound of voices. As the voices grew louder, he could tell the men were speaking Russian. From his elementary knowledge of Russian, he understood enough to know they were talking about money. There was the crunching of shoes on the pebbly surface of the trail, and then movement in his peripheral vision. In ten or fifteen seconds they had passed him. Carefully, he moved the branch off his arm. Ana's head was hanging above the bigger man's waist. Her feet were also about at waist level.

He straightened his arm, focused on the sights of the pistol, and squeezed off a shot at the back of the big man's left thigh. The pistol went off with a startlingly loud bark. The man dropped as though he'd been poleaxed, with Ana on top of him. Coombs moved the sights to the smaller man, who was whirling around and bringing up the rifle. He fired three shots into the center of his chest. The man staggered backwards, clasping the rifle awkwardly to himself. A fourth shot sent him over the edge of the path.

Coombs jumped to his feet. The bigger man was pushing Ana off him while clearing a pistol from a holster at his waist. Coombs fired two quick shots, then two more. The man lay still. As Coombs stepped closer, the pistol toppled out of the man's open hand to the dirt. Kicking it away, he knelt and checked for a pulse. There was none. He holstered his weapon.

Ana was unconscious. He cut the nylon ties around her wrists and ankles and checked her over quickly: good pulse, no obvious wounds, eye reflex normal. She was pale and dirty. Her hair was matted and her extremities were cold, but her neck and stomach seemed warm enough.

He turned back to the big man. First the pistol: a fine, stainless Makarov 9 mm. He extracted the clip. The bullets would fit his own pistol. Toss the Makarov over the edge, keep the clip. Check the pockets: two more fully loaded clips, keep those; a Leatherman-type utility knife, over the edge with that; a cell phone, keep that, might have numbers that could be traced, shut it off for now, though; something big and bulky in a jacket pocket—water bottle! Unopened! Excellent. That was one item Coombs had forgotten. He slid it into a front pocket. What else? Lip balm...car keys...nothing else useful.

He stood and looked over the precipice. The smaller man's body was barely visible halfway down, sprawled about in vines. OK, then. He rolled the big man over twice, and the two comrades ended up together again. Sorry, Ivan—there was just no time for the traditional rites. He kicked dirt over the puddles of blood on the trail, hunted down the ejected cartridge casings, and smoothed out signs of a struggle.

After changing the water bottle to a back pocket of his cargo vest, he gathered Ana in his arms and started back to the clinic. She was frighteningly light. In case she could hear he spoke to her.

"I've gotcha, shipmate. This is your old buddy, Rob. You're safe now. You're gonna be OK. We'll get you fixed up and back to your family in no time."

She wasn't quite as light after a half mile, but that was no problem for a Seal. He'd carry her all day if that were required. But when he rounded the last curve to the clinic, plans changed. He stepped sideways into some foliage and looked again. On the suspension bridge beyond the clinic, another olive-drab SUV was headed into Qotosh.

He knelt behind the cover and eased Ana to a sitting position on his left knee. The SUV bumped across the bridge, up the slope to the crest, and turned left toward the clinic. It pulled off and stopped by the first vehicle. Four men got out, shouldered weapons, and started toward the damned trail where he and Ana were. How did they know which way to go? Had to be the cell phone.

Shit! By himself, he'd take on four people in a situation like this if he had to, but not with Ana along. Dammit! Where to go? He sure as hell couldn't carry her 18 clicks to the next village, and even if he did, what then? Nor could he go back to Qotosh. There was only one way to go: up. The four would be at his position in less than fifteen minutes, but all he had to do was get Ana above the trail and out of sight and let them go by. If he could get back to the taxi still parked beside the clinic, they could be on their way to Huánuco and Lima before these humps realized it. He checked his watch and scanned the hill. Better get started.

After several minutes he realized the big man had had the right idea for carrying Ana. He draped her over his shoulder, freeing up both hands for parting vines and grabbing onto branches. In ten minutes they had climbed to roughly 100 feet over the trail. He was puffing. Altitude was not his friend. He laid Ana gently on a big patch of ferns and moved to a position where he could see the trail. Sure enough, there came the men, moving quickly around the curve...three of them. Three? Where the hell was the fourth?

There he was. The fourth mope was headed back to the clinic! A few minutes later he appeared on the Qotosh side of the hill, approached the clinic and took station behind a clump of bushes. Coombs could see him holding his rifle at the ready. Some smart bastard in his party had realized she might double back on them and posted a guard to watch for her. Coombs shook his head. He might have done something like that himself, that is, if he had been the type of sorry son of a bitch to try to hunt down an innocent young woman.

He watched another fifteen minutes until the three in the forward team disappeared around the next curve. It was only 11:25 am—too much daylight left to wait until nightfall to sneak into Qotosh, but there was no point in risking it anyway. They might bring in even more reinforcements. The only choice was to keep going up. But up to what?

Two hours later he and Ana had reached the top of their particular hill. It was rounded and relatively free of trees and undergrowth, an ideal spot for a helicopter pickup. Unfortunately, there were no helicopters available, and he and Ana were sitting ducks for any Russian-chartered rotary winged craft that might be poking around. Coombs needed a breather. He retreated fifty feet down from the top and laid Ana in a pile of leaves under the hollow of a tree. He allowed himself an ounce of water from the Russian's bottle and poured a little on a handkerchief and cleaned off her face. She sighed and moved her head a little. He dripped an ounce or so into her mouth. She didn't spit it out. She could have been asleep, as far as she appeared. He dripped in another ounce.

He sat back and weighed his options, which boiled down to one. He took out his cell phone and called Hleo.

Hleo was cool as always, allowing Coombs to explain the tactical situation concisely. When Coombs paused, allowing ten seconds for the relayed signal to make the round trip to the moon and back, Hleo had the question Coombs hoped he would ask.

"Chief Coombs, in your estimation would Ms. Darcy's escape pod be suitable for a rescue?"

"I believe it would, Counselor. We have no food and very little water and Ms. Darcy needs medical attention as soon as possible. I can think of no other way. It may be a delicate operation, however, and I would like to brief Matt Méndez personally on it, if possible."

"Certainly. I recommend you allow me to 'patch you through,' I believe the expression is. You will have a delay, but it will be absolutely secure. I shall listen in, if I may."

In less than a minute, Matt was on the line.

"Matt, this is Rob Coombs. First, the good news: I have Ana with me and she's not seriously hurt as far as I can tell. She's asleep at the moment. I'll explain how it happened later, because we have more urgent business right now. We are hiding from her pursuers in the Amazonian jungle of Peru, and it looks like the only way we can extract ourselves is with the assistance of you and the escape pod. Is that possible?"

He stopped talking and waited. It was awkward but he'd done it before. After a short pause, Matt came on, perfectly clearly.

"Wonderful news, Rob, the best! You're damn right I can get the pod up. Tell me what and how."

That was encouraging. Matt had seemed steady to Coombs when they'd met four years ago. It wouldn't help at all if Matt came unglued.

"Get a pencil," Coombs said. "We need food for Ana, you, and me, for two days, just to be safe. If you have any of those MREs left from our little adventure four years ago, toss them in. They're a little old but they should still be good. We need water for two days also, and maybe orange juice or something like that. Even milk might be good. Bring a first aid kit. Tell me what firearms you have on hand."

"I have two Ruger pistols, both single action, a .22 and a .357 Blackhawk. I have a .22 single shot target rifle, a .22 lever action rifle, a .223 semiauto Ruger ranch rifle, and a 12 gauge semiauto Browning shotgun."

"Bring the .357, the .223, and the 12 gauge, and ammo. For the shotgun, the largest shot size you have. I don't think we'll need any of that, but bring it just in case. Bring some warm clothes for Ana, a couple blankets, and a pillow. She's exhausted. She'll need a checkup first thing when we get back, so plan that out too.

"I'll take a GPS reading and send it to Hleo. You should be able to ease down right on top of us, but phone before you do so. You need to time it for a night pickup, as soon as it's fully dark if possible. There may be bad guys in the vicinity. Nightfall here is..." he checked his watch, "about four hours from now. I don't know if you can leave in the daytime or not, but Hleo will let me know when to expect you. You got all that?"

"Yeah, got it. Normally we take the pod out after dark, but this time I think we'll risk making an exception. I can head out over the desert. People are always seeing UFOs anyway, and the Air Force flies some strange routes around here too."

"Counselor Hleo, sir, can you estimate the flying time?"

"I can, Chief Coombs. First, Mr. Méndez, is the radar-absorbing paint on the escape pod in good condition?"

"It is, Counselor. Julio and I repainted it last month."

"Excellent. Then if you will allow me to direct your flight, I think we can use a high altitude, high speed track, Mach II, I think. Flying time will be two and a half hours."

"OK," said Matt after the delay. "That's good, gives me an hour and a half to gather the stuff and get set. Unless you have anything else I better get to it."

"Good deal, Matt. I wanna keep this smooth and fast. The Counselor will keep me advised of your progress. Safe trip, shipmate."

Please, let's have no glitches for once, Coombs thought, as he cautiously eased to a point where he could check the trail below. He watched for ten minutes and saw nothing, which was good. No news is good news.

He checked Ana again. She had drawn up her legs and thrust her hands between her knees. He collected bunches of leaves from the jungle floor and piled them over her. They would help keep her warm while concealing her. He piled more next to her. If the mopes happened to patrol by here he could quickly bury the both of them. If they were discovered anyway, he'd make sure there'd be as much hell to pay as he could possibly manage.

He gave Ana another tiny drink and sat and thought. OK: two more things to do. He dug out the three Russian clips and popped out the bullets, sliding them into his own three clips and dropping the extras in a pocket. Then he set his cell phone to vibrate. Wouldn't it be a pisser if it beeped while the bad guys were strolling by?

"Clio!"

There was no answer. She wasn't in her room. She must be in her shop. Julio went out the back gate of the patio. She was sitting against a tree with her arm around Raisin.

"Hey, Clio!"

"What?"

"Time for lunch."

"I'm not hungry."

"Dad says to come eat."

"Maybe later."

Julio shrugged and went back inside. A few minutes later Abuelita emerged. Kneeling slowly, with the help of her cane, she sat and leaned against the tree at Clio's elbow.

"You need to eat something, granddaughter."

"I'm not hungry."

"What if I told you your mamá was all right, that she'll be back with us soon? Would you eat something then?"

"She shouldn't have gone. Dad should have made her stay home."

"Mejor libre albedrío que vivir en las sombras." ("Free will is better than living in shadows.")

"Huh?"

"Your mother is brave. She wants to do good for people. No one can tell her what to do. And besides, she's all right. Te prometo."

"How do you know?"

"I asked La Virgen. I lit candles for her. La Virgencita won't let us down."

Clio leaned over and laid her head on her grandmother's lap.

"Además, donde menos se piensa, salta la liebre." ("Besides, when you least expect it, a rabbit jumps up.")

The old lady stroked her hair softly for several minutes. Clio sniffled.

"Now, come inside and eat something. I'll make you a...."

"Buela! Clio!"

Julio burst through the back gate.

"It's Mom! They found her!"

Clio was on her feet instantly.

"Are you sure?"

"Yeah! Mr. Coombs just called! Dad's going to go get her!"

"¡Gracias a diós! Ay, nietos, help me up. But slowly, slowly. ¡Te dije, nieta, te dije!" ("I told you, granddaughter.")

Inside, Matt was piling things on the couch: three plastic cases, two rifle-sized and one pistol-sized, two blankets, a pillow.

"Dad! Is Mom OK? What happened?" Clio screeched.

"Mr. Coombs didn't have time to tell the whole story, but Mom's OK, tired but OK. I'm going to zip down there in the pod and bring her back. You guys want to help? Clio, get a pair of Mom's blue jeans and a sweat shirt and some clean underwear and socks. And a jacket. Son, get the ice chest from the laundry room and put the orange juice and milk from the fridge in it. Buela, are you up to making some sandwiches?"

Everyone got busy. Julio, lugging the ice chest to the kitchen, had a question.

"What are the guns for, Dad?"

"Mr. Coombs said he'd probably not need them but there are still a few bad guys around down there, so it's better to have them just in case. Don't worry; I won't let anyone shoot us, or the pod."

"The pod's tough," Julio said.

"Yeah. You said it's made out of glass, right?"

"Yessir. Glass. It's real tough. Bullets wouldn't hurt it."

"Good to know," said Matt, heading to the bathroom to fetch the first aid kit. "But I'd rather not find out."

When he got back, Julio had another question.

"How are you gonna find her, Dad?"

"GPS."

"I wish she had a gravity tag."

"I do too. But she doesn't. Son, do you remember if the water tanks are full on the pod?"

"They were when we painted it."

"I'll check again before I take off. Why don't you fill a jug with water just in case? Put it here on the table. Then maybe you could help Buela with those sandwiches."

"Dad?"

"Yes, mija?"

"Here are the clothes. When do you leave?"

"In about an hour and a half. Mr. Coombs wants the pickup to be after dark."

"Can we go?"

"Better not, sugar. I'll just get Mom and hurry back. I'll call you when I'm on the way."

Julio and Abuelita brought over a stack of sandwiches in plastic bags.

"That's great," Matt said. "Son, how about dumping a couple trays of ice in here, please."

"Sure, Dad."

Abuelita stayed by the ice chest.

"Matt?"

"Yes?"

"What is 'the pod,' and how are you going to zip down to Peru and right back again?"

Matt stopped arranging sandwiches in the box.

"It's Ana's little Thoman runabout. It's time you knew about it. When this settles down I'll give you a ride. Let's load the car and you can drive me to it. I'll give you a quick tour before I take off. You thought you'd seen a lot in your life, Buela, pero nunca has visto tal cosa. ¡Pero nunca!"

The sun was getting low in the sky. It only shone through the low cloud cover sporadically anyway, so there was no excess of light on the ground. The canyon the river flowed through was already in shadow. It would be a chilly night.

Coombs had plenty of time to think. The chances were excellent that the men searching for them would have found one or more of the bodies of their associates. He thought of them as chumps but they shouldn't be underestimated. They were professionals—professional Russian military types, apparently. Somebody with a lot of money was going to tremendous trouble and expense to capture Ana Darcy. If they figured out that either Ana was knocking them off one by one or she had help, what would they do?

They'd not waste time going to the next village. They'd realize she was still nearby. They'd search for her. He brushed the leaves off himself and gave Ana another little drink. She spluttered a bit but swallowed. Then she sighed. It was good to hear her voice.

He got up carefully and scanned his surroundings. There was almost no breeze. He heard nothing. Staying low, he moved slowly and deliberately back to his earlier vantage point. It reminded him of deer hunting, staying concealed while looking and listening for movement. By golly, damned if there weren't flashes of light near the top of the second hill. It was getting too dark, and therefore too dangerous, for searchers to be out, but several people, no doubt that three-man team, were checking out that hill. Surely they would save the hill he was on for the morning. Surely. They were working their way down. That had to be futile. In this light a person could very nearly hide in plain sight. In another half hour it would be completely dark. They should be no problem for him tonight. He went back to Ana.

His pocket vibrated as he was covering himself with leaves. Remembering to hide the light the damn thing made when he opened it, he tucked his head under the leaves next to Ana.

"Yes?" he said quietly.

"This is Counselor Hleo, Chief. Mr. Méndez will arrive over you in thirty-five minutes."

"Good. Hold him at 1000 meters please, Counselor. I will call you when we're ready for his approach."

Should he check those searchers one more time? No. They were not likely to climb this hill just as it got dark, and if they did he'd see their lights first. He slid next to Ana and patted her shoulder.

"Not much longer, shipmate. Your ride out of here is close."

There was a peculiar vibration in the air. It wasn't the wind and it didn't sound like the pod, which he'd heard up close several times. The vibration got louder, taking on a pulse and finally a distinct whoppity-whop that gave it away: a helicopter! Louder, louder—where the hell was it? He sat up, shedding leaves. It had come from the direction of Huánuco. Now it was over the second hill, perhaps 500 yards away. Several lights shone down from it—not military-style searchlights, fortunately, but large, hand-held flashlights. It circled the top of the hill several times. The chopper must be covering the blanks left by the ground searchers.

Holy crap! If it flew over here things might get sticky. If it landed and people got out to search, there would definitely be pole-cat hell. He would see to it personally. It *was* coming over here! Coombs sank into the leaves, piling more over Ana. They were under a tree and shouldn't be recognizable from the air at night. Just don't land, sucker, don't land. Reflexively, he patted his pistol under his vest and felt for the extra clips.

The helicopter circled the top of the hill while one person on each side shone a light on the ground. Then it swooped lower and made another pass below him and Ana. Some of their leaves blew away but no beam of light happened to fall on them. It began a third circle lower down but the pilot evidently realized that put him too close to the second hill and he pulled away. Coombs heard it head toward Qotosh until finally the sound faded out. Dammit, he thought. We need to get the hell out of here!

Again hiding the light from his cell phone, he called Hleo.

"We're ready, Counselor. Have Matt descend slowly to the first coordinate I sent you. That's the top of a hill. Tell him to open the hatch at fifty feet and ease down slowly. I'll whistle when I see him and we'll climb aboard."

"I shall tell him, Chief Coombs. Stand by."

Pickups were always scary. Coombs had once missed the loop attached to a speed boat during a sea pickup one night and had had to swim three miles to shore. Night is my friend. Night is my friend, he repeated, standing slowly and listening with all his might. He stepped away from the tree and looked around—no lights bobbing anywhere. He looked up. Pure black overhead. He stood.

Five minutes. Six. Seven minutes. Was that a faint hum? Yes, that was it! The pod was 100 feet above, maybe less. He brushed the leaves off Ana and picked her up and headed to the top of the hill. The humming was louder. He could just make out the dark outline of the pod, and the open hatch, on the other side. He went around and whistled like a bird. The opening was head high.

"Down three feet, Matt," he whispered.

He laid Ana inside, grabbed the edge of the hatchway, and pulled himself in with her.

"Blast off," he whispered.

The hatch shut tight and he felt the elevator-like sensation of rising quickly. He could see Matt in the faint glow of the instrument panel. He leaned forward and patted his shoulder, shaking his hand when Matt extended it.

"Well done, shipmate," Coombs said. "Let's blow this dump!"

Five minutes into the flight, with Hleo setting the course, Matt and Coombs eased Ana into one of the folded-down rear seats and switched places. Coombs watched the instruments while Matt draped a blanket over Ana and washed her face and hands. It was obvious Matt was overcome with emotion, mumbling endearments and encouragement to her as he worked. Coombs tried to tune him out and give them privacy, hard as it was in such a confined space. Finally, Matt must have gotten her comfortable. He spoke in a conversational voice.

"Man, I was worried about her," he said.

"Yeah. Me too," Coombs replied.

"That dive! I was sure she'd drowned."

"You saw that?"

"Oh, yeah. It was all over the news."

"I didn't know that. But then I saw it in person. I would have tried to stop her, but I had no idea she was going to jump. The truth is those guys were all over us. I wouldn't have lasted long. They took off after she dived, so I guess she saved me as well as a bunch of other people."

"It looked like she said something to you before she jumped."

"Oh, yeah. Funny thing. I was so amped up keeping those guys back it didn't even register until much later. She said 'Tell Matt I love him.'"

"That's all?"

"Yup. We had zero time to waste. I think she expected to die. I thought about that the whole time I was searching for her. God damn it, that was hard."

Matt said nothing. After a few seconds he sniffed twice and dug a comb out of a pocket.

"Shoulda brought a brush." He began gently combing out her hair. "She's cold, but her clothes are dry. I think I'll just keep this blanket over her. Maybe get her to drink some orange juice."

He pulled a cup out of the ice chest and poured a little juice into it. Holding her head up with one hand, he tipped a little into her mouth.

"How much do you know about what happened, Rob?"

"I'm guessing she didn't swim that far. Had to have pulled herself out downstream a ways and made it some distance from the river, because the banks were searched pretty well. She probably wasn't in any shape to trek back. The doctor at the clinic told me a herder brought her in last night. The standard herd animal around here seems to be alpacas. I've seen them drag heavy loads on a travois, so maybe that's how he did it. She was out in the open two days. Long time."

"Jeez. I bet she's starving. She always was a big eater. High metabolism. That's probably why she's so weak. I'll see how much food I can get her to take."

She coughed. Matt wiped some droplets of orange juice from her face. Coombs continued.

"Whoever's behind this must've sent a dozen men. I'm pretty sure I took out one, maybe two, at the bridge Monday. Then this morning, Ana got three and I got two. "

"Three? She did that? How?"

"The doc called early this morning to tell me she had Ana. Before I could get there from town a car full of bad guys showed up and she headed for the hills. I caught up in time to see her put three men in the river. She was smart: started with the last in line, then the next, and the next, but the final two got the drop on her. She must have used up her last reserves of energy doing that, because that's when she folded. I got the drop on those two when they were carrying her back to their vehicle. Another bunch arrived about noon. They were still looking for her after dark when you picked me up. They had trucks, helicopters, all kinds of gear. We skedaddled up one of those hills and called Hleo. Boy, was I glad to see you."

"Christ!" Matt said. More softly, he added, "We owe you, Rob."

He began rubbing her arms and whispering to her. Coombs' eyes stung. He said nothing, turning back to the instruments. Outside it was completely dark. So this was what Mach II felt like. There was no bumping, no vibrating, and only the slightest hiss audible. Four years earlier he had learned to love the pod. Thinking of that gave him an idea. He switched on the radio and called Hleo.

"Counselor, this is Chief Coombs. All is well here. Ms. Darcy is still asleep. Sir, would you recommend the application of one of those medical units Ms. Darcy used on me four years ago? I don't know the name of it. She called it 'the doctor.'"

Ten seconds later, Hleo answered.

"Excellent idea, Chief. Below the collarbone is an ideal location. I can monitor the results through the pod's on-board maintenance system. I shall report to you what it finds."

"Will do, Counselor. You might also call the Méndez family and tell them that we're coming home."

"I shall, Chief Coombs. Good work, sir."

Coombs popped open a compartment in the bulkhead by his knee and found several 'doctors' tucked inside, along with other items he didn't recognize. He opened the packet, slid it out, and wormed his way back to Matt.

"What's that?" Matt asked.

"Some kind of fancy Thoman first aid device. See these tiny holes?"

The object, the size of a bar of hotel soap, had perhaps forty tiny holes in rows on one side.

"You stick it on the skin, and little needles come out and get to work. When I was shot, one of these checked me out and treated me. It supplied antibiotics and pain killers and I don't know what-all else. It doesn't take the place of a real doctor, like if surgery were needed, but Ana bandaged my arm and this thing had me up and going the next day. I showed you the scar, didn't I?"

He pulled up a sleeve to reveal a six-inch welt on his forearm. Matt shook his head.

"If Hleo suggested it, let's do it."

Coombs pulled Ana's shirt collar away from her skin and cleaned the area, sticking the pad on beneath her collar bone.

"There. That was easy. I wish I had a box of these."

"How long does it take?"

"I don't know. Not long. It tingles once those needles get going."

Coombs moved back to a front seat.

"I'll see if she'll take a little milk," Matt said.

Coombs heard her cough again. Matt spoke to her.

"Hey, babe."

Coombs looked back. Her eyes were open, barely. Good sign. He turned back to the instruments. He heard Matt say "Have some milk, sugar." He tried to focus on figuring out what the controls on the panel before him might actually do.

Some minutes later Ana coughed again, several times. The coughs gave way to crying. Weak as she was, the crying became louder, crescendoing to an astonishing, heart-rending moan of anguish. Coombs swiveled in his seat to look. Matt and Ana were holding each other tightly. He had never heard such an agonized cry from anyone, least of all Ana Darcy. She was clinging to her husband, sobbing convulsively, but he was able to make out what she said.

"Oh Matt, Matt!" she wailed, "I lost the baby, Matt! I lost the baby!"

Matt continued to rock her gently, his face empty. Coombs turned forward and stared into the darkness outside. He had been so relieved for her once he finally got her safely aboard the pod, but now his soaring mood crashed hard, very hard.

Whatever sorry son of a bitch had done this to her was going to pay, pay dearly, pay with his worthless, damnable life. He would see that done if that was the last fucking thing he ever did.

Chapter 14

Coombs held the pod at 500 feet over an all-night medical clinic in a strip mall on the edge of a town in northern New Mexico. Matt had called it "Hispaniola," or something like that. It was 1:30 am. The clinic was the only establishment open in the whole mall. Largely funded by an organization Matt and Ana had started, it was staffed by a doctor and several nurses. Coombs had watched the doc, who Matt had called from the pod, arrive about half an hour ago. When your main benefactor beckons, you come, Coombs figured, even if it was in the middle of the night.

Presumably the doctor and the duty nurse were tending to Ana. Coombs had heard Matt tell the doc on the phone that they'd had an accident while hiking in a nearby national forest and that Ana had suffered a miscarriage. She'd been tended to by another hiker who was an ER nurse, but the nurse had recommended that she be looked at by a doctor. Good cover story, Coombs thought, and not too far from the truth.

With time on his hands, he keyed the radio and called Hleo.

"Counselor, this is Chief Coombs. Ms. Darcy is with a doctor now. I am standing by, with further thoughts."

"Yes, Chief. What are they, sir?"

"I've been thinking about those who attacked Ms. Darcy. They were many, at least twelve, and well equipped, trained, and financed. I heard several speaking Russian. I have a cell phone from one of them. It has three numbers stored on it. They are...." He read the numbers off. "I suspect this attack may be related to the conflict Ms. Darcy and I had with the two Russian oil tycoons four years ago, over that business of proton weapons they developed from illegal trade information. It occurs to me that those gentlemen may not have been willing to let the matter drop. If so, more than likely they will try another attack in the future. I think it is time to end this once and for all, sir. Do you agree?"

"I do, Chief. In fact I have already begun an investigation. I am delighted but not surprised to hear that you and I are of one mind. The telephone numbers will help, but I have already learned enough to believe that your suspicions are probably correct.

"Allow me to make a suggestion, if I may. When Mr. Méndez rejoins you, with his wife, let us hope, he will probably call me with a report of the doctor's findings. In our conversation I shall mention that I need you to do our cause a service, and request that he lend you the escape pod for several days. Later, you may call me back privately, at which time you and I shall discuss possible plans of action."

"I'll do it. It's a pleasure to work with you, Counselor."

"And an honor to work with you, Chief Coombs."

He continued floating in midair, thinking strategic thoughts and remembering hovering like this years ago waiting for Ana to return from reconnaissance missions on the ground in Sedlakia. But now it was different: there had been a death in the family. Ana was wounded, and grieving. An account that was open needed closing.

Finally, the doors of the clinic swung open to reveal a person pushing a wheel chair out to the curb. Waiting a few seconds for a shiny pickup to clear the other end of the parking lot, he dropped the pod down in a dark corner and eased it to within 100 feet of the clinic, hovering just off the pavement. Matt met him in front of a darkened Mexican restaurant and transferred the sleeping Ana to a back seat.

As Matt hurried to return the wheel chair, Coombs heard the unmistakable sounds of a bottle clinking and rolling on a hard surface. Not more than ten feet away, a grizzled old man in ragged jeans and dirty t-shirt laboriously pulled himself to his feet from behind some ornamental bushes in planters on the sidewalk. He staggered closer and squinted at the pod with great effort. His mouth hung open as he took it in from bow to stern.

"¿'Onde 'stán las llantas?" he croaked.

Although garbled, Coombs understood the old fellow wanted to know where the tires were. A reasonable request: the pod did resemble an SUV, with the notable exception of tires. Why not add to his confusion?

"Mañana," he replied to the man.

"¿Q...q...qué?"

"¡Arriba!" Coombs repeated, more loudly.

The man tilted his head back and peered unsteadily at the open hatch extending over him like a giant wing. Just as Matt walked up the man reached out for the bush to steady himself and fell over the planter in a heap. Matt pulled him to his feet, brushed him off, and turned him toward the lighted doors of the clinic a short distance away.

"Allá, tío. Véte allá. Le ayudarán. Vaya con Diós, tío." ("There, uncle, go over there. They'll help you. Go with God, uncle.")

By the time the man gazed vaguely in the direction of the clinic and turned back to the pod, stumbling over the planter again, Matt had hopped inside and Coombs was raising it into the darkness.

"You reckon our cover is blown?" Matt chuckled.

"For sure. Soon as he calls the FBI, we're done for. What's the word on Ana?"

"I know the doc—good guy. He's in his second year with the foundation. We paid his way through med school in return for three years' service. He confirmed pretty much what that Thoman whatchamacallit found. She's dehydrated and anemic. Not enough to require a hospital stay, but she needs rest and lots of fluids. He gave me a prescription for an antibiotic. You said that doctor device supplied that so I don't know if she still needs the antibiotic. Maybe we can ask Hleo."

"Good idea. Let's get this thing to altitude and call him. He'll have to set the course to your place anyway."

"We'll have her home in half an hour. Man, oh man, will that be fine. I think I'll call the twins first."

"Yeah, good. That'll make their day." He yawned. "It'll make the day for all of us."

Forty minutes later, Coombs relinquished the pilot's seat to Matt for the final descent, taking the back seat next to Ana. Matt knew where they were setting down; Coombs had no idea. Ana, next to him now, was still sedated. She mumbled softly, but beyond the word "caldo" ("soup"), he couldn't tell what she was saying. He rubbed her hands.

"Almost home, shipmate."

Matt eased the pod down slowly until Coombs felt it settle gently to earth. As soon as the hatch opened, the biggest, scariest goddamn cat Coombs had ever seen outside of a zoo leaped in. It looked like a cross between a lynx and a mountain lion. Its ears were laid back, eyes burning, and it hissed at him.

"Jesus Christ!" said Coombs, automatically reaching for his pistol, which he had taken off earlier.

"Easy," Matt said. "That's Clio's cat. She won't hurt you. She hisses all the time."

"Damn!" Coombs whispered, keeping an eye on it. "Nice kitty, kitty."

Clio and Julio hopped in after it, with eyes only for their sleepy mother. Matt eased around them, picked her up, and carried her off into the darkness. Clio followed, one hand on her cat and the other on her mother's ankle. Two large dogs went with them. The cat was making strange trilling sounds.

Coombs, happy to be on solid ground and to have escaped a mauling, watched them disappear. Julio stayed.

"Thank you, Mr. Coombs."

"Huh?"

"Thank you for bringing Mom home safe."

"Oh. You're welcome, Julio. It was my pleasure."

Gratifying! No one had ever thanked him when he was a Seal.

"I'll show you the way to the house."

"Good. Let me grab some of this stuff."

With Julio's help it took only two trips to haul Matt's guns, the ice chest, blankets, clothes, and other baggage to the laundry room. Julio led him to the living room, where Ana, seated on a couch and wrapped in a blanket, was sipping something hot from a cup, surrounded by her family and three cats, two normal cats and the scary one. No one seemed the least bothered by it.

"Everyone OK?" Coombs asked.

"I think so," Matt answered. "Have a seat, Rob. How about something to eat?"

"Midrats," Ana said quietly, with a tiny smile.

Coombs laughed. Seeing Matt's confusion, he explained, "Navy phrase. Means 'midnight rations.' We had them on our big expedition four years ago. No, thanks—I need to be going."

"Have some coffee, at least. It's been a long night."

"Well, OK. Thanks."

He spent fifteen happy minutes watching a drowsy Ana drink soup, hug her children, and stroke her cats. He was dying to ask about the mountain lion with the spectacular ears but it didn't seem a good time. Finally, Ana agreed to take a hot shower and go to bed. Coombs made his farewells and headed out the way he had entered. Clio tagged along.

"Thank you, Mr. Coombs," she said.

"Glad to help," he replied.

"Where are you going?"

"I don't know, exactly. Hleo has something he wants me to do."

She led him to the laundry room and looked in the ice chest.

"Why don't you take this food? And the orange juice and milk? I'm sure you're hungry. We have another ice chest."

"That's very thoughtful, Clio. I think I'll do that. Thank you."

"I'll take you to the pod. It's dark out there."

Ten minutes later he once again was hovering at 500 feet. The lights of a decent-sized city were visible several miles away. He pulled out his GPS unit and pressed several buttons: he was south of Las Cruces, New Mexico—probably as good a place as any for Ana Darcy to live near. Modest little house they had there—nice. Sweet twins, a good bit bigger than when he'd last seen them. Both thanked him for his services, and one had seen to it that he'd taken some food away with him. How many kids would have done that?

Better call Hleo and work a few things out. Dammit, he was getting sleepy. He keyed the radio, if that's what it was. It worked like a radio, at least. Who the hell knew what it was?

"Are you there, Counselor?"

"I am here, Chief."

"Our friend is home. When I left she had eaten and was headed to bed. Her family is happy and well."

"Excellent news. My prayers have been answered. On behalf of the people of Thomo as well as myself, I thank you, Chief Coombs."

Everybody was thanking him.

"It was an honor to be of service, sir. Counselor, I have had a long day. I am eager to learn what you have found out about our adversary, but if it can wait until I have had a little sleep, I will be better able to focus."

"Certainly, Chief. I think you will be pleased with the developments. There may be opportunities that appeal to you."

"I look forward to it, Counselor. Now, sir, could I turn the navigation of this vehicle over to you? I would like to be in Miami before dawn, but what route I take to get there, and at what speed, I leave to you."

"I have control of all the pod's flight control systems. Sleep well, Chief."

Coombs looked at his watch: 3:15 am. Midrats were overdue. He reached for the ice chest and selected a sandwich. He felt the pod rise and move forward.

This was the first moment to himself since he got out of bed in Huánuco 27 hours ago. It had been an eventful day. He'd rescued Ana, but had to kill two men doing it. There'd been no choice and he'd do it again under the same circumstances, but he still wished it hadn't been necessary. It was necessary, though, just like it had been necessary for Ana to dump three in the river. Damn it, but there was no shortage of sons of bitches in the world. No matter what he did there would always be an endless supply, but at least one remained that he was going to try to remove. His love for Ana and her family left little choice. They needed to be free of that particular son of a bitch, at least.

The carton of orange juice was half full...or was it half empty? He yawned, uncapped it, and took a big slug. Gotta call Michelle, middle of the night or not. Check the cell phone battery—still three-quarters charged. It rang and rang. Finally, she answered.

"Michelle? This is Rob. Sorry to...."

"Rob! Oh, God! Rob! Oh, Rob, how is Ana? Is there any news?"

"There is. She's all right. She was found, and she's back with her family."

"Oh!"

After a series of muffled bumps, Michelle spoke again, hyperventilating.

"Oh, thank God, Rob! We were so worried. What...how...was she...oh, God...."

"Don't worry about that now, girl. I'll be in Miami this afternoon. Clear a spot in your schedule and I'll give you a full report, OK? But let's do it privately. The world probably thinks Ana's dead, and I don't know how she might want to handle that yet. Don't even tell your mother, until Ana says it's all right, OK?"

More sniffling. She was crying or coughing, possibly both.

"Oh, Rob, Rob. Such wonderful news. No, I won't tell Mom, not until Ana says to. Oh, Rob, of course I'll see you tonight. I can't wait. And Rob...thanks, Rob."

By 4:00 pm that afternoon, Coombs had had some welcome shuteye, a planning session with Hleo which got his old Seal instincts humming again, rented a car, and gone shopping. The company charge card now had $12,000 billed to it that he would have to explain to Darlene Pizzoli, his boss at World Security, but later. The Thomans were providing his transportation around the globe, at least.

Fresh clothes were the least of the purchases. The sedan rolled smoothly down the interstate thanks partly to 400 pounds of goodies piled in the trunk. He hated cars. Better to have chosen a pickup, but that would have left the new gear exposed to view, not a good idea. The oddest stop was at an antique dealer that Hleo had made him an appointment with. That purchase alone accounted for $3,500.

The exit was just ahead. He had no idea why Hleo had wanted him to meet Michelle at her mother's house, nor how he had known her mother was in Houston on business, but that was fine with him. The main thing was that it would be private.

Down a sculpted boulevard, left onto a smaller artery...glimpses of inlets, rows of sailboat masts, turn right down a residential street...and there it was, an imposing two-story home at the end of a circle. He parked in the driveway and rang the bell. It was raining lightly.

Michelle was in his arms less than two seconds after the door opened.

He patted her back gently. Her hair tickled his nose.

"It's OK, girl. It's over. She's all right."

"I'm sorry, Rob," she said, "I know. I can't help it. I felt so horrible all week. I was just sure she was...was...."

"I was too. But she's tough, Michelle. She had a hard time, but she's real tough. Tough and lucky."

"Oh, me. Come in, Rob. I have to hear it all. Something to drink?"

"Yeah, thanks. Anything with caffeine. Hot is good, too."

He sat at the kitchen table watching her make coffee. Outside the sliding glass doors, wet patio furniture punctuated a view of a lush lawn sloping to a narrow waterway. She looked good even without makeup and her face slightly puffy from worry. She'd cut her hair in a page boy, setting off her features nicely. She was pretty like a sparrow, not flashy but sweet, with intelligent eyes and precise lips. He loved the little lines on either side of her mouth when she smiled.

It took two cups of coffee to recount the week's activities. Her occasional questions revealed a lawyer's logical mind. By the time she said, "Do you think it was...?" he completed the sentence for her.

"...the same guy we ran into in Russia? Yeah, I think it was. Hleo thinks so too. He has about thirty pieces of circumstantial evidence that point right at him. There's little doubt."

"Well, then...."

"Yes. I know. Now, listen to me, Michelle. Four years ago, at the Williams' ranch in west Texas, I told you I wasn't a very nice guy. You thought I was kidding, but I wasn't. I'm going to find that guy and take him out. Hleo is going to help. What do you think about that?"

She dropped her eyes to the table. She wadded up her napkin. Finally she whispered.

"I don't know, Rob. Ana wouldn't want that."

He kept his voice soft.

"Maybe, maybe not. She already gave him a second chance, and we know what he did with it: helicopters and a dozen goons. There's every reason to think he'll try again."

She sniffled.

"She just wouldn't want that. I'm sure of it."

"OK; granted. Probably not. But I didn't quite tell you everything, Michelle."

He hesitated.

"Michelle, Ana was pregnant. She had a miscarriage sometime after she dived into that river."

Michelle began crying for real. Coombs handed her his napkin and gave her a minute.

"It's a tough situation, Michelle. Matt and I took her home early this morning. I saw their house, their twins, their pets. It's a simple little place, very peaceful. I don't want her to go through life worrying that that guy might find her again and finish what he started. You're probably right that Ana wouldn't want him stopped permanently. That's why I'm not going to tell her."

She stopped dabbing her eyes.

"Then...then why are you telling me?"

"Because I could use your help. Nothing dangerous or risky. I just need some support for what I'm going to do."

"Me? Why me?"

"Because you know Ana. Because you care about her. Because you don't need to be filled in on the background behind this. Because you can keep Ana's secrets. I could get someone from World Security to go along, but I couldn't tell him much about what we were doing. It'd just be another job to him. If it makes any difference, Hleo suggested I ask you."

"What would I do?"

"Basically, be the driver. There are some things Hleo can't do from the moon, things that take an on-scene person's perception. They're not difficult and they're not dangerous. And besides, I'd like your company."

A tear started down her cheek. She looked miserable. Coombs felt rotten.

"Look, it's OK if you don't want anything to do with this. But it's what I do. It's what the special forces do. It isn't all ugly, but some of it is, even though we do it for the best of reasons. I'm sorry, girl. I've felt drawn to you for a long time, but you didn't really know me. I'm going to do it for Ana's sake, but don't worry about it. I'll get me a driver."

She looked at his hands, spread out on the table on either side of the coffee mug. They were nice hands, with strong, square fingers. More tears rolled down her cheeks.

"So...so that's why you stayed in New York...never called. You thought I thought...."

"That's what I am," he interrupted. "I'm just a thug, a truck driving, country music loving, sneaking-around bomb-handling thug."

After a second, she reached across the table and laid her hands on his.

"Oh, Rob. Silly me. Silly you. I still think you're a nice guy. Actually, I think you're a great guy."

His eyes on hers, he turned his hands over slowly and pressed her fingers.

She sniffled and swallowed.

"I'll be your driver. Gladly."

He eased her right hand into his right hand in a handshake and covered both with his left. He smiled.

"Are you still packed for the Bahamas?"

"Uh-huh."

"That should do. We're going to a similar spot. But I still owe you a trip to Nassau."

"Just be careful on this trip, please."

"Piece of cake. It won't be a vacation, but I promise you it'll be an adventure you'll never forget."

"When do we leave?"

"Soon. Just after dark, in about..." he rotated both their hands to glance at his watch, "...an hour."

"An hour! It takes an hour to get to the airport!"

"We ain't goin' to no stinkin' airport. Get your things together. Bring some food that'll keep in an ice chest. And write a note to your mom. Leave her these keys and tell her you'll be back for the car in a few days."

"Wait! We're not leaving in your car?"

"Nope. Are you ready to rumble?"

She looked doubtful. He stood, took her hand, and she stood. He opened his arms and she leaned into him.

"Thanks, girl friend. Can I call you girl friend now?"

"For a little while."

"Probation? OK, I'll try to keep fooling you."

"You've been doing it for years."

She had a lot of guts to trust him on this. He kissed her, carefully.

Her complexion was lovely up close. He kissed her again.

"All right. Grab your stuff while I call Hleo. You'll do fine. Girl friend."

Twenty minutes later they were standing under the awning over the back patio, out of the rain. Michelle had a small suitcase and a plastic bag of edibles at her feet. Coombs' rental car had been backed to the end of the driveway.

"What are we waiting for?"

"Our ride."

"Here? What? A helicopter?"

"No. Be patient."

A half moon produced only a feeble gray light beneath the clouds. With the patio light off they could barely see lights across the waterway. They stood there, his arm on her shoulder.

"This is crazy," she said after several minutes.

"Presto!"

"Huh?"

"Look out there."

He nodded toward the waterway. A hump had appeared in the middle. It grew larger, shedding water. It looked like a surfacing whale. Michelle clutched his arm. He patted her shoulder.

"What *is* that?" she whispered.

"Just watch."

The thing, gray like the night, floated in the water.

"We're going in a submarine?"

Then it was floating *above* the water, one foot, two, three feet. It drifted toward them and stopped midway between the patio and the water line. They heard two soft mechanical crunches and a doorway opened out of it, rising into the rain.

"Oh, my god!"

"C'mon, let's go. Get in. I'll get my stuff out of the car. Look around, but don't touch anything. Sit in front."

"Oh, my god!"

Coombs popped the trunk and began lugging packages to the pod. Some were heavy. Finally everything was in. He locked the car, climbed in the pod, and began securing the equipment.

"Is this Thoman? It's like the Thoman shuttle, only it's tiny!"

"Couldn't be ours," he replied. "We're not smart enough. It's the escape pod from Ana's original moon station. It's how she came here in the first place. Didn't you ever wonder about that?"

"I thought she burned it."

"So she fibbed a little. Lucky for us. Only about six people know it exists. It's another of Ana's little secrets. This is how we went to Sedlakia four years ago. This is how Matt rescued us from a mountain top in Peru and got her back home."

He double checked to make sure no gear would come loose and eased into the other front seat.

"It's powered by gravity just like their other vessels. Ask me no questions about that, but it flies like a dream."

"I flew to the moon and back in the shuttle, but it was huge. This is like a sports car!"

"Your lucky day, girl friend. Before we get where we're going I'll show you how to fly it. It's about like driving a car."

"Oh, my!"

She turned in her seat to look at the wet grass outside before Coombs shut the hatch. He pressed a button on the instrument panel.

"Coombs here, Counselor."

In ten seconds the reply came.

"Did it arrive accurately, Chief Coombs?"

"Yes sir, it did, exactly right. Ms. Stratemeyer and I are ready to go. It's cloudy and misty here tonight, Counselor. If you can determine that the skies are free of aircraft, I think we can set a conventional course."

"I see no problem, Chief. Departure in thirty seconds."

Michelle leaned forward and looked through the windshield. It was so weird. Here they were floating two feet off the ground and she could see the next door neighbor's bedroom lights through the fence that separated their property. Across the waterway, several small boats bobbed gently at their moorings. The light at the end of the pier was blurry from the raindrops sliding down the windshield.

With no warning, the pod began moving upward. Acceleration pressed her back in her seat. Her stomach struggled to keep up. She grabbed Coombs' arm.

"Airborne, girl friend! Get ready for the ride of your life!"

Chapter 15

Matt had his limits as a cook. He had a small repertoire of basic dishes and he could follow a recipe, but he seldom struck out on his own. This noon meal would be one of the exceptions. On her second day back, Ana still wasn't eating as eagerly as she had before, perhaps due to the shock her system had undergone, but she would willingly eat soup. He would make her a soup to die for, a soup that would put the fire back in her eyes and meat on her bones.

Fact 1: she loved his family's recipe for frijoles.

Fact 2: he had a family-size container of them in the refrigerator.

Conclusion: turn them into soup!

First, he stepped through the living room to look out to the patio. Ana and Abuelita were sitting on a bench in the shade, chatting quietly. That was good. Ana hadn't wanted to talk to him about the miscarriage. That worried him. She hadn't even wanted to call her sister Ianthe, which Matt found odd. Usually, though, Ana knew what she was doing. Maybe Abuelita was helping her sort out her thoughts. Whatever the case, they had to eat. It was time to get cooking.

He dumped half the beans and bean juice into the blender, blended them smooth, and poured the slurry into a large saucepan. He did the same with the second half. The thick liquid smelled heavenly of oregano and comino. Next, fry eight slices of bacon, cut them up, and dump them in too. Yum! Now, add enough milk to produce a slightly more soupy consistency. Taste. Savory! He put the saucepan over low heat and looked in the fridge.

Aha! Mozzarella, to grate into the hot bowls of soup! Two avocados. ¡Simón! Delicious, and loaded with calories. He could make guacamole while the soup heated. There was a bag of tortilla chips in the pantry—good to crumble into the soup, with the grated cheese on top. Lunch was coming together. While peeling the avocados, he thought ahead to fruit and dessert: cantaloupe, and a blob of caramel chocolate ice cream to cool the palate. Ana would love it! Perfecto!

When the guacamole was finished he covered the bowl and set it in the fridge and checked the soup. Tiny bubbles were appearing around the edges of the pan. Stir. Taste. ¡Allí, madre! He turned the heat down a little more and headed to the patio.

It was almost hot outside, but the blinding desert heat seldom penetrated the cottonwoods along the river. Abuelita looked comfortable in a deep green short-sleeved house dress. She surely loved bright colors. Ana had on white shorts and a maroon t-shirt bearing the logo "Pipe Dreams" over a graphic representation of a row of organ pipes. The faithful Eleanor lay in the grass at her feet. He pulled up a plastic chair and sat down.

"¿Cómo vamos?" he asked ("How we doin'?").

"Hola, nieto," was all Abuelita said.

Ana said nothing. She was combing her toes slowly through Eleanor's fur. The tendons in her foot stood out on the backstrokes.

"Eleanor's not well," she said.

"I know," he replied. "Clio pointed that out last week. She hasn't been eating well. She just sits around. While you were gone we took her to the vet for some tests. I'll call after lunch and see if the results are in."

"I thought you were going to Cloudcroft this afternoon," said Abuelita.

"That's tomorrow afternoon, to interview some applicants for Dr. Sandoval's job. But I don't have to go, wife. I'd rather stay with you anyway."

"No, that's OK. Dr. Sandoval is leaving soon. We need a good person to replace him. Go ahead and go."

"Why don't you come along? It's a beautiful drive, past White Sands and up into the forest. We can buy some fresh cherry juice! We'll be back by dark."

"Well, I might. We could ask the twins. Would you like to go, Abuelita?"

"No, gracias, mija. I've been feeling lazy lately."

"Julio's working on something in Dr. Jameson's lab this week," Matt said, "but Clio might go with us."

Ana rubbed Eleanor's chin gently with a toe. The cat didn't budge. Her eyes were closed.

"She might," Ana replied after a minute. "She said there's a famous yerbería there somewhere. She could visit it and look at their herbs."

"Great. You all can shop while I'm in my meeting. I'll go ask her. She's probably in her workshop with Raisin. It's time for lunch anyway. You two head to the table and get ready for un caldazo de veras!"

Viktor Reznik was reasonably certain that Oleg would not be terribly upset over the loss of so many of his highly trained intervention squad. If Oleg had any regard for human life, Viktor had yet to detect it. As the person with direct responsibility for the squad, however, Viktor regretted it deeply. He'd always preferred to not stir up trouble needlessly, but hunting this woman, ancient Sedlakian queen or not, had produced trouble aplenty—over half the squad had not returned and none of those who had could say for sure what had happened.

The remainders of the second team had reported what little they knew: two men killed on the bridge, three more missing, presumably lost to the river, and the two leaders, the fierce Lebedev and the even fiercer Afrim the Assassin, shot to death. The woman, even if she had survived as the intercepted phone call indicated she had, could not have done that. Her bodyguard, the one who fought back so bravely on the bridge, might have, but it seemed unlikely. The second team had scoured the area for days and found nothing. He prayed Oleg would not demand a recitation of all the gory details.

He also prayed he would survive his trip to Oleg's yacht. He almost longed for that wretched little helicopter, as the hired launch slapped through the wind-driven waves to the outer harbor where the deep blue Galaxie lay anchored, serene in its lofty superiority to the tinier vessels present.

To his immense surprise, once he got aboard, the afternoon passed in increasing delight, thanks partly to several mojitos, but mostly to the idle sun-bunnies on the fantail, with whom he chatted gaily on matters of no consequence. Oleg was off in the ship's gig with their husbands and boy friends, diving for archaeological piffle. For a few hours, Viktor actually vacationed in the sun.

But it couldn't last. The gig returned and was unloaded. The diving gear was washed down, cleaned, oiled, and put away, the men went to shower, the women to dress, if one could call what few clothes they donned "dress," and supper was served. Captain Oleg was in an expansive mood, fully enjoying his role as über host. Viktor didn't get in a private word with him until hours later, back on the fantail. As they leaned on the rail, looking at the harbor lights and holding their snifters of cognac over the water lapping at the hull, he spoke in a low voice.

"She's alive. I can feel it. Find her, Mishka. No matter how long it takes. Find her."

A seagull squawked overhead. Viktor watched the lighthouse flash on the promontory across the harbor.

"I will," he said.

They were joined by a sunburned man with a greasy smile, a three-day growth of beard, and a champagne flute in his hand. Oleg nodded at him and spoke to Viktor.

"Two more days of diving! Join us, Viktor!"

Viktor took a sip of his cognac.

"Alas, I am no diver," he responded. "I find things on land."

"So you do," Oleg replied, "so you do."

Coombs had had his first good night's sleep in days. As soon as they had reached cruising altitude after leaving Miami, he introduced an eager Michelle to the basics of the pod, but his continual yawning led her to relent and they both went to sleep, leaving Hleo to navigate them safely over the Atlantic. He awoke at 4:00 am feeling well rested. Michelle still slumbered, her seat reclined back. He raised his own to a comfortable sitting position and studied the instruments. He'd never known what they were all for, but he remembered Ana using the small screen in the middle to visualize what was beneath them. There were four buttons underneath it, and three rotary switches. One of the buttons was green. He pressed it.

The screen that came up didn't resemble the black and white images he remembered. The display was pale blue. White lines ran all over it. He studied it a minute. It was a map of some kind. On a hunch he turned one of the rotary switches. The display darkened. He turned the next one and the image started to rotate. He turned it 90º, 90º more, and another 90º, and it became clear: it was the Mediterranean—there was the boot of Italy kicking Sicily, with the coast of Tunisia at the bottom. A yellow dot blinked over the space between Sicily and Tunisia. That must be the pod. He watched the dot several minutes. It was moving east southeast. Hleo was keeping them over water. They were headed toward the Greek islands. He tried the third rotary switch. The display zoomed toward the center. Good! Now he knew where they were and how to zero in on the destination.

He carefully wormed past Michelle and between the rear seats to the small lavatory aft and relieved himself. Turning on the water in the tiny sink, he was struck by a sudden thought and turned the water off to ponder. The pod was made to operate in space, where there was no gravity. Astronauts in the space station had to contain all water to keep it from floating around the cabin in droplets, but this was a conventional sink. The pod obviously made its own gravity. He'd never realized that. What a wonderful machine. He'd damn well better be careful with it.

Michelle was barely aware that Coombs had moved aft. When she heard the lavatory door click shut she blinked and stretched and raised her seat to look around. It was pitch black outside. Inside it was almost completely quiet, the only sound a faint hiss, perhaps from their speedy passage through the atmosphere, and a subliminal deep vibration, probably from the propulsion system. The most noticeable thing within sight was the small display screen on the instrument panel: a map or chart of some kind. She recognized the southern end of Italy, which any school kid would recognize, or should. Rob had told her they were headed for the "Med," and that was where they seemed to be after only six hours sleep or so.

Why was she here? Basically, she was was here because she was going to help Rob kill someone. Her throat tightened at the thought. She wanted to believe Rob and Hleo knew what they were doing. There was no doubt they were devoted to Ana. The man they were after had tried to kill Ana twice. He had money and capable, dangerous people working for him, and both Rob and Hleo were sure he would keep trying. But it was also true that Ana wouldn't endorse what they were going to do and she wasn't at all sure herself. Blast it, she was a lawyer. Would she kill a person to keep him from murdering Ana? The lawyer in her said if that someone were in the act, yes, she would. But if he were merely walking down the beach, would she then? That was an entirely different legal situation.

Was she doing this because of Rob? He had been wary of her falling for him, but he wasn't a thug, in spite of what he said. He was more a soldier, even though he was no longer in the military. She'd known him four or five years and worked with him several times. He was a good man: considerate, moderate in his habits, gentle, courageous, decisive, and yes, admit it, handsome, a good dancer, and he liked her. Plus there was that dimple in his chin.

But those were not sufficient reasons for her to become an accessory to murder. If this mission caused her to think differently about Rob, then so be it. She was doing this for Ana, friend of Earth and its people, and her personal friend and mentor from another planet.

The lavatory door clicked open.

"Hey. Mornin'," he said. As he eased past he squeezed her shoulder lightly. "How you feel?"

"Good. I slept better than I thought I would. I see we're over the Med. What's the plan?"

"We're headed for the Greek islands, roughly in this area." He tapped the right side of the screen. "We'll set up a base and I'll reconnoiter and take action if feasible. Then we're gone, easy as that."

"It can't be that simple."

"It never is. That Peruvian episode is a particularly bad example. First thing to do is check in with Hleo. Shall we?"

She nodded and he switched on the radio.

"Chief Coombs here, Counselor. I see we're approaching our destination. Would you happen to have a weather report, sir?"

"I would, Chief," Hleo answered, after the ten second delay. "No storm systems are expected for the next 36 hours, though there may be isolated rain showers. Winds will vary from zero to twenty knots. Currents in the area will be from three knots to zero depending on the tides. At this time, an hour before sunrise, marine weather stations report light sea fog."

"That's good news, Counselor. If possible, I'd like to find a small island or shoal in an isolated area just at sunrise, to allow Ms. Stratemeyer an opportunity to practice maneuvering the pod at low altitude."

Coombs winked at Michelle.

"I see several possibilities, Chief. However, all are less than 1000 meters from populated coastline. The fog may provide cover. You should make the final visual determination before your approach. One more thing, Chief. All these islands are densely populated. I have been unable to locate any sufficiently isolated beach areas which might serve as a land base for the pod. You may decide the matter for yourself, but if necessary the pod can remain out of sight at altitude, and make a water pickup when required. I suggest that for the moment you take advantage of the dim light and fog to conduct your training."

"Will do, Counselor. Thank you, sir. Coombs out."

He turned down the radio and checked the display screen.

"Looks like we're nearly there. Hleo told me the target's yacht was moored in the outer harbor at Paros. That's this island here. See? There's the two harbors, inner and outer. There's the strait between Paros and the island to the west."

He studied the screen a few seconds and zoomed in a bit.

"OK, the yellow blinking dot is us. This green one would be the yacht, and this one," he pointed at a dot near the coast of the island next to Paros, "must be the location of the wreck they're diving on. That'd be some distance from the yacht, a pretty good boat ride in open water."

As they watched, two dots popped up close together off the northern point of the adjacent island.

"Hleo did that, I bet. Those would be the sand bars where we can practice," he said. "OK, let's drop down slowly and see how the fog looks. All we need is ten or fifteen minutes for you to catch on to handling this thing in close quarters. I promise you, it's easy. You'll get the hang right away. Ready?"

Michelle resisted swallowing even though her mouth was dry. She nodded.

"OK, here we go. Easy does it!"

Ana said little on the way to the vet clinic. Eleanor was lying on her travel bag in Ana's lap, eyes shut. The cat's fur was long and extravagant as ever, though it no longer glowed in the sunlight. It looked dry. Matt stroked her at a red light and felt her side vibrating.

"She's purring," he said.

Ana nodded.

"Cats purr when they're happy. Also when they're hurt. Or afraid."

Ana carried her into the clinic in her arms, not bothering with the bag.

Dr. Susan Franklin was a sweet-faced woman of 50 or so with pale blue eyes and graying hair neatly braided down both sides of her head. After a friendly greeting and a glance at some papers on a clipboard she turned to the examining table.

"Hello, Eleanor," she said softly. "How we doin', girl?"

She felt expertly down the cat's body, looked into her eyes and ears and mouth, and checked her temperature. The cat meowed briefly but otherwise registered nothing.

"Eleanor's an elderly girl," she said to Ana. "Do you know how old?"

Ana shook her head.

"She was a stray. At least fifteen. Maybe seventeen."

"Well, she's a sick kitty. We've run all the tests we can do or send off, but the results were negative. Typically, older cats suffer from hyperthyroidism, kidney disease, or even leukemia. The blood test usually catches leukemia but it didn't this time. Sometimes the test is wrong, though. We could do that one again. Barring that, the only other recourse would be to send her to the veterinary school at Sul Ross State University or even Texas A&M University, both in Texas. They can diagnose and treat things we can't. But," she hesitated, "their treatments are generally experimental, and often hard on the animal, especially an elderly one. There's no guarantee. And it's very expensive."

"You must have a guess what she has, doc," Matt said. "What do you think?"

"Neoplasia, most likely."

"What's that?"

"It means 'new growth.' Basically, cancer."

"So the experimental treatments would be...?"

"Probably chemotherapy. And radiation. Those are hard on people and even harder on a small animal. And an older animal, well, an older animal might not survive it."

"What are our other choices?"

"She doesn't seem to be in too much pain now. You could just wait." The doc smoothed the cat's fur. "She's not eating and not grooming herself. If she doesn't start eating, she'll continue to decline. The pain may increase but it may not. You could wait and see."

Matt moved his arm around Ana's waist. He went on.

"If the chemo and stuff stops the cancer, what kind of life would she have afterward?"

"I don't want to mislead you. The odds against it working are long. But if it does, it takes a lot out of them. A younger cat would have greater powers of recuperation. An older one, well, she wouldn't be like she was."

Matt knew the answer to his next question but he asked it anyway.

"Is there anything else?"

"Yes. We can give her an injection. She'll simply go to sleep...."

They thought about that a few moments.

"She's had a good life," Ana said softly. "I don't want her to suffer any more."

"I don't either," said Matt.

"What we do is inject a barbiturate into the cephalic vein in a front leg. It won't hurt her at all. Would you like some time to think about it?"

Ana shook her head.

"No. I'm sure. Eleanor has already decided."

"You can be present if you wish, or not."

Matt felt sure Ana would want to be elsewhere, but he was wrong.

"I want to be here." She sniffled. "Eleanor would do the same. For me."

The doc left to prepare the injection. Matt thought about that. He felt himself blinking. He pulled Ana a little closer. She bent over the still form of Eleanor and whispered something. It sounded like Luvit, her native language. He had no idea what she was saying.

The doctor returned, administered the shot quickly, and left them alone.

With his free hand, Matt pulled out his handkerchief and blotted his eyes. Ana laid her hands on Eleanor, stroking her gently under a jaw with a finger. They stayed that way for what seemed a long time. Finally Ana set her cheek to Eleanor's head. After a few moments she straightened up.

"She's not purring any more. She's gone."

Matt could tell. She was just a furry little body, nothing more. Something had gone out of her. He wanted to cry. He wanted Ana to cry. He wanted to hug her. Her eyes were glistening, but she remained composed.

"You can call the doctor," she said, and sniffled again.

"OK," he said.

He kissed her temple. Sniffing himself, he went to search her out.

Ten minutes later he held the car door for Ana, cradling a small bundle in her arms. Once on the highway, still shaken, he tried desperately to think of something non-stupid to say. He reached for her hand.

"That was peaceful."

She nodded, looking at nothing in particular.

"What did you say to Eleanor?"

"I don't know the English word. It's a poem. It's traditional. From a song. A farewell song."

He realized he knew next to nothing about Thoman customs regarding death, or pets, or lots of things. He knew the Thomans' early existence had been perilous, and many had died. They still tended to have large families. Their whole society nurtured life in general, all life. Was the discussion of death to be avoided? Was that why Ana refused to say much about her miscarriage? Too often he had simply assumed that she had adopted the ways of his society in their entirety, but upon reflection that was unlikely, and maybe impossible. So which of her customs did he need to be aware of now, and how should he deal with them?

"She was such a great cat," he said, at a loss but plunging ahead. "I remember when I was waiting for you to return from the South Pole. I didn't know where you'd been or how you you'd got there or would come back. I thought you might drive up in a taxi. I was in the yard looking up and down the highway when I noticed Eleanor inside on a window sill. She was looking straight up, and that was where you were, of course: overhead, in the pod. Eleanor knew."

No response.

"I don't know if I ever told you, but she knew whenever you were on television. Like when you addressed the United Nations General Assembly, she hopped up on the couch and watched your speech with me."

Still no response. A block later, he added, "Remember when I went to your harpsichord lesson once? Eleanor went along, in her bag. She sat on the bench next to you. Dr. Kirkpatrick wasn't even surprised. And remember those kids who were petting her while you waited for me at the bus stop by the university? Nothing ever bothered her, did it?"

Another half block went by.

"No," she said. He could barely hear her. "Eleanor was a good friend."

Michelle was bored and disgusted and she blamed herself. She'd never thought to bring anything to read, or even her iPod. She'd been cooped up all afternoon with little else to do but think, and while that had its benefits, they were fading fast. She should have foreseen there'd be long periods of time while Rob was off reconnoitering and she was waiting for him. But how could she have known?

Rob must have been on operations like this plenty of times, but this was her first. The pacing was strange, with moments of great excitement amid long spells of utter boredom. Their departure—her first flight in the pod—had been thrilling, as had learning the basics of operating it. Then she had slept peacefully during the flight across the Atlantic, only to be nearly petrified to practice handling the pod close to the ground. Fortunately, it turned out to be as easy as Rob had said it would be. It was about like driving an electric golf cart, if that golf cart could maneuver in three dimensions instead of just two.

Then Rob had scouted for a place to park the pod. He'd come up with an idea she'd never have thought of. From the air, as the fog thinned, it was obvious both islands had no unpopulated areas. It seemed to her there was no place set up a base on land at all. But Rob noticed that there were steep cliffs at several points facing the strait between the two islands, cliffs perhaps 200 feet high. Several of them seemed to be below private property, with elaborate houses set on large plots of land where they could overlook the strait. Coombs noticed that the cliffs were extremely rocky, with piles of large, rounded boulders resting on each other. He thought it extremely unlikely that anyone in one of the big houses would pay much attention to the all-too-familiar rocks below. If anyone on one of those estates looked east, it would be to scan the waterway. Why not "park" the pod among those boulders? The pod was a dirty, brownish black, not unlike the rocks, and it had no sharp corners to attract the eye.

But first, before the fog lifted, he had her hold the pod on the narrow beach while he unloaded his gear. She recognized some of it—scuba tanks, fins, mask—but several other items were new to her.

"What's that?" she said, as Coombs pulled a cylindrical object out of a box. It was a little wider than one of the oxygen tanks, and twice as long.

"It's a scooter."

"A what?"

"An underwater scooter. I'll show you."

He removed two heavy, car-type batteries from the pod, opened a cover in the scooter, and installed them.

"Here. Watch this."

He put a hand on the handle at one end and pushed a button. A propeller at the other end began whirring inside its shroud.

"See? It'll pull me through the water, three or four miles or so."

"Cool! And what's that?"

He was strapping a long plastic tube to the scooter.

"A self-defense item. Hleo thinks I need it."

He tucked all the gear behind some smaller rocks.

"OK; that's done. Let's get the pod in place and start watching."

Coombs found a spot less than half way up the cliff where the pod could rest between two boulders, one a little bigger, and the other a little smaller, than the pod, where they sat and chatted and took turns keeping an eye on the strait below them.

It was a lovely summer morning and the strait had more traffic than Michelle expected: fishing boats, several small freighters, three cabin cruisers, and two odd-looking sailboats. Rob said they should look for a "captain's gig," the kind of snazzy speedboat that would be worthy of being carried on a super-yacht.

An hour and a half later, he spotted a good candidate: a small, streamlined craft traveling fast in the right direction, bouncing over the swells, leaving a foamy wake behind.

"That's it," Coombs said.

"How can you tell? Have you seen it before?"

"Nope. Hleo said the guy's yacht is dark blue. That boat is dark blue. Makes sense they'd match. No other dark blue boats out there that I see. Gotta be it."

They watched it pass below them to their right. There were four people in it.

"Aren't you going to go after it?"

"No hurry. The spot they're headed to is about a mile south from here. They'll stay there until late afternoon at least. That is, if Hleo's green dot is correctly positioned. We'll just have to see."

They watched until the boat disappeared around the point of the next promontory.

"Well," said Coombs, "what say we have a little lunch? I'll give it an hour to settle, like my momma said, and then head over there and see what's what."

Two hours later, Coombs had scootered up the coast far enough to realize Hleo's coordinates were off, unfortunately. Hleo had placed the dive site one mile away, but it was more like two. Moreover, he had been heading against the tidal current, and the tide was slowing, meaning it would reverse soon and the trip back would also be against the tide. The charge indicator on the scooter showed the batteries were two-thirds gone. Bad sign.

The good news, if it was good news, was that he had the blue launch in sight, anchored about a half mile offshore, by a bright yellow buoy. From the shallows, his monocular revealed two men in the boat. One was bald and the other fat. The tall, lean Oleg must be below with the fourth.

He took a minute to study them and contemplate what he was about to do. His job description had been EOD, explosive ordinance demolition: bombs, in other words. Hand to hand fighting and stalking terrorists were things he'd never done, except in training. It wasn't good practice to question a mission while in the middle of it, but he took a moment to reflect on the one time he'd "met" Oleg. Oleg had tried his best to kill Ana, but she had driven him into the ground. She could easily have killed him, but she did not. Michelle was right that she still wouldn't want to, even if she had the chance.

However, he had also seen the lengths to which Oleg would go to get his revenge. They were considerable, and given his resources, limitless. With Oleg alive, Ana would never be safe. If he had fought Oleg himself instead of Ana, he would have finished it. Ana and Matt would have their baby. Bottom line: the time to close the book was now.

While he watched, a head appeared in the water. The two in the boat hauled the person in. Whoever it was pulled off his face mask and took a long slug from what looked like a wine bottle, before shedding his oxygen cylinder. He was out of shape, with a pronounced paunch. Considering the snootful of wine he was consuming, he probably was going to stay out of the water for a while. Neither of the others was dressed for diving, at least not yet. Oleg must be by himself down there. That wasn't good diving practice. Oleg would soon have cause to regret it.

Coombs ducked under, cleared his mask, and hung on as his scooter moved him toward the buoy. The water was not terribly clear. Visibility was fifty to a hundred feet, but that would work to his advantage. Furthermore, the bottom was irregular, with great clumps of seaweed waving in the current and piles of rounded rocks here and there. The shipwreck they were diving on would probably be nearly invisible—best to look for either the line from the buoy, or for bubbles, or for Oleg himself.

Following the compass heading for three-quarters of the distance he estimated, he slowed and parked the scooter behind one of the larger rock piles. He let out a tiny green buoy just a little higher than the seaweed and tied it to the scooter. Next, he retrieved what he'd told Michelle was Hleo's "self-defense" item from its tube and strapped it to his back. It was ungainly and not something he would have ideally chosen, but he knew why Hleo wanted him to have it. Finally, he checked the compass again, chose a large rock on one side and an outcropping of coral on the other to triangulate his starting point from, and pushed off.

He had to proceed slowly and carefully so as not to unexpectedly pop into Oleg's vision, but he couldn't take so much time that another diver might come down to join him. Given the current, the buoy might be 100 meters downstream from the place it was tied. On his third pass, well out of sight of his starting point, Oleg came into view through the murk: a tall, slender figure in a dark blue wet suit. He was barely visible, scraping up a cloud of debris with a clawed tool and stuffing something into a mesh bag.

Coombs swallowed and took a long, slow breath. This was it, now or never. He looked up—no sign of any descending diver. OK, Ana, he thought. This is for you.

Michelle yawned. The lonely afternoon was getting to her. She could chat with Hleo—switching on the radio was simple enough. But no, she had nothing urgent to bother him with and she really needed to keep an eye out for Coombs' return. Where was he?

The sun was getting lower in the west. If she went down to the beach, then she couldn't hear the radio. Coombs had taken his cell phone in a waterproof pouch, so he could call Hleo if there were trouble, and Hleo would then radio her. She dare not miss that.

She compromised by standing outside the pod where she could stretch, still watch the beach, and also hear the radio. First, she checked the strait through the windshield. It wouldn't do for some nearby mariner to see a woman emerge from a rock. The only vessel in sight was a fishing trawler with nets in the water, just offshore on the other side of the strait. No problem. She got out and limbered up, scanning the gentle swells below carefully.

A little of that was enough. The sun was about a half hour from setting. Should she get back in the pod? Where was Rob?

Still trying to decide, and beginning to worry, movement below caught her eye—not in the water, but on the narrow beach to the right. The light was poor and the figure, walking slowly in her direction, was in shadows. Someone out for a walk? Unlikely. She moved nearer the hatch to be ready to jump inside.

It was a man, but not a casual pedestrian. Instead of looking at the sunset or the waves, he was looking up into the rocks as he approached. It was Rob! She almost shouted, but hesitated. If someone were on the edge of the cliff above, that wouldn't be smart. Instead she began stepping down carefully between the rocks to meet him. He saw her when he was 100 yards away and waved. When she reached the bottom she looked back up the cliff. The pod had practically disappeared in the gloom. Rather than running to meet Coombs and maybe losing it she waited for him to reach her.

It took several minutes. He was trudging more than walking. He looked exhausted. She ran to him and hugged him.

"Rob! I was getting worried! Are you OK? Where's your equipment?"

"Yeah, I'm fine. Their anchorage was two miles away, not one. I scuttled all the gear, deep-sixed it. Had a little trouble with the tides. Against me both ways. The scooter gave out on the way back. Couldn't swim against the current. Swam ashore and hoofed it. Should've asked Hleo about the tide times."

His voice was grim. Something was wrong.

"Well, did you reconnoiter? Won't you need that equipment?"

"No. We're finished. We can go home."

The implication sank in.

"You mean...?"

"It's over."

"Oh, Rob!"

Reflexively, she seized his arm.

"First time to do anything like that. Wasn't much fun."

"Ooh."

"He had a diving accident. Let's get out of here."

She wrapped her arms around him and held him tightly.

"Oh, Rob! Ana's safe, Rob!"

After a few seconds he lifted his own arms and hugged her back so tightly she could hardly breathe. He was shivering. He laid his head on her shoulder. She could feel his breath under her ear.

"Rob, Rob. She's safe, Rob. Ana's safe!"

She was vaguely aware how ridiculous she sounded. She rubbed his shoulder blades. They held each other a long time. Eventually, he took a deep breath and drew back. His eyes were tired. He held her face between his palms and studied her. Slowly, he relaxed a little. He pulled her head to him and kissed her forehead.

"C'mon, girl friend," he said, finally, "it's dark. We can go home."

Matt poured a splurp of milk into his coffee and smoothed out the newspaper on the table in front of him. The morning sun cast slanted shadows from their cottonwoods way out into the field on the other side of the old, two lane highway. Clio was busy at the other end of the table, working on a design for the cement marker they would cast for Eleanor's small grave, freshly filled in the night before, next to the marker for Mork, Clio's previous cat. Her present cat was curled up in the corner by the dishwasher, methodically cleaning her face after her breakfast of chicken parts and Science Diet Large Cat Chow (which cost more per pound than ground beef).

He glanced up at a quiet "Psssst" from the hallway. Julio was beckoning to Clio. She left her project and accompanied her brother to the back of the house.

The day looked to be hot and dry. What else? They lived in the desert and it was July. He was reading an article about city council hearings. The Community Watch organization wanted to block off certain residential streets. The theory was this would make it difficult for strangers to cruise anonymously through neighborhoods, leaving the areas appreciably safer. Worth a try, he thought.

"OK, Dad. We gotcha."

It was Julio and Clio again. Clio had something on a small tray and Julio held a bottle of alcohol and a cotton ball.

"Take off your shirt, please. Time for your gravity tag."

"Uhh, well, how about later, mijos?"

"Now, Dad. We got each other last night. Mom too. She didn't mind. You won't either."

"I might, a little, but it's hard to argue against now. You had a good idea about that, son. All right. Be gentle with me."

He peeled off his shirt. Julio cleaned a spot and Clio "shot" him in the muscle behind his arm. It stung, but he'd been hurt worse. She taped a piece of cotton over it and he put his shirt back on.

"Thanks, mijos. I sure wish we'd done this weeks ago, for Mom's sake."

The unmistakable popping sound of tires on gravel and barking dogs signaled a visitor. Clio ran to the kitchen window and peered out.

"Expecting someone?"

"Harry's going to stop by on the way to work and pick up some horse liniment."

"Oh? Is that him?"

"No. It's Dr. Dave."

She went back to her project and Julio hustled the medical supplies to the back of the house.

Matt allowed himself a tiny smile as he tucked in his shirt. Clio had told him Harry was still being bothered by local gang members, so he had visited Hank Stallman and talked it over. The result was that Harry was now getting rides to and from work with Stallman's bookkeeper, Mrs. Flores, who lived in Las Cruces. Matt insisted on covering her extra time and expense. He'd never got around to telling Clio.

He opened the front door before Dave could ring the doorbell. Ana was still sleeping.

"Morning, Dave!"

"Hi, Matt. I'm early, I know. I apologize. I told Julio 9:00, but I imagine he's pumped and so am I. If you've got some more of that coffee, though, I could pump up a little more."

"Sure, got plenty. Come in!"

Matt had forgotten about Raisin, who sprang to her feet, ears flat, bared her fangs, and hissed loudly.

"Oh, *Sh...damn!*"

"No sweat, Dave. That's Clio's cat. She always does that. She doesn't mean anything by it."

"Yes, she does, Dad," piped Clio, innocently. "That hiss means 'watch out, or I'll hurt you bad.'"

"That's about what I figured," Dave whispered, frozen in place and watching out the very best he possibly could.

"C'mon, kitty. Let's go get Julio."

The cat took several steps to follow, stopped and hissed over its shoulder once more, and then flowed after Clio.

"What in God's name was that, Matt?"

"It's a caracal. Sort of like a house cat, but bigger. Much bigger. Forty pounds. Wilder. More dangerous."

"You're shittin' me," Dave said, under his breath.

"Yeah, a little. She's really a pussycat. OK, a big pussycat. Just don't threaten Clio and you'll be all right. Probably."

Dave was a kidder. It was a thrill for Matt to be able to kid him back, and a special thrill to have Clio help out.

Dave shook his head over his coffee.

"'Clio's cat.' I swear, I don't know where you found those twins. I've never seen two kids like them."

"Yeah, they're pistols, all right. But you're at least part of the reason. You tutored them for years."

"True. Starting early helped a lot. But you and Ana have a light touch. You give them room, and boy, do they run with it. I don't really tutor Julio any more. We're sort of like partners now. Has he told you what we're doing?"

"Not exactly. Something with batteries, right?"

"Yeah. That kid is incredible. He knows so much physics and chemistry, not to mention math. Don't misunderstand this, but he hasn't had the background that a scientist with graduate degrees would have. He's read a lot, for sure, but not everything. He just has a feel for it. He built a little robot bulldozer, I guess you know."

"Right. I taught him basic welding, and he made most of the frame and blade himself."

"It's small, but it must weigh 75 pounds. It takes a lot of battery to make it go. So he's been working on that. He's tried several types, most recently lithium batteries. Last month he said he wanted to add yttrium to the substrate of the plates inside. That's a rare earth element used in phosphors and lasers. I have no idea how he came up with that, but he convinced me to to try it. I blew a third of my annual research budget to get a lab to make him some batteries with that modification. Ion deposition, and all that—very expensive.

"The damn thing worked! We got a twenty-five percent power increase out of the batteries! And a five percent decrease in heat! With the potential for more, after a little modification! Do you know what that means?"

"Umm, that his bulldozer can destroy our barn?"

"Well, yeah, maybe. No, lithium batteries have applications in electric vehicles, Matt: cars! We're going to patent that process, him and me. He had the idea and I did the calibrations and testing and handled the data documentation. I'll bet you the car manufacturers will jump on this with both feet! It could be worth tens of millions, Matt, probably more, way more!"

"Sheesh," Matt exclaimed. He shook his head. "Oh, well. I'm bigger than he is. I can still take him."

Dave looked over Matt's shoulder.

"Morning, Julio."

"Hi, Dr. Dave."

"You ready? Got all your stuff? Journal, notes, documents?"

"Yessir. Not the documents. You said you'd bring those."

"Oh, right." He patted his shirt and pulled a folded paper out of the pocket. "Here, Matt. Sign this, please. There'll be more once we've seen the lawyers."

Matt looked it over—standard document, saying he was Julio's father, Julio had his permission, yada, yada. He signed it.

"Thanks," Dave said, folding the paper and putting it back in his pocket. "We should be back after we have some celebratory pizza for lunch."

"Good. Son, we'll be off to Cloudcroft in an hour or so. We should be home by supper time. Call us if anything comes up. You might look in on Abuelita, please."

"Sure, Dad. See you later."

He watched them drive off as another car pulled in. Clio appeared from around the corner of the house to meet it. With her taking care of that, he looked in on Ana. She was sitting on the bed, looking out the back window, absently rubbing Foosh's head. Foosh was the last of their original cats.

"Hey, babe. Buenos dias. ¿Amaneciste bién?"

She barely nodded.

"How about some breakfast?"

"OK."

She stood and stretched. She was wearing a long night shirt that used to be two sizes too big for her. Now it looked four sizes too big. There were hollows where her neck met her collar bones. With the sun streaming through the window behind her, her silhouetted thighs were positively skinny.

"I need a shower first."

He kissed her.

"Good deal, sugar. I'll get stuff started."

Back in the kitchen, he stared at the refrigerator door before opening it. This wasn't good. He was going to have to do something.

Outside, the dogs ran to accompany Clio and Harry and Raisin to the barn. Rani was feinting and yipping at the big cat. Raisin hissed twice, but on the third approach she suddenly charged, sending the dog into panicked retreat. Rani raced away, bounding around the yard in a big figure 8 only to zoom back for another attack.

"What are they doing?" Harry asked Clio.

"Playing."

"You're kidding."

"Haven't you ever seen a cat and a dog play?"

"Well, yeah. But not like that. That dog could get hurt."

"Raisin slapped Rani once, but I treated her. It hasn't happened again."

"Good thing!"

While Clio gathered the tubs of liniment and the animals tried to get along, Harry thought back to his recuperation in this very room. One of his ribs still ached.

"How's your mom?" he asked.

"Oh, pretty good. She had a hard time. She's still getting over it. Here, you can carry these."

Each balancing two plastic containers, they headed to the car.

"How much does Mr. Stallman owe you for this?"

"I had to spend $175 for the ingredients. Two of the herbs come from South America, and they were expensive. I'm sorry. It's a lot of money."

"Not really. You should see what Mr. Hank pays the vet for horse medicine."

"Well, let me know if it doesn't help. You can bring it back if it doesn't."

"The sample you gave me completely healed his best quarter horse. You could sell lots and lots of this stuff."

"It took a long time to make. It was messy, and smelly. This is about a gallon. It should last for months."

Mrs. Flores popped the trunk and Harry carefully set the four containers inside.

Clio brushed her hair out of her face. The sun behind her turned it into a glorious golden aura. He gathered his courage and tried to sound casual.

"Hey, would you like to spend the day at Stallman's sometime? We can pick you up and bring you back, easy."

"Sure! Let me figure out a day and I'll call you."

His heart soared. He wanted to give her an abrazo, but didn't dare. Shake her hand? No, too close to the house, too stupid. Someone might see. He felt like a lump, but he did nothing.

"OK, great! See you then."

The drive to Cloudcroft took a little over an hour. Matt always loved the long climb from the searing desert floor up into the forest and the mountains. Cloudcroft was a small town and it would be hot there, too, but the thin, dry air was somehow more comfortable. For one thing, there was no sand to reflect the burning sun up from the ground, like there was in the desert. Tourism was big in Cloudcroft, especially during the winter ski season. In July, it was easy to find a meeting room in a nice hotel, and the Mobile Migrant Education executives would enjoy the moderately upscale accommodations.

The trip went well. Ana wasn't interested in the scenery, but she and Clio chatted pleasantly enough, and seemed to have a good time at the buffet lunch the program provided. Afterward, Matt walked them to the car. He had worried a little about letting her drive, but she seemed alert, if not vibrantly so.

"Don't worry about hurrying back. I have a book." He patted the soft attache case under his arm and kissed his wife. "I'll meet you in the lobby. Have fun shopping!"

For once, Clio was prepared for a shopping trip. Doña Dolores had given her the addresses of three botánicas between Cloudcroft and Tularosa, twelve miles north, and even called the proprietors to tell them a young friend was coming to shop for her. A little Anglo girl buying medicinal plants might cause questions, even if she spoke good Spanish. Clio had found the addresses on Google Maps, and printed copies to bring along.

The biggest and oldest of the botánicas was in a rambling adobe building on the Hispanic outskirts of Cloudcroft. It was closed for lunch. They drove on to Tularosa, where they located the other two establishments, smaller but each interesting in its own way. Clio shopped enthusiastically but carefully in both, and then in the one in Cloudcroft on the return leg. Her mother waited patiently in the car the whole time.

Clio bought oshá and alta misa de la sierra; she bought ajeño and tronadora, good for diabetes; she bought ponil, the native aspirin, astragalus and mullein, turmeric and olive leaf extract in bulk, all immune system boosters; she bought konjac and pokeweed, for the skin, feverfew, comfrey, ephedra, yerba buena, and toloache, a kind of nightshade and very potent medicine, and a dozen more. When she added four large bags of maguey agave and two of ocotillo blossoms (for sore throats), to the dozens of smaller bags in the trunk of the Corolla, there was no room left and she was out of money. She had spent all her mother's money as well.

"Thanks, Mom," she said, fastening her seat belt.

"Did you find everything you wanted?"

"Mostly. That last store even had some Chinese herbs, but we're out of money. I can get those on the internet."

"I saw an ATM machine around the corner. I need to stretch. Let's walk there and get a little cash."

The ATM was halfway down the block, between a boarded-up business and a bank, which looked closed, at 3:45. Six or seven high school-age boys smoking cigarettes in an alley eyed them as they walked past, but Ana paid no attention.

She walked straight to the machine, fumbling for her card. She was tucking away her cash when Clio shouted.

"Hey!"

Ana whirled to see a boy with an arm around Clio, a knife in his other hand. Two more boys were headed toward her at the ATM machine while the fourth stayed behind her daughter.

"OK, mami, hand it over," said the one on the left. That was the last thing he said.

Ana looked sharply at Clio, turned up her eyes, and fainted, falling to the ground.

At least that's what the boys thought. By the time she hit the ground the boy who held Clio became aware that some number of his fingers had been broken and the girl had the knife.

Ana landed face down, arms braced against the sidewalk, and whipped her legs under the two boys who were closest to her. She was on her feet again almost before they landed, dropping on one knee into one boy's stomach and delivering a chop to the throat of the other. Clio's attacker stood dumbfounded, grimacing in pain. The fourth boy turned and ran for the alley.

Ana caught him before he had gone ten steps. As Clio screamed "No, Mom!" she tripped him from behind. He fell full speed to the sidewalk on his face, crying out as his head bounced to reveal a massively bloody nose. Ana returned to the knifeless boy with the injured hand, her eyes blazing. The kid stared at her in horror.

"No, Mom, don't!" pleaded Clio.

Ana pushed off one foot in a lunging motion and thrust a fist into the boy's solar plexus. He doubled over and fell to his knees, retching.

"Mom! *Mom*!" Clio screamed. "That's enough! You said only do enough to protect yourself! *Stop*, Mom!"

Ana glared at the four boys on the sidewalk. She spoke in Luvit.

"*Môje desh órhozh nikhda!*" ("No one threatens my children!"), adding in English, "Let's go."

They headed around the corner to the car. The alley was empty.

Clio got in on the passenger side, ignoring her seat belt. She stared at her mom. Ana shut her door and burst into tears.

Matt consulted his watch: 4:00 pm. That must be some shopping expedition. But that was OK. He was happily absorbed in his book, Tony Hillerman's *The Dark Wind*. One of his summer projects was to reread the entire series of mysteries, and this one, featuring Officer Jim Chee, was one of his favorites. He had about three chapters to go and was wondering if he should have brought the next book too, when he saw Ana's Corolla pull up out front.

The car smelled like some exotic, third world barn. Ana slept most of the way back while Clio studied the scenery. Neither smiled. Ana looked exhausted and Clio unhappy. Not good, not good. Ana probably wouldn't tell him what was wrong. Clio might, when he could ask her privately. Dammit, he was worried.

Ana was healthy enough—two doctors had said so. The miscarriage had been a terrible, terrible tragedy, but he could think of no reason she wouldn't share her feelings about that with her husband. It must go deeper. Maybe it was something cultural that he was failing to pick up on. But she didn't even want to talk to her sister. Should he call her himself? Bad idea, probably—not smart to mess around in someone else's family. Well, he could call Hleo. That would be a good place to start.

Another idea was nagging at him...what was it? He almost had it...something he'd been thinking about just a few minutes ago....

His cell phone buzzed. He quickly worked it out of his pocket—it was the pocket under the seat belt—and answered.

"Hello?"

"Dad?"

"Yes, son."

"Uh, Dad...."

"Yes, son, what's up?"

"It's Abuelita. She started having lots of pain. I called 911. An ambulance came and took her to the hospital. Can you come home soon, Dad?"

Chapter 16

"Matt?"

"Yeah."

"This is Rob. Rob Coombs."

"Hey, Rob."

"Am I catching you at a good time?"

"Well, yes and no. My grandmother just had surgery for appendicitis and we're sitting around waiting for the docs to give us a report."

"Oh, jeez, I'm sorry, man. You want me to call back later?"

"Naw. I'm just pacing up and down the hall right now. What's up?"

"I'm ready to bring your, uh, your vehicle back, but maybe this isn't a good time."

"Well, hang on a sec."

Coombs heard muffled voices in the background and then Matt came on again.

"What time are you going to arrive?"

"Uh, in about an hour and a half, unless you'd rather I not."

"No, that's fine. The kids are tired. I'll take them home and meet you there."

"Same place as last time?"

"Perfect. See you there."

"Best wishes to your grandmother."

"Thanks. I appreciate the thought. She's 90, but we should all be as tough."

"You said it. Take care."

Michelle, hearing only Coombs' side of the conversation, found her thoughts running ahead of her. They'd been cooped up in the pod, following the progress of the night a third of the way around the globe, for over ten hours, and she was getting sick of it. Her butt was numb.

She found herself sorting through her feelings for the man next to her, her good friend, her "boy friend." Or was he, really? He had just killed someone, for heaven's sake, probably in cold blood. He still seemed upset, talking little, not relaxed and comfortable like he usually was. Yet she too was invested in what he had done. Part of the burden was hers. She wasn't even certain how she felt about herself now. Yes, it had had to be done, for Ana's sake, but even so....

Could she have done it herself? No, of course she couldn't. It had taken someone like Rob to actually do the dirty work. That had to be bothering him. But it wasn't fair. He shouldn't have to take all the guilt on himself. He deserved to have someone to help him deal with that. Well, that could be her share of the job. She owed him that much, whatever she decided about their relationship.

"Michelle? Did you hear me?"

"Huh? Oh, sorry, my mind was wandering. What did you say?"

Coombs tucked the cell phone in his shirt pocket.

"I said Matt's at a hospital with his family. His grandmother was just operated on for appendicitis. They're waiting for the doc to give them her status. He's going to duck out to take the twins home and he'll meet me. Are you sure you still want to go along?"

"Oh, uh, yes. Sure! I'm loving this pod. I'll go anywhere in it, any time."

Coombs began to radio their plans to Hleo so he could adjust their course and speed. Michelle scooted forward in her seat to try to match up the city lights far below with the lines scrolling across the little display screen. Hopefully, the shift of position might get a little feeling into her rear.

Matt braked at a red light by the hospital. Julio, in the front seat, spoke in the darkness.

"Dad, is Abuelita going to be OK?"

"I think so, son. It was fortunate that you were there to check on her, and that you called 911 right away. Good job, mijo. She's so stubborn, she might have gone to bed in pain if you hadn't. That could have made it much worse."

"I meant OK after the operation."

"Yeah, well, because she got to the hospital in good time, her appendix hadn't burst. That meant that the operation could be simple. They didn't have to make a large incision. They inserted a laparoscope through a small hole in her abdomen. They just snipped her appendix off and pulled it out and that was that."

"Ewwww."

Julio was the squeamish twin.

"She should be up and around in a day or two. Her vital signs were good, but we're waiting to be sure how she is when she comes out of the anesthesia."

The light turned green. He eased the Corolla down the boulevard.

"I'm not too worried about Abuelita. I'm more worried about mom. Mija," he looked at Clio in the rear view mirror, "what happened on your shopping expedition this afternoon? Mom seemed upset on the way home."

"Oh, well, uh, I must've spent too much time shopping. She got tired, I guess."

"Hmm."

"Dad?"

"Yes, son."

"Mom's been different ever since she got back from her trip. Is that because of the miscarriage?"

He had always tried to be honest with his children, and not sugarcoat things. This was one of those times. He thought a second.

"I don't know, son. Could be. She's seemed sad, lately, maybe depressed. I'm not sure why, or what to do about it. I wish I knew."

Clio spoke from the back seat.

"She's not depressed. A curandera would say she has *mal de alma*."

"'Soul-sickness?' What's that?"

"It's hard to describe. But they treat it."

"How?"

"Doña Dolores has done it a couple times. It's complicated. It wouldn't work on Mom."

"Why not?"

"Well, it's religious. The patients are Catholic. Mom isn't."

"Oh, I get it. Doña Dolores uses church-based rituals, with saints and stuff?"

"Uh-huh. But she helped an Indian once. He wasn't Catholic."

"Yeah? What'd she do?"

"She sent him back to a healer from his tribe, in Arizona, I think. He did it."

"*Yeah!*" Matt shouted, startling both children.

"Sorry," he said, in a normal voice. "I didn't mean to yell. You just reminded me—earlier today I was reading a Tony Hillerman novel. There's a Navajo policeman in it who wanted to learn to be a medicine man. He helped conduct a ceremony they call the Blessing Way. It's used for much the same purpose, to restore balance to a life that's lost its harmony." He thought about that a half block, and added, "Would you say Mom has lost her harmony, mija?"

"Uh-huh," Clio said quietly. "I think so. Maybe."

He drove another half block.

"I don't know as much about Thoman culture as I should, guys," he said. "All societies have certain rituals, like weddings, graduations, funerals, and stuff. You two might know more about Thomans than I do. Do they have lots of ceremonies?"

Julio nodded but Clio spoke first.

"They do. They have all those, and a bunch of others, like for menarche."

"What's 'menarche?'" asked Julio.

"Uh...." Matt began.

"It's a fertility ceremony, for girls," Clio finished.

"Well, that's good to know," Matt said. "I think I'll ask Uncle Hleo about rituals. He should know if his people have something like a Blessing Way ceremony. We could see if we could adapt it for mom, you think? Maybe we could borrow some Navajo ideas, too. You guys want to help?"

Clio answered first again.

"Sure, Dad. I could ask Doña Dolores about her Indian friend."

"Great, mija. Do that. I'll ask Hleo about Thoman customs. Maybe we can come up with something to help Mom."

"New Mexico?"

"Right, southern New Mexico. See those lights off to the right? That's Las Cruces."

"I always wondered where they lived. I never would have guessed."

"They live near there. A little south. Hleo's setting us down slowly. There aren't many lights where we're headed, but it's about right...there."

Coombs pointed and then put his hand on the controller, in case Hleo couldn't sense the ground as well as he could in person. The lights slowly spread out as the pod got lower, but enough mercury vapor lamps and porch lights were visible here and there to reveal they were descending toward a dark stretch along a curving road. The pod slowed even more. The lights began winking out as they were obscured behind features on the approaching ground. In the faint starlight, Michelle detected trees close around them. Then she saw a rooftop, with a cupola on top.

"Oh, my goodness."

They felt a faint bump.

"Here we are," Coombs said. "I hope."

He opened the hatch. Matt and the twins were waiting in the dimness, surrounded by animals. Michelle, nearest the opening, eased out carefully, her fanny shooting pains throughout her body as she stood.

"Matt! Clio! Julio! It's so good to see you!"

She hugged them all, and held out a hand to the animals.

"Such lovely dogs, and such a gorgeous cat!"

The dogs crowded on either side. Raisin cautiously extended her head and sniffed the hand. Michelle scratched her jaw and rubbed the dogs' heads.

"You must be part wild animal, Michelle," Coombs said, stepping out behind her. "That cat nearly ate me for dessert. Hi, guys!"

He shook hands all around, animals excepted. Matt gestured toward the house, a pale shape in the darkness.

"You gotta be tired, folks. Head on inside and relax. I'll put the pod in the barn and join you. You can get your stuff out of it later. Mijos, please show our guests to the house and tend to what they need."

He pulled open the barn doors and climbed into the pod as Michelle's fading voice sounded across the grass.

"My, but you two have grown! You're nearly as big as I am."

The twins led them through the back gate to the patio. Michelle noticed the dogs remained outside, but the cat followed Clio as if she considered herself the equal of the humans. After a pit stop in the back bathroom, they headed to the front of the house.

Michelle was dying to see how the Méndez family lived. She had no idea of their personal wealth, but Ana routinely handled hundreds of millions of dollars from her charitable funds. She was certain they could afford a lavish lifestyle if they wished.

To her surprise, the house had a none-too-large central living area, with what passed for a living room facing the porch on the patio, and a dining table behind, next to the kitchen. All three areas made one irregular space. The furniture was sturdy and simple, somehow western looking, arranged about a shiny wooden floor with a number of large rugs with Indian patterns woven into them. There were several bookshelves and a flat-screen TV most of her lawyer friends would find rather too small. Built into one of the bookshelves sat a computer and peripheral machines. The kitchen was neat and clean, with modern, if not cutting edge, appliances. She estimated that a party of ten or twelve would have maxed the room out. She instantly felt comfortable.

The twins actually took their drink orders and fixed them glasses of iced agua de Jamaica, which Michelle had never heard of. Clio explained that it was made from "an infusion of the calyces of the hibiscus flower," that it contained vitamin C and minerals, and was used from time to time as a mild diuretic. It was more than she wanted to know, but she was impressed by Clio's erudition and delighted with the cranberry-like flavor.

Coombs was sipping his while browsing the bookshelves by the TV when their attention was drawn to a profound ripping and scratching from one corner. The big cat was sharpening its claws on an oval sisal mat Michelle had noticed before. It didn't fit the decor, but now it made sense. The animal's claws looked like the needle-sharp tines of a weeding fork. She was about to ask Clio about the cat when Matt entered through the patio.

"Y'all doing all right?"

"We are, thanks," said Coombs.

"Wonderful," added Michelle. "I love this drink!"

Coombs had a question.

"How'd you know we were about to land, anyway, or were you just waiting around out there?"

"Raisin," Matt said. "Clio's cat. All of a sudden she wanted outside. We were expecting you any minute, but she knew."

"I'll be." Coombs uttered, suppressing the "damned" for the sake of the kids. He'd seen lynxes attracted to the pod too, years earlier. It was a mystery.

"Would you like some, what was that Navy word for late night food?" Matt asked.

"Midrats? I think I'm good. Michelle?"

"I'm fine, thanks. We had a snack in the pod, not too long ago."

Matt noticed Julio, sitting quietly at the dining table, turning his head to yawn.

"It's getting late, folks. How about staying the night, or even a couple of nights? There are four spare bedrooms in my grandmother's house."

Coombs smiled.

"Oh, I kinda need to be getting back, I think."

He looked at Michelle.

"Can we take a rain check? I have some vacation days coming," she said. "I'm feeling a serious need of some beach time."

She glanced back at Coombs, who took the cue.

"You need to get your grandmother back on her pins. If we can call us a taxi out here, we'll head to the airport tonight and be out of your hair."

"Sure, you can have a rain check, but why don't you just ride back to town with me? I'm going anyway—I need to collect Ana. There's a taxi stand at the big hotel by the hospital. I can drop you there. I warn you, though, the fare from there to the other side of El Paso is breathtaking. I could take you myself tomorrow."

"Nah, that's all right. We're not packed for a visit. Another time would be great. The fare will go onto my expense tab. By the way, Hleo said he'll report to you on our doings in a day or two."

"Sure, no problem."

"Please tell Ana we're sorry we missed her," Michelle added. "We'd love to visit when we all have more leisure time."

"I will, of course," Matt replied. He winked at Clio and Julio at the dining table. "Kids, thanks for your help. You can hit the hay now, and don't worry about Abuelita. We'll catch you up on her in the morning."

He watched his children say farewell to their guests, acquitting themselves politely and appearing to mean it, but he also noted Coombs and Michelle. She had said "*We'd* love to visit." He had noticed their glances at each other when they'd been talking over their future plans. Interesting! He'd been a reporter. He recognized a subtext when he saw one.

Matt tossed down his pencil and looked at the clock: 10:30 am.. He got up from the computer and poured himself another cup of coffee. Ana had left at 9:00 to drop Clio off at Doña Dolores' place to deliver her share of the herbs, and then she was going to the hospital to visit Abuelita, the morning after her emergency surgery. He had an hour left, more or less, until he had to find something else to be doing when Ana returned.

Back in his chair, he read over the notes he had scribbled while emailing back and forth with Hleo. Apparently, Thomans had all kinds of customs and ceremonies, but nothing specifically for a person with possible deep-seated emotional problems. They seemed to deal with such things medically or theologically, but neither of those avenues were terribly promising in Ana's case. It occurred to him that Thoman society was not that different from his own in that regard. Neither one had a place for "mal del alma." It was difficult to judge from Hleo's rather formal writing style, but once Matt described what sort of ceremony he had in mind, Hleo seemed to understand. He said he would put something together and send it to Matt's computer in a day or two.

Matt had already thought of the second promising idea Hleo mentioned: to talk to Ana's sister. Ana hadn't wanted him to, but now he had changed his mind. It would be better to do this face to face, but there was no other choice. He picked up the phone and dialed their New York apartment.

"You have reached the Zimmer residence. We cannot take your call right now."

He hung up. Crap. What message could he have left? "This is Matt, Ana's alive but so depressed I'm worried about her?" No way.

He flipped through his address book and dialed the number of the newspaper Scott often worked for. A robot took him through his options. No, dammit, he didn't know the party's extension. Yes, dammit, he'd dial in the name. By the time he'd punched in Z-I-M-, a real woman came on the line.

"I'm sorry, sir. Mr. Zimmer will be on vacation until next Wednesday. May I connect you to his editor?"

No, ma'am, never mind.

He sat back and thought. Scott had just finished a multi-part piece on famine and revolution in southern Africa. It had to have been stressful. As best he remembered, Ianthe had accompanied him. If they were now on vacation, it didn't seem likely that they'd choose to travel again just for relaxation. More likely, they'd want to be alone in peace somewhere—probably at their vacation home at the Williams ranch in west Texas, between Alpine and Fort Stockton.

Should he call? No. Much better to talk this over in person. It was all of a half hour flying time in the pod, and the pod was 150 feet from him, in the barn.

He would do it tonight.

When Clio and Ana returned at 2:30, Matt and Julio were fooling around with sticks in the shade behind the house.

"What are they doing, Mom?"

"I have no idea, daughter."

"How's Abuelita?" Matt asked, as they emerged from the car. Both were sweating. There was a reddish patch below Julio's left ear.

"She could be better," Ana replied. "Tired, and not too...what's that word she uses? Perky?"

"They said she was supposed to come home today, but they won't let her go now," Clio grumped.

"Clio got into an argument with the doctor."

"Her blood pressure was too high. She needed a blood thinner."

"How did you know it was too high, mija?" Matt asked.

"From her pulse. I check it all the time."

"The doctor said they were treating for her blood pressure," Ana pointed out.

"Yes, Mom, but that's different. She needs a blood thinner!"

Trying to defuse things, Matt said "Well, let's hope they know what they're doing. Julio and I will go check on her before supper. You can come with us, mija."

"Her food wasn't that good, either. We had lunch with her," Clio said.

"Green Jello," Ana added, "Brrr." For some reason she'd always hated Jello—something to do with cows, Matt thought. She couldn't even stand the sight of it. She went on, "I'd better get those things she wants from her house before I forget."

"Check the dining table first," Matt said. "I put the items I collected for her there."

Ana nodded and disappeared into the patio. Clio looked closely at Julio.

"What happened to your face? What were you doing with those mops?"

"Dad and I were fighting."

"It's a long story," Matt said. "One of the things I found in Abuelita's house was Abuelo's bastón. That's it over there." Leaning against the house was a stout stick, nearly as tall as Matt. The top ended in a baseball-size knot. "That was Abuelo's lucky bastón. It's made out of oak. He used to carry it into the fields when he went to check on things. When he got old he used it as a cane. I found it in her house and thought I'd take it for Abuelita to touch, to bring her a little of his luck. She'd like that. Julio wanted to see it, and we got to playing around.

"It reminded me of the pugil sticks I used to use in the Army. A pugil stick is a long shaft with padded ends that you can use to fight with without hurting anyone too seriously.

"We found some old mops in the laundry room, and I taped them together in pairs, after tying the heads down to cushion the ends. See? You hold it in both hands, like this, and you can block your opponent or smack him, if you're clever. See?"

He demonstrated a few moves in slow motion, stopping short before he whacked Clio with one end of his odd-looking weapon.

"Julio and I had a good workout. He got me, low, a couple times, and I got him high, once. Hence the red spot."

"And that was fun?"

"Yeah!" said Julio. "I want to learn to be good with these. Only we'll make better ones."

"Right. We broke one of the mops," Matt said.

"That's crazy!"

"Well, what can I say, mija? A dad and his son—gotta mix it up sometimes. At least he didn't throw me on my butt, like a certain daughter did recently. Ahem." He looked in the direction of the patio and lowered his voice. "Hey, mija, did you get to talk to Doña Dolores about the blessing ceremony?"

"Uh-huh. She had some good ideas."

"Great. Listen, if you come with Julio and me to see Abuelita this evening, you can tell me what you learned. Also," he glanced again at the patio, "After you guys are in bed I'm gonna sneak out in the pod and go see Aunt Ianthe. They're at their house in west Texas. I shouldn't be gone but a couple hours, but I need to fill her in on our plans. I imagine she'll want to be with us for the ceremony. Mom's been sleeping soundly lately, but if she happens to wake up and wonders where I went, she'll probably ask you guys. Tell her, oh, tell her I couldn't sleep so I took the pod back to the hangar, all right? Then text me on my phone, so I'll know. OK?"

It took the twins a second to absorb that. They looked at each other before Julio spoke.

"Sure, Dad."

Sneaking away turned out to be no problem. Ana was tired after a day of visiting and driving around and went to bed early. The twins followed soon after. A half hour later he eased into bed fully clothed. Ana only sighed and rolled toward him, her hair flowing over her face. He kissed her softly, waited a few minutes, and then got up carefully and headed to the back of the house.

Clio was asleep. Raisin was curled against her, raising her head only to blink in the bright orange beam of his keychain light. Julio was reading in his room by the light of one small lamp.

"I'm off, son," he whispered.

"OK, Dad."

"Don't stay up too late. See you in the morning."

Good old pod—from fifty feet, silent as an owl. He eased it into the air and headed west southwest, staying low and slow over the Organ Mountains. To be on the safe side he crossed over to the Mexican side of the Rio Grande, where traffic from the El Paso airport would never penetrate. The pod had been on two long trips since he and Julio had painted it (assuming Rob and Michelle had been on a long trip). When they had time, he'd get Julio to test it to be sure it was still absorbing radar signals completely—better safe than sorry.

With the lights of El Paso behind him, he accelerated to 500 mph and entered the GPS location for the Zimmer house below Fort Davis. It was only about 250 miles away, less than a half hour flying time. Only a handful of lights were scattered across the desert at night. Nearly all were along the highway, and even those were few and far between. There wouldn't be many near Fort Davis, either, since the locals were careful to cooperate with the observatory and not pollute the night air with too much light.

When he was getting close he called their number on his cell phone. A woman's voice answered.

"Hello?"

"Ianthe?"

"Yes."

"This is Matt."

"Matt! How are you?"

"Fine, thanks. Listen, I hope I didn't wake you."

"No, of course not. Scott and I are playing chess."

"OK, great. Hey, I'm nearby. Would it be all right if I stopped in for a minute or two?"

"We would love it! Please do!"

"I'll be there in ten minutes. Thanks!"

There'd been no choice of moonlight, but fortunately there was only a quarter moon over broken clouds. It was just enough to make out the house, nestled by itself in the foothills of the Davis Mountains, as the pod slowed over the coordinates he'd entered. He set it down in front, next to their car.

Ianthe answered his knock in jeans and a blue t-shirt. Her dark hair was tied in an informal pony tail, a style he'd never seen her use before. She wore no makeup and was barefoot. She'd come a long way since the repressed, super-formal days of her first marriage. She was a striking woman: her face had some of the same, penetrating features as her older sister, but being taller, and with her darker hair and eyebrows, she would have stood out more in a crowd. The diminutive Ana could modify her own normally pale features and become unrecognizable with little trouble.

Ianthe hugged him warmly and he remembered to kiss her on both cheeks—air kisses for strangers, real kisses for family, was the Thoman way. A firm handshake was enough for Scott, also wearing jeans, a khaki shirt, worn loafers, and a good three days of beard stubble.

Ianthe was looking out the door.

"That looks like...."

"Right. That was Ana's escape pod."

Scott stepped to the door for his own look.

"It's the coolest thing, Scott. I'll give you both a look before I head back. I can't stay long." He paused. "It's about Ana."

Ianthe nodded and shut the door. Matt had expected his words would make her anxious, but she was cool as always.

"I understand. Please sit down. Something to drink?"

He saw a beer bottle by the chess board.

"A beer?"

"I'll get it," said Scott.

Matt chose a seat to the side of the board. Scott was back with the beer in less than a minute. The only thing to do was start.

"Ana's alive and well. She's back home."

Ianthe nodded again.

"We know. Hleo told us. He felt he had to."

"Wow. I'm glad. I was worried about you guys being worried. Ana told me not to tell you, or anyone."

"Yes. I expected that."

"You did? Really?"

"Yes. It relates to a family matter, Matt. I'm not sure I'd have felt differently in her place, but I've lived in society here long enough to know that a painful situation on Thomo might be seen differently on Earth. There's very little that's new anywhere, really."

"Aah," Matt said, sitting back in the chair. "It was obvious something was bothering her, a lot, but she didn't want to talk about it. I bet Hleo didn't tell you she was pregnant when she dived off that bridge, and that she lost the child soon after. He knew we took her to a doctor right away, but we never told him why."

"That's terrible, Matt! I'm so sorry," Scott said, as Ianthe nodded.

"No, he didn't mention that. But it tells me exactly why she would be feeling troubled."

"Clio says the faith healers she knows call it 'soul-sickness.' They have ceremonies to treat it that are often successful. I didn't think medicine or psychiatry would be that helpful. That's why I'm here, to see what suggestions you might have that would help us create a healing ceremony for her."

"That's a lovely idea, Matt. I'm sure we'd both want to help in any way we could."

"Count on it. Anything," Scott nodded in agreement. Ianthe twiddled a captured pawn in her fingers and went on.

"I should fill you in on a bit of Darshiell family history. You don't know this either, husband." She paused a beat. "Ana has probably talked about our father, hasn't she?"

"She has," Matt said.

"But she has said very little about our mother, yes?"

"That's right. I wondered about that."

Ianthe picked up another pawn and began rolling them one over the other in her hand.

"Her name was Maerl. She was a remarkable woman, extremely energetic and intelligent, and the most senior Warrior in the Teihern clan. 'Warrior' is an office, not an occupation, you see. When she married Heoren Darshiell, it united the two largest and oldest clans on Thomo. The celebration was planetwide, the biggest in our history. Shortly after, when signals from Earth were detected, that, together with their marriage, was considered a clear sign of our destiny, that we should launch a unified expedition to find our original home."

She paused and studied Matt over the chess board.

"Did you know that our sister Anneyn, your Ana, was a twin, Matt?"

He was thunderstruck.

"No! She never mentioned that!"

"Yes. Under Thoman custom, each child would have become the head of each clan. It was a further sign of destiny. The first child born would head the Darshiell clan and the second the Teihern clan. But," she set the pawns down, "her twin brother was stillborn."

"Ooh," said Matt.

"From our earliest days on Thomo, when our numbers were so reduced we almost died out, human life has been sacred to us. To lose an unborn child, for whatever reason, is a source of great shame, not only to the family but to the entire clan. And when that lost child was to head one of the two most senior clans, it was a disaster for the entire planet."

Ianthe set down the pawns. She picked up a rook.

"The political chaos that resulted took years to resolve. The effort to mount the expedition was in jeopardy. Our father used all his political skills, and those of his advisers, to maintain unity. Planetary affairs were slowed, as were the preparations for the expedition, but they continued nevertheless.

"Another child was born a year later, a girl, Onela. Two years later, I was born. Anneyn was to marry into the Teihern clan. Onela was to head the Darshiell clan. But Anneyn refused three suitors. Our father, desperate to fulfill our destiny, managed to make other arrangements. He proclaimed that Anneyn would be the one to conduct the expedition, removing her from the clan hierarchy. Onela would take her place, and her first child would marry a Teihern. I could not, because I had been promised to Herecyn's clan, and to retract that would have been an unforgivable insult. It was Herecyn's decision to accompany the second expedition to Earth, which I why I am here."

She looked sideways at Scott.

"I have never regretted that, any of that."

Zimmer shook his head slowly. Ianthe looked directly at Matt.

"After six years of marriage, in the face of unrelenting criticism, our mother, distraught and despairing of her remaining years, committed suicide. This is perhaps the greatest wrong one can do in Thoman society. It is considered murder. The censure never goes away. I'm sure it affected our father until his dying day, as it will his daughters until our final days. Especially dear Anneyn, who was old enough at the time to feel the family's shame." She paused again.

"On Earth, I felt the opprobrium lift from my soul. No one knew our secret, and even had they known they would not have felt its weight as they would have on Thomo. I am sure sister Anneyn found similar relief, that is, until her tragic miscarriage, when the whole sad episode of our family's history and our shame seemed to repeat our earlier misfortune. I am certain that is the source of her 'soul-sickness,' as you have termed it."

She set the rook down.

"It is a fitting name."

Matt had no words. He noticed his untouched beer as if for the first time. He took a swallow and set it down gently. Ianthe was still looking evenly at him.

"So," she said, "let us consider how we may serve our honored sister and wife."

Airborne again, Matt checked his watch. He would make it home a little before 3 am. Worrying about Ana and Abuelita had been stressing him, but he wasn't sleepy. He hadn't expected to feel so enlightened by the visit. Now the problem was much clearer. Poor Ana! At first he'd thought she'd been depressed from the miscarriage, and perhaps she was. Now, thanks to Ianthe, he knew that it had also brought back old memories of their family's terrible problems, especially her poor twin brother, born dead. And if that weren't enough, Abuelita's problematic recovery from surgery, worrisome in itself but recalling her own mother's sad fate, further compounded both miseries. The pill didn't exist that would cure that. Not good, not good.

The pod rifled through the dry night air as the few lonely headlights threaded their way along the highway below. He found himself mulling over Clio's and Ianthe's ideas about the healing ceremony. They were helpful, but the process still had not come together in his mind. There were two more avenues to be pursued. Now that he thought about it, Ianthe might well benefit from a little healing herself. Come to that, so might they all.

Chapter 17

Harry Saenz tossed down his last gulp of milk and washed the plate and glass in the sink, setting both in the drainer. It was 8:14 am. His mother would be at work now, answering the phone and greeting her coworkers as they arrived. Mrs. Flores would be arriving on the half hour. She was always punctual—she was a bookkeeper, after all.

He stepped to the front window, cautiously pulled the drape back, and looked down the street to his left. The only thing moving was their neighbor, Eloy Gonzales, unlocking his S-10 and raising his lunch box to his wife. She waved back from their porch.

He let the curtain fall back and moved to the other side of the window, repeating the maneuver. Nothing on that side either...no, wait. Down near the corner was that black Escalade with the tinted windows, looming ominously and out of place in all its body shop glory.

Crap! That wasn't the local gang, the Tirilongos. It was the big shots from El Paso, their distributors. What the hell were they doing on Belva Way, and at this hour of the morning? He'd been fairly successful at avoiding the Tirilongos although he'd had to modify his lifestyle a good bit—no running errands to Mr. Silvas' tendajo and no visiting friends—but he figured that situation would ease once school started again. So what were these gangsters doing here?

He stood back from the curtain. There was no way he was going to take Clio to work if those pendejos were anywhere near. The policemen had told them to call if anything looked funny. That Escalade looked way funny. He flipped open the cover of the phone book, studied the number of the Doña Ana

County Sheriff, and dialed. They'd been pretty good about driving by every so often. He'd ask them to come take a look now.

If that didn't work he'd call his mother and have her call them. He couldn't imagine anyone disobeying his mother.

Matt parked in front of San Albino church at the north end of the historic Mesilla plaza even though he might have parked closer. It was a little early for tourists to start clogging the area, but he didn't need the distraction of hunting a better spot.

The morning sun sent the shadow of the bandstand in the middle of the plaza almost to the bookstore on the far corner. He walked down the left sidewalk in the shade, past struggling trees with trunks whitewashed to shoulder height, and turned in at the Native American Gallery of Art, one of a block-long line of adobe store fronts, between an unmarked ancient wooden door on one side and a souvenir store on the other. It was 9:20. He nodded at the woman stocking pamphlets in a rack near the back of the gallery and began browsing.

The works of art on display included many ceramics and paintings, but there were also examples of astonishingly fine basketwork and cases of resplendent silver and turquoise jewelry arranged down both walls.

He noticed none of it.

All he could think about was la esposita, his little wife, and her alarming lack of interest in the things that usually absorbed her. He was getting an idea of what to do for her. The question now was how best to go about it.

He was barely aware of standing before a strikingly colorful woolen textile, glowing in reflected sunlight, when the sound of boots on the wooden floor and a hearty greeting startled him out of his reverie.

"Hei, Matt! Have you had breakfast?"

It was the man he'd come to see, Melvin Bisti.

"Hei yourself, doc! Yes, I have, thanks. ¿Cómo estás, esta mañana?"

Dr. Melvin Bisti, professor of sociology and a national authority on things native American, raised a steaming paper cup of coffee to him.

"Good! How about some coffee? Could you use some of that?"

"Sure could. Good idea!"

"Follow me. My treat."

Dr. Bisti waved a friendly hand at the woman in the back, saying, "Hei, Ellie," and led Matt two doors down to a tiny café where he saw Matt supplied with the beverage in question, and then back to the weathered door on the other side of the gallery. He handed his cup to Matt while he dug out his key and unlocked the door.

Bisti was a compact, barrel-chested man of about 60, with graying hair tied back in a pony tail and a broad, lined face the color of an old saddle. He was wearing a maroon western-cut shirt over pressed jeans and a bolo tie sporting a large bright green opal two inches below the collar button. A full-blooded Navajo, in addition to being prominent in regional Indian affairs, he was also a renowned, published scholar on the native cultures of the southwest. His English was accented, but not as an Hispanic's would have been. He spoke deliberately and musically, treating his s's with great respect.

As Bisti ushered him into the open air passageway Matt reflected on the oddity of consulting this man on a matter he was also consulting with a high-level advisor to the ruling family of a planet twenty-five light years from Earth. Hleo might not have been amazed, but Melvin Bisti surely would have been.

The passageway, shady in the morning light, widened to a small tiled patio where two benches sat to either side of a small fountain under ornamental shrubs. A blue parrot eyed them skeptically from a cage littered by fragments of fruit and seeds. The earthy adobe walls around them radiated the coolness from the night before.

"We could go in my office, but why not sit here in the open air?"

Each took a bench. Matt sipped his coffee and set it next to him.

"Is this about the school?" Bisti asked. He was on the board of Juarez Academy and had worked with Matt and the other members for several years. He was a family friend. Matt shook his head.

"No. It's personal. It's about Ana."

"Ana? Bless the dear lady. How is she?"

"Well, not so good. I'm worried about her."

"Oh." He sipped his coffee. "I'm sorry to hear that."

"Yeah. She had a miscarriage, for one thing. Just between you and me."

"Oh, no. That's terrible, Matt. What a shame. My condolences."

"Thanks. But there's more to it than that. It's hard to get a handle on. Basically, I'd say she has the blues. If you know what I mean."

"The blues?"

"Clio says curanderas call it 'mal de alma.' It doesn't seem like anything that medication or psychiatry would help." Matt stirred his coffee with the little plastic stick. "I've been re-reading those Tony Hillerman stories this summer. That business about the healing ceremony struck me. I wondered if something like that might help Ana."

"Hmm," Bisti said softly. "Well, it's possible. If she were Navajo."

"Exactly. I understand that. I just don't know how the ceremony works. If there might be some features of it that could be adapted, perhaps. I hoped maybe you could give me an idea."

"Ah." Bisti set his own coffee down and leaned back, his face thoughtful. Matt knew he never rushed into anything. He waited.

"Well," Bisti said after a long minute, "I guess you'd say there are preconditions. Mainly three. There's the belief system, there is the community, and then there's the ceremony." Another twenty seconds passed. "Hillerman is pretty accurate, if not exhaustively so. Navajo symbology is extensive, and all good Navajos know it well. That's a given. That's a big part of the evocative content of the ceremony."

He brushed invisible dust off his thighs.

"I'm sorry if I sound like a lecturer, but I am a lecturer. What is Ana's belief system?"

"I was afraid you would ask me that. It's kind of embarrassing, since we've been married thirteen years. I'm not sure. I know she believes in a supreme being, or maybe spirit. But she doesn't follow the tenets of any religion I'm familiar with."

"That could be a problem. A big part of the effectiveness of the ceremony depends on the power of association, you see."

"Sure. Makes sense. I do know some of her associations. Have you ever conducted one?"

"Me? No, not me. I wanted to, when I was a young man. I studied for it, like Chee, in the book. I just didn't have what it took—the presence, the 'force,' maybe. I was too analytical. So instead I became a scholar. Now I work with the biligana at the university—my white brothers. I've attended quite a few ceremonies, though."

A mockingbird fluttered down to light on the edge of the fountain. The parrot emitted a rusty squawk.

"Whatever Ana's beliefs are, drawing on them would probably help."

"Yeah. You mentioned the community?"

"Friends. Witnesses. That's as important as the beliefs. Your people have this too. It's a feature of biligana twelve-step programs, you know, supporters, so the person knows he, or she, isn't alone, that they care about him, or her. That's a major part."

"Yeah. I thought so. I can handle that. What about the ceremony itself?"

Bisti shook his head slowly.

"That's complex, very hard to describe. It's a combination of a lot of things. The idea is to get the person out of himself, or herself, kind of zoned out, but comfortably so, if that makes any sense. It's done in a small space, to concentrate the effect. Music is a part of it—drums, chants—and visual stimuli, like sand painting. Both have powerful symbolic value. There's also reduced light, and scents. A small fire is often burning, with incense. It can go on for hours. It's not unlike hypnosis, I would say. In the hands of a skilled practitioner, the participants emerge feeling drained, cleansed. The outside light brings them back to the world, but they're not the same any more.

"I can't imagine how you would do this for a non-Navajo, Matt. I wish I could, for Ana's sake."

They sat there a minute. Matt studied the leaves stuck to the tile around a metal drain. The mockingbird splashed in the fountain briefly and took wing, disappearing into the sky.

"I think that helps," he said. "A lot of it is the mood, the atmosphere, isn't it?"

"Yes, it is." Bisti paused. "You said this was between us. So, just between us, I have a video of a Blessing Way I sat in on two years ago. I had to get permission from the participants to tape it, and promise not to show it in public. You're not the public; you're a friend in need. Would you want to see some of it? I have it in my office, right down the walk here."

"Claro que sí. I bet a little would go a long way to convey the general idea."

"Right. A little is plenty. Especially since you don't speak Navajo."

An hour later Matt was back in his truck by the church. He sat there with the windows down to let the hot air out, thinking. Then he jotted down some items in his little notebook: have another consultation with Hleo; go see Fito and nail down renting his place; call Ianthe and the others—tons of stuff to do, and not much time to do it. Better get going.

He started the engine, let the oil pressure build up, and switched on the air conditioner. The immediate next thing to do was think about lunch. He was too preoccupied to have much of an appetite, but if Ana still wasn't interested in food, he needed to come up with something tempting enough to get her eating.

Ana was close to tears when she left the hospital, mostly because her beloved Abuelita was so discouragingly unresponsive, but also because she didn't like hospitals in general. Of course there would be suffering and pain there, but even so, the level of medical care was not as advanced as what she had grown up with. Most of those patients would not have been in a hospital at all on Thomo.

Except for her mother. That was too painful to think of. She forced herself to count the elevator buttons.

It didn't help that she detoured through the maternity ward, expecting the sight of so many newborn babies to cheer her up. The actuality was the opposite.

She had to concentrate to remember where she had parked her Corolla. She dropped her keys, put the car in the wrong gear at first, and had trouble safely negotiating the concrete spiral out of the parking garage. Blotting her eyes with a tissue and concentrating desperately on her driving, she managed to pull out onto the street without embarrassment. There was little traffic on the street behind the hospital.

She was alone, utterly alone, more isolated than when she'd landed on Earth and squads of armed men had been chasing her. Then, she had known no one, but it felt worse now because she did have friends and loved ones. Those among them who might conceivably help ease her pain were the very ones who either wouldn't be able to or wouldn't want to: not poor Matt—it hurt to see how worried he was for her—not Ianthe or Rothan, certainly not Hleo. The only person she could confide in was in the hospital, and fighting for her own life. It was such a....

Oh! That's a red light! How had she not seen that! She mashed the brake pedal quickly. The tires protested but the car stopped, two feet over the white line, just as the light turned green. The pickup behind her squealed to a stop, delivering the lightest bump to the back of her car. The driver honked his horn. She pressed the tissue to her eyes again with a shaking hand. The driver honked again, longer this time. Checking the cross-traffic, she accelerated through the intersection and pulled into a parking spot along a row of stores.

The driver of the truck, a forty-one year old sometime-handyman named Rudy Jaramillo, pulled up behind the Corolla. There was no parking slot available, so he stopped halfway into the lane of traffic. As he did so, his twenty-three year old, 300 pound, son, Chote ("Shorty"), leaped out of the passenger side and began slamming his hands on the trunk of the little Corolla, rocking it up and down. He had to get control of that hot-headed kid, and fast. Chote had a bad anger management problem.

He got out and quickly ascertained his prized vintage Chevy pickup had sustained no damage. The Corolla had only a cracked tail light housing.

The driver of the Corolla opened the door and got out. It was a woman, a young, small woman with long, flowing hair, in new jeans, athletic shoes, and a long-sleeved silver shirt, open at the collar. Chote was now directing a tirade of insults down at her. Twice as large as his father (his nickname was ironic), with a head shaved bald, and a puffy, scowling face, he loved to loom over normal-sized people, the better to enjoy their discomfort. He stepped to within boxing distance of the woman, continuing to berate her. Rudy noticed she was not cowed, however. Quite the contrary, she was eerily composed, feet apart, weight on her toes, arms held slightly away from her sides, hands relaxed and ready. Her head was turned slightly down, but except for her eyes riveted on Chote's face, her own bore absolutely no expression.

Moving up behind his son, Rudy looked more closely. Several hitches in prison and on the run had made him an expert reader of faces. Hers showed no inkling of fear, despite Chote's aggressive closeness and his threatening gestures and obscenities. She stood absolutely still, radiating controlled, lethal potential. Chote was too involved in his own performance to notice she was measuring him like a rattlesnake, eyes burning, waiting the moment to strike. Rudy had never seen anyone look as threatening as this woman did. Somehow he knew in his guts that if Chote actually touched her, she would seriously hurt his stupid boy.

He grabbed his son's arm, hard.

"Chote! Coolate, Chote! Ain't no thing to beat up a little woman! You want your parole officer to put you back in with your brother? We don't need none a' that. No harm done, vato. Get in the truck. ¡Ahorita pronto! ¡Muévate!"

His dumbass son continued to puff with hostility as they drove off. The woman was still standing there, facing the spot where Chote had stood, only her scary eyes cutting in their direction. Rudy could swear his truck steered a wide berth around her by itself. A chill prickled the back of his neck. ¡Diablos! He'd cross himself as soon as his son couldn't see him do it. What was this pinche city coming to with people like that loose in it?

Ana came to herself some seconds after the truck was gone. She sat back in the car, feeling the delayed anxiety surging in her soul. She was always steady during a crisis, but she usually paid for it afterward. She closed her eyes and breathed deeply, feeling her heart pounding in her breast.

This was such a terrible day, one of a succession of terrible days. After several minutes she got out of the car and looked at the back end. One of those plastic things over a tail light was cracked, but that was the only damage she could see. Julio could fix that easily. A tidal wave of grief nearly overcame her. She leaned on the trunk. If that stupid, stupid man had come within five inches of her she would have...she would have.... A tear appeared on the trunk between her fingers. She wiped her cheeks with the back of a trembling hand.

A door slammed nearby, followed by a jingling bell. A woman walked out of a storefront forty feet away. She was stout but nicely dressed, her heels clicking crisply, and her hair was freshly permed. Ana looked at the store. A painted sign on the window said "Dreamers—Curl Up and Dye."

It was a hair salon. Ana watched the woman sashay proudly down the sidewalk. She must be expecting to meet someone. A lover? Girl friends? Co-workers?

Facing the stores on the other side of the street were older, ugly hospital annexes. It was a drab, seedy part of town. Her dusty old Corolla with the cracked tail light fit right in. She looked back at the stores. Thoman women never messed with their hair. Never. It wasn't done.

Ana walked to the salon and pulled open the door. The bell jingled.

"Yes, ma'am?" said a woman at the counter.

Ana looked around. On the walls were large posters of models sporting a wide variety of hair styles.

"May we help you, ma'am?" the woman repeated.

Ana studied the posters, jaw muscles flexing.

"Ma'am?"

"That one," Ana pointed. "I want that one."

"Uh, *that* one? Are you sure?" the woman said.

Ana glared at her. The woman's eyebrows raised a half inch. She looked to the back of the salon.

"Yes, ma'am. Tomás has a chair open. Right this way."

"Order me a beer when I'm about halfway back, will you, please?"

Michelle nodded as Coombs waded out into the surf, selected a wave, and launched himself into it. God, he had fine muscles across his back. He was about the strongest man she'd ever known. And the handsomest—that dimple! It was embarrassing how that attracted her.

He had settled into a steady stroke, already a hundred yards from the beach, headed for the tiny island they had both swum to not an hour before. It had to be a half mile away. One round trip was a good workout for her, but not for Rob. She hadn't done well with the waves, being more of a pool swimmer. Rob had said something about staying in shape. Perhaps it was logical for former Seals, after all, to swim in the open ocean.

She leaned back and sipped her fruit punch. The shade of the palm trees and the light breeze off the ocean was heavenly. The beach was blindingly white even through sunglasses.

This mini-vacation was a welcome break, even if it wasn't quite perfect. Rob was a great companion, but they hadn't exactly bonded. Their lovemaking was wonderful, but somehow that's all it had been—a mutually welcome and delightful physical diversion, accomplished with care and respect. Still, it had not been the union of souls she would have welcomed. Rob seemed reserved somehow, and to be honest, she was herself, as well.

Maybe it had something to do with the frightful mission they'd been on so recently. She thought they'd got past that, but perhaps not. Perhaps it was unfinished business.

The cries of sea gulls nearby caught her attention. A stone's throw away, two young girls were shouting and tossing bits of bread up to the birds, hovering on the breeze over their heads. Not a piece of bread made it back to the beach.

The tiny island, the size of the average par five golf hole, was deserted. Coombs waded out of the water whipping his arms back and forth to keep his muscles loose for the return trip. It would take maybe ten minutes to walk all the way around the narrow beach. He marked a clump of palm trees at the other end as the spot to swim back from, so the gentle current would put him back by Michelle. He began walking.

She was such a sweet woman. He regretting having involved her in his dirty doings. As it turned out, he could have conducted the mission by himself and no one would have known but Hleo—and his unfortunate target, of course. He'd served six full tours in his career, gone on a dozen missions, and never had to kill an unarmed opponent before.

He thought back to the ghastly feeling of watching Ana dive into that river, an instinctive act of such incredible selflessness that it still took his breath away. And those goons who had come after her—they were armed professionals, they had meant her ill, and they deserved what they got, and so did the s.o.b. who had sent them, unarmed or not. He didn't regret any of it. Except for Michelle.

He arrived at the clump of palm trees, whipped his arms some more, waved at Michelle, and headed back into the water.

By the time he touched sand again he was feeling a definite burn throughout his body. That was good. When the water was waist deep he stood, smoothed his hair, and set a course for the beer he could see on the table next to Michelle. She waved, her cell phone to her ear.

He took two welcome swallows while she finished the call.

"OK, then," she said, "we'll see you about eight."

He discreetly stifled a beer burp.

"Who was that?"

"Matt. He says Ana needs us back there. Tomorrow." Her face was serious. "The Zimmers will meet us at the airport. I'll get my mother to clear the extra days with your boss if you need."

He didn't have to think about it.

"Won't be a problem. I'm ready if you are."

"OK, Fito. I'll try to get by this afternoon but I've got a ton of things to do, so if I don't make it, I'm sure it'll be fine. We'll see you tomorrow night. Muy agradecido, hermano."

Matt set the phone down and jotted yet another note on the sheets of yellow paper before him. Across the room, Julio was still riveted before the computer, eyes fixed on the screen, only his mouse hand flicking quickly. He'd been playing solitaire ever since lunch—Matt glanced at his watch—over an hour.

"Mijo."

No response.

"Son!"

"Yessir?"

"Are you OK, mijo?"

"Sure, Dad."

Matt scooted his dining chair around to face his son.

"You worrying about Mom?"

Julio's face fell perceptibly.

"Is she gonna be OK, Dad?"

"I think so, son. Everybody has ups and downs, even your mother. But Mom's tough. And we're gonna help her."

"Who were you talking to?"

"Fito Dominguez. He owns the little tavern just this side of Mesilla."

"Were going there?"

"For the party for Mom. You know, the healing ceremony, sort of."

"Why do we have to go there? Why don't we have it here?"

"Here's too familiar. It needs to be a strange place, but a friendly place."

"But that's a beer bar!"

"Not this Thursday. Fito doesn't have much business during the week, so he rented the whole place to us for a private party. He has a small meeting room that should be about right—it even has audio and video equipment, and a good sound system. You'll see."

Julio didn't look convinced.

"What about Abuelita, Dad. Is she going to be all right?"

"Of course she is. She had a simple operation, but no operation is that simple when the patient is 90. She's slow getting over it and they want to watch her closely for a few days until she gets some strength back. Mom's with her now. We'll hear how Abuelita's doing when she gets home."

Matt checked his watch again.

"And now, son, if you'll let me have a turn at the computer, I need to see if Hleo's data is downloaded yet. If it is I need to burn it onto a DVD. That's going to be a big part of the ceremony. You can play solitaire on your own computer, can't you?"

"Can I watch?"

"Well, yes, you could, but I think it would work better if everyone sees it for the first time together, tomorrow night. That's what Dr. Bisti recommends. OK?"

"OK, Dad," Julio said, clearly disappointed.

"It might help if you let me know as soon as you hear Mom drive up. She's the one who really mustn't see any of this."

"I will, Dad."

Matt watched his son walk dispiritedly out to the patio and head back to his room. He picked up the sheaf of yellow papers, reviewed the top page, and slid them into the folder next to the computer. He sat down at the keyboard and sighed, hoping that he hadn't been wrong to show Julio more confidence than he felt himself. The kids were as stressed as he was, maybe more, since they had little idea what was going on. At least Clio was getting a break being at Stallman's with Harry for the day. It pained him to see them worrying.

This whole healing ceremony business was getting to him. The Navajos had a thousand years of tradition behind theirs. They could rely on it to work. Dammit, he couldn't. He had to wing it. At least Melvin Bisti, Hleo, and Ianthe had thought it worth trying. One thing at a time, Méndez: concentrate. He focused on the monitor and started clicking keys.

Whoa! Hleo had been busy! There were nearly five gigabytes of files in the new folder Hleo had set up. What the hell were they? He didn't recognize any of the file extensions. VOB files? Hleo had said to burn all of them onto a DVD. That was easy enough. He slipped a blank DVD into the disk tray and began the process.

While the data copied he called the Esquire Motel, a mid-level inn popular with tourists visiting Mesilla and within walking distance of Fito's place, and confirmed the reservations he'd made the day before. He pulled out his to-do list, crossed that off, and checked the next item: retrieve the DVD player and projector from the hall closet, put them in a tote bag with an extension cord, and put the bag back in the closet. Now he'd have a backup machine if Fito's system failed.

The disk tray had slid open. The copying was done. He pushed the tray back into the machine and waited while it whirred and clicked. The movie-playing software opened. He clicked "play," and sat back to watch. Music began blasting out of the speakers. He turned the volume down to a whisper as pictures began to flash on the monitor. What the hell? A slide show? Surely Hleo hadn't sent him a four hour slide show?

He clicked to the next track of the movie, and the next. Finally, there was a person dressed in a blue, Thoman-style robe, saying something into the camera.

At the bottom was a crawl in English. He'd just started to follow along when Julio whispered from the patio.

"She's back, Dad."

"Thanks, son. Good work."

He stopped the movie and ejected the disk, slipping it into an envelope and pushing it into his folder with the notes. He closed the software, clicked to the screen saver, and headed to the kitchen.

He was drying the blender with a dish towel when he heard the patio door open.

"Hey, babe," he said, turning to face her, "how's Ab...," and paused in shock.

She'd cut her hair! She'd cut the hell out of it! Her beautiful hair, that he loved so much! It was gone! It was a...a what? A page boy? Barely below the ears, with spiky tufts sticking out all around? He couldn't conceive of her doing such a thing. It looked awful. She looked awful.

"Uh, you cut your hair!"

That sounded stupid the second he said it.

"Yes," she clipped, "I did. Abuelita's no better. I'm not sure she knew who I was. Clio was right all along. Medicine here is so primitive!"

Without another word she stalked straight to the bedroom.

Chapter 18

Clio clapped her hands in delight as the two quarter horses thundered past the finish line. Harry shouted "Yeah!" and pumped his hand in the air as the two powerful animals slowed to a gallop and continued around the track.

"Deep Six did it!" he said. "Your horse won again!"

"He's not my horse."

"Yeah, but he was nothing until you fixed his gaskins with that funky liniment. Now he runs confident and strong. He's got style!"

"He was growing too fast. Those muscles just needed to relax. You helped train him."

"Let's go see if they need help with the horses, and then find Mrs. Flores and head back, OK? It's getting late."

They climbed down from the small viewing stand and began walking to the stables. The sun, an hour from setting, was directly in their eyes.

"Why does that goo of yours smell so nasty?"

"Probably the dimethylsulfoxide. That's the base for the other ingredients. It smells like sulfur."

"Die-what?"

"It's a solvent, made from wood. Vets know about it. It's good by itself. It might have helped you with your bruises, but it can burn bare skin unless it's diluted. If I'd had the liniment when you needed it, I'd have tried it on you. It mostly soaks in."

"Horse liniment on Harry. Sure, why not?"

Mr. Stallman was chatting with another gentleman outside the stables. A pickup with a horse trailer was parked nearby. The jockeys were walking the horses the final furlong.

The man, a tall Hispanic with a handlebar mustache and embroidered guayabera over crisp black jeans and shiny boots, was saying, "Dammit, Hank, Mr. Zerk beat your horse bad last month, but there's no doubt that yours is the best today. That's a good horse, and good training."

"Yeah, Tony's an ace. Got good horse doctors, too. No injections or anything. Here comes my horse fixers now." He winked at the approaching youngsters. "Fixed up his hindquarters, they did."

"I might make you an offer for that horse, Hank."

"No hurry. Take your time. Let's do this again next month and see what happens. Make sure he's still getting faster."

They shook hands and the man opened the gate to his trailer and retrieved a horse blanket while Stallman shouted into the barn.

"Tony, will you close up when you're done?"

A voice inside said something. Stallman turned to Harry and Clio. He nodded in the direction of a woman standing outside the little office building.

"Mrs. Flores loves a good horse race too. Come on, guys. It's time to wrap this up and let you three go home."

Together in the backseat, Harry and Clio happily reviewed the evening's match races while Mrs. Flores headed north up Highway 28.

They'd traveled less than five minutes when Harry became aware a car was passing them. He barely had time to register that it was a black Escalade before it veered into them with a loud scrape, forcing their car off the road. The last thing he remembered was Mrs. Flores screaming, the car swerving toward a clump of trees, and a violent crash.

Clio was dazed, but aware of being pulled out of the car and hands patting over her body. One of them removed her cell phone. She heard it crunched into pieces, felt herself tossed into another vehicle, Harry tossed in with her, and then all was blackness.

She had no idea how long it took her head to stop spinning, but when it did she realized that the darkness was not because it was night. They were in the back of an SUV whose rear windows were tinted black. There was a panel between them and the front of the vehicle, but she could see slivers of light around the edges.

She checked Harry over as best she could in the dimness. His arms and legs felt sound, and his head moved easily, side to side with the swaying of the vehicle. He was breathing. She patted his cheeks and chest and talked to him. Finally, he began to come to, groaning and stretching his limbs.

"Wh...what happened?" he said.

The thumping norteño music on the other side of the partition made whispering unnecessary. A normal speaking voice was barely enough.

"This car ran us off the road. Whoever was in it grabbed us."

"Ohh, nooo," Harry moaned.

"Do you know who they are?"

"Yeah. ¡Ai! My chest hurts—seat belt, I guess. Yeah, they're drug dealers."

"Drug dealers?"

"Yeah. They supply that gang that's been after me, that shot at us. We're in real trouble now. I'm sorry, Clio!"

"Why would they want you?"

"One of the neighborhood gang told me these guys were their suppliers. He shouldn't have told me that. They're afraid I'll tell the cops."

"Oh, Harry!"

"You got your cell phone?"

"No, they took it. They smashed it."

"What're we gonna do, Clio?"

"I have no idea, Harry. None."

The ride was interminable. There were periods of normal driving and periods of stop and go driving. It was hard to tell how long they traveled—an hour or more, certainly. Finally, at one of the stops, the vehicle backed up. Then the engine shut off. It rocked as people got out.

The back lid opened. Six men were standing there, four with pistols drawn.

"You," one of them said. He grabbed Harry's ankle and pulled him rudely out of the SUV. Forcing one of his arms behind him, he pushed him into the building they had backed up to.

"You, chica. Vamos," said another.

There was nothing Clio could do but scoot out the back, where she was grabbed like Harry and marched after him. She got a glimpse of a trashy walled parking area and the shabby back end of some concrete block building, before she was forced down a freight entrance and into a small warehouse. Cases of beer were stacked head high down both side walls. Her captor pushed her across the room to a metal door which he thrust her through, stepped back, and shut the door. Harry was sitting slumped on a row of beer cases.

A quick glance showed the room made a good choice for a prison cell. It was also of concrete blocks, with no windows nor even a vent for air. A bare light bulb hanging from the ceiling was the only illumination. The door was metal, hinged from the outside, and shut tightly.

The men had been rough looking, most wearing wife-beater shirts, as if proud of their arms and shoulders and tattoos. Harry groaned and rubbed his chest. Shakily, Clio sat next to him. The room was stuffy and smelled of stale beer. She wondered what had happened to Mrs. Flores. Three cockroaches scuttled along one wall. She couldn't stop shivering.

Matt and Ana and Julio were having a late snack, or rather, Matt and Julio were having a late snack. Ana was too jittery to eat. It didn't help to have Raisin crouched on the back of the couch behind her, haunches and elbows higher than her back, eyes wide, tail twitching. Her majestic black ears pointed this way and that, their long black hairs swaying like tassels.

"She should be back by now."

"Yeah, she should," agreed Matt. "She said something about staying to see some test races once the afternoon cooled off a bit. Maybe they were slow to get started."

"I'll call her," Ana said.

She walked five steps to the kitchen, snatched the cordless phone from its charger, and punched in the numbers.

"No answer," she said, after a few seconds. "She must have her phone turned off."

"Pass it over," Matt said. "I'll call Stallman's office."

There was no answer there either.

"Hmm. Well, it's late. The office must be closed." He stood and gathered the plates on the table. "I'll put this stuff up and then drive down there and see for myself. Son, wipe the table, please."

He had just set the dishes in the dishwasher when the phone rang. Ana answered in a flash. She listened a long minute, asked "When can we visit?" and then laid the phone down gently.

"Who was that?" Matt asked.

"The hospital," she said, sitting down again. "They've moved Abuelita to intensive care." She slammed the table with both hands. "*Zhad!*" she shouted. One of the candles fell off the centerpiece. She slammed it again. "*Zhad!*"

Raisin raised up on her front paws, ears laid back, and hissed. Matt knelt by Ana, laying an arm around her waist, thinking of Ana's poor mother and her stillborn twin brother. Julio rubbed Raisin's shoulders, trying to settle the cat down a little.

"Did they say why?"

"I don't know. Something about blood pressure. There's a visiting hour at 9:00, but I'm going now. I'll make them let me in!"

Tears leaked down her cheeks. Matt hugged her tighter.

"OK, sugar. I'll go get Clio and we'll meet you there."

"I need to change."

She got up and ran to the bedroom.

"You better go along, son. Try to keep her calm."

Raisin, responding to the rubbing, nevertheless hissed again.

Ana was back in minutes, wearing jeans and a burnt orange shirt. She sat at the table and began lacing up her flats.

The phone rang again. Matt picked it up, glanced at Ana, and pressed the speaker button.

"Hello?"

"Mr. Méndez?"

"Yes?"

"This is Policarpio Flores. You know, the husband of Lola Flores. She works for Mr. Hank."

"Yes, sir. How do you do?"

"I'm fine, Mr. Méndez, but my wife, she is banged up a little. She had a wreck coming back from work this evening."

"No!"

"Sí. The airbag, it hit her pretty hard. The hospital let her go, but she still dizzy. She think a car force her off the road. She's not sure, but she think someone take Harry and your daughter, maybe to the hospital. Have you heard from them?"

"No!"

"Well, she sort of think they go back the other way, you know, toward Canutillo, or maybe El Paso. If you not heard from them, then maybe you better check the hospitals, or call the police, ¿qué no?"

"I will, Mr. Flores. Thank you very much. Our best wishes to your wife, sir."

He set the phone in the charger. Raisin was staring at Ana, eyes wide. Ana looked far more dangerous. Matt's mind was whirling. They wouldn't be in a hospital. A Samaritan would have taken Mrs. Flores too, or waited for an ambulance. This sounded bad.

"Which cops would we call? New Mexico? Texas? City? County? No way to tell."

"The pod," she said, her voice flat.

"The gravity tag!" Julio added.

"Right," Matt said. "You got your cell phone, wife?"

Anna nodded. Matt patted his jeans.

"I have mine. Julio?"

"I'll get it."

"OK. Let's go."

They didn't notice Raisin until she jumped into the pod with them. No one thought to object.

"You fly, son."

Julio took the far front seat and began throwing switches. In minutes they were rising above the cottonwood trees toward scattered clouds and perhaps a third of a moon. It was windy, but mercifully, no dust was blowing. Matt briefly regretted not bringing a pistol, but then realized the last thing he wanted was a shootout over his daughter. When they located her, if she was someplace other than a hospital they'd call the local police, wherever that was. He didn't remember picking up his grandfather's bastón—had Julio?—but there it was, on the floor between the seats.

"We never tested the gravity tags, did we?" Matt said.

"No," said Ana, "but they have to work. I've never used them, but the scanner is simple enough to operate."

"I hope so," Matt replied. "You better sit up here by the instruments. I'll move back."

They changed places. Julio set the radio to the local air traffic control frequency.

"How high should we fly?" he asked.

"Hleo estimated a twenty mile range," Ana said. "If we fly two miles up, we can cover forty miles side to side."

"Good," Matt said. "At two miles we'll be invisible from the ground, moon or no moon. Son, let's search from here south along the Rio Grande down as far as Ysleta. A thirty or forty mile swipe should cover the most of the area. If we get nothing we can move over and do it again."

"How fast, Mom?"

"Not too fast. Forty or fifty miles per hour." She was fiddling with knobs on the instrument panel. "It's on. This screen will show when it's detected."

"Does it scan to the sides, or in all directions, Mom?"

"I can aim it. I just scanned behind us. Now I'm pointing it ahead and to the sides. It's less a...atten...weak when it's focused."

"Attenuated," Matt said to himself.

Long minutes passed. They drifted over Chamberino, La Union, and Canutillo. It was completely silent in the pod. More minutes crept by. Ana concentrated on the little display screen. Matt, leaning forward from one of the back seats, his head between his son and his wife, alternated between the screen and the ground ahead.

The scattered lights below thickened into glittering strands, collecting along the Rio Grande and Interstate 10. In the near distance, El Paso was a glowing mat of shimmering colors. It would have been beautiful if they had been in the mood to appreciate it.

"Any air traffic, son?"

"No sir. Flying's restricted over populated areas. There could be medical helicopters. They'd be much lower."

"Oh!" said Ana.

"What?" said Julio and Matt in unison.

"A contact. Ahead, seven miles. Maybe eight."

"Which side?" asked Julio.

"Right."

"Right? Are you sure?" Matt asked.

"I'm sure. Why?"

"Because that's gotta be in Mexico. In Ciudad Juárez."

"So what?"

"Well, for one thing, they have thirty different kinds of police over there. Even if I had their phone numbers, which I don't, I wouldn't know which bunch to call. They might not have trained SWAT teams like we have over here, if you could even trust them. Many are corrupt."

"Corrupt?"

"Yeah, in the pay of drug smugglers. The Las Cruces police told me the local gangs were getting into drug dealing. If they went to Mexico, I'd bet this has something to do with those kids who bothered Harry. Maybe they had something against him. I bet Harry's the one they were after."

He thought a second.

"If the druggies took them into Mexico it must have been to some sort of headquarters. I don't want to think what we might be getting into. It could be a real mess."

"Clio is already into it," Ana said, her voice tight. "We're going to get her out."

"Yes, we are," Matt conceded. "But if they're in Mexico, we're totally on our own. Let's check it out. We'd better be very careful."

"You sound like Rob Coombs."

"Probably for the same reason," Matt replied cryptically. He had seen Coombs make Ana an honorary Seal because he had been so impressed by her abilities in combat. He said a silent prayer that Coombs' opinion was correct. Tonight he might find out.

Holding her ear to the door, Clio could hear occasional bits of conversation in the warehouse. Over the course of an hour she put several things together. She and Harry had been taken by a combination of a group of drug dealers and several Tirilongos, the gang from Las Cruces. The Tirilongos intended to impress their suppliers with their concern for loose ends, and the suppliers intended to similarly impress the big shot cartel members, the Zetas, with their ruthlessness. They were waiting for the Zetas to arrive. Much of the rest of what she heard was about what various members were going to buy with their money, how they were smarter and more dangerous than their competition, and, incongruously, the ranking of local soccer teams. They were drinking: she could hear beer bottles clanking frequently. Several broke, amid much laughter. They didn't mention what they intended for their captives, but Clio had no illusions about that.

When footsteps approached the door, she ran back to sit next to Harry. She put an arm around him. The door opened. Two men with pistols studied them briefly and stepped back for a third man, who entered. He had two plastic Pepsi bottles.

"Tenga," he said. "It's gonna be a while."

He handed one to each and walked out. The door slammed.

"Oh, good," said Harry, uncapping his and taking two big gulps.

Clio looked at her bottle and then at Harry's. She grabbed his away from him.

"Don't drink that!" she said.

"Why not? I'm thirsty!"

"Look at it! The seal's been broken. See mine?"

She looked more closely. There was a tiny white residue on the bottom. She unscrewed the cap. She sniffed it, stuck a finger into the neck, tilted the bottle slightly, and touched her finger to her tongue.

"This stuff isn't right, Harry. They've put something in it. Don't drink any more."

"Well, OK."

She thought a minute. The taste was familiar, a vague bitterness with a hint of lemon and copper. She couldn't be sure what it was, but it certainly wasn't all Pepsi.

Why would they give them drugged sodas? If they wanted to kill them, they could just shoot them. She decided to watch what happened to Harry after his two swallows. She could copy his reactions but keep her wits about her. She carried the bottles to the back of the tiny room and poured about half of each behind some cases of beer. Then she set one by Harry and the other close to her.

"Remember: don't drink any more, OK?"

Harry looked at her. He blinked slowly.

"OK," he said, finally.

Time passed slowly. Neither had a watch. Clio listened at the door as best she could, but learned little more than that every other word their captors used was profanity. She couldn't listen for long because Harry kept falling asleep. Every few minutes she had to rub his arms and back and beg him to stay awake.

She was doing that for the fifth or sixth time when there were voices close on the other side of the door. Quickly bracing Harry against the wall behind them, she leaned against him and shut her eyes. The door opened. Footsteps approached. She opened her eyes sleepily. Three men again, one with a gun. One grabbed Harry and another seized her by one arm and hauled her to her feet. They were dragged into the larger room and dumped in dirty white plastic chairs.

Remembering to let her head wobble slightly and keep her eyelids half shut, she took in the scene. There were a lot of men in the room: four on the opposite side, near where they had been marched in, and three closer. The men in back were holding beers, smirking and wise-cracking. She recognized the closest one: Mando, the kid who had hassled her and Harry before the drive-by shooting. The second nearest was not much older than Mando, with a wispy, ragged mustache and tattoos on his forearms. The third was older and sloppy fat. Both he and Mando held pistols.

"OK, Lito," said the fat one, gruffly. "Ees your gang. Hágalo." ("Do it.")

Lito tossed his head insolently and slapped the pistol against Mando's chest.

"Toma," he said. "Tu lo chingaste. Fíjalo." ("Here. You screwed it up. You fix it.")

Mando clasped the pistol clumsily, turning it over in his hand as if he'd never seen a pistol before. He looked trapped. Lito raised his chin.

"¡Tíralo!" ("Shoot him!"), he spat out.

Mando looked down at the pistol. It was shaking in his hand.

"¡Pendejo!" ("Dumbass!") snarled Lito, grabbing the pistol away from the frightened boy. Pushing Mando to one side he stepped in front of Harry. Harry's eyes were half open but his face remained slack. Lito glared from Mando to Harry, and raised the pistol.

"What can you see?" Ana asked.

"Are we directly over the gravity tag?"

"Yes."

"I see a bunch of back streets, lots of low buildings. Few lights—not many businesses open, if that's what they are. Little or no traffic. Too dark to see pedestrians. The building under us faces the street but there are no lights on in front. There's dim light in the back...seems to be a walled parking area, opening on an alley. There are three vehicles parked there. The buildings on both sides have similar parking areas...but no vehicles. The building is longer front to back than it is wide."

He checked the screen Ana was watching, showing rows of black and gray rectangles, and a single glowing green dot: their daughter, please God. He looked through the windshield again.

"Looks like Clio is in the back third of the building, to the right, if one were going in through the parking area."

"Let's get down there."

"To check it out, remember?"

"I remember."

"Son, can you bring the pod to within a foot of the roof right about where the dot is?"

"I think so, Dad."

"Stop a little short. Don't bump the roof."

"Nossir."

With his hand on the controller, alternately looking out the window and at the display screen, Julio eased the pod gradually downward, nudging it ahead and to one side slightly. Covering that last 100 feet was the longest thirty seconds of Matt's life.

"OK, Dad."

"Well done, son. Ready, babe?"

She had never looked more ready.

"We'll ease to the edge of the roof and see if anyone's below. If it's clear, we'll look for a quiet way down and peek inside. Right?"

Raisin had appeared at her side. She laid a hand on the cat's shoulders, her face grim.

"Bait'anà," she murmured ("Sit").

"OK, son, pop the hatch."

Ana and Raisin slipped out before it was halfway up. Matt followed.

"Dad!" Julio whispered.

"What?"

"The bastón."

"Oh, yeah."

Julio handed it out to him. He hefted its solid weight. Abuelo's lucky bastón. It might come in handy. Who knew?

"Take the pod up high enough to where you can see us if we wave at you from front or back," Matt whispered. "Leave the hatch open."

"I will, Dad. Be careful," but his father had disappeared into the gloom.

Matt could see well enough in the moonlight combined with the weak city light reflected off the pollution in the air, but where the hell was Ana? And Raisin? He looked around as the pod's vibrations faded overhead. He was the only one on the roof. Tiptoeing to the back of the building, he cautiously peeked over. There were the three vehicles, in the faint light of a bulb in the entrance somewhere underneath him.

He looked more closely. To the left, on the far side of a big pickup, was a shoe, with a leg attached. He moved to his left, to see around the truck. It was a man, lying face down. That looked like Ana's work. How had she got down there? Maybe via the dumpster just below. Cautiously, he lowered himself over the edge, feeling for the dumpster with his feet. It creaked slightly but took his weight. He dropped softly to the ground—dirt, thankfully, not gravel. The man had one arm under him, the other splayed out, hand turned under at the wrist. He was still as a sack of grain.

He eased around the dumpster to the back entrance and knelt, leaning slowly to peer around the edge. The light was coming from a room twenty feet down the passageway. Halfway down it, Ana was crouched behind some boxes with her hand on Raisin. Feeling for each step, he moved next to Ana. Raisin was trembling, her powerful haunches cocked, ears pointed toward the voices inside. Several male voices were laughing. Ana signaled: two men to the left, two to the right. He understood instantly. He motioned that the two on the left were his and the two on the right were hers. She would want that side. That's the side Clio should be on. She nodded and turned back to the room.

And then all hell broke loose.

While Lito was taunting Mando, Clio was fighting panic. She couldn't let them shoot Harry, but what could one girl do against six armed men and a boy? She was paralyzed by helplessness. Her mind was not working right. She'd had none of the drugged Pepsi, but she felt as fuzzy-headed as if she had.

Something was calling to her, some sensation. What? It wasn't a voice, not a smell. *What was it?* Frantically, she tried to concentrate. Some tiny corner of her brain was trying to get through to her consciousness. A sound? A *sound!* Yes! It was a faint, low hum she could feel rather than hear. Was that...? Yes! It had to be! It was the pod!

She started in shock, but no one noticed. The others were watching Mando and Lito. The pod! That meant.... She almost cried out. Lito raised the pistol.

Hardly knowing what she was doing, she stood suddenly and hissed from the back of her throat, showing her teeth, as loudly and as harshly as she could, directly at Lito, distracting him. She glared, took two steps forward, and hissed again, and from behind them came the reply: a hair-raising, inhuman scream. Lito whirled around as a golden thunderbolt with fangs and claws hit him square in the chest, tumbling him to the floor. Locked together, man and beast rolled over and over in a frenzy, both screaming bloody murder. Her mind clicked into gear: she kicked Mando in the crotch for the second time in two weeks and turned to the fat man, backing away and waving his pistol, trying to get a clear shot at Raisin. Clio hissed again, raising her arms and shouting "Dhava!" ("Attack!"). While the man gaped at Clio in confusion, Raisin sprang at his face.

Matt heard the hiss, but he wasn't expecting it and didn't know what it was. Raisin did, however, instantly rocketing out from under Ana's hand in a heartbeat, streaking into the room screaming like a banshee. Ana followed immediately, with Matt, taking a half second to process things and grasp his bastón, close on her heels.

Ana's man was closest. It hadn't yet occurred to the man that his most immediate threat was from behind—he was watching Raisin's attack, dumbfounded. Just as Ana landed a flying jump against the side of his knee, Matt encountered his man on the left, who was also gaping at the cat and her prey. Using the upper end of the bastón, he cracked him as hard as he could on the back of his head. The man dropped like a stone, revealing the man beyond him, throwing down his beer and grabbing a pistol out of a shoulder holster. With his right hand Matt whipped the lower end of the staff up against the man's forearm, sending the pistol flying, and immediately brought the left end down sharply over his ear, one-two. The man collapsed. Such a great weapon, Matt thought, whirling to see Ana's second man clutching his throat and sinking to his knees.

He checked the room. It was already over: seven men were down. Three were out cold. One was rocking in pain holding a dislocated knee. One near Clio was rolling back and forth with his hands between his legs, and two were moaning in terror where they lay, in shredded clothing, leaving blots of blood on the floor as Raisin growled ominously at them. Ana and Clio were sobbing and embracing.

He took a second to whack the head of the man with the bad knee, settling him down considerably, and to slide the various firearms away from their owners with one end of the bastón.

"What's the matter with Harry?"

"They drugged him, Dad. He'll be all right."

"OK, then. We need to go, guys. Now."

He handed the staff to Ana, tossed Harry over his shoulder, and led them out back.

"Julio's overhead. Wave at him, mija."

The pod was at ground level in less than a minute. Matt loaded Harry into the backseat. Ana was slow to get in.

"What?" he asked her.

"Those men. We can't leave them like that."

"The hell we can't! Just watch!"

"No, Matt. At least call an ambulance!"

"Sugar, those guys and their kind have murdered over a thousand people so far this year."

"Maybe so, Matt. But we can't let someone die. I couldn't stand that."

"Hell, who would I call? Superman? Oh, all right—I have an idea. Get in. I'll be just a minute."

The outside man was still lying where he'd fallen—the eighth one they'd thumped, he realized, as he rifled the man's pockets. Sure enough: he had a cigarette lighter. He took that and the bandanna around the man's head and walked to the pickup in the back corner of the little lot and opened the hood. In the dim light of the lighter he located the fuel line. He snapped the lighter shut and started flexing the metal tube back and forth until it broke. He pushed the end coming from the tank toward the ground. The smell of gasoline told him what he needed to know.

Scooping a handful of dirt into the middle of the bandanna, he tied the corners together and soaked the bottom in the gasoline spreading under the truck. Stepping back a few yards, he lit the bandanna and tossed the smoking mass into the puddle. It ignited with a thump that moved him back an extra yard or two.

He jumped in the pod.

"Vamos," he said, shutting the hatch. "The faster the better, son."

Ana was looking at him.

"That'll bring the fire department," he said, unasked.

Julio realized he was actually on his first solo flight, in a one-of-a-kind billion dollar escape vehicle made on a distant planet, no less, but he was far too scared to enjoy the experience. He preferred to think through problems before working on them, but they had had to rush headlong into this one, and he hated that. A tight knot was forming in the pit of his stomach. There was no way he could let his family down. They had no one else to rely on. What if they got in trouble? What if they died?

From a hundred feet above he could see the front and the back of the building, but if they stayed against either wall he'd miss them. He eased the pod up another twenty feet. It was dark down there. He might be able to see a group of people, barely, but probably not if they waved or signaled.

He spent twenty seconds adjusting the scanner. The black and white display showed objects below according to their distance, closer ones lighter and farther ones darker. A little focusing produced nice outlines of the roof, the vehicles, and the wall around the back. People would be gray fuzzy spots, he supposed. Oops! There were *four* green dots. Clio's dot was where it had been, but now he could see three more dots just inside the building, not moving. Surely there were bad people somewhere there too, but without gravity tags they would be invisible. There seemed no point looking out the windshield when everyone was inside—but no, he needed to make sure no one else was approaching. He checked left and right quickly and then returned to the screen.

The dots had moved! Two were further inside the building and two were now at Clio's position, all moving irregularly. What was going on? The ache in his stomach redoubled. Now the dots came together. Was that good? Or had they been rounded up by bad guys? After a few seconds, the dots moved toward the back of the building. He looked out the windshield. Yes—there were people down there! Waving or not, he maneuvered the pod toward the ground.

His father's head appeared at the bottom edge of the hatch, then his shoulders, a body over the left one. Oh, of course: it was Harry. He steadied the pod while his dad stepped in, laid Harry in a back seat, and retreated. Clio climbed in next, checking Harry, who looked to be asleep. She took the second front seat. Raisin jumped in next, issued a muted hiss of greeting, and disappeared between the backseat and the lavatory bulkhead.

"Is Harry OK?" he whispered.

She nodded, turning in her seat to look out the hatch at their parents, arguing outside. Julio read Clio's moods as easily as she read his. She was scared and jumpy, but upset about something more, too.

"What's wrong?"

"Mom. She's different. What happened to her hair?"

Before he could reply, his mother climbed in. She hugged them both, hard, and squeezed in with Clio. Even though he'd seen their mother earlier in the evening, Clio had a point. In her agitation, her short, spiky hair made her look almost deranged.

"Mom, you OK?"

She was looking out the hatch. She nodded without turning.

They waited.

"Where's Dad?" he asked.

"*Lovashe hovori*" ("Speak Luvit"), she whispered, glancing back at Harry, adding "*He's coming.*"

As several very long minutes passed, the knot in his stomach grew bigger and bigger. They needed to leave. He could hear Raisin licking herself in back somewhere. He was on the point of saying something when a low whump ruffled the air in the pod and flickering yellow light illuminated the vehicles around them. His dad jumped into the backseat and they departed. Julio had a jillion questions, but they'd be home in ten minutes. He'd concentrate on flying for now.

The best part of the return trip was when he'd leveled off and was smoothly accelerating to 300 mph. In the silence, his father reached forward in the darkness and gripped his shoulder, adding a couple of pats.

He would always remember that moment. That was when he started to become a man.

Chapter 19

Matt carried Harry, groggy and mumbling, to his truck and belted him in. He finished as Julio was closing the barn doors. Clio was headed in his direction, carrying a small bottle. She was weeping. He knelt and hugged her.

"It's over, sugar. We're all fine. You did good, girl."

"I know, Dad," she sniffed. "I'm OK. It's Mom. She's in my shop. Can you go talk to her, please?"

"Sure. What's in the bottle?"

"They gave Harry a sedative. This will help him get over it."

"OK, daughter. I'll run Harry home soon as I see Mom. Don't worry about him. I'm sure he'll be fine."

He headed to the barn, pausing only to give his son an abrazo and tell him what a good job he'd done with the pod. He found Ana leaning with both hands on the counter of Clio's shop, her hair wild, orange shirt half pulled out of her jeans, staring fiercely at the counter top. He could see why she upset Clio.

"Babe?"

She jumped at the sound of his voice. That was upsetting in itself. She stared at him.

"It's over, love."

He gathered her to him. She resisted, holding herself stiff in his arms.

"We're all safe, sweetheart."

He patted her back. She was shaking—not trembling, but pulsing with nervous energy. She pulled back. He kept his hands on her shoulders. Her eyes were glittery and her voice had an edge.

"I know we're safe, and thank the stars for that, Matt. This should never have happened. It never would have happened if Clio had stayed away from Harry. This, this place is so violent! And, and your medicine is so primitive! And...."

Her voice tapered off and she burst into tears. He pulled her close and wrapped his arms around her.

"I know, babe, I know. We've had a rough patch these past weeks. But it's over now. Let's go clean up and get some sleep. It's late. We'll feel better when we're rested. C'mon, love."

She grabbed a tissue out of the box on the counter and blotted her eyes. Matt guided her out of the shop toward the house.

"I'm going to take a shower. Then I'm going to check on Abuelita."

"It's the middle of the night!"

"The intensive care section never closes."

"They won't let you see her. We can phone."

"No phone. They'll just brush me away, or off, or however you say it. Stupid prepositions! Even your language is hard! I want to see a real person. I'll make them talk to me!"

"Well, if you insist. I've got to run Harry home. Take the twins with you. They shouldn't be alone right now. Please?"

He hugged her again and kissed her wet cheek and opened the patio gate for her.

"It's gonna be OK, wife. It really is over. You'll see."

Matt had unexpected good luck returning Harry to his mother. He was sure she'd be frantic and maybe have called the police, but she wasn't and she hadn't. After they put Harry to bed, she explained her son was occasionally late coming home and sometimes stayed at the stables all night, nursing a sick horse or helping with a birth. Since he didn't have a cell phone, and access to Mr. Stallman's phone wasn't always possible, she had learned to not worry about him. She was predictably upset at Matt's slightly revised account of the auto accident: the trip to a Texas hospital from a good Samaritan, and Harry's treatment in the emergency room, which included a strong sedative. In a burst of inspiration he cautioned that the doctor had warned the sedative was excellent for pain but sometimes induced hallucinations, so Mrs. Saenz shouldn't worry if Harry was a little confused about what had happened to him. He promised to check on him the next day, adding that his insurance would cover any expenses.

He congratulated himself as he drove away. That little tale would fly with poor Mrs. Flores too. She was the one who might have medical expenses.

That took an hour, but he spent fifteen more minutes to swing by the hospital parking lot, looking for Ana's Corolla. The only entrance at that time of night was the emergency room. Two ambulances and a couple dozen cars were parked outside it, none of them Ana's. He headed home, feeling trembly himself.

It was 1:40 am. Jesus, what a night. Now he had an Ana story he might tell Coombs sometime, instead of listening to Coombs tell Ana stories. Thinking how events could have transpired differently gave him cold chills. They probably hadn't killed any of those thugs, but he didn't much care. Let the Mexican EMTs worry about them, if they cared to. He finally and definitively understood Coombs' high regard for Ana's abilities in a tight spot, even while he also understood why Ana had nearly come unglued when they arrived home. The recent crises—the kidnapping attempt, the miscarriage, Abuelita's surgery and difficult recovery, and Clio and Harry's godawful kidnapping, not to mention their harrowing rescue—would be enough to give anyone the fantods. Add in the memories of her stillborn twin brother and the tragic suicide of her mother, and it was a miracle she was still functioning at all. Ana was desperately stressed, but if Melvin Bisti was right, that could work to her advantage. She might be more easily affected by the healing ceremony.

Once home, he checked on the twins as usual, a ritual he found strangely comforting. Clio was sound asleep, Raisin stretched along her far side, blinking sleepily in the light of the tiny orange flashlight, one muscular forepaw over Clio's outstretched arm. He tiptoed to Julio's room, visualizing that same cat ripping into two armed thugs not four hours earlier. Pound for pound, a cat had to be about the most ferocious beast in the world. And other times, maybe the sweetest. Julio was asleep too, twisted in the sheet, but Matt roused him gently.

"Son. Son. Wake up, son."

"Hmm...umm, huh...Dad? Wh...what...."

"Did you learn anything about Abuelita?"

"Huh? Oh. Uh, yeah. They said she was doing much better." He rubbed his eyes. "They're gonna move her to a regular room tomorrow and if she's still OK they'll let her come home."

"Excellent. Thanks, son. Did Mom calm down any?"

"Maybe a little."

"OK, good. Go back to sleep, mijo. See you in the morning. Sleep well."

It was late afternoon by the clock, but the middle of the afternoon by the sun. Julio closed up his shop, passed through Clio's, and paused at the doorway. The dogs outside the door raised their heads hopefully. His sister was sitting cross-legged in the grass under the shade of a cottonwood, twiddling a stalk of grass against Raisin's head. The cat, flopped down in comfortable cat fashion, ignored the grass for the most part, only twitching her ears. As Julio watched, the animal bit perfunctorily at the annoyance twice, when it became too much to stand. He walked closer. The dogs followed.

"Tister."

No response.

"Whatcha doin'?"

"Nothing."

He sat down with her. The dogs sat too, a respectful distance from Raisin, who ignored them.

"What's the matter?"

She shook her head imperceptibly.

"You still upset about last night?"

She shook her head again.

"C'mon. What?"

"Oh, just Mom."

"What about her?"

"She's been after me."

"Yeah? Well, she's had a hard time...."

"So have I! That's no reason for her to gripe at me!"

"When did she gripe at you?"

"Last night. When we got back. And then, after lunch."

"What about?"

"About...stuff."

"What stuff?"

"About Harry. She said this was all Harry's fault. She doesn't want me to see him any more."

"Yeah?" He watched the grass twirl against Raisin's head. "Well, it kind of was, wasn't it?"

"It was not! It wasn't Harry's fault at all. He couldn't help it. I mean, Mom wouldn't have had a miscarriage if she'd stayed home like I wanted her to. Whose fault was that? I didn't gripe at her!"

"Hmm."

Julio had many strong points, but analyzing human affairs was not one of them. Both his sister and his mother seemed to have their reasons. Reconciling the two was beyond him.

Raisin raised her head suddenly and swiveled her ears forward, the tufts at the ends bobbing jauntily. The dogs sprang to their feet and sped toward the front entrance. Twenty seconds later Ana's Corolla turned in. It passed behind their house to reappear at the back, the two dogs racing ahead. Their parents got out. Ana headed into the patio. Matt walked over.

"Hey, guys. Everything secure here?"

"Yessir," said Julio.

"How's Abuelita?" Clio asked.

"On the mend. She's almost the Abuelita we know and love again. We can bring her home tomorrow."

Clio's face lightened up noticeably.

"And guess what? Guess what they gave her yesterday."

Clio glanced at Julio but said nothing.

"A blood thinner, just like you told them to. Her blood pressure went back to normal and the infection went way down."

"Way to go Tister," said Julio.

"Dad?"

"Yes, mija?"

"Do we have to go to that ceremony tonight?"

"You mean, you don't want to go?"

Clio looked at her knees. Julio kept a poker face. Matt sensed some unknown chemistry at work.

"Sugar, I don't want to order you to go. It's not like that. Mom's in pretty bad shape. She's hurting and she needs our help. I know you want to be a part of that. Besides, I think you'll have a good time and you might even learn something. There'll be some things that'll surprise you that you don't want to miss. Trust me on that, daughter. Please?"

Julio spoke up, nicely diffusing the issue.

"What do we wear, Dad?"

"I think clean jeans and a nice shirt or top would do. Someone important will be there."

"Who?"

"It's a secret, son. You'll find out in a few hours."

"Did he say a blue RAV-4?"

"Yup."

"I see it. Coming around the turn, far lane."

Five minutes later, Rob and Michelle were in the Zimmers' backseat, leaving El Paso International Airport, headed toward the Trans-Mountain Road.

"How you guys doing?" Coombs asked

"We're fine, thanks," said Scott, over his shoulder.

"How's Ana?" Michelle asked.

Scott glanced at his wife.

"Not well," said Ianthe, turning in her seat. "You know about the miscarriage, don't you?"

"We do," said Coombs.

"Of course you do," Ianthe replied. "You rescued her in Peru. Thank you, Scott. That was very brave of you."

"Ana did her part," Scott replied. "She was incredible."

"We also know Matt's grandmother is sick," Michelle added. "Ana's very fond of her. That has to be worrying her."

"It's even more complicated," said Ianthe. "Both of those things tie in to similar events in our family history on Thomo. I'm sure Ana finds it all terribly sad. She won't even talk to me about it."

"Not even to her sister?"

Michelle didn't have a sister. She thought sisters shared everything.

"No. Matt came to see us and I explained it to him. I am sure that Ana feels crushed by events. He's planned a whole evening to try to help her. Such a sweet man."

"I didn't know that," Coombs said. "What did Matt say when he called, Michelle?"

"He said Ana needed us, tonight, and that Scott would meet us at the airport. That's all."

"That's all we needed to know," Coombs said.

"You got that right," Scott replied, glancing at the side-view mirror. "We're her family now."

The motel they checked into, an hour later, a well-preserved adobe relic of the 1950s, was clean and basic. Scott and Ianthe declined a snack, but Rob, on the advice of the motel clerk, walked with Michelle to the Mesilla plaza, where they had a taquito and a beer and then took a turn around the square. It was an hour and a half until their function with Ana, twilight would come slowly, and the dry, warm air was perfect for walking.

After window-shopping the numerous stores on the plaza, most closed, they sat one of the benches to one side, now completely in shade. A handful of people were walking around it much as they had been. Several small children whooped and shouted on the bandstand in the center. Michelle was not saying much.

"What is it, girl friend?" Rob asked, after several minutes' silence.

"What's what?"

"You're pensive. Something's bothering you."

"Oh, not really." Fingers interlaced in her lap, she rubbed one thumb back and forth over the other. "I don't know."

"C'mon. It's Greece, isn't it?"

A ground squirrel was examining a gum wrapper at the edge of the sidewalk. A kid ran by and it dashed into its burrow.

Coombs spoke again.

"If it makes any difference, I can't stop thinking about that myself."

She nodded imperceptibly.

"Yes, I know. I helped. I wanted to. I just didn't know I'd feel this way afterward."

"Yeah. Me neither," he murmured. "I've trained for damn near everything, but not that." He sighed. "I wish there'd been another way."

A white-haired couple walked by. The man wore a Panama hat and carried a cane. He and the woman held hands. She smiled at them as they passed.

"I'm so sorry," Michelle said as they passed beyond earshot. "We can't change it. It's just there, between us, isn't it?"

"Yeah, it is." He laid his arm on the bench behind her shoulders and looked at her profile. His voice was husky. "I don't want to lose you, girl friend. You're the best thing that's happened to me in a long time."

Her reply was almost inaudible.

"I don't want to lose you either."

A shiny red Ford pickup turned onto the street on the opposite side of the plaza. It burbled to a stop at midpoint and a boy leaned out the window and shouted, "Hey, Lupe! Lupe!" Three girls wandered over and began talking with the boys in the cab.

"Well," Coombs said, patting her shoulder gently, "Let's go meet Ana tonight and see whatever Matt has planned for her. Maybe it'll give us a different outlook on things. Shall we?"

Clio and Julio were cleaning up after supper. Clio was loading the dishwasher. Julio watched her while he wiped the table and straightened the place mats. He kept his voice quiet.

"You OK, 'mana?"

Clio fit a salad bowl on the back of the bottom rack and nodded, but said nothing.

"Mom's feeling better, ¿no crees?"

He had seldom seen her so somber. It worried him. Clio kept her voice down as well.

"She barely talked to me."

"Yeah, but...."

He stopped as their father walked in from the patio at the same moment their mother entered through the front door with a large bundle in her arms. Matt took it all in.

"Whatcha got there, babe?"

"Sheets to wash. I want Abuelita to come home to a clean house."

"That's nice. Get 'em started, and then we can change for the reception."

She didn't slow down as she headed headed for the laundry room at the back of the patio.

"I just don't feel social, Matt. You go without me. I need to work on Abuelita's house."

She continued through the patio down the hallway past Julio's room. Clio looked at her brother, who was looking at their father, who looked at both of them.

"I didn't plan for that," he said. "I'm gonna have to improvise."

He studied the rug for a minute and disappeared toward their bedroom.

Clio felt momentary hope that maybe she wouldn't have to go either, but immediately realized that whatever was ahead had been planned expressly for their mother, it was a big deal, and it involved other people. Canceling it was out. But her father would never force her mother to go, so what could he do?

Matt returned from the bedroom.

"These are the keys to Mom's Corolla," he said, opening a cupboard door and placing them inside. "I've got to leave for a little while, and I don't want her driving away so I'm hiding her car keys where you guys know where they are. I'll be back in less than half an hour. I've got my phone. You all are in charge, OK?"

He left through the front door. Julio watched through the window as Matt started his truck and drove out the gate, turning right. Clio peeked down the hallway. The light was on in the little laundry room the other side of Julio's room.

"What do we do, J-man?" Clio whispered.

"I dunno. Hope nothing bad happens?"

In the twenty minutes Matt was gone the only thing that happened other than the muted churning of the dishwasher was that their mother carried a load of laundry dried earlier back to the bedroom. From the shadows on the bedroom wall, it looked like she was folding clothes.

Finally, the lights of the returning truck appeared in the driveway. Clio joined Julio at the window. Two people got out, but in the twilight they couldn't recognize the second person. Without a word, both moved to other places in the room and looked busy.

Their father ushered the visitor through the door: a solid man, nicely dressed in gray slacks and blue shirt, not as tall as their dad, and heavier through the middle. He had thinning red hair and a round, fair face. He beamed when he saw them. They stared in puzzlement. He spoke.

"*Vnuki vyznani!*" ("Honored grand-niece and nephew!")

"*Shtryshek slovutne?*" ("Esteemed Uncle?") Clio whispered, astonished. It was her Uncle Rothan, but without his beard!

He embraced them both warmly, laughing and adding two real kisses for Clio, not air kisses. Clio thought she remembered that was done for women, not for children, and felt herself blushing.

"You honor our house, Mr. Ambassador," Matt said with a big smile.

"The honor is mine, Most Esteemed Nephew in Law, mine completely, I assure you," he replied. "Young sir, young lady, how handsome and lovely you are, and how you have grown since last we met!"

As he spoke he held out his hand to Clio, kissing it when she placed her hand in his. Laying a gentle hand on Julio's shoulder, he beamed at them both.

"Thank you, sir...uh, esteemed Uncle," mumbled Julio, awed by the appearance of their famous extraterrestrial relative, all the way from his important duties at the United Nations in New York City.

"Ana!" Matt called to the back. "We have a guest!"

She rounded the corner from the bedroom in ten seconds. Her hair was neat, if short, and she was wearing khaki shorts, flip-flops, and, fortunately, a new, pale blue t-shirt with "The Thistle and The Shamrock" in the center. She came to a halt, her eyes widened, and her hands went to her throat.

"Oh!" she gasped. "Oh!" she exclaimed again, bursting into tears and and running to hug her uncle.

She got four kisses. Clio counted: one on each cheek, with the cycle repeated. They spoke a torrent of Luvit she couldn't quite follow, exchanged more kisses, and her flustered mother ran back to the bedroom. In the ensuing silence, Matt cleared his throat.

"Honored son, honored daughter," he addressed them with a twinkle in his eye, "I think it's time to get ready to go."

Despite her reluctance to attend a social event in a beer bar with her snappish mother, Clio was nevertheless curious about the affair as someone keenly interested in the healing arts. She had a general idea of how a Navajo Blessing Way ceremony went, thanks to Doña Dolores' description, but what she found at Fito's El Rio Bravo Tavern was not remotely similar. The gathering resembled one of the parties her parents gave from time to time, except in this case the guests were extraordinary.

There was Uncle Rothan, relaxed and jolly without his beard, joking that its absence was his disguise. There was her mother's sister Ianthe and her husband, Scott Zimmer. Aunt Ianthe looked considerably different from the last time she'd seen her, less nervous and formal, genuinely friendly in an adult sort of way, and dressed comfortably in pressed slacks and frilly white blouse, with her long hair braided and pinned behind her head. Her husband looked a bit out of place, Clio thought, not like a local person. He wore tasseled loafers, brown slacks, a fancy polo shirt with an embroidered monogram, and his hair looked expensively layered. He was a big-time journalist, so maybe that was how they looked. He was pleasant, but now that his wife was so personable, he took second place in her estimation.

Friendliest of all were her mom's old acquaintance Michelle Stratemeyer and Rob Coombs, who seemed to be a couple. Michelle, in a cute burgundy sun dress with thin braided straps, was fun and light-hearted. Rob, who she remembered from a previous get-together at the Williams ranch in west Texas, was some kind of security person or bodyguard. At the Williams ranch he had been practically a cowboy. Tonight he had on pressed, new jeans and boots, and a crisp dark green western shirt. He was relaxed and unaffected, if not exactly talkative.

Whichever it was, healing ceremony or cocktail party, it already looked like a good idea. It had taken her mother many minutes to stop weeping for joy at seeing so many old friends. They spent an hour and a half mixing and catching up but for once Clio didn't mind. She talked with everyone. So did her brother, who was normally a bump on a tree in groups.

It was strange. The place was just an ordinary beer bar: small, with neon beer signs and trophies for bowling and pool on the walls. It even smelled like beer. Her father, of all people, was the bartender, passing out beer, wine, and sodas and chatting happily with everyone. She observed her mother having a glass of wine. Now that she knew the difference between wine and vodka, Clio thought a little wine might be a good thing for her, medically speaking. Her Abuelita had taught her that.

The nine of them filled the small space with jolly camaraderie until her father dinged a wine glass with a spoon and invited everyone into the next room for the evening's program. Program? Oh, right: the DVD, Hleo's DVD! J-Man had told her about it. He'd sworn he hadn't seen it, that their dad didn't want them to. She shot a glance at her brother, who shrugged subliminally.

The back room of the El Rio Bravo Tavern was smaller than the front. There were only a few low lights, but Clio could make out tables pushed against a far wall and nine chairs arranged in an arc before a large screen. Music was playing, one of those fugues her mother used to practice on the harpsichord, Clio thought, but she hadn't played anything in a long time. Her father seated her mother near the middle, Uncle Rothan to one side and himself to the other, and then checked to make sure all were comfortable and had a beverage handy.

Clio couldn't tell how long they sat and listened to the music, chatting quietly, but it was a long time, perhaps a half hour. She recognized many of the selections as among her mother's favorites, most of them soft and peaceful. Many were fugues. Her mother loved fugues. One piece she didn't recognize startled her mother—she clutched Rothan's forearm. He patted her hand and leaned over to whisper something to her. Clio guessed the music was Thoman. It was followed by several similar-sounding ones. Her mother said something to Ianthe in Luvit, but Clio couldn't hear the words. Ianthe smiled and nodded.

Eventually the music grew louder, becoming a whole orchestra playing an exhilarating piece that sounded like a movie theme. The screen illuminated to reveal swirling grayish-white clouds of fog which thinned after a few seconds to reveal a spectacular aerial panorama of a coastline, passing rapidly under the camera. That scene dissolved into one of a forest, then a vast plain with herds of antelope, to a desert, to snow-covered mountains, to assorted cities. She recognized a few: New York City, Cairo, Rome, San Francisco, Melbourne. Each scene—there might have been as many as a hundred—lasted fifteen or twenty seconds. The music continued throughout. Clio had seen similar panoramas before, but not presented in sequence like this. The effect was beautiful, like a fireworks display. After yet another long shot of a coastline featuring cities, ports, and ships, the camera panned skyward, through puffy clouds, higher and higher, until the curvature of the horizon was visible, the blackness of space above.

That scene dissolved to the heavens, studded with stars. Planets swept by slowly—there went Mars, Saturn, and Jupiter. Was it animation? Clio couldn't tell, but she was entranced. Together with the music, the effect was almost hypnotic. The planets disappeared. Stars seemed to move past, slowly. Clio checked the people beside her. They were as rapt as she was. Could this be part of the ceremony?

Several minutes passed. One small star took the center of the screen. It grew larger. More planets flew by. The camera settled on one in particular, a white and blue cloud-wrapped ball not unlike Earth, but with two moons, a large one and a small one. It grew and grew, bigger and bigger, until it filled the screen and there was a curved horizon with an atmosphere, then a vast expanse of water, and finally, a coastline.

Once again, as in the beginning, there followed a sequence of overflights: deserts, mountains, plains, herds of animals, giving way to more settled vistas:

croplands, industrial complexes, and cities. The cities, she noted, were smaller and more compact than the ones before, not tapering off to thin edges, but with distinct boundaries, sometimes several smaller cities in the same shot, connected by lines—roads or rail lines?—she couldn't tell. Her mother was leaning forward in her chair, hand to her mouth. Rothan had a hand on her shoulder. By squinting against the reflected light from the screen, Clio could see Ianthe, on the far side, eyes fixed on the images, fingers tight around the arms of her chair.

Suddenly, the camera turned down into one of the cities. The ground flew up in most alarming fashion as buildings and streets became clearer and clearer. The camera was headed toward some kind of stadium or amphitheater but the picture faded back to fog, the music crescendoing to a thunderous climax. Then all was silence. Clio heard several exclamations to her left, and a little embarrassed laughter.

The fog roiled ten seconds, twenty, before clearing a little, partially revealing something obscured deep in the background. The image resolved gradually: it was a human, an adult male, wearing a striking robe. He had a beard and gray hair, white at the temples. The robe was deep blue, with gold bands running up the sleeves to the shoulders. Shorter gold bands lay across them at the shoulders, making a golden T on each side. The man stared into the camera with vigor and dignity.

Clio saw her mother gasp and half stand.

"*Hleo Vazhni!*" she exclaimed, "*Nitelni nuskutech!*" ("Honorable Hleo! It can't be!")

Uncle Rothan seemed taken aback as well. He was shaking his head slowly.

Could that actually be Counselor Hleo? Clio thought he had passed away about the time her mother left Thomo, and existed now only inside a computer on the moon. She and Julio had talked with him personally online, and knew he spoke and thought like a real person, except that he wasn't, really. How was this image possible? If Hleo had created an animation of himself, it was a very good one. He looked impressively authoritative.

The figure began speaking in Luvit, in an elderly, resonant bass voice. Clio had learned household Luvit from her mother. She could read Luvit text with the help of a dictionary, but this was another matter altogether. His words were in verse, for one thing: the word order was unusual and some of the particle endings and conjugations were unfamiliar. She had never heard many of the words, so it was hard to grasp the gist of what was being said. Fortunately, there were English subtitles. When the figure paused dramatically, she heard Michelle whisper to Rob Coombs, "It's Hleo. It's that epic poem he wrote!"

Clio turned back to the screen, forcing herself to concentrate on the sound and the subtitles at the same time.

"*Be with us, we pray, o ye stars, as you were with the bards of old, with Cirigh, with Vrestan....*"

Hleo ran through a long list of Thoman poets and their tales of heroes and struggles, victories and defeats, the great epic poems of the past. Clio knew nothing about those, but she took the opportunity to practice scanning the subtitles for meaning while listening to the Luvit verse. She missed the first few sentences, but by the time Hleo moved to his real subject, she was getting the hang of it. His words had a rolling cadence, like waves, that carried her along almost in spite of herself.

"*It is fitting, o Heavenly Spirit, that we dedicate our tale to you who have witnessed it.*

"*Our hero's story traced its path through your vast domain, under your enduring presence, o stars.*

"*Hear my verses, we pray, O Celestial Muse!*

"*My song is of your Eternal Cycle:*

"*I sing of beginnings. I sing of endings.*

"*I sing of beginnings that become endings,*

"*And of endings that are beginnings.*

"*All that is new shall be old. All old shall be new.*

"*We spring from you, o stars. To you we shall return.*

"*I sing of the circle; I sing of completion;*

"*I sing of Destiny!*

"*Hear me, o Beloved Spirit, hear me and bless our song.*

"*Hear me, and bless our fate!*"

Clio shot a glance at the three Thomans in the group. Ianthe was staring at the floor. Uncle Rothan's eyes were closed. Her mother was bent over, face in her hands. Her father was looking sidelong at her. He winked.

Hleo moved from his opening litany to a recitation of the generations of Thomans. There were a lot of them, but he marched steadily through, naming clans, tribes, and noteworthy people, men and women. Names of members of the Darshiell clan cropped up frequently, as Hleo's image on the screen gave way to a series of artwork, photographs, and portraits.

A set of eloquent verses on the values of civilization and on the heroes who embody those virtues led to others on the detection by Thoman antennas of promising signals emanating from the direction of Earth. His voice took on more urgency. He described the way the discovery galvanized all Thomans, and their tremendous efforts to mount an exploratory expedition. The words "fate" and "destiny" occurred increasingly. He described the technological challenges as well as the political and financial agonies of the effort. He described the uniting of all the clans to fulfill their common destiny. Pictures of important people, most notably her mother's parents, apparently as newlyweds, standing before a huge crowd, flashed on the screen. To Clio's right, Julio whispered, "Cool!" She sneaked a glance to her left. Her mother was leaning into Rothan, who had an arm around her.

Clio agreed with Julio: it *was* cool. She'd never considered the massive effort required to send someone to a distant planet in another solar system, to a planet that might be—or might not be—where her people had come from. The sequence of pictures continued: classrooms, engineers, industrial production, meetings, and more people. She saw her grandparents again, with three little girls. One had to be her mother, Anneyn, with her second sister Onela, and Ianthe, who was tiny, chubby, and barely walking. Another furtive glance at Rothan—he held Ana close against him, one hand tenderly stroking her hair.

Hleo's verses were building to a climax. Clio felt a chill run down her back when she realized where this had to be headed. The videos showed tests of rocket engines and the building of complex machinery, gantries and giant rockets blazing upward, a huge interplanetary vehicle being assembled in orbit, swarmed over by platoons of workers in pressurized clothing, as Hleo thundered line after line about the destiny of the people coming to pass under the united clans.

There were scenes of a grand banquet. The camera zoomed to pan the head table as Hleo lauded Heoren Darshiell, who guided his people to their culmination, and his daughter Anneyn, sitting next to him, who would bring it to fruition. She stood and bowed as the camera pulled back. There was no sound from the clip to go with the poetry, but the attendees were standing and applauding. That scene dissolved to another of an elaborate outdoor ceremony before an enormous crowd, where it appeared Anneyn was being blessed before her departure. She looked tiny and young and frightened to Clio, but only because she knew her so well. To all appearances she was smiling bravely, bowing and waving, and then stepping into an ungainly bus-like vehicle that carried her toward a rocket on a gantry.

The next clip was an aerial shot of a long, low coastline with a wide, white beach. The beach was deserted and undeveloped, waves breaking along it in angled rows of long ripples. In the hazy distance, not far inland, a tiny light sparkled, growing brighter and brighter. The light moved slowly upwards, rising on a thick column of smoke. As the camera neared, it could be seen to be a large rocket blasting into the sky. The camera panned up to follow it as it got smaller and smaller and smaller, fading to a dot.

Clio's eyes stung. Her mother had always been just her mother to her. She'd never thought about what it might have felt like to leave one's home planet forever and head out into the universe alone. The realization gave her a major lump in her throat.

The animations that followed were much the same as the opening sequence but in reverse, a journey across a corner of the galaxy, a yellow star and planets, Earth's moon and the tiny Thoman moon base and then the blue marble of Earth, growing larger and larger, as the poem built to its conclusion. Clio began to notice an odd disparity creeping in, between Hleo's verses and the English subtitles. The spoken couplets praised the Darshiell clan and especially Heoren, her grandfather, and her mother in the most lavish terms. The subtitles were more muted, less laudatory somehow. When she reflected that the three native Thomans watching would hear the undiluted version while the non-Thomans would be reading the less florid translation, she realized that might explain it: a poetic version for the Thomans, and a less elaborated one for those from Earth.

As the visuals moved in on Earth, the poem returned to the themes of fate and destiny. On behalf of all clans, one brave, young Thoman woman from the Darshiell clan was single-handedly bringing thousands of years and 160 generations of millions of Thomans full circle, back to their home, transforming and improving the lives of the populations of both planets. Never again would their people be separated.

But, Hleo continued, this was not the sum of the triumph. The end of one "Eternal Cycle" was merely the start of another. The courageous young woman, (unintelligible) Anneyn Darshiell (Clio didn't understand the elaborate honorific Hleo used with her name), had begun the next cycle on her own initiative, by marrying: formally and corporeally uniting all Thoman clans with all the clans of Earth. The children of that union, a symbolic two in number, would be the beginning of the next, even more glorious cycle in the two-planet super-clan of all humanity.

The epic concluded with a ringing incantation to the Heavenly Spirit, to fate and destiny, and to the immortal heroes who will always be celebrated as long as human civilization endures. An image of the sky, galaxies wheeling through incomprehensible space, faded slowly to black. Only the music remained.

Clio turned to Julio. He was as stunned as she was. For once their twin communication system had nothing to communicate. They too were a part of this grand epic—the poem was for them, as well. The implications of that could not be comprehended. Julio saw something behind his sister and raised his chin a fraction of an inch. Clio turned.

Uncle Rothan was standing. Their mother had the fingers of one hand over her mouth. Rothan faced Ana, slowly let himself down on one knee, and took her other hand. She shook her head in protest several times, but got to her feet, sniffling. Rothan began speaking what must have been extremely formal Luvit. Clio picked up only a few words, but he seemed to be acknowledging her status somehow. He asked for something. She swallowed and mumbled several phrases. The only words Clio caught were "blessing" and "dearest and most honored uncle." She laid a hand to his head, he arose, and they embraced tenderly. Then Aunt Ianthe performed the same rite. Clio was dumbstruck. Scott Zimmer had moved beside his wife. He kissed her mother's hand and hugged her. Michelle and Rob Coombs embraced her next. Her mother stood as if in a trance.

Clio, her emotions a roiling jumble, went to her mother and leaned into her and hugged her hard. Her mother hugged her back even harder. Clio could feel her mother's ribs as she fought for breath. Julio followed Clio.

Matt was last. Ana looked into his face, burst into tears, and fell into his arms.

Chapter 20

Rob and Michelle were sitting in a glider on the cement patio behind Abuelita's house. It was mid-morning, Friday. Most of the yard was in solid shade. Beneath the canopy of leaves a dark gray rain curtain from a thundershower was visible over the Organ Mountains, twelve miles away. Low rumbles of distant thunder rolled through the trees every so often. Rob's left arm rested on the curved back of the glider, lightly against Michelle's back. From time to time he rubbed her shoulder.

"Did you find the cantaloupe?" she asked.

"Yup. In the fridge. Very good."

"Was anyone else up?"

"I saw Scott, shaving. Told him about the breakfast layout in the kitchen. I wonder who set it out."

"Matt?"

"You think so, or you know so?"

"That's a guess. There were no napkins. I found some."

"Ah."

Coombs planted the heel of a boot on the cement and started the glider moving back and forth.

"So, what did you think of the show last night?" she asked.

"Unreal. To think that Hleo wrote all that. Unreal."

"Did you follow it?"

"Pretty much. Probably not as well as you. It made me realize something. I...."

He paused as the two ridgebacks, emerging from behind Matt's house, saw them and trotted over hopefully.

"Hey, dogs," he said, reaching into his shirt pocket and pulling out a folded tortilla. "I thought I might see you this morning."

They sat, bright-eyed, ears cocked, while he tore the tortilla into quarters. He flipped pieces right and left, the dogs lunged, and the treats were gone. He tossed them the last two, with the same result.

"Sorry, guys. That's all."

He slapped his knee twice. Rajah came to be petted. Rani, finding Coombs only had one hand to spare, went to Michelle, who patted her carefully, keeping the dog's wet nose away from her hand.

"You were going to say, about realizing something?"

"Oh, yeah." He started the glider moving again. "See, I've been a soldier most of my adult life. You hear a lot about patriotism and fighting for your country, but the bottom line is soldiers fight for their buddies. Your squad does the job, you cover your buddies and they cover you. You do it right and everyone stays alive, you hope. It's a major bonding thing. My acquaintance with Ana has been like that. We went on a difficult, extended mission together years ago—I told you about that; it had to do with finding and destroying a couple weapons—and we did it. It was dangerous. She couldn't have done it without me, and I couldn't have done it without her. But together, we did it. I don't know if she feels like I do, but I feel we bonded during that mission, on a sort of professional, soldier basis. Same deal getting out of Peru. It took both of us. Honestly, she would have made a terrific SEAL, except for the possible lack of brute strength. She wasn't that good with firearms, either, now that I think about it.

"Anyway, to me she's been this fellow soldier, one of the best. That's how I thought of her. But that show last night...." He shook his head. "I realized she was way beyond just a soldier. She's a pioneer. Even more than that. She's history, world history, world history on two worlds. I'm seeing the bigger picture now, know what I mean?"

Michelle said nothing. Coombs went on.

"I mean, she's more than just a person. Her life means something to her people. And to ours." He paused a beat and spoke more softly. "I'm not saying that very well. She's important to all of us. I'm not proud of what I did for her last week, but I'm glad I could help her stay alive, because we need her. I had to do it, and I'm glad you were there too. I needed you, more than you know."

He pulled her closer and patted her shoulder. She rubbed his thigh.

"I'd do it again too," she whispered.

"So what about you?" Coombs said after a pause. "You lived on the moon. You're old friends with Hleo. You savvy the lingo. Did you follow it?"

"Yes, but it was very formal and must have had some old or poetic-type words. I needed the subtitles. When I was staying in that moon station, Hleo helped me read through several of their...."

The screen door to Abuelita's house slapped shut behind them. It was both Zimmers, looking relaxed and summery.

"Morning, Rob, Michelle," Scott said, smiling conspiratorially. "How are you, this morning? Good, it would seem."

"Very good, thanks," Michelle replied, returning the smile. "Did you all sleep well?" Both nodded. "Love your hair, Ianthe—so beautiful. Have you seen the Ambassador this morning?"

"He's having breakfast," Scott said. "He was delighted with the taquitos. I showed him how they're assembled. He's having a second at the moment."

"We were talking about that poem last night," Coombs said. "I've never heard anything like it. It was impressive."

Ianthe nodded in agreement.

"Yes, it was. Believe it or not, that would have been the short version," she said. "Almost all of them go on for hours, some all day. I'm certain the Counselor omitted many sections last night."

"No kidding?"

"There are thirty-two major epics in Luvit, thirty-three now. This one is sure to become one of the two or three most important. The Counselor did a wonderful job creating it. I always thought of him as a soldier and adviser. I didn't know he was also a poet...a bard? Is that the word?"

"That's the word," Michelle said.

"Back home, they're recited on festival days and studied in schools. They're popular. They're an important means of uniting the clans into one people."

The screen door slammed again. Rothan Darshiell stepped out, looked around the compound, and headed their way. At almost the same moment, Matt appeared on his porch, saw the group, and joined them.

"Morning, folks, Mr. Ambassador," he said. "Everyone OK this morning?" There was a general chorus of agreement. "I really appreciate your presence yesterday and today," he continued. "I'm sorry it was on short notice, but it was so helpful to Ana. Your generosity was most helpful."

"To the contrary, sir," Rothan said. "Your efforts on behalf of our niece were exceptional and praiseworthy. We are most deeply in your debt, honored nephew in law."

"Is she still asleep?" Michelle asked.

"No, she's been up a good while. She was torn between coming out here to join you or fixing a meal for everyone. She's in the kitchen putting lunch together."

"Oh!" Michelle exclaimed, "I'll go help!" She jumped to her feet. "Thanks for the good breakfast, Matt."

Matt chuckled, saying to her retreating figure, "You're welcome, but that wasn't me. Julio and Clio took care of that." He looked at his watch. "I have to run to town briefly. My grandmother is being released from the hospital today, and she'd kill me if she missed meeting you all. She'll kill me twice if she has to eat another hospital meal." He jingled the keys in his hand. "I'll be back in an hour and we'll have us a fine lunch, if I'm any judge."

Michelle was about to knock softly on the screen door when what she saw inside caused her to stand aside and hold it open. Julio thanked her and passed through, pulling one end of a wheeled ice chest. Clio followed, carrying a pitcher of purple agua de jamaica and a stack of plastic cups. Ana was at the kitchen counter, using a knife to slide small pieces of meat from a cutting board into a bowl of dark liquid. She smiled when she saw Michelle.

Michelle greeted her in Luvit, hardly knowing why. Ana replied in English. That was fine with Michelle, who switched too.

"That was such a fabulous poem Hleo wrote! You must be thrilled!"

"Not really. It's embarrassing. That's partly why I haven't greeted our guests yet this morning."

"Oh, no! You shouldn't be! It was majestic, so beautiful!"

Ana turned back to the counter and began fussing with food. She really was taken aback. Michelle had never seen her at a loss like that.

"Anyway, I came inside to help. Something smells great. What? Limes?"

"Yes, limes, and soy sauce, and I just crushed some toasted sesame seeds. Is that it?"

"Maybe. I just had breakfast but it makes me hungry all over again. What can I do?"

"Oh, take this bunch of cilantro and pull the leaves off and rinse them. They're going into the relish."

Michelle washed her hands and began stripping the fragrant leaves off their stems, thinking as she did so. There were some things she just had to know.

"Are you going to let it out that you're still alive?"

Ana stopped stirring for a moment.

"Yes, eventually. I feel so badly for Dr. Schwartz. He talked me into that Peruvian tour. I'm sure he feels terrible about what happened. He needs to know I'm alive, and that it wasn't his fault."

She resumed her mixing, more slowly, but said nothing more. Michelle went back to pulling leaves. Thinking carefully, she spoke again.

"You know, you have been so important to me in my life, more important than my mother, maybe. I can't tell you how upset I was when I heard about that incident in Peru. I was a total wreck. Was it...terrible?"

Ana looked into the bowl she was using. She stirred once and stopped.

"Yes. It was. I don't remember much of it. The water almost knocked me out. I thought I was going to die. It was so cold. I don't know how I pulled myself out." She stirred whatever it was once more. "I must have slept; I don't know. I remember hearing a helicopter, but I had no strength to move. I slept some more and then it was the next day. I remember pulling myself uphill. I don't know how far. I think I was delirious. A man, I think he was an old man, found me at nightfall. He took me to the doctor at the clinic. That was where...where...I, I lost...."

She dropped the spoon and bent over the bowl. Michelle sprang to her feet to hold her. She could feel Ana trying not to cry. She felt wretched for having asked.

Shoes sounded on the porch. Quickly, she released Ana and turned on the water in the sink, rinsing the cilantro shreds off her hands and hoping to intercept whoever it was.

There was a soft knock and Rothan entered. Ana gasped and quickly mopped her hands and face, launching into an elaborate Thoman greeting. Rothan smiled, raised a hand in a "stop" gesture, and hugged her affectionately.

"English, please, Honored Niece. Let us be informal, always, shall we? Nothing has changed, my dear."

Ana clasped her hands together, smiling weakly.

"I hope I see you well this morning, dearest niece?"

He removed a piece of paper from his pocket and unfolded it.

"Counselor Hleo sent me this," he said. "I think you should see it."

He passed it to her. Michelle saw it was a printout of a newspaper article. She heard Ana's intake of breath at the same time she saw the top line: *Kathimerini English Edition,* over a picture of a stern looking man in a coat and tie. The headline of the article said "Gazprom Executive Drowns in Diving Accident Off Paros." Michelle froze. Vivid memories flooded her brain while Ana skimmed the article, the sheet quivering in her hand. She clasped it to her breast and looked up at Rothan.

"Alas," he said quietly, "bad news for one is good for another. I think you may finally be at peace, dear child, you and your family."

Ana stepped to her uncle and hugged him without a word.

Michelle looked at the dish towel in her hands. Coombs was right. Ana's life was worth what he had done. He had definitely done the right thing. She was proud to have been a part of it.

Two hours later, Clio and Julio were in the kitchen. Julio was packing ice around a container of pistachio ice cream in a small tub while Clio sprinkled confectioner's sugar over two trays stacked with Mexican wedding cookies.

"That's all the ice," he mumbled.

"We shouldn't need any more," Clio said. "If we do, there's more in Abuelita's refrigerator."

He jostled the ice cream container lower in the tub. "It's nice to have her back," he said a little louder. "You'd never know she'd been sick except for that cane."

"She put on some makeup. She's had a good time. I think she likes Uncle Rothan."

"Yeah. He likes her too. Maybe it's his manners. He's pretty old-fashioned." He laid a dish towel over the ice cream and the tub. "Did you hear Dad say her doctor wants to talk to you?"

"Uh-huh. He probably wants to gripe at me. I don't want to ever see him again."

"Dad said he wanted to know how you knew about the blood thinner."

"I don't care. I don't want anything to do with him. He was a big doody."

"I didn't like him either." He moved to one side and peered at an angle out the window over the sink. "I think they're ready for dessert. Mom's laughing again. I haven't seen her laugh so much in a long time."

"That was a funny story Rob told. Everybody laughed at that."

"Did you know Dad is going to take Abuelita up in the pod tomorrow night or the next night?"

"Yeah? She'll love that, even better than the balloon ride."

"For sure." He scanned the items on the table. "You wanna take this stuff out there?"

"Um, let's take the cookies first. I can't carry both trays. We can come back for the ice cream and the spoons and bowls."

Outside, the adults had mostly finished eating. They were pushed back from the tables but were still chatting. Ana was giving Ianthe a tour of the garden. The cookies were welcomed by all but Coombs.

"Thank you, no, Clio. I gotta have a few more of those fajitas first. Slide 'em this way, please, Scott."

"Sure. Here you go. Matt, however did Ana fix the pork for those burritos?"

"She said she caramelized it and topped it with a relish of crushed sesame seeds, cilantro, and key limes. I think that's basically it."

Zimmer shook his head.

"I thought I knew something about New Mexican Mexican food, but that was a new one on me. Tangy, man! Delicious!"

"It's not exactly New Mexican. I have no idea where Ana got the idea. She comes up with some wild combinations. It might be Korean, or Vietnamese, or anything, really."

The slightest breeze wafted the smell of the dying charcoal fire over the group. A rumble of thunder passed through the cottonwoods. Rothan looked up into the trees.

"Don't worry, Mr. Ambassador," Abuelita said, brushing cookie crumbs off the table cloth. "That shower is moving south. It won't bother us."

"I am certain it would not dare, Mrs. Méndez," he said, reaching for another cookie. "Such perfect peace must not be disturbed."

Ana and Ianthe returned from their garden tour. Ianthe was smelling several leaves pinched in her fingers. Zimmer checked his watch.

"We're coming out just right. We'll get you to the airport in good time, Mr. Ambassador. You all too, Rob and Michelle, unless we can convince you to spend the weekend with us at the ranch."

"We'd love to, another time, Scott," Rob said. "We still have some beach time in the Bahamas left—hate to waste it."

Everyone's attention was diverted by Julio, who set a heavy tub on the table with an audible "Oof!" He removed the towel from the top. Michelle leaned over to look.

"Ice cream!" she exclaimed.

Matt stepped out his front door and paused a moment to appreciate the lowering sun, a stunningly brilliant salmon, glowing through branches and distant shreds of cumulus clouds. He liked evenings about as much as mornings, surely because of the way the sun, low in the sky, showed through under the trees, making the house and grounds glow as if enchanted.

The drapes were pulled back from Abuelita's bedroom window—she was up from her nap. They'd have a snack with her once the cleanup, now in progress, was finished.

Clio hurried past him with an armful of tablecloths.

"Thanks, sugar. You've been a huge help today."

"Sure, Dad," she said, continuing her beeline to the house.

Ana was sitting in the glider, shoes kicked off. She seemed to be smiling at her toes. He eased down next to her.

"Hey, babe. What's so funny?"

"Hmm? Oh, nothing. I was thinking about Hleo."

"What about Hleo?"

"You know him. He doesn't have much of a sense of humor. He almost never laughs or makes a joke. So, I was thinking that his poem was really kind of funny, but that he couldn't have meant it to be that way."

Matt hadn't found it funny in the least.

"Funny? How so?"

"You have to understand, Matt. Ever since I was a little girl I've heard our epic poems recited on holidays and special occasions. They were about some very remarkable people, and incredible events. I never thought what the real truth behind them might be."

"The real truth? What do you mean?"

"Well, now, there's a poem about me. I never dreamed there'd be a poem about me. Our friends last night seemed to believe the whole thing. It was strange."

She leaned her head on his shoulder. He pulled her close.

"Strange?"

"Yes. You know—I told you. I wasn't a good daughter. I wasn't a good Thoman. I didn't fit in. I wasn't happy. I caused problems. That's why my father sent me here—to get me out of the way. I was scared, but otherwise I was happy to leave. And then, after I got to the moon, I disobeyed the Council's orders by coming here. I should have been banned from the clans for that. Once I was here, I got into trouble again, and then more trouble. And now I'm a hero of the people and there's a great poem about me. Little Thoman children will have to listen to it some day.

"I wish I could tell them it's all nonsense, to pay no attention, but I can't. They're too far away and they haven't even been born yet. And so here I am, with my dear husband, watching the sunset."

He pulled her harder against him.

"Reminds me of Jello."

"What?"

"Yeah, Jello. Did you know I like Jello?"

"You do? I didn't know that." She pulled back and looked at him. "What does that have to do with anything?"

"You don't like Jello. You hate Jello."

"Well, so what?"

"Exactly. So what? I like it. You hate it. But it's still Jello. It doesn't care. No one cares."

She searched his face for two beats.

"Oooh. I see."

"Besides," Matt added, "most of the founding fathers of the United States were troublemakers. I think that could be said about most of this planet's high achievers." He smiled. "I think it's supposed to be that way."

She freed her arm and laid her hand on his neck, tugging him gently.

"I guess you're right. Thanks, Matt."

He was about to kiss her when the twins, followed by Raisin ten feet behind, returned. He kissed her anyway. Julio went to the trash can, twisted the liner tight, and tied the plastic ribbon around it. He pulled it out of the can and began dragging it across the grass toward the back of the barn.

"Thanks, son," Matt called after him. "You guys were great today."

Clio unfolded a new trash bag while Raisin hunkered down to sniff Ana's shoes. When Clio whipped the bag through the air to open it fully, the cat flinched but then suddenly sat up, eyes alert, ears turning this way and that. The long black hairs on the tips of her ears leaned to the south in the breeze.

Matt looked at her closely. She was wrinkling her nose in the oddest way, raising her upper lip, partially revealing her fangs, while she turned her head one way and then the other. He'd never seen a cat do that.

"Daughter? What's this cat doing?"

"Huh? Oh. She's flehmening."

"She's *what*?"

"She's smelling something. Not smelling, exactly. It's a special sense organ cats have. They smell pheromones or something. No one's really sure."

The cat sprang to her feet and squalled alarmingly, ears fully back. Everyone jumped. She took off like a shot, leaping easily to the top of the seven foot north wall around the compound. She froze, hindquarters high, front quarters low, looked north, hissed loudly, and leaped off the wall out of sight.

"What the hell?"

"I'll catch her, Dad," Clio said, dropping the crumpled liner in the trash can. She looked at the dogs and commanded, "Sit!" They sat.

"Mija!" Matt commanded. "Here. Take my cell phone. Call us!"

"I will, Dad," she said, grabbing the phone and running to the back gate.

Julio watched her run past.

"I'll go up in the loft and watch her, Dad!"

He abandoned the trash bag and raced to the barn, leaving Matt and Ana to stare at the open back gate and barn door.

"I'll get the cordless phone," Matt said. "Let's hope we don't need the pod to track down Raisin. I'll lock the dogs in the patio. Rajah! Rani! Come!"

When he returned with the phone, the yard was deserted. In response to his shout, Julio's head appeared at the south loft window.

"We're up here, Dad."

When he joined Ana and Julio at the north window, Julio pointed.

"She's in that clump of trees by the water gate."

"Damn! I better..."

Before he could finish his sentence, Clio appeared. The trees were a good 300 yards from the compound, too far to shout. She stepped away from the trees, faced north, and whistled. The shrill peep was barely audible downwind. She whistled again and disappeared back into the underbrush around the trees. A minute or two later she emerged again, carrying something. She whistled to the north once more and began walking back to the compound.

"There's Raisin!" Julio exclaimed, pointing again.

The cat had come out of the next clump of trees beyond. She looked back over her shoulder before heading after Clio, stopping every ten or twenty yards to turn and hiss, or so it looked. They could hear nothing at that distance.

They met Clio at the back gate. In her hands were two tiny kittens, pale blue eyes barely open, mewing piteously. Both were white, with the lightest silvery fur on paws, faces, and tails. Clio was weepy.

"A coyote killed their mama," she said, close to tears. "Raisin got him before he could kill the kittens."

The big cat appeared at the gate, her muzzle and paws splotched with blood. She checked the compound carefully and, finding no threat, sat and began methodically cleaning her face and paws.

"Good God," said Matt, under his breath.

Julio had eyes only for the kittens.

"Aww, lemme see one," he said.

Clio handed him a kitten. They looked healthy enough, not fat, but not skinny. They windmilled their little arms in the air, tiny claws extended.

"I'll set up a box in the barn for them," he said.

"I'll get some milk and an eyedropper. After they eat we can bathe them and get rid of the fleas. Then we'll go bury their mother."

Paying no attention whatever to their parents, they headed into the barn. Ana and Matt looked at each other. Ana smiled.

"There's our next generation of cats," she said.

Matt watched Clio and Julio disappear into the barn, heads down, shoulder to shoulder, cradling their kittens.

"Yep. And there's our next generation of Méndez-Darshiells."

Ana's face brightened into the radiant smile he hadn't seen for weeks. She reached for his hand. He wrapped his arms around her and squeezed. She smelled like baby powder. He inhaled deeply and whispered in her ear.

"We fit together perfectly, don't we?"

Harry's great job as a horse trainer earned him enough money to cover his tuition at Juarez Academy and maybe save enough for a used car by the time he got his drivers license. He didn't really need to work at Mr. Silvas' neighborhood tendajo any longer. But he liked Mr. Silvas, and the man wasn't getting any younger. Harry's mother told him Nicho got by with the aid of Social Security, that he liked having something to do, and helping his friends and neighbors made him feel useful. So Harry decided to work a couple hours at the tendajo every Saturday. Nicho only paid him $5 an hour, but Harry didn't care about that. What could you expect from a man who remembered the Depression and kept framed pictures of FDR, JFK, and the Virgen de Guadalupe on the wall behind the cash register?

Harry was a better arranger of merchandise than Nicho anyway. This Saturday he had rehung the costales, the bags field workers loaded with the produce they picked, the gorras (caps), and the better-looking western hats so that the flashier ones would be more prominent. He also straightened the small selection of magazines: *TV Guide*, the weight loss and horoscope magazines, and the tabloids. One of these, *National Star*, caught his eye with its lurid headline: "Starchild Made Queen of the Shining Path Guerillas!" The front page contained four large color photographs of the "starchild," the term all the tabloids used for Ana Darcy, the woman who came to Earth from the planet Thomo. Everyone knew who she was. Everyone had heard she had been killed in Peru, though her body had not been found. That detail was gold for the tabloids.

Two of the photos were from twelve years earlier, when she had stunned the world with her performance in the Olympic Games. One was a sexy tabloid-quality shot of her standing on the 10 meter platform in a sleek swimsuit. Another showed her holding up a gold medal, while wearing five others around her neck. The third showed her at the podium of the United Nations, looking gorgeous and serious at the same time. The fourth was a blurry still from a video, of her famous dive from the bridge in Peru, her arms outspread, hair streaming behind, framed by the ropes which suspended the bridge over a rushing river.

The photos hit Harry like a bolt of lightning: Jesus! Starchild looked just like Clio! He checked to see what Mr. Silvas was doing. He was bending over the freezer box, sorting the ice cream bars and frozen pizzas. Harry pulled the magazine out and flipped to the story. The first few paragraphs jibed with what he remembered from the TV news broadcast that he and his mother had seen, but it soon veered off into its "exclusive" findings. The starchild had been missing two weeks. The reporters were sure no one but possibly an Olympic gold-medal high diver could have survived such a drop.

So the *National Star*'s expert reporters had gone to Peru and dug out the rest of the story: the Shining Path guerillas, on the ropes from a series of attacks by government forces, were determined to become the preeminent revolutionary force in the world, the Third Reich of guerillas as it were. To accomplish this, their leader, one Comandante Enrique, decided to create a royal family that spanned two worlds. Accordingly, he plotted to kidnap the starchild, take her to his jungle capitol, and marry her. There was a grainy black and white photo of a group of guerillas, standing in the jungle. In the center of the group, Starchild was standing next to the Comandante before a priest, or so it appeared. Their union would found a royal revolutionary family that would…uh oh! A customer entered the store. Harry put back the magazine as Nicho came to greet one of his old friends.

He kept bustling with the items in the magazine rack but he couldn't keep his eyes off the cover of the *National Star*. Just like Clio! Come to think of it, Clio's mother had had some sort of problem while traveling recently—Clio had been terribly upset about it. But her mother came home; Starchild was missing, and probably dead. And anyway, what were the odds that Clio's mother was the woman from another planet? C'mon, like a woman from another planet would be living in Las Cruces? Ridiculous—she'd be living in Hollywood, or New York City. Or a castle somewhere.

People did look like each other, sometimes. His mother's brother was a dead ringer for Luis Aguilera, the famous Mexican singer. People even asked him for his autograph. It happens.

But still. There was something weird about that family, especially the mother and daughter. He stood up as the cash register dinged and the customer departed. Before him was the Virgen on the wall, her eyes turned down at him. ¡Eso sí que es! Now he knew who he could ask about this, and he could do it this very afternoon.

Forty-five minutes later, when the bus swayed into the long curve to the right before the Méndez place, Harry scanned the grounds carefully as he passed by. Their car and truck were there, but he could see no sign of life. Well, it was

Saturday afternoon. He knew Clio was all right—she'd called that morning to check on him, but she had supplied no new information beyond that. Even so, he was sure, despite having been drugged, that they had never gone to a hospital, yet that was what Clio said had happened, just as her father had told his mother. But that was wrong! How had they done what they had done? And why wouldn't they admit it?

The bus passed through a shady pecan orchard, then a tiny village. On the other side of the next little community was where his grandmother Dolores lived: La Doña, Doña Dolores. He rarely visited her. More often, she visited them, since she periodically shopped in Las Cruces. Normally a kind, reserved, woman, he knew her to be intelligent, insightful, and decisive. Those were the qualities he needed this afternoon.

Doña Dolores had no schedule, attending to those who needed her whenever they arrived. He found her watering her herbs, but she readily invited him into her kitchen for a drink. Before opening her refrigerator, she paused to study him.

"I think something is bothering you, grandson."

"Yes, ma'am."

"I think it has to do with that young friend of yours, my assistant, Clio Méndez."

"Yes, ma'am."

"You have feelings for her, but you do not understand her."

"Yes ma'am. I mean, no ma'am."

Doña Dolores set a cold Dr. Pepper before him. She poured herself a glass of water and took a seat on the other side of her kitchen table.

"Bueno, grandson. Desembúchate" ("Unburden yourself.")

And he did, the whole story, from meeting Clio at school, to their visit to this very house, to his securing an excellent job at Stallman's stables, to his problems with the neighborhood gang. He concluded with his confused recollection of the horrible kidnapping of the previous Wednesday, adding the contrary version told by Clio and her father.

His grandmother was a superb listener, subtly leading him on with raised eyebrows or chin, a tilt or shake of the head, or a faint "hmm."

When he reached the end, he stopped. She was neither stunned nor mystified as far as he could tell. Instead, her eyes narrowed the tiniest bit.

"¿Y pues?" (And so?"), she said.

"Well, I mean, I mean...how did they find us way in the back streets of Juarez? How did her mother and father beat up eight men with guns? How did we get all the way back to Las Cruces from Juarez in just minutes? It's impossible, don't you think? I was never in a hospital! What happened? Who are they?"

Doña Dolores shook her head slowly.

"Ay, grandson. The only One who knows the truth is God. You do not know the truth. I do not know the truth."

She picked up her glass of water and studied it against the window. Then she set it down.

"I know a few things, however," she continued. "I met her mother once, at the community center. I would have known her even if we had not been introduced. She has the same eyes as her daughter, deep eyes, powerful eyes. I sense the same light around her that her daughter has. It is strong, very strong. En mi vida, I have only seen one other person with that light, but never a mother and daughter such as these. I cannot say if the mother has la tocha like her daughter, but she has compassion. She is a good person. I do not think you need to worry about what is true, grandson. God knows the truth, and we must be content with that."

Harry watched a droplet of condensation run down the can of Dr. Pepper.

"Yes, ma'am," he said, after a minute. "I just can't help wondering. Could they be brujas?"

"No. I promise you, they are not brujas. Brujas are of the Devil. Esas, no son."

"I don't mean brujas del diablo. Aren't there white witches?"

"¡No! ¡No hay! Sí, there are those who say they are brujas blancas, pero no son. They are desgraciadas who wander around in the forest worshiping rocks and trees and the seasons. Es pura tontería" ("That's all nonsense").

"Well then, could they be, I don't know, saints?"

"No. Imposible. The saints are Catholic."

"Well, what do you call people who are not Catholic who do impossible things that are good, then?"

Doña Dolores' eyes twinkled.

"There is only one other possibility that I can think of, grandson. Angels?"

"Sherry, please. Bristol Cream."

The waiter nodded and looked to Viktor Reznik's nephew, who also nodded.

"Two sherries. Yes, sir."

The waiter disappeared.

"What a fine meal, uncle. Thank you! I would never have tried the, uh, Spigola arrosto alla ligure without your recommendation."

"I discovered it in Monaco," Viktor replied.

"Did you discover the sun there, too?"

"The sun? Ah, no. You mean my coloration? No, that came later, on the Galaxie."

"Yes, of course. Oleg's yacht."

"The unfortunate Oleg, may he rest in peace."

"Most tragic," Aleksei replied, stifling further comment while the waiter returned and placed two snifters before them. Once he left, Aleksei continued. "I hope his loss will not affect your position with the company."

"Indeed, it may. It appears my department may be moved up to the same level as the other divisions of Gazprom. I may well be promoted."

"Wonderful news, uncle!"

"Yes, if it happens. I rather think it will."

"Are you announcing that yet?"

"No! At present, it is another one of those secrets I mentioned. To your health and fortune, dear Aleksei."

They savored the aromatic wine a moment.

"Connections, money, and secrets, you said. I will not forget that, uncle."

"You have the first, you have some of the second, and you will encounter the third, as you enter the business world, Aleksei. Nurture them all. I hope you understand why I cannot share my secrets with you now, or ever."

"Of course, uncle. As you so wisely said, had you done so, they would no longer be secrets!"

Once their fashionably late lunch concluded, Viktor bade farewell to his nephew and decided to walk the five blocks to his next destination. The weather was chilly and cloudy—not at all like the Mediterranean—and he was comfortable in his suit. It was good weather for reflection. Having coached his nephew a bit on career matters, he found his thoughts turning to his own career.

He had been most sincere in his advice to Aleksei. He had parleyed Oleg's obsessive death wish for that unfortunate young woman into his own personal success. His plans would have succeeded no matter what had happened to her. He still could not believe that Ana Darcy, the famous philanthropist from another world, would have invaded the Serbanov estate and humiliated the younger Serbanov with a sword—Oleg's primal icon, of all things.

At the same time it could be not denied that the natives of the tiny country of Sedlakia believed they had seen someone who looked very like her, who they expected to protect them from the depredations of his employer. They even had a photograph of her. That they chose to think she was the returning queen of their ancient royal family was patent nonsense. But he had to admit that the evidence indicated she appeared there as if by magic and disappeared the same way. It was inexplicable, but he could not accept that the event had been paranormal in any way.

But why attack Oleg? Even if she arrived and departed from his estate by similarly inexplicable means? It made no rational sense.

He had no personal enmity for poor Ms. Darcy. He rather hoped she had survived Oleg's efforts.

He found himself at the door of Sukhanov Imperial Antiques. The receptionist, a steely-eyed, well-dressed matron, remembered him.

"Good afternoon, Mr. Reznik." After a quick word on her phone, she said, without a smile, "Mr. Godarian will see you now," and clicked his way through the door to the inner sanctum.

Artur Godarian, highly recommended expert on Soviet militaria, greeted him warmly. A dignified man with silver hair, erect bearing, and a suitably Armenian nose, he looked the part of a dealer in military antiques. After the requisite social niceties, Godarian produced a long, black case and passed it to Reznik.

"This is a fine exemplar of an eighteenth or nineteenth century Cossack saber, Mr. Reznik," he intoned. "Such weapons were made by the same exacting methods over at least two and a half centuries, which is one reason it cannot be dated precisely. Additional reasons are that the regimental badge on the hilt is missing, and the grip, while appropriately fashioned of sharkskin, seems to be a later replacement, probably because grips suffered severe wear from use.

"Nevertheless, whatever its provenance, it is genuine, and in reasonably good shape. Should you desire to sell, we would be prepared to offer you two thousand Euros for it."

Viktor declined politely, proffered the proper words of appreciation, and returned to the street with the case under his arm. Still in a thoughtful mood, he headed back to his car in the valet lot behind the restaurant.

So the sword was genuine. He had been tempted to keep it as a souvenir, but now the better idea seemed to be to add it to the collection in the display case in Oleg's office before it was cleaned out. It might thereby end up in the collection of Cossack weapons on the walls of the Serbanov estate. He smiled at the irony. There was absolutely no way a woman, whether dead or alive, resurrected queen or modern philanthropist, could have left it deep in the chest of her long-time antagonist, thirty meters beneath the surface of the Aegean Sea.

Or was there?

Perhaps he should rethink his prejudice against the paranormal.

Made in the USA